EDGE OF DIVERGENCE

STEFANIE CHU

CANARI PUBLISHING

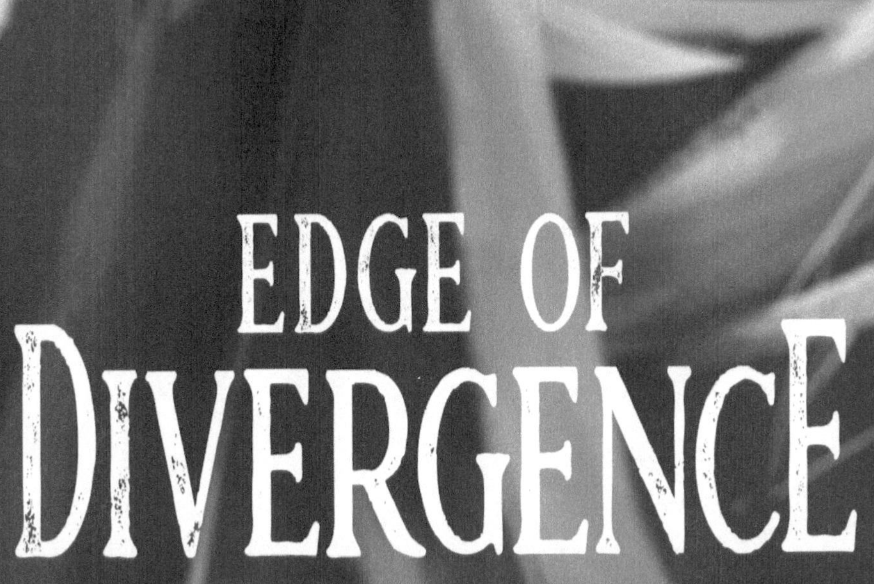

EDGE OF
DIVERGENCE

This is a work of fiction. Names, characters, places, and incidents are drawn from the author's imagination, and any resemblance to actual persons, living or dead, business establishments, events, or locales is entirely coincidental and not intended by the author.

Copyright © 2024 by Stefanie Chu

Canari.

All rights reserved.

No part of this book may be reproduced in any form or by any electronic or mechanical means, including information storage and retrieval systems, without written permission from the author, except for the use of brief quotations in a review.

First Edition: June 2024

ISBN: 978-1-7377125-3-4 (paperback)

Cover by *Booksmith Designs*

Map by *Janas Art Fantasy Illustration*

I'm meant to be your piece until I die.
No one wants to be alone.
I'll leave my soul by your side.

Though we fall apart between hell's divide,
I will seek you for all time,
And smile together underneath the stars.

Till I die, by your side.

The Alliance
of Althaea, Minetta, and Valenia
CANDELA SEA
MORENTA
NARVI
SOLI
AGNA
AVON
KNIGHTS ESTATE
AKOUN
BAY OF MINETT
VENNE
SOLARIN
SAON
OBAN
OON
MALINO
KESTREL BAY
FAUNA
FALUM
MERSA TRIBE
TRIBE OF AEGISES
TRIBE OF UMBRAS
VISCARIAN TRIBE

ALTHAEAN SEA
ALTHACITY
ALTHA HILLS
ALLETE
ELEGEN
EVALEEN
KISHNIN
EKVELT
NAMANI
RHEA
DESDEMONA
YOUNTILLA RIVER
ALTHAEA MAIN
NANAKA
ENDINE
ALTHAEA MAIN
NAIAD
GANMALI
OLINA
OPHALLEN
GULF OF ORIS
AKE URABE
AXILLAIRE
XERAN
TRIBE OF CELTAS
BELLIGMN TRIBE
ZLAN TRIBE
ALYSSI
THE HEARTH
TRIBE OF PARAGONS
N
W
E
S

THE ALLIANCE

Empire of
ALTHAEA

Councilors
ADDER & SUZAN

ALTHAEA MAIN
Leader: Gaven

AXILLAIRE
Leader: Yoah

EVALEEN
Leader: Landon

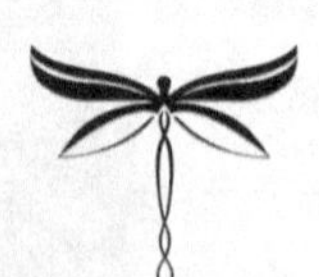

ALTHA HILLS
Leader: High Priest

NANAKA
Leader: Noire

OPHALLEN
Leader: Cole

Empire of
MINETTA

Councilors
DAREH & NOVINHA

AVON
Leader: Shiba

SAON
Leader: Ryland

OBAN
Leader: Hilda

Empire of
VALENIA

Councilors
TAREK & JULIE

Tribe of
PARAGONS

Tribe of
AEGISES

Tribe of
UMBRAS

Tribe of
CELTAS

PROLOGUE

It was strange, really, that sound. Like distant echoes reverberating in my ears. My eyes tightly shut, I couldn't piece together the events leading to this disarray, but all I desperately yearned for was that haunting noise to cease. The bitter cold clawed into my bones, rendering my body too feeble to muster even the faintest movement. So, I lay there, in eerie silence, awaiting...

My body jerked as I choked on something that felt like I had a lump in my throat. My chest heaved, met with a painful resistance, and my limbs throbbed in ways entirely unfamiliar. Every cell in my being came to life with a brutal awakening.

A crimson droplet seeped into my eye, stinging with the acrid reminder of chaos and bringing forth a metallic taste that lingered in my mouth. It dawned on me – I was dying.

Specks of yellow, orange, and black light swirled into my vision. When they began to clear, I found myself gazing at the ground, and strangely, enveloped in warmth.

I brushed my hand over my eye, and my awareness surged like a sudden revelation – there was far more blood than I had anticipated. I traced from my forehead down to my cheek, realizing I had lost vision in one eye.

I couldn't accept it. Dying? Not like this, not here.

"Get up," I snarled at myself. "You can't...you ca..." My voice faltered.

Helpless, I turned my head to the source of the light. The ringing in my ears was now replaced by the chaotic roar of a colossal fire devouring what had once been a warehouse. Lifting my trembling hands, I witnessed a gruesome map of burns and cuts etched across my arms. My memories rushed back – why I was here, what I must do. My thoughts, once bright and optimistic, now traversed a darker path.

"Mirari," I whispered, casting another glance at the blazing warehouse. Those flames, cruel as the association might be, reminded me of her. Who would she have left if I were to perish here?

My eyelids grew heavy, but I fought to stay awake. I couldn't let Mirari down. Begrudgingly though, I couldn't let Gaven down either.

Gaven. I scoffed. Why should I think of him? He left behind his Minettan roots to become an Althaean region leader. His dream had trumped his family, and when someone left you like that, it was a clear message – they weren't coming back. Every shared memory would be consumed by the flames of the past.

As much as I resented Gaven for running off and abandoning us, I felt a lingering obligation to protect him. Perhaps it wasn't what he would have wanted, but deep down, I hadn't entirely given up on the dream that the three of us would reunite. Mirari was right. He was still family.

I clawed at the ground, but only managed to grasp a handful of soil under my nails. Cursing myself, I wished I weren't so powerless. I was no regional leader, no noble. Perhaps my desires, my life, were too minuscule to matter in anyone's eyes, not even in the eyes of the gods. My very essence seemed to be slipping away, vanishing into the overwhelming void that eclipsed the flames of light.

"The three of us..." my voice trailed off. Was it a fantasy beyond my reach? I imagined myself embarking on the journey to Althaea, completing what I had sworn to do. Did I ever make it there? I told myself I did, even if it wasn't true. It was the only way to make dying more bearable.

Each breath was a harrowing battle, as if I were grappling with a beast that refused to be tamed. My eyelids descended, and I sensed the last vestiges of my strength leaving my body.

Whispers in my ear – were they real or not? The lord of death had arrived to escort me to the other side. I was certain of it. They spoke in a language unfamiliar to my ears, but the words offered a soothing closure to my journey. I welcomed it. Should I have? Could they complete what I couldn't? It felt as though they responded, and the last thing I heard were the words: *ning-ürip*.

PART I

CHAPTER ONE

"Is this real? Are you really—" She choked on her words, unable to finish her sentence. Awareness was a gentle tide rising slowly over Mirari. She tried to shake the grogginess from her mind, but it clung like cobwebs. Shoulders tightening, she tucked her head down and clutched at the back of his shirt. No, he was real.

Salathiel.

He laughed. "Truly, I am here."

He leaned back, but she was quick to grasp his arms, unwilling to let him go. She stared at him and doubt crept over her. He looked good. Hardy. His dark hair had a healthy sheen. His coral eyes crinkled not from age, but from a gentle smile. He hadn't aged a day since the last time she'd seen him, but he now had a scar over his left eye that worried her. She shivered again.

Salathiel shook his head with a gentle smile. "But you. You're freezing." When he tucked the cloak back around her shoulders, fretting over her with familiar care, she burst into tears. Hallucination or not, he was here.

"I thought you were dead! Where have you been? How, how—"

He hushed her. "We can talk about it later." Settling his arm around her shoulder, he asked, "Can you stand?"

She nodded, though she wasn't sure if she could. When she tried, pinpricks stung her fingertips and drying blood tugged her shirt.

Something was also adding weight to her body. She reached inside her pocket and found two renastōnes, faded from their brilliant green. She couldn't recall having a spare, or even using one.

When she didn't move, Salathiel helped her to her feet and she leaned heavily against him.

"We need to get you somewhere safe."

She balked. She wasn't sure if there was somewhere safe for her. People were looking for her and she knew – regardless of her past relations with Gaven – all traitors met the same fate.

Forcing aside her shame, she admitted, "I… can't. I… helped the rebels." She didn't think Salathiel would be happy. He always chastised her in the past for sticking her nose in places it didn't belong. And now, what he had always feared had happened. "I know it was dumb, but… I…"

Salathiel brought her close into another hug.

"You help people. That's what you do. If you didn't, would you even be Mirari?" This brought cold tears to Mirari's eyes and it stung her cheeks, but it was not for long before Salathiel wiped them away. "You keep that up and your eyes are going to freeze shut."

He moved to stand in front of her and bent his knees.

"What are you doing?"

"Hop on," he said, motioning toward his back. "I'll give you a lift."

"I can walk," she humphed, clutching the cloak.

He smiled as if he could hear her thoughts. "You may not be as small as you used to be, but I can still carry you."

She huffed but conceded when it didn't look like he was going to be moving anytime soon.

"Fine," she grumbled and climbed on his back. Lifting her easily, he started walking. She tucked her head into the back of his neck to block out the cold. "Let me know when you get tired. I really don't mind walking."

If he responded, Mirari didn't hear. With her arms wrapped around her brother's neck, warm and safe and loved, Mirari was drifting in and out of consciousness.

She muttered, "Where are we going?"

"I know of a place where you can recuperate," he said. "It's safe, don't worry."

"Where?" She glanced behind her, but there were just as many trees ahead as they were behind. She couldn't even tell which direction they were headed.

"Valenia."

Her head whipped back around to look at him. "Valenia?"

"Indeed. No one will even think to look for you there."

She couldn't argue with that. She glanced behind her with one final, regretful look, silently saying goodbye. While there was nothing but scorn and death in Althaea for her now, the time she'd spent there wasn't meaningless. She wished her friends well, even if they didn't feel the same.

***

To Mirari, the trip to Valenia seemed both too long and too short. The country was beautiful, living so close to nature. Houses were built into the trunks of massive trees. Moss grew along stone buildings and bridges formed along exposed roots. As fascinating as it all was, it was difficult for Mirari to enjoy the scenery. The battle in Aias, the argument with Gaven – it weighed on her. She slept a lot, but it was always an unpleasant, restless sleep. She often woke from dreams that whispered of fire and death, covered in a sheen of sweat, while she shook with an anger toward Gaven that she was quick to dismiss.

A hand landed on her shoulder, startling her, but she unstiffened when she realized it was only Salathiel. They were sleeping under the stars and the trees cast a dark shadow over his face.

"Are you all right?" he asked.

"Yeah, I, yeah." She swiped her hand over her face, pulling down her hood and bringing her legs close to her chest. She opened her mouth to explain, but bit back the words.

The fire inside of her.

Her status as a traitor.

The empty spot in her heart.

Her dreams were nothing. The true terror was in her waking days.

"Mirari?" Salathiel called.

"It's fine. Just a nightmare."

He looked at her with an open face. Not pressing, but giving her room to talk. No one else treated her like that. By the Gods, she'd missed him.

She sighed, "Gaven hates me."

"I doubt it," he said, running his hand through her hair.

"You didn't see how he looked at me. He was, he was…" She couldn't go on, unable to put into words the disgust she'd seen on his face.

"We don't have to talk about it."

She was glad that he didn't say he told her so. There used to be a time when they'd been on opposite sides of the same argument. Salathiel had been angry with Gaven, assumed that he had become a changed man and wanted nothing to do with them anymore, while Mirari assured him that Gaven was just busy being a region leader. If only she had listened to him then, she wouldn't have been suffering so much now. How could she think that after being years apart, Gaven would stay the same?

"Lay down," he said. "We have an early start tomorrow."

"How much longer?" she asked, feeling the strain of her sleepless nights.

"Not long."

***

SALATHIEL'S DESCRIPTION failed to capture the majestic beauty of their hideaway. He had told her it was a cabin in the mountains. She didn't expect it to be etched *in* the mountain, the back disappearing into the side of a cliff. Steps had been carved into the mountainside so subtly that she hadn't noticed them until Salathiel pointed them out. She tilted her head back, admiring the rustic front with large bay windows. Her hood fell back, and for the first time since finding Salathiel, she let it stay that way.

"Come on," Salathiel said. He began ascending the stairs. Mirari took another look around before bracing her hand on the cliff face and slowly ascending after him.

The cabin was high enough in the mountains that they could look down on the canopy of trees in the local forest. Birds swooped down below, trilling a soothing song back and forth to each other. There was no one around them for miles in either direction. She had one way to go, and that was wherever Salathiel led her. She finally caught up to him near the top of the stairs, and he opened the side entrance of the cabin.

Inside, it was large and expansive, extending to the right, deep into the mountain. The huge windows illuminated the interior well. It was both charming and elegant. Mirari stepped inside, spinning around to take it all in at once. Aside from the birds outside and Salathiel walking comfortably across the stone floor, it was completely silent. No dust on any surfaces either. Even though it was empty now, it hadn't been for very long.

Mirari walked around, running her hand across the rugged stone walls. Looking closely, she could see the gray stone had flecks of some kind of faintly glowing gem. She wondered how

Salathiel came to find such a beautiful place. She had many questions for Salathiel now that they didn't have to keep rushing. It was time for Mirari to get some answers.

"Is this your place?" Mirari asked. "Is this where you've been living?"

"Not exactly," Salathiel said, walking down the hallway. He opened one of the doors and motioned toward her. "You can take this room."

She didn't budge.

"Salathiel." He glanced up at her but turned away at the look on her face. "Where have you been all these years? I… I looked for you." She dragged her hand down the stone wall, clenching her fist down by her side.

"I'm sorry, Mirari."

That wasn't what she wanted to hear. She just wanted to know why and understand him. Had he ever gone back to Solarin and looked for her? How did he get the scar on his eye? She wanted answers, not an apology. If she could only understand, she wouldn't even need an apology. She was inches from him now, and she tried again.

"Salathiel. Please, just tell me what happened to you. Did you look for me?"

He wrapped his arm around her shoulder. "I looked for you as soon as it was safe for me to do so. I promise. Hey." He waited until she met his gaze. "I found you, didn't I?"

But how had he found her, she wondered. How had he known where she was in that forest when she didn't even know herself?

With his arm still around her shoulder, he steered to the door he'd indicated earlier. "Here. Just rest. We've been traveling for a long time now. You can relax." He pushed the door open and looked at her. "How long has it been since you've had a chance to relax? Years?" She looked away, feeling suddenly weary.

"There are some things I can't answer yet, but I will in due time."

Though it wasn't the response she wanted, she let herself be pulled into the cozy bedroom.

"What *can* you tell me?"

He sighed and she thought he was going to refuse her again. "The cabin doesn't belong to me. It belongs to my benefactor. After that last job in Solarin... I ran into some trouble. I was injured. She took me in and helped me. And now she's going to help you." When Mirari opened her mouth, he held his hand up. "I can't tell you who my benefactor is, but know that she wants to meet you. When that can be arranged, I'll be able to answer the rest of your questions. Is that enough?"

"I suppose." Trying not to sulk, she sat down on the bed, bouncing slightly on the plush surface.

"Good. Now get some rest. I'll be back soon."

"Wait," she cried, jumping up when he turned to leave. "Where are you going?"

"I have to get some supplies before the snow gets bad." Mirari knew she was being irrational, but she worried about being separated after they'd only just found each other. "I won't be gone long," he said. "You know it's safer if you stayed here."

"Yeah." Her shoulders slumped. "I understand. Hurry back."

"I will."

Mirari collapsed backward onto the bed and stared at the ceiling. She sat quietly, alone, and the silence agitated her. Waiting for Salathiel to return... again? She quickly sat up and shook her thoughts away. Getting to her feet, she looked around the bedroom searching for a distraction. Anything would do.

The room was large. With the bed taking up a significant proportion of the room, it had a cozy atmosphere. A small nightstand stood to the right of the bed and a chest of drawers close to the door. The stone walls sparkled with some embedded gems like twinkling stars. It was cute, but Mirari felt claustrophobic with the door closed.

Slipping out, Mirari explored the rest of the cabin. As she got farther in, cabin felt like a misleading term for the chalet. It was huge. There was a large kitchen, a sitting room, three bedrooms not counting the one for her, and a stone stairway that led to the second floor.

Upstairs, she found a library. Perhaps she could find something to occupy her mind while she waited for Salathiel. Floor-to-ceiling shelves were bursting with novels and textbooks. Plush chairs sat underneath the window, inviting her to sit.

She walked down the aisles, searching for something to read. Instead, she found a door tucked away into the far corner. She glanced around, but, of course, there was no one to see her. It felt a bit like snooping, but when she twisted the handle, the door was unlocked. Shrugging, she walked in. She wanted to know more about who had been helping her brother all these years.

The hidden room was nothing nefarious, just an office. It was fairly small compared to the other rooms in the house. Aside from the singular chair, there was only a large, oak desk covered in papers. Mirari was about to leave when she caught sight of a seal stamp.

She picked it up, looking more closely and muttered in realization, "The Council." She dropped it and grabbed a few letters that lay on the table. It was signed by Councilor Dareh. The next was from Councilor Suzan, and they were both addressed to a fellow councilor.

That was where Salathiel found her, still looking over the letters.

"Mirari?" Salathiel called, sticking his head through the doorway. "There you are." He looked around the room. "What are you doing in here?"

She turned to face him. "Sal, is this Councilor Julie's home?"

"I already told you—"

"They'll execute me, Sal."

Salathiel bit his lip. When he didn't answer, she ran out of the room. She made it halfway down the stairs before Salathiel caught her wrist. She turned to look up at him.

"Mirari, it's okay," he said. "We can trust her."

She scowled, "Stop dancing around my questions and just tell me what's going on already." Mirari tried to shake off his grip, but Salathiel held on tight. "Trust her? Trust you? How can I—"

She paused when she realized her mistake. Salathiel *was* the last person she could trust, and he didn't deserve those words.

He sat down on the stairs and with his grip on her wrist, tugged her down next to him. He didn't seem offended at the slightest. Instead, he took a deep breath and began, "Do you remember when Kylah was at our place? When Councilor Julie took care of the assassins?"

Mirari furrowed her brows. She had nearly forgotten that they had all met at one point. "Just because she helped us that one time doesn't mean we can trust her," she said.

"She saved my life," Salathiel said, and reminded her, "and she saved yours too. At least listen to what she has to say. You owe her this much."

Mirari crossed her arms and stared down the stairwell. She didn't want to get into an argument with Salathiel like she did with Gaven, but she wasn't convinced. Councilor Julie was unpredictable and known to act on her own, against her duties to the Council, the people of Valenia, and even her own allies.

In a softer tone, Salathiel continued, "You've heard of the Blessed, right?"

Mirari's head whipped around and she clenched her hidden hands tight enough to hurt. "Y-yes. Of course."

"They were responsible for the attack on the Grand Ball, and they're only growing more powerful."

"The Defiants," Mirari said, correcting him.

"The Defiants?"

"T-that's what people are calling them. To differentiate them from the other members. Even they want to stop them."

Salathiel mused over the name. "Fair. You seem to know a lot about this."

Mirari shrugged. Was this the time to talk about the Blessed? Larger questions were at hand, and she had to bring the conversation back around.

"But what do the Defiants have to do with Councilor Julie?" she asked.

"Julie has known about the Bl—, ah, the Defiants for a while. She knows who the leader is, and we're trying to locate her now."

Mirari frowned. "If she knew about the Defiants, does that mean she knows the rest of the Blessed are innocent? Why didn't she tell the rest of the Council?"

Salathiel scoffed. "She knew they wouldn't listen. To them, no member of the Blessed is a human being, Defiant or not. That's why she's doing this on her own." He turned to her. "That's why she's going to ask for your help."

"Wait, me?" She pointed to her chest.

Salathiel laughed at the look on her face. "What? You don't think you're important?"

"...No?"

He laughed again. "Well, you are. You can help a lot of people." He sobered. Then, he turned away and mumbled, "You're the only one who can stop them."

At least, that was what she thought she heard him say. "Huh? Come again?"

"Julie can explain everything better. She'll talk to you when she gets here." He slapped his legs and stood up. Grabbing her arm, he tugged her to her feet.

"And I'm supposed to just wait?" Mirari asked as he pulled her down the stairs and into the living room.

"Well, first, you can help me put away these supplies, but then, yes."

She turned her head to the right and scowled. They passed a window and she saw her eyes glimmer in the reflection. Mirari froze, letting go of Salathiel's hand. He turned back.

"Mirari? Is everything all right?" She took a small, slow step toward the window, but it was gone. "Is there something out there?"

Mirari shook her head, hiding behind a smile. "Oh, no. Just… just a bird. Come on." She ran ahead of him, running away from what she'd seen. "Those supplies won't put themselves away."

CHAPTER TWO

Gaven stood before the Council at the Hearth once again. Ostensibly, it wasn't a trial, but the similarities were not lost on Gaven as he was observed by the councilors from their high thrones. The six of them stared down at him impassively as they discussed the situation between them. In the beginning, they had remained stoic and somber, but as always, the debate soon became heated. Even though he wasn't the one they were deliberating upon, he'd been dragged in as soon as the chaos died down.

The meeting was about the trial that had brought them all to the Hearth in the first place. The leader of the Blessed, Eoin, had been captured by Gaven, tried, and sentenced to death in short order. Then, in the walk between the court and the gallows, he'd simply disappeared – just walked out as far as anyone could tell. There hadn't been any fighting or bloodshed, and no guards were missing or dead. The conclusion was simple: someone helped Eoin escape. There was a traitor in their midst.

"What of that girl," Councilor Tarek said. He motioned to Councilor Julie. "The one you mentioned."

"Mirari Zanette," she answered. She stared him down, then

at the rest of the councilors, reminding them that she was right all along.

Gaven gritted his teeth, but he kept his face impassive.

Tarek nodded along. "Didn't you say she spent a lot of time in Aias?" Gaven was brought back to the forefront as they questioned him. "Are you sure she is dead?"

"You think she faked her death and helped the blacksmith escape," Dareh said, musing.

Out of the corner of his eye, Gaven could see Hime grab Dorain's arm when he jumped to his feet.

"They're trying to blame Mirari," Dorain hissed, but it wasn't much of a whisper. Gaven could understand his frustration. He was thankful that the Knights still supported Mirari.

"She was stabbed in the chest," Gaven said, pointing to his chest. "Fatal. No one can survive a wound like that without a healer." He gestured to a soldier on the sideline, sweating profusely. "I have a witness if you'd like to question him."

"That won't be necessary," Dareh said. "I agree. Such a theory seems far-fetched." He smirked at Gaven. "After all, why put the blame on the dead when there's another more logical explanation standing before us."

Novinha followed, "Let's not forget that Region Leader Gaven helped the rebels during the siege."

"What are you saying?" Suzan demanded. "We already established that it was Laikos' doing."

"Only that birds of a traitorous feather, flock together," Dareh said.

"Do you have feathers in your ears, featherpit?" Adder responded, half rising. "Region Leader Gaven is not on trial. He was the one who brought the blacksmith in for trial."

"Where were you when the Blessed leader escaped?" Tarek turned to Gaven.

"Talking with the Knights," Gaven said. He nodded toward

the assembled Knights. Lifting his hand to his bruised lip, he said, "Region Leader Shiba had something to say."

All heads were turned to the stands. Shiba had his arms crossed and chin held high.

"There you have it," Suzan said. "Can we stop wasting time and focus on what's really at stake? The leader of our enemy has escaped and we still don't know the extent of the Blessed's power."

There was some grumbling and the discussion continued for some time. Though, at the end of it all, they didn't get much farther than when they started. Only one thing was agreed upon: focus on finding Eoin.

At the end of the trial, Suzan took Gaven to the side to speak to him privately.

"Do you truly not know anything about this Eoin?" she asked.

He scowled. "I don't."

She settled him down with a look. "Calm yourself. I'm only asking if you remember anything Mirari might have said to you. Did she visit any other place besides Aias? Did she mention another name besides the blacksmith?"

Gaven's hand ached with how tightly he was clenching his fist behind his back. He truly hadn't known what Mirari had been up to, but he wouldn't call that incompetence. Was it so wrong to trust the person he chose as his partner?

Inigo…

Mirari…

Maybe it was wrong.

He shook his head in response, and Suzan cursed under her breath.

"Your Grace, Councilor." He met her gaze boldly. "I swear to you, I will find the one who attacked the Grand Ball, the leader of these dissidents, and I will bring you their head."

She exhaled heavily and nodded. What else could she do? "I'm counting on you."

Resolved, he turned sharply on his heels. He met Fangbane's eyes across the room, but the masked man was being crowded by the other Knights. There was no need to talk to them, and he had enough today.

Fangbane resisted looking into the Knights' minds, to save himself the headache. He could already see the fury on their faces to know what their thoughts were.

As soon as the meeting concluded, the Knights swarmed him, demanding answers, demanding an explanation he just didn't have. He was verbally bombarded with their disbelief and despair. He could only imagine the chaos of their thoughts. Looking up, he caught Gaven's eyes briefly over Suzan's shoulder, and then they were both gone, leaving Fangbane alone with his Knights. Their thoughts were tugging him back.

Does Gaven even feel any remorse?

We've let Mirari down. How could we let him escape?

This can't be happening. Not again.

Fangbane exhaled deeply, his mind drifting to his family at the estate, where they were peacefully distant from the drama unfolding before him. When he returned to the present, Dorain was filled with righteous fury.

"Why didn't you say anything," Dorain demanded. "They slandered Mirari's name."

"You don't really believe Mirari would betray us, right?" Neo said, brow furrowed as he hovered over the Knights.

"Lord Fangbane," Lucan asked tonelessly, "is… Mirari really gone?" He was naturally pale, but now he was practically color-less. Fangbane winced, imagining the full-blown horror that hid behind Lucan's white-tinted glasses. He knew it was exceptionally hard for him to hear. Lucan had lost his cousin, found her, and then lost her all over again.

"Are you still defending that flatty?" Shiba scorned, turning everyone's attention away from Lucan. "He should've protected her, and he gets to walk free like he does every time. When are you going to stop giving Gaven a free pass, Fang? He needs to be held responsible for this!"

"Will you shut it already?" Kylah hissed. "It isn't always about you. For once, can you think about what Mirari would want us to do?" She must've hit a nerve when Lucan stood up.

"I… I need some air. Please excuse me for a moment." Lucan bowed and staggered toward the open doors. That face couldn't fool Fangbane – he could tell his mind was beginning to spiral into a dark place, and reasonably so. Would Lucan keep Mirari's secret now that she was really dead? Would he have her buried as a Hale?

Ha. Buried. There wasn't even a body. Only Gaven could tell them what happened, and his anger was too raw for Fangbane to glean anything from him.

He clapped his hands, bringing the Knight to focus. "We need to talk about what we'll do now," he said. "With the leader of the Blessed back out there, we need to prepare for an escalation of rebels again. That's—" He cut himself off at the sharp spike of anger coming from the right. Dorain was sitting with his arms crossed. It was almost nonchalant and collected except Fangbane could see his knee bouncing with barely repressed energy and no small amount of anger. "Do you have something to add?"

"Aren't you changing the subject?" Dorain said, leaning forward. On his shoulder, his bright-eyed kestrel mirrored his movement. "Yes, the Blessed leader has escaped, but the Council thinks, for some reason, Mirari had something to do with it. They're blackening her name, and we don't even know what happened?"

"The kid has a point," Shiba said. "I understand if Gaven has nothing to say to the Council, but at the very least he owes us an explanation about what happened to Mirari. He seems to be hiding something."

Fangbane spread his hands and shrugged. "I lack the power to keep Gaven any place he doesn't wish to be, and trust me, he is as distraught as we are."

That might as well have been a lie. The truth was, Fangbane was unable to read anything from Gaven. Pain? Worry? It was all blank. Unless Gaven came clean about what happened to Mirari, he would keep that secret to himself. There was no other way around it.

Fangbane could see that his answer was unsatisfactory to the Knights, but he didn't think the truth would be more readily accepted either. Whether or not Gaven was there with them, they weren't going to get any answers him. The best Fangbane could do was keep the Knights cordial with each other long enough for cooler heads to prevail.

"As for Mirari..." Fangbane continued. "Finding out what happened to the blacksmith will do a lot more toward clearing her name than just arguing here. The Council—"

"Yes. We all heard," Shiba said, rolling his eyes. "The leader of the Blessed was served to them on a platter and now they expect us to clean up their mess." He growled. His voice deepened with anger, but the volume stayed the same. "One of our own is dead and they expect us to fix their incompetence."

It was more than that, Fangbane knew, though he was reluctant to say. The fate of the Knights was split among the council, and ordering the Knights to find out what happened to Eoin was also a test of faith. Dareh, Tarek and Julie wanted to see them fail, to prove their existence useless. Suzan was giving them a chance – a chance to prove that even if Mirari was a traitor, she was just an outlier in the Knights. The rest of the council agreed with her.

Fangbane knew that telling the Knights to tread lightly going forward wasn't going to engender any positive feelings. For Hime, Dorain and Lucan, it would hurt them and their family name to be doubted after all they had contributed to the Knights. For Shiba and, to a lesser extent, Neo, they'd be outraged to have their honor doubted. Kylah would, no doubt, withdraw, wary of being recast as a villain after trying to rehabilitate her image. It was best if Fangbane kept that knowledge to himself and just gently steered his Knights through the minefield that was the Council's scrutiny.

"If you believe it's the Council's incompetence that let Eoin escape, then prove it," Fangbane said. "We'll do as the Council suggested and investigate how he escaped between the courtroom and the gallows. If it was a traitor, find proof."

"What are your thoughts?" Dorain asked. "Do you believe it was a traitor? Do you believe Mirari was a part of some… some larger conspiracy?" Dorain got to his feet to stare Fangbane down. "You talk about finding proof, but no one presented it at the trial before they decided she was complicit with the Blessed."

"She was spending time in Aias, where the rebels were hiding," Shiba said. "That was more or less confirmed, wasn't it?"

Whirling on the region leader, Dorain looked almost incandescent with rage. "She went to some village and that makes her a traitor. That's what you think?"

"I didn't say that," Shiba said, even-toned. It didn't last. Each word rose in volume as his own frustration leaked through. "I'm saying that little idiot probably had some misguided idea about helping and didn't think about how it looked. And now she's dead and can't explain herself. You tell me. What am I supposed to think? Because I don't know."

Shiba's breath was heaving and he only settled when Neo placed a hand on his shoulder. He may have appeared enraged, but Fangbane could read that he was concealing a deeper level of distress. He did this whenever he thought of…

Mecate…

Shiba was imagining scenarios that would have led a gullible Mirari into Aias in the first place. He seethed, blaming Gaven for not keeping a closer eye on her.

"Right now," Fangbane said, turning everyone's attention back to him, "there's too much we don't know about what happened in Aias and what Mirari did." He flattened his hand on the table and leaned forward as everyone's gaze reoriented toward him like flowers seeking the sun. "Needless speculation and arguments won't get us anywhere."

Dorain stayed tense and angry, not willing to concede just yet.

Hime, ever the peacemaker, placed her hand on his shoulder to ease him back into his seat. "Lord Fangbane is correct. We mustn't argue among ourselves. It's not helping anybody, least of all Mirari."

The others slowly unwound and Fangbane quickly ran through their surface thoughts.

Kylah's face was blank while her mind rolled with turmoil. Unlike the others she wasn't blaming Fangbane or even Gaven. He picked up an interesting thought, something about wishing she had listened to what Mirari said. What else did she know? She turned her head so the long curtain of golden hair shielded her expression from view. Whatever it was, he couldn't get it from her now.

Neo worried for both Shiba and Kylah. Neo worried Shiba would spiral like he did after Mecate's death. For his love, Kylah, he worried about her trying to take responsibility for things outside of her control. He was right about both. Fangbane almost pitied him for the heavy, responsibility he had placed upon himself, but it was what made him a good friend.

Hime's thoughts were on the Knights, especially on how hard

Dorain was taking the news. Her vibrant ocean-blue eyes darted around the group. She worried that the discord would seep in and fracture their group. To be honest, Fangbane had the same fears but he would do everything in his power to keep them together.

As for Dorain…

Though Dorain had chosen to stand down at Hime's insistence, his thoughts were still fairly antagonistic. Fangbane probed deeper to get a clearer picture. His heart sank as Dorain's thoughts filtered through.

He's a coward. We're not going to get anywhere like this. Dorain's thoughts turned to his father and they lacked the usual scorn he held for his father's ideals. *Maybe there's actually something my father can teach me. At least he stands up for what he believes in.*

Fangbane internally winced. To be considered less than Dareh in terms of principles and values was… worse than an insult. The Knights were Fangbane's cause. Bringing an end to strife was the belief that had drawn him and Starlight together in the first place. Fighting with everyone who disagreed with him was counterintuitive. That being said, he could understand Dorain's anger.

It was a relief when the door opened and Lucan returned to them. Fangbane wouldn't say he looked better than when he'd left, but there was a sense of grim commitment to him. He looked around the room, noticing the tension among the others.

"Did I miss something?" he asked.

Fangbane shook his head. The truth would be had in time. Until then, he knew what they had to focus on. "I was just saying that while the Blessed are still an active threat, we need to investigate how their leader escaped and where he might go next."

Shiba snorted and got to his feet. "Yeah, *that's* what we were discussing."

"Oh and we just have to accept that Mirari was a traitor," Dorain added sullenly.

Lucan twitched, but somehow managed to maintain his composure.

"I see," he said.

Fangbane sighed. "For now, we have to accept that we can't change anyone's mind with words alone," he corrected before the argument could escalate again. "What we can do is recapture the blacksmith and find out the truth of his escape."

Lucan didn't say anything, and Fangbane narrowed his eyes. He could be a problem.

"Do *you* have any objections?"

"No, that's fine," Lucan said. *I will find out what happened to Mirari.*

With no obvious support, Dorain huffed and headed toward the door.

"Where are you going?" Shiba demanded.

"To investigate. That's all we can do, isn't it?"

CHAPTER THREE

Erel sat atop her horse, back straight and face somber. In the distance, the Hearth sat in the center of acres of carefully maintained Valenian land, and the guards walked the grounds, typically attentive, but comfortable with defensive barriers to assist them in their duties. That comfort was disrupted earlier today when Eoin escaped.

Erel was familiar with the guard's routines and defensive measures, having had multiple chances to examine them in the many roles she affected – guards, servants, dignitaries, even a council member for a few months. She observed their new countermeasures with much curiosity, if not to distract her from the nerves swirling in her stomach.

She breathed a sigh of relief when she saw Gaven walk to the stables where his mount waited. The guards watched carefully, but didn't follow him. But then, Lucan greeted him at the stable, no doubt with a few choice words. Erel bit her lip. Time seemed to pass slowly, but as soon as Gaven was able to get Lucan off his shoulder, he sprinted away from the Hearth, down the road, just out of sight from the guards.

He slowed his horse to a brisk trot as he got closer to Erel, and she fell into an easy step beside him. Glancing over, he raised his eyebrow and she nodded to his silent question. His shoulders slumped. That was one thing taken care of. They rode in silence for a little while.

Gaven kept his senses extended and glanced behind him routinely. It wouldn't be unusual for the council to send spies after them. Fortunately, they were alone.

He nodded to Erel and she pulled ahead slightly, leading the way off road. She took him to a long-abandoned fort, hidden in a thicket of trees. The forest had reclaimed the land and huge oaks pushed aside the crumbling stone and burst from the roof of the fort. They dismounted and he handed the reins of his horse over to his second.

She accepted them but kept her heavy gaze on him.

"Speak," he prompted. "What's on your mind?"

She blinked and turned to look at the fort. "Are you sure about this?"

He snorted. Of course he wasn't. Erel knew that since his fight with Mirari in Aias, he had been fighting his own thoughts.

Shaking his head, he said, "Isn't it a little late for doubts?"

"We could still turn it around. If we find a body instead of a fugitive, no one will doubt us."

Gaven shook his head. "If I want answers, this is the only way I'll get them."

Erel didn't argue with him. Earlier that day, they arrived at the Hearth with more than the intention to watch Eoin's inevitable death sentence. Gaven had a ludicrous plan, and Erel didn't know if it was designed with the best judgment. She trusted Gaven, but if they were caught, the consequences would be dire.

"This won't take long," he said, rubbing his raw knuckles. He spoke it like a promise as they entered the fort.

Erel secured the horses and took on the form of a soldier. This one was tall and muscular with a dark, thick beard, a proper

Althaean soldier. She followed Gaven inside and stood guard by the hole in a wall where she had a view of their horses and the entrance. It wouldn't do for them to be found here.

Yesterday's trial sat in her mind. She had taken the form of a royal guard she had cunningly dismissed and guided Gaven to the dungeon. After he gave Eoin a good beating and took him to the stand, Erel took her place by the door and waited until it was time to escort Eoin to the gallows. His face was starting to swell – a brilliant subterfuge planned by Gaven to keep Eoin's thoughts on his pain. There was a mind reader in the room, after all, and Eoin knew he wasn't going to die today.

Though she had impersonated people thousands of times, this was the most challenging act she had done by far, and she found it hard to keep her breathing steady. She took note of the attendees and hoped no one had their eyes on her. Gaven wasn't handling it any better. He was standing in the shadows cast by rows of seats and out of sight from everyone when she heard his heart rate slightly increase. His face was set in stone, a somber frown affixed to his features. Underneath the facade, she doubted anyone else could see his nerves, and if they did, they might attribute it to nothing more than anxiety about being back in the Hearth where his fate had been decided.

Erel knew that on top of their lucrative plan, Gaven was carrying a larger burden than ever. His aura was like a candle's flame fighting a windstorm. He acted as if nothing had changed, but his lifeline – his partner – was now gone. It affected him, and he didn't want to admit it.

After Gaven denied the Council's accusations of Mirari, Eoin was ordered to be executed immediately. Straightening her back, Erel walked confidently forward. She grabbed Eoin by the arm and ordered him up. He looked at her warily, but she gave him no choice as she hauled him to his feet. It was all going as expected… until the Knights swarmed Gaven.

"Keep moving," she said, dragging Eoin forward. Their

window of opportunity was shrinking, and now she had to do this on her own. As they walked down the hallway, Eoin's gaze darted around, no doubt looking for the place that would lead to his freedom. Halfway toward the gallows, she dragged him down another hallway. She could sense his heart rate picking up and the thick muscles in her grip tightened in anticipation of an attack.

"Don't even think about it," she hissed. "If we're caught, you're dead. Understand?"

"I thought—"

"Quiet!" Fortunately, he got the hint and remained quiet while Erel led him to the servant's entrance. The bag she left was waiting for them and she grabbed a cloak to throw over Eoin's head.

They kept their heads down as they snuck out of the Hearth. There wasn't much time. The Councilors would soon notice that Eoin hadn't made it to the gallows. After they gained a little distance, Eoin also got some confidence.

Enough to say, "This wasn't the plan."

"You think His Honor would tell you the real plan?"

The bluff barely worked. They had told Eoin that members of the Blessed would create a distraction to help him escape. The truth was that it was just her and Gaven. They were on their own.

"How far do you plan to get with just the two of you?" he said when they ducked out of sight from a group of guards racing toward the Hearth.

"Silence, you disgraceful peasant," Erel hissed. She carefully waited for the guards to look in the other direction before forcing Eoin into another sprint toward a thick forest.

This was stupid. Reckless. But he was right – how were they supposed to pull this off alone?

When they finally reached the horse Erel had tied down, she helped Eoin onto the saddle and kicked the steed into a bolt.

"You must really trust the region leader," Eoin said, "to risk so much for him."

She scowled at him. "Do you want to talk or do you want to escape?"

Eoin finally subsided, allowing her to focus on getting them out of there safely. It took them longer than she wanted to make it to the abandoned fort she'd found. She took a moment to catch her breath before directing Eoin inside. It was dark and damp, but Eoin didn't complain or fight when she chained him to the one sturdy wall inside.

"What now?"

Erel exhaled. She couldn't believe she did it. She spoke, "Now you wait for His Honor."

<hr>

Eoin glanced briefly at Erel – to him, she was a new face. She thought about his words and took it as advice – it would be best if Eoin believed Gaven had many comrades on his side. They couldn't let him believe that there was a chance of escape.

Staring down at Eoin, Gaven spoke in a calm voice. "You'll tell me just what lies you filled Mirari's head with."

Eoin seemed cooperative at the moment, but in truth, she knew little about this man and what he might do. She couldn't take any chances, not after coming this far.

Eoin said, "No lies, Your Honor. I speak the truth to those willing to hear."

Perhaps for the first time since the Grand Ball, even if it was just a little, Erel could tell Gaven was at ease. He sat down on a stump, looking every inch the region leader he was and sighed.

"Speak then."

CHAPTER FOUR

Not far from the Althaean–Valenian border stood a large town called Byham. It was by no means a metropolis, but like most towns in Valenia, it had grown around the forest it inhabited with winding roads that either looped around the foliage or through the trunk of a particularly large tree. In the thick of winter, the sunlight bore down through the bare trees. It wasn't known for much other than its abundant natural resources exported, and often smuggled, from Valenia – a sweetshop for spellcasters like Kylah.

"We're here," Neo said. He ran his large hand through his hair, looking adorably befuddled. "Do we just ask around for the Blessed?"

Shiba snorted. "Yeah, sure. Just point me to your nearest terrorist please."

Neo rolled his eyes and nudged Shiba. "Let's just find the mayor and see what they have to say."

Crunching the dead leaves, Neo and the other Knights walked into town in search of any connection to the Blessed. They were silent, speaking no more than a few words at a time, focusing on whatever dark thoughts consumed them. It was a few weeks after Eoin's trial and they had no leads on his whereabouts.

At a glance, it looked like the Blessed was winning and the Council was left in checkmate. Violence across the land was ramping up thanks to the Blessed, or by rabble-rousers. Neo couldn't really tell. All were trouble in his eyes. The Council certainly did their part too. The executions continued, on a much grander scale now. Squads of soldiers were stationed across every region to terrorize the people in the name of peace. The uncertain stability of the nations created doubt not only in the Knights but in the people across the empires. Neo felt some of the same influences in Byham – uneasiness, doubt, fear.

The Knights no doubt had it worse. Mirari's absence placed their synergy on a thread. It seemed to have dawned on them that any of them could meet the same fate – that the seven Knights would gradually diminish over time. By the time the Blessed was put to an end, who would be left?

Neo forced himself to acknowledge it – Mirari's death – but not all the Knights were willing to do so. He glanced at Lucan walking quietly next to him. For the past few weeks, he swung wildly from hope that she was alive somewhere, to despair, all tinged with a hint of disbelief. When Fangbane told the Knights to investigate Byham, he'd suggested that Lucan sit out. Lucan had declined. He was grimly focused on finding the Blessed. He was no doubt also participating to find answers for personal reasons.

Hime approached a woman hanging her wet clothes on a line. "Excuse me." The woman started, whipping around in a snap enough to rip the cloth in her hand. "Ah, I'm sorry. I didn't mean to startle you."

The woman glanced from Hime to the rest standing behind her. Her fear escalated and was followed on the heels by suspicion and dread. She took a step back, holding the ruined cloth in front of her like an ineffectual shield.

"What is it?" she asked in a trembling voice.

Hime held her hands up. "There's nothing to fear. We're with the Knights and I just want to ask you a question."

This doesn't do much to soothe the woman. A creak sounded and the woman's eyes widened. "Stay inside," she whispered without looking back at the door.

A mop of curly hair peeked out. The child pouted, whining, "Mama, I—"

"I said to stay inside," she snapped and the child disappeared, slamming the door. In the quiet aftermath, the woman held her shaking hand out, blocking their view of the door. "What is it? What do you want?"

Perturbed, Hime could barely speak. "Could you direct us to your town's mayor?"

The directions were given, terse and anxious. There was no chance for a guide, so they were forced to find their way based on fearful directions. The woman's reaction to their presence was not unique. As they walked through town, mistrustful glances followed, with locals quickly disappearing into their homes at the sight of the Knights. It was worse than Neo had thought. The Council was getting out of hand if people held as much fear of the protectors as they did of the Blessed.

"I can't believe it." Dorain stared around the town in shock. "How could things have gotten so bad?"

Hime patted him on the back, but it didn't appear to do much to soothe his anger. He lowered his head, hands clenched by his side.

"We have to do something about this," he said.

"We are—"

"Not enough." He exhaled harshly, glowering at the street. "I bet this is what Mirari saw across Althaea. I bet she tried to stop this and—"

"Enough, Dorain," Shiba said. He kept his gaze to the front, scanning the empty streets.

"Why?" Dorain stopped, turning to face the rest of them. "You don't really believe Mirari was a traitor, do you? She would never turn her back on the people she was protecting."

Neo watched Shiba's hand clench into a fist. He could feel his partner holding back a strong urge to silence the young one. Neo huffed, dissipating the anger he felt in his heart, and relaying the feeling back to the sender. That was enough to get Shiba to release his fist.

No, Shiba didn't think Mirari was a traitor. Believe it or not, had he known what was going on in Althaea Main, he would've rushed over to help Mirari in a heartbeat. But he didn't, and that regret was a heavy feeling that even Neo found difficult to carry. And whenever someone spoke her name, it just made the guilt worse.

Neo had told him that, though unfortunate, Mirari's situation was inevitable. If she survived the battle in Aias and stood up to the Council for their practices, the Council would've silenced her rather than admit their mistakes.

"It doesn't matter," Kylah said.

Neo looked at her. Of course she understood; she knew all about being scapegoated and was familiar with the genuine sense of helplessness. Truth often carried little authority – most of them had seen it. They had accepted the reality of politics, but not Dorain. He was yet to witness what it truly meant to be powerless.

Dorain turned on her and huffed, "How can you say that?"

"I only meant that now's not the time or the place." She tipped her head back. "We're here to help people, not argue amongst ourselves."

"Kylah's right," Lucan said. "We need to focus on our current duty." With crossed arms, he stared down at the youth challenging him to retort.

Dorain looked dissatisfied but fell back into step with them.

Neo gave Kylah a small smile. His large, warm hand grasped hers and gently squeezed.

"We're almost there," he said as he guided them forward.

It was later in the day when they finally found the mayor's house among the tangle of streets. Hime's earlier encounter had shaken her and it was Dorain who approached the door and knocked. It was a few minutes, and many more knocks later that the door finally opened. A wizened old man appeared in the crack and stared at them.

"What do you want?" he croaked.

"Apologies for dropping in like this," Dorain said with surprising grace. Then again, being with the Knights for years had matured him to some extent, if not from being a councilor's son. Despite their differences, he must have picked something up from his unlikeable father. He flashed the badge on his chest. "We're with the Knights, and we need to speak with you."

"I don't know anything," he said, starting to close the door.

Dorain quickly placed his hand in the gap. It was a good thing he was taking the lead. If Neo had done that, the old man would have surely keeled over in shock.

"Sir, we just need a minute of your time. Our lands are under threat and we need your help."

The man glanced at them. "I already told you, I don't know anything. I can't help."

"You've heard of the Blessed, haven't you?" Those words weren't as forbidden as they were just a few months prior. Through the door, Dorain pressed his questions, gently but persistent. Dorain had a young face, eager and approachable, that usually put people at ease. It was better than Shiba's harsh mannerisms or Kylah's cynicism, but this time it wasn't working. Regardless of Dorain's sweet-talk, the old man remained adamant that he didn't know anything about the Blessed, Aias or Eoin. After a while, they had to concede that they wouldn't get anything out of him. If they kept pressing, it would only be considered harassment.

Sighing, Dorain stepped back. "Very well. Thank you for your time."

The man harrumphed and shut the door.

"Now what?" Dorain asked, turning back.

"I suppose if there's no more information to be gathered from here, you should report what we learned to Fangbane," Lucan said as he stepped away from the door.

Frowning, Kylah touched his arm so that he turned to look at her. He didn't look nearly as frustrated as she thought he would. "You aren't coming with us?"

"I have business to attend to," he said, tugging on his sleeve.

Shiba scoffed, taking a step toward him. "Just what kind of business?"

"Hale," he answered shortly. "I'm still the head of my household. I have duties."

Kylah watched Dorain's brow furrow, but he didn't interject.

"And I'm still the region leader of Avon but I'm pulling my weight for the team," Shiba said. His shoulders grew tense and Hime stepped forward, lifting her hands between the two of them as he spat, "Are you going to abandon us like a coward?"

Lucan didn't respond to the challenge. "I assisted you this far. Is there anything else to be done here?" Shiba's lip curled, but he didn't say anything. "As I expected." He tugged on his cloak, straightening his already neat clothes. "I'll take my leave then."

No one had anything else to say. They could only watch as Lucan turned and went in a different direction.

Shiba snorted. "Fine. Let's go."

Shiba stalked away and the rest simply fell into step behind him. Kylah glanced back, but Lucan was already out of sight. Neo knew what she was thinking; she hoped Lucan wasn't obsessing over clearing Mirari's name. Everyone was, to some extent, even Neo. But sometimes the truth didn't matter no matter how much you wished otherwise.

Dusk had settled over the town, and it seemed the people had disappeared along with the sun. The Knights were silent, but so were the streets, except for the discordant noise of heavy footsteps out of place among the Knights. Even through the dead leaves that littered the road, they couldn't be concealed.

Kylah started to turn when Neo stopped her, draping his arm over her shoulder. He leaned down to whisper warmly in her ear.

He leaned back, nodding at the questioning look in her eyes. They were being followed, had been since they'd left the mayor's house. "There's at least ten of them."

"More up ahead," Shiba added.

Kea returned to Dorain's tense shoulder. She flapped her wings and cooed.

"Three," Dorain said. He flicked his wrist and his bow extended in his hand.

"Don't be stupid," Shiba said with a warning glance at the younger man. "What do you think beating up a bunch of peasants is going to do for our reputation?"

Dorain scowled but kept his bow lowered.

Kylah patted Neo's arm and he nodded, stepping away from her. Tucking her hand into her cloak, she checked for the potion vials she kept against the lining – two green, one blue. She hoped they would never be put to use.

As they walked farther out of town, Neo hoped that their spies only believed they were leaving town. It was a foolish hope, of course. They passed a cascade of tree roots, and three men stepped out between the openings, blocking the way forward. Their weapons were laughable – two pitchforks and an ancient short sword. Shiba couldn't contain his smirk.

Hime held her hands up. "Peace, kind men," she said in her calm voice. "We don't want any trouble. My comrades and I were just leaving."

Neo could have told her that it was pointless. If they cared that the Knights were leaving, they would have just stuck to the shadows to watch them.

An arrow whistled through the air.

"Look out!" Dorain shouted.

Without taking her eyes off the peasants, Hime pivoted her hand in the direction of the arrow. The point of the arrow began to crystalize, until it was heavy enough to fall to the ground. The bandits in front rushed forward with a storm of arrows overhead.

Neo raised his hand toward them, and a barrier shimmed in front of Hime. The arrows bounced off harmlessly, but it wouldn't be enough for the archers hiding high among the trees and rooftops. They stuck out their heads one by one, readying their bow. Dorain stood next to Hime, aiming his bow at the snipers above.

"Your orders, My Lord?" Neo asked Shiba.

One of the men tripped as a shadow grabbed his legs and felled him like a tree. He bowled into another bandit and they both hit the ground.

Shiba spat on the ground. "Do we even have a choice?"

With a dagger in his right hand, he charged toward the next assailant. Kylah and Neo attended to the bandits approaching from the rear. A large man shot forward swinging an axe at Neo's head. Ducking, he grabbed the man's arm, halting him in place like a brick wall. Something cracked and the man was thrown backward. He hit the ground and didn't get back up. Others swarmed to take his place. Heedless of their fallen comrade, they stepped right over him. If he wasn't dead from the fall, he was now.

This was the state of the Alliance. Ever since Eoin escaped, the Knights were met with no choice but to take the lives of those who attacked them, innocent or not, and this had become their norm. Blood and death coursed through the valleys and met no border.

Lifting her cloak, Kylah pulled forth three vials, holding them between her fingers. Her eyes searched for the right moment.

While Neo was engaged with a burly man with a scarred face, Kylah lifted her hand and tossed the green vials in a line one after the other, ahead of the incoming bandits. They shattered on the ground, spilling a pale green liquid that splashed across their legs and boots. Raising her hand, Kylah ignited the toxin with a burst of fire. The bandits buckled under the noxious fumes, screaming as their lungs burned from the acrid scent.

If the bandits retreated, they could escape the worst of the fumes and would recover within the week. However, they didn't care. They threw themselves forward until Kylah had to dance back out of reach of their weapons. Their eyes reddened and blood pooled in the corner of their mouths, but they kept advancing.

Neo intercepted them, grappling with the closest two. Another tried to go around him and he kicked the man. Ducking, he forced the one on the right down and tossed the other back into the crowd. They kept coming. A few slipped around Neo and stared at Kylah with dead eyes.

Stand down," she demanded, pulling forth her last vial. "You cannot win. You'll die if you continue."

"We serve a higher purpose. We will not falter."

Behind him, more bandits were creeping closer. A dozen? Maybe more.

Neo realized these were more than just bandits after coin. They couldn't be reasoned with. Kylah must've thought the same when she backed up another step and nearly bumped into someone – Hime, if the chill emitting from the icy crystals surrounding her hands was any indication.

Resigned, Kylah chucked the potion at the feet of the attackers. It exploded on impact, a very small blast, sending shards of glass and liquid flames licking up their legs and across their skin.

Neo wasn't a child that had never seen death before, but watching their bodies light up in the night filled his stomach with discomfort. One of their companions fell to the flames, and to Neo's surprise, the others kept advancing.

He furrowed his brows. Why?

"They won't stand down," he heard Hime cry.

"Then we'll make them," Shiba said, not that Neo blamed him. There really was no other way.

Another civilian fell over, his body encased in ice. Hime covered Kylah as she reached in her left pocket for a blue crystal. The Knights could keep fighting, but should they? Was there a point where surrendering would've been a better option? Neo would've considered it, but he thought the others may not; certainly not Shiba. As the Knights, they weren't supposed to show weakness. So, unfortunately, against Neo's will, the fight continued.

The Blessed – for what else could they be? – threw themselves endlessly into battle, going so far as to trample over their own fallen brethren. They were frenzied, pressing close with wide eyes and blood-stained hands.

The fight seemed to have no end. That may have been in part due to the fact Neo avoided creating any fatalities – no more lives needn't be lost tonight. But he could see the Knights growing fatigued, especially Kylah. She had never had to use so much kore at once. The crystal in her hand turned dull, and she scrambled for another one in her pocket. She held a yellow crystal in front of her and cried out as a string of lighting struck forward. Her shoulders slumped as she heaved, then turned to the next target.

Bringing his fist to their stomachs, Neo added two men to the pile of dead or unconscious bodies on the ground. The last one fell over with an arrow in his chest, and they all took a moment to catch their breath. Bodies decorated the now silent field. One such body was staring at Kylah, sprawled on the ground with blood pooling under his head. When Neo looked down he could see the boot of another behind her.

He stepped in between her and the carnage and touched her shoulder. "Are you all right?"

"I'm fine," she said. She gave him a once over, looking for any injuries he might have. Bruises blossomed on his bare arms and he had a cut on his forehead that trickled blood down his dark face. She wiped the blood away with a cloth and ignored how close their faces were. "I have something for that."

She put away the cloth and looked down at one of the glass bottles around her belt. She hesitated. Something was off. Missing.

The boot by her foot was gone. She had a moment of panic before the ruffian lunged out from the roots behind. She turned her head as a dagger aimed for her chest.

"Kylah!"

The blade bit in deep. Blood splashed across Kylah's face and trickled down Neo's arm where the dagger was buried in the muscle. Like an iron band around her chest, he pulled her away from the crazed man.

As soon as she was clear, Neo plucked the dagger from his arm like a splinter and returned it to the man – jabbed in the throat, and he fell backward, dead.

Kylah didn't have a chance to look at Neo's wound before he turned her roughly in his arms and hugged her close. Heart beating like a drum in his ear, he didn't know if it was hers or his. It didn't matter while she was in his arms.

Kylah closed her eyes, and when Neo tightened his grip on her, tears began to stream down her face. All this time, he could tell Kylah was trying her best to hide the discomfort of killing civilians, being blamed for something she didn't do, and being treated like a monster. She had already been through all of that, and Neo had promised to never let her feel that way again. He had failed.

"Neo," Shiba called.

Kylah lifted her head at the sound of Shiba's tense voice. She glared at Neo's harsh partner, but found he wasn't watching either of them. Instead, he was looking up into one of the windows overlooking the street. Her head followed his gaze, and Neo did too.

They were being observed. Not by more enemies. In the long run, that would have been easier. Instead, townspeople and merchants were staring down at them. Neo didn't know if they had seen the entire fight. They knew what it looked like from their view. The Knights were surrounded by bodies of civilians.

"It's not what it looks like!" Dorain started, but Shiba cut him off with a wave of his hand.

"We should get going."

"We can't just leave," Dorain said. "They think we've—"

"There's no point." Shiba snapped louder than usual, and Neo could feel him growing discouraged. He hid it well on his face, as he always did, and the others didn't need to feel Shiba's heart to know to take him seriously.

Shaken, Hime spoke up. "Well, shouldn't we try?"

Dorain nodded and waited for Shiba's orders.

"There's nothing you can say to convince them otherwise," Shiba said. Turning on his heels, he began pacing away from town.

"No!" Dorain retracted his bow with a snap of his wrist and tried to keep up with Shiba's pace. "It's not fair. We didn't— They attacked us first."

Kylah's gaze fell to the ground. "Not if it affirms what they already believe," she said. "To them, we're no different from the Council."

She was right. As far as the town was concerned, this was what they expected the Knights to do.

Hime scanned the bodies around her. She carried a frown, but not the same kind that Kylah had. Knowing her, she was checking to see if there was anyone alive that she could heal. When she turned and began following Shiba, Neo knew the answer.

"Come on," Neo said as he started walking, pulling Kylah with him. She conceded, but kept her head lowered and dragged her feet.

Shoulders slumped, the Knights hurried from the town under the fearful scrutiny of its people.

CHAPTER FIVE

Lucan had decided to take matters into his own hands a long time ago. A few weeks ago when Gaven's trial ended and the Knights discussed their next steps, Lucan left the room to recollect himself. Dorain was putting up a fight trying to protect Mirari's name. Lucan agreed, but he wasn't as courageous as Dorain. He grew lightheaded at every mention of her name, and he took his weakness outside.

He stalked the hallways, heading to the exit. His hands clenched and unclenched and his breath felt tight in his chest. There was no telling how much longer he could last suffocating under the Council's roof. Instead of ordering his carriage to be brought around, he turned down another corridor, looking for a closer exit. He found bright sunlight streaming through from under a door, and pushed it open.

The earthy scent of hay filled his nose along with the strong odors of horse and sweat. His footsteps were silent as he walked through the stables filled with the mounts of those who were in attendance for the trial. He tried to focus only on the soft nicker of the horses. As he walked, some of the horses thrust their snouts over the gates, looking for treats and pats.

Outside the paddock where his horse rested, he paused. Bracing himself against the gate, he leaned over to take breath and another. Hot breath ghosted over the back of his neck.

"Saddle my horse," he heard a familiar voice say.

"Right away, Your Honor."

Lucan lifted his head. Gaven was standing at the stable's front entrance, tugging on his gloves like he had no care in the world. Lucan brushed away his horse's curious nibbling and stalked over before he knew what he was doing.

"You," he said with a snap in his voice, a tone that surprised himself.

Gaven glanced over. Cold. Curious. Unconcerned.

"Where are you going?" Lucan seethed while crossing his arms.

"I'm not sure how that's any of your business," he said. "But I'm going back to Althaea Main. I have duties there if you've forgotten."

"What about your duties to your partner?"

Gaven's eyebrows lowered over his blue eyes and he stared at Lucan like a bug was buzzing in his face. "My… partner." His jaw flexed. "I've done my duties to…" He glanced at Lucan again. "Mirari."

The stablehand approached with a saddled white stallion. He hesitated when he saw Lucan and Gaven speaking. Gaven turned away, holding his hands out for the reins to his mount. Lucan had no intention of just letting him walk away.

Swiftly, he stood between Gaven and the stablehand. "We're not done talking."

"I've nothing left to say." Gaven stepped forward like he was going to bowl right past Lucan. Lucan grabbed his arm, forcing him back a step. Behind him, the stablehand let out an audible gasp.

Lucan knew he was inviting a political disaster, but he didn't care. So what if Gaven was a region leader? Lucan Hale could weather the storm. It may not be what Mirari would have wanted – to bully answers from someone with the strength of his name – but for her he was willing to use his family name.

"What happened in Aias?" Lucan demanded. He felt Gaven's muscles tense underneath his hand but Gaven only jerked his hand free from Lucan's grip.

"Were you not listening? I've said all that needed to be said."

Lucan didn't move, rooted to the spot in front of Gaven. How could he? "So that's it? You'll just let them say whatever they want about Mirari, without standing up for her? Defending her? Do you not care?" Gaven stared at him coldly. "Have you *ever* cared?"

"Do not—" Gaven cut short his admonishment, visibly restraining himself. "Do *not* talk to me about caring for Mirari," he said, biting off each word. He took a step forward, preparing to push past Lucan who dropped his hand to his belt where his dagger rested. He could hear the stablehand behind him draw in a harsh breath as Gaven paused, finally meeting Lucan's eye.

It was monumentally stupid to try to physically pit himself against the Valiant Tiger. Lucan knew this. This went beyond politics. Lucan's cousin was dead and Gaven knew something about it. He refused to let Gaven walk away like nothing had happened. Gaven waved his hand and Lucan heard the stablehand step farther away.

"You knew," Gaven said. "You *knew*." He repeated the words more softly. "Of course you did. You two were so close."

"What are you talking about?"

"Her *name*."

Lucan drew back with a frown, shaking his head. "So what?"

"So *what?*" Gaven parted his lips to speak, but then he slammed his mouth shut and the anger in his eyes recoiled. He took a step back. "I was her partner. I deserved to know."

Lucan snorted. "She didn't owe you anything. And rightly so. Look what kind of a partner you turned out to be."

Gaven shifted his gaze to look beyond Lucan as though it was beneath him to even give Lucan his attention. "I've nothing left to say," he said. "Especially to you. The Council was satisfied with my testimony and that's all that really matters."

Lucan was outraged. He had just enough self-control to not raise his fist. Though, he wanted to – he wanted to force Gaven to his knees and demand answers from him. He would not be ignored.

But he allowed Gaven to push him aside like he was nothing more than lint. Gaven took the reins from the stablehand, dismissed him, and hopped onto his mount.

Lucan stood in front of the horse with his arms crossed.

"You're going to tell me what I want to know."

Gaven sneered. "And if I don't?"

"I'll have my answers one way or another. Perhaps I should seek an informant." Lucan tapped his chin, pretending to think. "What's the name of that old partner of yours? Inigo, right?" The corner of Lucan's mouth perked into a grin. "I'm sure he'll have a lot to say, wouldn't you agree?"

Self-righteous fury lit up Gaven's blue eyes. From what Lucan knew, Gaven and Inigo Tepis had not parted on good terms. For a businessman like Inigo, money would be the easiest way to get him to talk. And Lucan had lots of it.

"Are you threatening me?"

"I am *promising* you that I intend to find out what happened. One way or another. Are you refusing to cooperate?"

Gaven rocked back and nodded with something like agreement. "Go ahead," he snarled. "Talk to Inigo or whomever you want, if you can handle the truth."

Lucan clenched his hands and watched Gaven ride away without a backward glance, arrogant and alone.

If he thought Lucan was bluffing, he was sorely mistaken. Mirari wasn't a traitor. She was good and righteous and if Gaven had cut her down for standing up for what she believed in, Lucan would make sure he wished he'd died instead.

LUCAN WAS DIRECTED to a room in the back at the town tavern. To his relief, he was the first to arrive.

The room was small and private. It was just large enough for the square table and two plush velvet benches on either side. The room was warm enough that he could take his cloak off as he sat down. He selected the bench facing the door to give himself the advantage.

He hadn't been worried about being late to the meeting, but being early. He didn't want to be seen fumbling in front of a man like Inigo Tepis.

Lucan took a deep breath. As though summoned by his thoughts, the door opened and Inigo was granted entry into the room. Lucan rose to greet him, and if Inigo was annoyed that Lucan had beat him here, he didn't show it.

"Did I keep you waiting?" Inigo asked as he took his seat. Lucan paused to answer as the waitstaff poured them both a rich red wine. Tepis wine, of course. It was a bold choice considering he was wearing a fine white suit. Lucan wondered how long Inigo could hold that confidence. Lucan took his glass and swirled the wine a few times. Bringing it up to his nose, he took a deep whiff, nodded, and set the glass back down.

"Not at all. My other meeting finished early. You are simply on time." But no one ever got far just being on time.

"I hope your other business was fruitful."

"Let's just say I expect this one to go better."

Inigo laughed. "I'll do my best."

They toasted and Lucan managed a single sip before setting the glass aside. "Delicious."

"Thank you," Inigo said with a little bow. "I hope I'm not being too forward in asking what this is about? I was quite surprised that you reached out to me. Though, of course, I'm always willing to do business with the Hales."

He gave a sharp smile like he had blades in his mouth.

Lucan was not fond of Inigo Tepis. Even when Gaven had abolished the Separation Law, he hadn't rushed to start a business relationship with the man. Inigo was shrewd, smart. As a Hale, Lucan could respect his business sense. His personality left much to be desired. Lucan thought he was a bit slimy – a sawgator lurking in murky waters – but he kept his thoughts off of his face.

"And I'm happy to do business with the House Tepis," Lucan said in response.

Inigo motioned toward the wine. "If the bottle is to your liking, I think we can set up a trade route between—"

Lucan held up his hand before Inigo could continue. "As I said, I'm happy to do business with House Tepis but perhaps on another occasion. I'm here on a more…personal matter."

"Oh?" Inigo leaned forward as if he smelled blood in the water. "How can I help?"

"I heard you were the person to talk to if I needed information."

Inigo smirked. "I'm a good listener," he said with false modesty. "And sometimes I hear things. That's all."

"Have you heard anything about M—" Lucan bit his lip. "About the region leader's partner?"

"Which one?"

"Gaven Zanette."

Inigo blinked and Lucan thought he had actually surprised the man.

"His…partner?" Abruptly, he threw his head back and laughed. "Is that what this is about?" He clicked his tongue.

"After all I tried to teach him, he still hasn't learned the art of being subtle, has he? Is this the best Gaven can do?" He lifted his hand like he was reciting an oath. "I swear, I gave Gaven the only copy. No one else knows she had a fake name."

Lucan was glad Inigo was facing away. It gave him a chance to regain his composure. Lucan knew there had been something odd about Gaven's story, and his lack of remorse began to make sense.

Inigo crossed his arms and shook his head. His amusement only grew. "I knew he'd be upset, but all I wanted was for him to break the partnership. I didn't think he'd kill the girl. On occasion, he manages to surprise me. I'll give him that."

Kill her? Over her identity? Lucan did his best to hide the twitch in his eye and shake those thoughts away. If Mirari was truly dead, Gaven would be burdened with unimaginable pain – the curse from a paragon's bond. But he seemed normal, unremorseful even. Either Gaven broke their partnership before killing Mirari, or…

She was still alive, and Gaven knew it. She was out there somewhere and, perhaps, he couldn't bear the shame of the Council knowing that he let her slip. And now he was going to finish the job.

Too many questions were unanswered, but Lucan had a good lead. All he knew for certain was that Gaven was responsible for whatever happened to Mirari. He couldn't be trusted.

Lucan cleared his throat to draw Inigo out of his own amusement.

"Thank you, I think I've heard enough," he said, rising to his feet.

"You'll report back to Gaven then." He waved his hand. "Go on. Let him know that his secret is safe with me."

"I assure you, I do *not* report to Region Leader Gaven," Lucan said coldly. He drew himself up to his full height to look down on Inigo's smug face. "I'm Valenian and I find discussing the death of a young woman to be uncouth at best."

Inigo's mouth dropped open as he realized he had made a mistake.

"I'll be taking my leave," Lucan said.

"Wait," Inigo reached out toward him.

"We have nothing left to say." Slipping out from the bench, Lucan grabbed his cloak and swung it over his shoulders.

"Wait," Inigo said again. Lucan didn't spare him another look. "You said you wanted information, didn't you? I have some knowledge you might find interesting."

"I doubt it."

"Then perhaps you need to audit the weapons your family is shipping out." Lucan paused, halfway to the door. When Inigo spoke again, the smirk was clear in his words. "I heard there were some missing hāstal weapons. You wouldn't want the Council to suspect you're a rebel sympathizer, would you? I don't know what other conclusion they might draw if they were to find Hale weapons with those dissidents."

Lucan's movement was ominous as he turned and fixed a steely gaze upon him. Inigo was leaning against the back of the bench with one arm thrown over the side. Slimy might have been too nice of a description. Lucan inclined his head in a stiff nod.

"Thank you for the warning. I'll take your leave now to conduct a review of my family's trade deals and I assure you I'll be quite thorough. If there's so much as a single box missing, I'll find it." He narrowed his eyes, taking a step toward Inigo. "And I'll find whomever let it slip away," he vowed. "I'll levy the full force of the Hale name to *destroy* this person." He waited until Inigo's smile faded. He straightened and turned back toward the door. "It's as you say. We don't want those weapons to fall into the hands of the rebels."

He didn't wait for a response from Inigo. There was nothing

else he wanted to hear from that serpent's mouth. If there was a missing shipment, he hoped Inigo *did* have something to do with it. It was his fault Mirari was on the run and he fully intended on making him regret it. Whatever name she went by, Mirari was still his cousin. He would always look out for her.

CHAPTER SIX

Dorain was restless and angry, pacing in his quarters at the Estate, too unsettled to sit. He was still geared up for a fight, but with whom? Dorain couldn't help feeling that they hadn't done the right thing. But what *was* the right thing? He only knew for certain that the Knights weren't doing enough.

Byham had a noticeable pall and what the Knights did wasn't unique or unjustified. Dorain had heard about whole villages slaughtered under the suspicion of a connection to the Blessed. The Council was overzealous, going after the Blessed, and the ones being affected the most were regular people. The Council was rounding people up in droves and civilians were lucky if they were allowed a trial.

He scoffed. If allowed, they all ended with the same sentencing.

Execution.

Dorain drove his fist into the wall. The pain shook him into clarity. Sitting around wishing to help was pointless. He needed to do something. He slipped out of his room, looking for Fangbane.

The Knights' Estate was decadently spread, but Dorain was

used to it by now. Five years ago, it was just a handful of them: the Knights, Fangbane and his family, and occasionally Region Leader Gaven. They had gained a surplus of volunteers on the island after defeating Laikos. But with the rise of uncertainty, and manslaughters, many returned to their homes either in fear of the Knights or from acceptance that they had little time left and wished to spend their final moments with their families. Those who stayed still believed that the Knights were an image of peace and unity. They were blind to the harsh reality. Dorain believed, much like his fellow comrades, that the Knights were now just another puppet under the Council's strings.

Movement in the courtyard caught his attention, but it was only Fangbane and Starlight's child, Sarkan. Maybe this was for the best. Anyone else might have questions about Dorain's wandering. The child was playing in the dirt, digging a hole that would have gotten Dorain a scolding when he was that age. Starlight must be in the kitchen – it was the only time Sarkan could roam unattended.

Dorain laughed at the caught look on Sarkan's face. Maybe some things weren't so different.

"Hey Sharky," Dorain called out.

Sarkan tucked his hands behind his back, as if hiding his smudged fingers would make Dorain blind to the dirt on his pants.

"Um, yes?"

"Do you know where your father is?

Sarkan's face scrunched up. "Uh-huh. His office. The one by the library."

"Okay, thanks."

"You're welcome! Um, you're not going to tell…"

Dorain laughed again, but shook his head. A sobering feeling came over him. "No, but you should get cleaned up."

"I will!" His cheeks perked up, and to Dorain it felt like

Sarkan's ignorance of the world was the only thing keeping the island afloat.

Dorain knocked on Fangbane's office door. A voice quickly granted him permission to enter. The room was dark, as usual, but there was enough light peeking through the curtains for Dorain to make out Fangbane's mask. He was composing a letter when Dorain took a seat across from him. Dorain gripped his pants so tight his knuckles turned white, and he waited for Fangbane to meet his gaze. He stared intensely, almost wishing that his thoughts could physically strike Fangbane like a bolt of lightning.

Fangbane lifted his head, nodding once before setting down his quill. He intertwined his hands and braced them on his desk. "Is this about Byham?"

Dorain forced his hands to relax. "It's not just about Byham," he said. "People are dying. Shouldn't we be doing something, anything to help? Isn't that our duty as Knights?"

Fangbane nodded. "Of course. Finding Eoin—"

"I'm not talking about the Blessed," Dorain snapped. He lifted his hand to rub his forehead. "I mean, it's not just about the Blessed. The people in Byham, the people in every region, they're scared of us. Maybe even more than the Blessed! Don't you think that's a problem?"

"Of course," Fangbane said immediately, then took a deep breath. "There is a road to peace without violence, but that road needs a foundation. Our society is faulted by an unpleasant terror that is plaguing our minds, yours and mine alike. That's why we must find and eliminate that source of fear. Only then can we restore clarity and find peace. Find Eoin. That is our first step in creating the best possible outcome."

Dorain furrowed his brows. He didn't quite agree with Fangbane's oversimplification. He knew that there was another path that didn't involve bloodshed. Then, something clicked, and he leaned forward.

"Do you think that's what Mirari did?" he asked. "If what the Council said is true, if Mirari was in Aias, she must have found something, right? Or someone?"

Fangbane sighed. "Dorain, you mustn't speak like that."

"Why not?" He slammed his hand on the arm of his chair. "Why can't we speak of her? Why are you all acting like she's worse than the Blessed? Doesn't she deserve our trust and support, especially now that she can't defend herself?"

Fangbane took another breath. "It's not so simple."

"Isn't it?"

"I don't believe that Mirari was a traitor. If there's a chance to clear her name, I'll be the first to take it." He regarded the half-finished letter in front of him without really seeing it. "But right now, that's not feasible. As far as the Council is concerned, Mirari is a traitor, and our alliance with her is in danger. If they hear you or any of us speak of Mirari in a positive light, it could jeopardize the Knights' existence."

Dorain clenched his fist. He wanted to rage at the unfairness of it all, but he knew that acting childish would not get him what he wanted. "Fine, but what about the Council?"

Fangbane tilted his head. "What do you mean?"

Dorain jumped to his feet, arms spread wide. "What are the Knights going to do about the Council? The terror they're instilling in the people? The executions? What about that? Should we just let them continue, continue to support them even if it goes against our ideals?"

"Of course not, but—"

"But what? You're sucking their weasel."

"Dorain…"

For once, Dorain held his tongue, waiting for Fangbane to finish his response. Dorain enjoyed watching him struggle. It forced Fangbane to acknowledge that there was, in fact, an issue, an issue that he had been sweeping under the rug instead of confronting. Dorain knew Fangbane didn't have an answer, and he wanted him to squirm as he tried to come up with one.

Fangbane touched his mask, then slowly nodded. "Very well, you're right. I will talk to the Council."

Dorain laughed mirthlessly, sinking back into his chair. "That's it?" he said. "More talk?"

"For now, yes." Dorain looked away, shaking his head as Fangbane continued. "The last thing we should do is set ourselves up as enemies of the Council. A hard stance against them will only lead to more chaos. We worked hard to be legitimized by the Council, and we should remain on their good side." The silence stretched between them. "Dorain? Do you understand?"

"Oh, I understand all right." Dorain got to his feet. He took his badge off, and slapped it down on the table. "And I have a better idea."

Fangbane stared at it. "Dorain, think before you act."

"I did think about it. For weeks. I'm the only one who *has* been thinking since Mirari died. I thought joining the Knights was a way to help people." He let a heavy silence fill the room. "And to have comrades I could rely on. People I could trust." He slid the badge across the desk. "Now, I know the truth. I can't do this anymore."

"Dorain, please. Reconsider." He tried to push the badge back to Dorain, but Dorain shook his head. "What will you do?"

Dorain was pained to say it, but it had been on his mind for some time. "I can do more good working with my father than just waiting for something to change with you."

Holding his head high and his back straight, Dorain left the room with the door wide open, forcing Fangbane to turn away from the blinding light. His eyes drifted to the badge on his table – another one gone.

Reaching into his pocket, Fangbane pulled out Dorain's discarded badge. He spun it around in his hand, feeling the dents and valleys underneath his fingers. The Knights could survive this, he knew. It was only a temporary setback. He tucked the badge away.

He had arrived at the Hearth now, ready to face the Council. He knew they were here – he heard murmurs coming from the courtroom. Without a guard to escort him, he took a deep breath and pushed open the golden doors leading into the courtroom.

To his surprise, five other men were in the room. They were not standing trial, but delivering some information. The room went silent and all heads turned to Fangbane. He hesitated and bowed twice.

"My apologies," he said. "I'll wait out—"

"Please, join us, Fangbane," Suzan said, gesturing to the center of the court. "This concerns you."

Fangbane tilted his head. What did these men have to do with him? He carefully stepped forward. He was now close enough to see an aviary crest embellished on the men's shoulders – the neighboring region of Saon. His mind flickered to a particular person. Could it be?

Not so obvious, Father.

Fangbane scanned the faces of the men. There he was, a man, far younger than the rest, who looked at him with tired sapphire eyes. He was handsomely fit in frilled attire, the way he always preferred. Turning away, he lowered his head, showing off the brown curls over his heavy brow ridge.

How long had it been, Fangbane wondered. Little seemed to have changed about him, and it carved a smile on Fangbane's face.

"A pleasure to see you, Lord Fangbane," one of the men spoke. He reached out and shook Fangbane's hand. Fangbane must've seen these men before, but he could not recollect their names. The only person he cared about was Sorren.

Keep your eyes on the Council, he advised. *Your loyalty will be challenged.*

Fangbane nodded to himself. He would heed Sorren's warning, as he always did. His eldest son had the gift of clairvoyance. Sorren had always considered it a curse, much like Fangbane did his gift when he was a child. But unlike Fangbane, Sorren appeared to still be ashamed of his ability. He was adamant about keeping his ability, and relationship with Fangbane, a secret from everyone.

Sorren wanted a quiet life, and his parents honored it. He rarely reached out to them since he left – may as well have disowned them – but Starlight knew he expressed his care in other ways. Fangbane could hear it in his thoughts.

Fangbane's confidence grew knowing that he could count on Sorren to get through this meeting with the Council. Sorren had become an advisor to the region leader of Saon. Perhaps he knew more about the situation than Fangbane.

"What may I help you with?" Fangbane asked, looking up at the councilors.

"Have you made any progress on locating the fugitive?" Dareh asked. Based on the smirk on Dareh's face, he had seen and was enjoying Fangbane's misery. It seemed Dorain had been successful in returning to his father's side. No matter their contentious relationship, Dareh must have been thrilled that Dorain was no longer a part of the Knights. The thought was bitter and Fangbane had to focus on his reason for being there. He had to follow through on his promise to Dorain and try to reason with the Council.

"The Knights are working diligently to locate Eoin," Fangbane said. He heard huffs of disappointment.

To Dareh's left, Tarek and Adder had their arms crossed. They seemed annoyed to be there, or was it because of Fangbane's presence? Novinha was whispering something in Suzan's ear. Her hair was draped across half her face, shielding Fangbane's view, and Suzan was nodding in response. Councilor Julie was absent, as usual. The aura around him tinged like the stench of fermented molark, and this meeting was anything but delectable.

"The Region of Saon has seen an increase in murders," one of the Saonian men said, directing his attention to Fangbane. "We understand that the Knights are busy, however we feel that they are not doing enough to help us."

Fangbane furrowed his brow. What was he? A babysitter? It was not his duty, nor the Knights, to solve every inconvenience in the empire.

"We are doing the best we can," Fangbane said as calmly as he could.

"With all due respect, Lord Fangbane, not enough."

Fangbane huffed.

He must've heard Fangbane's dissatisfaction. "Allow me to clarify," he said, gently waving his hands. "The Council has ordered region leaders to suppress the violence by killing all who oppose authority. The Knights, however, have been letting the rebels go with warnings." He pursed his lips. "Arguably, the rebels are dominating the Knights."

"Ridiculous," Fangbane scoffed. "Our methods are diligent and precise. We don't slaughter those who have nothing to do with the Bl—" He cleared his throat. "The rebels."

"Diligent?" Tarek said with a pinch in his voice. His white brows pulled together. "Tyrants are running loose. Our prisoner is yet to be caught. Where exactly is the diligence in the work you speak of?"

Show restraint, Sorren communicated to Fangbane. *You need to prove that you are still suitable to lead, or else they will tear the Knights apart.*

He knew Sorren was right, but it was easier said than done. Sorren wouldn't know it since his ability always paved the road for him. He rarely experienced an outcome he did not foresee.

Fangbane kept silent as Tarek tore him apart. Tarek leaned forward with his interlaced hands on the table.

"Let's not tax simple minds," he continued. "I feel for the people, really, but sacrifices must be made for the peace of our empires." He looked around the room. "We can all agree that that's what our aims are."

The Councilors nodded, and Fangbane was glad he was wearing his mask. What would be the point of peace if there's no one left alive to enjoy it? These sacrifices never seemed to affect the Councilors. He kept all these thoughts to himself.

He had one ally, Suzan, but she was unlikely to yield to his idea. She had watched her region and protege suffer from the damage inflicted by the Blessed. Fangbane knew his chances of convincing the Council were close to none, but he had to try.

"Peace is indeed the goal, but I think a little more restraint is necessary," Fangbane said. "I worry that this zealotry from the soldiers will have the opposite effect on quelling the rising rebellion."

He could tell his words were not getting through to them when Suzan shook her head. He knew in that moment that whatever chance he had of convincing the Council was lost.

Looking down at him, Suzan spoke, "We must make it known that rebels like *them* will not be tolerated. If the people fear our so-called zealotry, they'll be quick to reveal the dissidents in their midst."

"Violence will only lead to more violence," Fangbane said.

"Don't be naive," Dareh jumped into the conversation. "The rebels aren't going to hold our hands. They'll only cut them off. They grow in power by the day, ravaging our lands, and to be frank—" He paused, turning his attention to the other councilors. "What good are the Knights if not to handle these threats?"

Dareh's remarks were not unpredictable. They were exactly what Fangbane had hoped to avoid. But no matter how much he could predict the outcome, he had foolishly hoped differently. He would try once more.

"My Knights have traveled across the three empires in search of those who are responsible for all this destruction. While they have not yet captured the fugitive, they have the people's trust and cooperation." Fangbane nodded to himself. He believed every word he said, even though their most recent incidents proved otherwise. It was only temporary, he told himself. The Knights would regain their glory. "We can and will find *them* without needless bloodshed."

The councilors were silent.

Novinha spoke up. "And then what?" she asked, leaning back in her chair. She rested her head on her hand. "Do you think you'll be able to *talk* the rebels into laying down their arms?"

"It's our duty to try."

Adder frowned, rubbing his temples. "Half-measures don't help anybody. Arguably, you're making things worse if you are seen to stand against our orders."

Suzan looked apologetic but firm when she nodded. "A leadership divided only brings chaos to those who look to them for guidance."

"Well said, Councilors," Dareh said. "Since the Knights' inception, it seems that the unrest in our lands has only grown worse." Fangbane caught an unpleasant thought from him. *Perhaps it's time the Knights were disbanded.*

Fangbane scanned the other councilors. Adder was deep in thought, and Fangbane heard him think, *Those Knights would be better served elsewhere.*

Fangbane tried to keep his composure, though he felt like everything he and Starlight had accomplished was slipping through his fingers.

"The Knights have proven themselves invaluable in the past," Sorren said. Fangbane looked up. He was surprised to hear him speak. Sorren lowered his head into a bow. "They stopped Laikos after he placed half of our empire's leaders on their deathbeds. When the time is right, I have faith that the Knights will capture the one responsible for this insurrection."

Sorren had always disagreed with the way his parents approached justice, but even if their methods were different, Fangbane knew that his son believed in the same goal – their society had to be fixed. Instead of joining his parents as vigilantes, he sought to shape ideology from the inside, as a politician. Not long after discreetly aiding Fangbane in the Althaean Siege, he found a seat beside the region leader of Saon. He didn't want to be involved with the Knights, but Fangbane knew he supported the idea. He funded most of the Knights' Estate.

Fangbane was happy for Sorren's support, but those words didn't affect Dareh.

"One success over a dozen failures," he said. "Not a good look." He gestured to the councilors. "We're looking to the future. The future of our lands. The future of our...children."

Sorren nodded. "If it eases His Grace, then may I suggest that the Knights swear their loyalty to the Council?"

"What?" Fangbane hissed.

Play along. You don't have a choice.

Fangbane wanted to argue with him, but his son couldn't read minds. There was never a point in arguing with him – he saw the future, and he always made the right decision. No matter how obscure his plans were, it always placed them on the most desirable path. It was up to Fangbane whether or not to take it.

"A fair offer," Novinha said. She squinted at Fangbane and her eyes revealed light wrinkles when her nose turned up. "Well? Will you and the Knights stand with us?"

Another quick scan of their thoughts revealed that the situation had been resolved in their mind already – the Knights failed to capture Eoin and now their honor was at stake. Before Fangbane could defend himself, Suzan cut in.

"The Blessed's numbers are growing and will only continue

to grow," she said. "They will become bold if they perceive any weakness from their enemies. As far as I see, you…no, we…can achieve the best possible outcome if we work together. Will you work with us, Fangbane?"

"*For* us," Dareh corrected with a grin smudged across his face. Suzan shifted her eyes, almost as if she was about to protest.

Fangbane could understand the force behind a united front. He could see it right before his eyes. But when he created the Knights, he swore they would remain independent, unwavering by the biases plaguing the Council and leaders of the empires. But was this inevitable? In war, there were only two sides, and right now people were doubting where the Knights stood – as the Council's right hand or as allies of the traitorous Mirari, and the Blessed.

"You said yourself your current methods have been unfruitful," Adder said. "Combined, we can crush our enemies and remove the threat of the Blessed once and for all."

Suzan nodded. "If you worry about the morale of the people, then join us. When they see that the Council and the Knights are unified, it will reassure them."

The Council never agreed on anything, until now, and Fangbane felt pressured to conform to their unity. If he denied them, he would make the Knights an enemy of more than just the Blessed. He turned to Sorren, who responded with a firm nod.

Fangbane let out a deep sigh, then bowed his head.

"Very well. The Knights are at your disposal."

"And the Knights will not act until asked, understood?" Dareh had a big grin as he looked down on Fangbane.

Fangbane gritted his teeth. Then what were they supposed to do?

CHAPTER SEVEN

A large stack of reports wobbled precariously on the table when Gaven sat down. Sighing, he rubbed his eyes. Reports were coming in from all over Althaea Main and they all contained the same message. Violence was growing with each passing day and the Council's no-mercy policy was doing little to curb it. He anticipated an eternity of looking through the stack. Groaning, he pushed away from his desk and stood by the window. Haynes was running a squad through drills in anticipation of a mobilization order. They were good men and women — reliable and hard-working to defend their land. They did as they were ordered because that was the role they played in keeping peace in Althaea Main.

There was a time Gaven knew his role in bringing peace to Althaea Main. That knowledge had grown murkier over time. He glanced back at his desk and his lip curled. He dreaded returning to those papers without a solution.

He wanted to blame the Blessed for the discord Althaea Main was facing. It would be easy to. It was expected. However, he had done what Mirari had – help the Blessed. He had listened to Eoin and now the blacksmith's words were circling his head like vultures over carrion. He believed, to a degree, that there was something darker out in the world – something more powerful than an old blacksmith and more dangerous than an empath.

Focusing on the Blessed and harassing the peasantry was less than useful. It was dangerous because it allowed the true mastermind to operate from the shadows and amass unchecked power. He realized now that he had wasted his time, and that perhaps… Mirari was right.

Gaven ran his hand over his stubble, pressing his knuckles to his chin. What Eoin told him was infuriating, terrifying. The idea that the one who had possessed him was not only still alive and well but also spreading their darkness through his people… He couldn't stand it. He couldn't stand knowing and doing nothing. He stared at his reflection in the mirror and watched a terrible idea come to mind.

The one responsible was named Soteria. According to some of the reports that rested on his desk, whispers hinted at the woman's ability to endure a thousand slashes. Gaven rolled his eyes at the fantastical claim, yet, considering her elusive nature, he couldn't entirely dismiss the notion. After all Eoin had shared with him, nothing felt too far-fetched anymore.

There was a knock at the door and he was relieved to dismiss, at least temporarily, this bout of insanity. Straightening his back, he watched the door in the mirror's reflection.

"Enter."

The door opened and Erel peeked her head in. She looked around but only stepped across the threshold once she confirmed that he was alone. She was holding a stack of papers shoulder height and Gaven's shoulders deflated.

"Just put them there," he said, returning to his desk and sitting wearily in his chair. The reports hit the desk with a solid thump. "More reports?" he asked, though it wasn't really a question. What else would they be?

"You got it," she said. When he motioned, she dropped into the seat across from him and propped her legs up on the desk.

"Anything noteworthy?" he asked, absently flipping through the papers. He was thankful, at the very least, that she always made sure the urgent ones were at the top of the pile.

She was a beat slower than usual to answer, and he glanced up at her. She met his gaze, and raised her shoulders. "More violence. More revolts. More of the same."

"That's it?" he asked, not quite believing it.

"You've probably already heard, but there's a letter from Fangbane in there."

He frowned and gave the stack a more thorough look. Indeed, there was a post from Fangbane. He held it up, but didn't open it. Why would Fangbane send him a letter? Why not just contact him on the comstōne? Not that Gaven was inclined to answer his call.

"What's it say?" he asked.

She scoffed, laying her hand on her chest. "Are you accusing me of reading your mail?" He raised a brow, and she dropped the act. Still, it took her a while to respond. "It's nothing you need to answer. It's only a formal missive about the Knights."

At her prompting, he ripped the side of the letter and pulled the paper out. He scanned it and then read it again before crumpling it in his hand.

"Is this a joke?"

With a bemused lift of her shoulders, she stared at the ruined paper. "Didn't seem like it."

He shoved away from the desk and started pacing from one end of the room to the other. "So now the Knights are the Council's puppets?"

"Aren't the region leaders already the Council's puppets?"

"All the more reason the Knights should remain separate." She conceded with another shrug and left him to ruminate in silence.

He first thought of Suzan. She was the one who had urged Fangbane to create the Knights, and he was surprised to hear that she would support such unification. He would always respect her and follow her orders as his mentor, but Suzan was not a lone voice on the Council. Perhaps Adder had said something to convince her? Then there were Dareh and Novinha, who were regular voices of dissent. Tarek and Julie, who were voices of monetary gain. As a whole, he didn't trust the Council. How could he? They rarely had people's best interests in mind – they couldn't from their high thrones.

What he didn't understand is why Fangbane would concede to them. What upper hand did the Council have? And why now?

His thoughts must've been apparent to Erel when she spoke, "You've heard about Dorain, right?"

"Dorain?" He stopped to look at her. "What happened?"

"He left."

"Left?"

She hummed. "Yeah. Left the Knights. The letter mentions a change in personnel. I think he is talking about Dorain."

Gaven thought he was talking about Mirari. He sat back down. "Do you know why he left the Knights?"

"From the gossip among Dareh's servants, Dorain was fed up with Fangbane's passivity. He's back at his father's side because, reportedly, Dareh can be relied on to get things done."

"And is that his true reasoning?"

"We would need to ask the boy himself."

Sighing, Gaven ran his hands through his hair. That dark, oppressive feeling was more prevalent than ever. "Even though I have my duties as region leader, I always thought the Knights could do some good." He snorted and turned to look out the window. The battle in Aias seemed to be the beginning of the end. "Mirari was the glue that held the Knights together. Without her…"

"They are falling apart," Erel said, and hesitated to finish her statement. She sighed, "As are you."

He casually waved a hand and reached for the reports. "If that's all, I should get back to these." To his surprise, Erel didn't immediately leave. "Was there something else?"

"I, no," she said, speaking slowly as though she were choosing her words with care. "I thought you would at least scowl over that." She dropped her legs and leaned forward. "I didn't think you had any fond feelings left for Mirari."

Now it was his turn to pick over his words. "I did what I had to do."

Erel nodded without arguing. He scrutinized her, gauging her thoughts on Mirari.

Mirari was labelled a traitor because reports said she'd been spending time in Aias and the Council wanted someone to blame. It was nothing more than rumors and conjecture. The two of them in this room were the only ones who knew the truth. Mirari really had sided with the Blessed during the final battle.

Now they had more information.

Gaven tapped the stack of papers. "This chaos. What do you think is causing it?"

She frowned. "The Blessed, of course."

He was slow to nod along with her response. "Even with what Eoin said? You don't believe it?"

Her eyes darkened; a haunted look in her gaze. "The Blessed? The Defiants? It doesn't matter what they're calling themselves," she said tersely. "They're dangerous. Even if they're not causing it, the Council plays a significant role in the unrest. Even then, they're thriving in it. The death and dissent. That's exactly what they want. Believe me."

Perhaps that was the only answer she could give. Erel was the last surviving member of the Belligmn Tribe, the tribe of shapeshifters. She'd witnessed the destruction of her home, friends, and family. All were killed by Laikos, a member of the Blessed.

"You must have felt betrayed when you learned Mirari was spending time in Aias."

She shook her head and a dark look passed from her eyes. "It was a shock, sure," she said dryly. "Arguably, you were more betrayed."

He braced his elbow on the arm of his chair. "Really?"

They stared at each other for a moment. The truth sat between them unsaid. "I'd say so, yes," she finally spoke. "Considering how it ended."

Images of his fight with Mirari trickled in his mind. His stomach twisted recalling the moment he ran a blade through her chest. He had refused to touch that blade since, and it made its home in the drawer of relics taken from the Blessed. To him it was cursed – a reminder of the coward he was.

"You wouldn't have done the same thing?"

Erel bit her lip. "I wasn't in the same situation. I don't know what I would have done." She leaned forward, now staring him in the eye. "Don't doubt yourself. It leads to madness."

But Gaven was mad. He could never hate her, let alone have the courage to kill her. The reality was he would've killed himself before hurting her. But unfortunately, Gaven was still alive.

Gaven copied her pose and lowered his voice. "What if it's the opposite? What if I let Mirari live? Should I doubt myself then?"

Erel's eyes widened. "Did…you?"

Gaven pulled away, slumping back into his seat. He pulled out his top drawer and threw a renastōne on the table. Erel knew that she had given him two for the battle.

Her eyes widened, and she stuttered, "I- I thought you used that on yourself."

"Did I have an injury, Erel? You're more observant than that."

She collapsed in her seat. He sighed, knowing that she wouldn't approve. They knew Mirari had sided with Eoin, chose the Blessed over him, and Gaven gave her a free pass. Was her life truly that valuable? Saving her was a selfish and disgraceful decision, and would cost him his life if anyone found out. But holding such a secret, while the people around him blamed him for failing to protect Mirari, was starting to consume his mind.

"Well?" he asked when she didn't take her eyes off the stone. He tightened his hand into a fist, needing to know what Erel thought. "Do you think that was wrong?"

"Mirari's alive," she said. Closing her eyes, Erel exhaled deeply. After a long, silent moment, she lifted her head and nodded. "I'm glad."

Gaven unclenched his hand. "You're…glad?"

She hummed. "Yeah." She looked him over and snorted. "You look surprised."

"She's a traitor."

"You and I both know that isn't entirely true."

Gaven paused, then scoffed, "I distinctly remember you warning me against trusting her."

"Hmm, no, I didn't."

He gaped at her. "Erel! Yes, you did."

"I cautioned you against being too trusting of her. Huge difference."

Gaven raised his brow. "Is there?"

Grinning, she nodded. Next instant, she dropped the joviality. "I'm serious, Your Honor. Even with all Mirari did, the lying, sneaking off to Aias, I never thought of her as a traitor… How to explain?" For a moment, she seemed overwhelmed. It was a look he'd never seen on her before. "You know I can shapeshift."

"Of course."

"It's more than that though." She waved her hand, and her body changed to Haynes' appearance. In his deep voice she continued, "I do this by copying their aura." He nodded. "I can do this with any person I've seen, but…" She bit her lip. "There's only been three times in my *life* that I haven't been able to shapeshift into someone." She mirrored her appearance into the man in front of her and held up a finger. "The first was that assailant who attacked you, right before the battle in Rhea." Another finger went up. "You were the second, but only during that time when you were possessed." The final finger rose. "Then…it was Mirari."

He frowned. "Why? What does that mean?" He had known about the first two, but Erel hadn't told him about Mirari. Did she also have selfish intentions in wanting to keep Mirari safe? He didn't bother to question it, now that he knew that they were on the same side.

"I don't know," she said with helplessness in her tone. She returned to her natural form, her cascading hair shielding the frustration on her face. "I wish I did. I like Mirari. I see the good in her, but it's whatever's inside her, whatever blocks my abilities… I'm not so sure about."

"I see." With this new knowledge, his plan seemed a little less wild. "Erel, I need a favor."

CHAPTER EIGHT

Eoin paced around his confined bunker. It was partly to keep his blood moving and his body fit, but also because there was nothing else to do in his new prison. There was a small window out of reach, even if he jumped. At night, he could see familiar stars, and during the day, he could hear the bustle of people speaking with familiar accents. A soldier had transported him to this bunker during the night in a covered wagon. He couldn't be sure, but he thought he'd been brought to the outskirts of Althaea Main.

Eoin hadn't seen the region leader since their talk in the abandoned fort. He thought he'd gotten through to Gaven, but weeks had passed and he was still a captive. He was eager to speak to the region leader again. It was his best chance at convincing someone with power about the threat Soteria posed to Althaea Main and beyond. Gaven seemed receptive to Eoin's words. Eoin knew that if Gaven intended to reject what he'd said, Eoin would be dead. It was a good sign that he was still alive.

Sighing, he sat down in a chair. He leaned forward, bracing his elbows on his knees. He had no idea how much longer Gaven intended to keep him locked up. Eoin regularly received food and water, so he hadn't been forgotten. To his surprise, a new person delivered his rations each time. Whenever he tried to question them about Gaven's return, or even just his verdict, he received the same blank stare.

The exact same blank stare. There was something familiar about each of Gaven's soldiers. When he looked at them, he got the feeling that he knew them. Not well, of course – they weren't old comrades of his. In fact, they were all so vastly different, he couldn't know them from the same place. Still he couldn't shake the feeling. Hours after the soldiers would leave, he was left with a nagging sense of familiarity.

Sighing to himself, he shook his head and started pacing again. They'd probably all been trained to give him the cold shoulder if he tried to ask any questions. Anxiety kept his feet moving. Another night was falling. Another day gone. He couldn't do anything except listen for the terror of his people. He had to remind himself that, right now, he was doing all that he could. Even while he itched to do something, it was most prudent that he be patient and wait for Gaven's judgment. He wouldn't be held indefinitely and waiting would be better in the long run. He was a fugitive on the run from the Council. He didn't want to add an angry region leader to the list of people after him if he escaped.

He was under the window when he heard the screech of metal as the outside lock turned. He braced himself. He didn't know who it was, but the guards usually came around sunrise; this was unusual. The door swung open and it was yet another oddly familiar, strange soldier who stepped through. And following behind him, Eoin was relieved to finally see the man he had been waiting for.

"Your Honor," he greeted, careful to cover his surprise.

The man glowered at him, as wary as he'd been in the fort, but without that stark hatred. Gaven was wearing a cloak over his simple tunic and breeches. A couple of bags were slung over his shoulder. He dropped one of them on the ground and kicked it over to Eoin.

"Here," he said.

"What's this?" Spare clothes, rations, waterskins, and bandages. He'd have thought Gaven was releasing him and providing supplies to help him, except the region leader was obviously dressed to travel. Eoin put the pack over his shoulder. "Going somewhere?"

Eoin watched the muscle in Gaven's jaw jump as he clenched his teeth. He spoke like the words were hard to get out. "The Defiants are an imminent danger that can't be allowed to continue unchecked." These were the words Eoin wanted to hear, but he could tell there was more. "You will help me find and stop them."

"I admit that's not what I expected," he said, staring at him across the room. "Why would you deploy me, over your army?"

Gaven set his bag down and leaned against the wall. "Even if I'm the region leader, I can't do whatever I want. There's a hierarchy I'm bound to. You think I can just tell the Council they've made a mistake, have you exonerated, and send you on your way?"

"You're going rogue." Eoin couldn't hide his grin. "Just like your old partner."

Gaven scowled and huffed, but held back. "I am loyal to my people. I'm doing what's best for them."

"I never said you weren't." Eoin glanced at Gaven's bag. This time he backed up until he was leaning against the wall, mirroring Gaven's position. "When you say you want to work with me, you mean you want to work with the Blessed?"

"Yes."

"You're joking."

Gaven growled, waving his hand. "You know very well that this is a serious matter."

"The joke is you think I'm going to tell you where my comrades are." That drew Gaven up short. "How can I trust this isn't a scheme to reveal other members of the Blessed? How can I trust that you are not working with the Council right now?"

Gaven thought about it, crossed his arms and nodded. "You're going to have to take the chance. Just how much do you want to stop the Defiants, who blacken the name of the Blessed and corrupt your ideals? How much do you want peace, hmm? What are you willing to sacrifice for it?"

The question reminded Eoin of when he'd first met Gaven in person. Though possessed of that dark spell, he was much the same then as he was now. They'd had a similar conversation when Gaven asked Eoin to trust him. Back then as it was now, Eoin would, no doubt, acquiesce. Gaven was right that Eoin would just have to take that chance; the other option was to remain imprisoned and do nothing. Though, he wasn't going to make it easy for the region leader.

"Enough stalling. Make your choice," Gaven said, taking a step forward. "Help me, unless you'd prefer to rot here until I defeat the Defiants on my own."

Eoin didn't laugh, even though he knew Gaven was bluffing. If it were possible for Gaven to find the Defiants on his own, Eoin doubted Gaven would be talking with him at all. Gaven had too much pride to ask for help from someone he perceived to be a former enemy unless there was no other choice. Perhaps that was enough reason for Eoin to ally with him for the moment. The question was, was that reason enough for Eoin to bring his comrades into this?

"I have a concern," Eoin said and Gaven frowned. "You won't remember, but I've asked you this before." Gaven's face darkened. "I hope this time I can get a proper answer."

"Ask," Gaven ordered.

"Why are you doing this? What do you hope to get out of this? Fame? Glory?"

"Neither," Gaven said with a shake of his head. "I'm doing this because it's my duty. I took an oath. If I am to be executed for doing the right thing, then so be it. That's something you understand, isn't it, soldier?" He nodded pointedly at Eoin's side and Eoin ran his hand over the dragon talla. Gaven stuck his hand in his pocket, fiddling with something. He didn't seem to be aware of it as he continued speaking. "When I first allied with the Knights, I didn't have a choice. It was my punishment for participating in the Siege. I soon learned to appreciate what the Knights stood for and took my recruitment as an opportunity to do more." He looked down and hastily released whatever he was holding, taking his hand out of his pocket.

Eoin was still hesitant. Didn't Gaven have that squad of trusted soldiers that delivered Eoin's supplies? Eoin realized there was something only he could do for Gaven. Pushing away from the wall, Eoin adjusted his bag. He slowly walked across the room.

"I think there's something you're not telling me," he said. "All of what you said may be true, but it's not what spurred you into action. I would gladly sacrifice my life to stop the Defiants, but this isn't just my life I'll be risking. I have few comrades left, I'm not quick to sacrifice them just to get out of this place." He stopped in front of Gaven and said, "Your Honor, why are you really here?"

The words were pried from his lips. With a firm stare, Gaven responded, "I'm looking for someone."

"Someone taken by the Defiants?"

"It was *you* who took her from me." Gaven's expression softened, and he slowly shook his head. "But... I was the one who drove her away, and it's my responsibility to bring her home."

"Mirari's alive?"

Gaven responded with a single nod. Shocked, Eoin rocked back on his heels. He thought back to the battle that led to his capture. While Mirari had started the fight by his side, she took on Gaven alone and that was the last he saw of her. He assumed that Gaven took her life, and Eoin's theory was confirmed when Gaven acknowledged her death at the trial.

"I thought you killed her," Eoin said.

"What else could I say? She had sided with you, with the Blessed. If she was caught, she would've met the same fate as you." He ran his hand over his face and his shoulders slumped.

Eoin understood. "You protected her…even though you were on opposite sides." Their argument had been real, but now Eoin knew that Gaven didn't have the heart to kill his partner. The pain of watching the empires call Mirari a traitor, perhaps even the guilt of running a blade through her, had driven him over the edge. And now, he needed the Blessed's help in finding her because he couldn't let anyone else know that she was alive. He would lie to the Council and leave behind all he had worked so hard for just to reunite with her. That was Gaven's deepest secret, and he had entrusted Eoin with it.

"I understand now she was trying to do the right thing," Gaven said. "I think she's still trying to do the right thing. If we find the Defiants, I think I'll find Mirari again." His hand slipped into his pocket again and his face hardened. "There," he said gruffly. "That's why I need your help. Anything else?"

"One thing."

Gaven scowled. "What now?"

Eoin smirked. "Won't people notice the region leader missing? How do you intend to run around the countryside with me?"

"You needn't worry about that." He lifted his hand before Eoin could speak. "That is my business."

Eoin wouldn't get anything else out of him. Regardless, Eoin was satisfied. He didn't trust Gaven, but he trusted that they were working toward the same goal. For now, that was enough.

"Very well then. Let's find the Defiants." Taking one last step forward, Eoin extended his arm. Gaven wasn't quick to respond, but he nodded and clasped Eoin's forearm, over his talla. "And Mirari."

FANGBANE GAZED OUT HIS WINDOW, savoring the serene view of the snow-top mountain range. It offered a poignant complement to the fading vibrancy of the Knights' Estate. The silence in the halls deepened day by day. He could hear the laughter of his child, often followed by Starlight's jests, and it provided a fleeting respite. He was grateful for this precious time with his family, but he couldn't help wondering if he was just masking his problems.

Lucan was the first to leave, if that even counted. He had slipped away long before Fangbane could grant his formal approval. He hid behind business matters, returning to his former life as a Valenian businessman and seemingly erasing all traces of his knightly past.

Shiba's black carriage was pulling out as Fangbane caught another glance out his window. He didn't get so much as a goodbye from him, only a glance over his shoulder. Over the last couple of days, Fangbane reluctantly observed his Knights depart one by one. They unanimously agreed that their time would be better spent at home, carrying out their duties to their respective regions, until an urgent order was received.

Hime was the first to propose this idea, refusing to remain idle while other regions teetered on the brink. She chose to confront the mounting chaos in Alta Hills, despite the harsh rejections she encountered from the very villagers she vowed to aid.

Kylah, though sharing Hime's longing to leave the estate, reacted to the violent encounters in the opposite way. She dismissed any discussion of Eoin or the Blessed, hiding in the sense of security that Neo seemed to provide to her. She departed with Neo and Shiba back to Avon without hesitation.

"They will be back," Starlight said. Fangbane didn't notice her leaning against his door until he heard her voice. She didn't seem worried about the Knights; she was worried about him. Her smile brought comfort to him. "This isn't the worst thing that's happened to us."

Fangbane chuckled. That much was true, and much like every adventure they had been through together, he knew they could overcome this.

PART II

CHAPTER NINE

Mirari spent the past month reading the vast collection of books available at the cabin. It was a little different from her normal taste, but she didn't mind learning about ancient cultures and folklore. She was more surprised that Julie took an interest in such things.

Even though Mirari's wounds had healed and she rarely left the cabin, Salathiel volunteered to do most of the housework. It reminded her of the time before he had disappeared – just the two of them, living each day. No wars. No drama. She was happy, and she felt like she hadn't laughed this much in years.

And yet...

Salathiel still hasn't explained why he went missing. She tried to not think much of it; what mattered was that he was here now. They could live as if the last five years didn't happen, and Mirari was okay with that.

Salathiel routinely went out to pick up supplies for them. Every time he returned, she had to bite back the urge to ask him if there'd been any news from Althaea. She couldn't help wondering and worrying. When she'd left with Salathiel to come to this mountain retreat, she'd thought she'd washed her hands of Althaea and its hardened people. They didn't want her care and compassion, so why bother?

That didn't stop the thoughts from swirling in her head when the sun peeked through the windows, when she was trying to sleep at night, and any time in between. Was Eoin dead? He must be. The Council would have executed him if he hadn't died at Aias. What of Gaven? And the Knights?

Lucan… Should she send him a message? Was it safe to do so? If Gaven intercepted the message, would he…

"Mirari?"

She snapped out of her spiral. "Yeah?"

"You all right?"

She nodded quickly and looked around. "Of course."

She'd been standing in the kitchen with a clean plate in her hand for who knew how long. Blushing, she pushed the plate into the cabinet and faced Salathiel. He was dressed to leave again but he had a larger bag on his shoulder.

"Where are you going?"

Sighing, he looked exasperated. "You weren't listening to me at all?"

"Ah, remind me?"

"I got a message from Councilor Julie," he said.

She perked up. She had been going crazy just waiting and waiting. Salathiel had promised she could do something to stop the Defiants. She didn't know what that could be, but she was ready. She still wasn't sure how she felt about Julie, but she was willing to work with her if it would put a stop to the Defiants. "What did she say? Is she coming here?"

Salathiel pulled on the strap over his shoulder. "We're going to her. If you'll just get ready already."

"Okay." She headed down the hallway to her bedroom. "Where are we going?" she called.

"There's a village not too far from here. It's important that you see it."

It was nothing more than a pile of rubble. Abandoned and aged with time. Salathiel didn't look surprised. She could hear the trickles of water coming from a nearby stream, and it drew her closer. Mirari found skeletons among the debris. Animals had made their homes in some of the dark crevices. Mold grew on some of the exposed walls. It had to have been like this for decades, maybe centuries.

"There she is," Salathiel said, pointing.

Julie was standing in what could have been the village center, waiting for them. The rubble was arranged in a circle around the clearing. Decked in plated paragon armor that glistened like gold even under the pale winter sun, she looked much like what Mirari expected a councilor to look like – cold, regal, deadly.

They came to a stop in front of the older woman. Mirari was only here because Salathiel had asked her to give Julie a chance. She didn't trust her, but she wanted to know what the councilor wanted with her.

When she met Julie's gaze, a strong feeling welled up inside of her. She couldn't name it or explain it. While she was wary of the councilor, the feeling she had was closer to… hate. Her eyes burned and she had to blink rapidly to suppress this strange rage.

"Councilor Julie," Mirari greeted. The cold wind helped her cool off. "You wanted to speak with me?"

Julie harrumphed. "Yes. Let's not waste time." Mirari nodded, turning her head for a brief moment to hide her distaste for the woman. "I want to talk about your…ability. The flames."

Mirari opened her mouth, but no sound came out. She didn't know what to say. Whirling around, she glared at Salathiel who, until that moment, had been standing quietly by. "You told her?"

He lifted his hands and shook his head. "No, of course not. It's not like that."

"You said you wouldn't say anything." She bunched her hands into fists to hide the shaking.

"He had no need to tell me," Julie said, drawing Mirari's attention back to her. "I thought you would want to know how your powers came to be, but if you would much rather squabble with your brother, don't let me stop you."

Shocked, Mirari turned to Julie. Her voice quivered. "How… much do you know?"

"I've been there since the beginning, child."

She looked down at her hands, fearing the destruction they could wrought. She had almost given up hope. When Fangbane had asked her to join, he had pitched the idea that her flames could be managed. That she shouldn't let them control her life. Five years later, her fighting skills had vastly improved and still she was at the whim of this fire inside of her.

Whatever she touched could end up like this village.

"I want to know everything," Mirari said.

Tucking her hands behind her back, Julie contemplated the decimated village. "Do you know where we are?"

"No."

"This village used to be home to the Belligmn Tribe. Over thirty years ago, they were wiped out by the Blessed due to a… disagreement." Mirari scrutinized with a more discerning eye, shocked at the damage that had been wrought. "People chalked it up to a simple feud over religion, but there's more to it than that."

"What does it have to do with me? That was before I was even born."

Julie hummed and started walking. At Salathiel's nod, Mirari jogged over to keep up. "Who you are was decided before you were born. Your abilities are not a curse you were saddled with, but a divine gift you should embrace."

"Whatever I have…it has killed people." Her parents and all

the rest of the passengers on the kōnvoy. She almost killed Gaven, twice. "It's dangerous."

"Indeed, it is dangerous, but it serves a purpose." They came to a stop in front of a large, stone slab with words engraved on it. She motioned and Mirari took a step forward.

"What is this?"

"Read it."

THAT DAY WHEN A CLARION CALLS, the Goddess of Devotion,
she hears a plea. A wail like reliance of truth,
that makes her spare the boy. Out of potion,
to bestow upon, the mortal mercy for pitying youth.

NOT KNOWING THE CONSEQUENCE, our dear God become a great risk;
for a mere child to behold the power of ning-ürip, a captive
of uncontrolled caliber grows to be a part of a matrix.
This cheers joy with chaos, an ever-damning curse adaptive

TO TURN the villagers into an obsessed soul. A killing pandemic
alarms the earth, as the black tar propagates the mirth, of the ways
of Cygnus' dissent. The Goddess of Fate remonstrates an emic,
and cleanses the boy, bless akü-kene, with the touch of her plays.

THE OTHER OF GODS THEN, annoyed by the Goddess' interference with mortals,
curse them, the once friends, with a reincarnation of 100 years' immortals.

Mirari got to her feet, frustrated. The words hadn't answered anything. Julie's eyes were soulless and she nodded.

"He was a kind boy," she said. "Pure in every way, loved by

every soul. But his fate was met when he was swept away in this river trying to save another." She swung her hand in the direction of the sound of flowing water. Mirari found it hard to imagine – there was hardly any water left. Just how old was this story?

Mirari rubbed her forehead. Still, what did this have to do with anything? Julie heaved a sigh as if having to explain herself was taxing.

"The boy was blessed with *ning-ürip*," she said, "or what people call these days, dark aura, a gift of life. But it has earned a bad reputation through the ages, simply because, when the power is abused, it becomes an ability to subvert another's will."

Mirari turned her gaze to the ground and her brows furrowed. Yes, she had heard of dark aura – Joachim had suspected it had something to do with Salathiel's disappearance – but without proof, she had dismissed it as nothing more than a myth. No one had brought it up since, and she had forgotten about it. Julie's story made sense to her. Gaven. That poor man from Eoin's story. They wouldn't have taken things to the extreme if it wasn't for this dark aura.

"Your people are wasting time chasing after the ones you call the Defiants," Julie said. "They are nothing, a ragtag group that will dispel once their source is out of commission. If you want to win, you find the boy."

Mirari nodded, biting her lip. "You're saying Soteria has dark aura. We only need to kill her to stop the Defiants."

"Very good."

Mirari huffed. She thought of Eoin, how he'd done his best to impart his knowledge. She hoped she could carry on his legacy and stop this woman.

"How do we stop her?" Mirari asked.

"Your flames can dispel *ning-ürip*. Only you can negate Soteria's abilities with your own and stop her once and for all."

Mirari shuddered. "But…"

"But what?"

"I…can't control it. I've never once been conscious when it happens."

"You don't have any control over it because you've always shied away from it instead of embracing its power. A sword is dangerous in the hands of the ignorant. You must practice."

Mirari had no choice but to agree. It made sense and if she was really the only one who could stop Soteria, she had to be ready.

"I trust when the time comes, you'll be ready to face Soteria without all of that…" she flicked her fingers dismissively, "fear." Mirari gritted her teeth, but before she could say anything, Julie said, "I will let Salathiel know when she has been found. You will practice to control your flames."

Julie turned to Salathiel. He crossed his arms and gave her a look of confidence as if he knew what she was going to say.

"I told you," he said. "I'm seeing this to the end."

Julie glanced at Mirari one more time, whose attention was now fixated on the abandoned village.

"Then for your own sake, I hope this works." Julie said, then turned away.

Mirari wasn't listening. She stared at the crumbling tents of sticks and mud and wondered about the people who had lived there. If what Julie said was true – that dark aura is what caused people to act irrationally – then she knew her flames were the only solution. Looking at her bare hands, she couldn't see how she would do it, but she had stopped Gaven during the Althaean Siege. Surely, she could do it again.

When she turned back, Julie had left. She scowled at the empty space next to her. Salathiel came up behind her and squeezed her shoulder.

"I know you can do it. And I'm here. You're not doing this alone."

She sighed. "How in the world am I supposed to practice?"

"For starters, you can lose that negative attitude." She glared at him, but he only nodded. "I'm serious. If you don't believe you can do it, then you won't. And Mirari?" He waited until she was looking at him. "I believe you can do it." He took her to one of the decaying huts and stood behind her. With his hands on her shoulder, he said, "Deep breaths. In the past, what did you feel before the flames took over?"

"Anger?"

"Okay, good. Is there anything that makes you angry now?"

"Yes." Julie dragging her out to this abandoned village. The pressure of being the only one who could stop Soteria. Gaven. Inigo. "A lot of things make me angry." Her hands clenched into fists so tightly her knuckles ached.

"Then tap into that. That anger can be useful. However, you have to control it. You can't let it control you."

He took her hand and held it until she loosened her fist. "Close your eyes and just breathe. Feel your breath. Be here, in this moment, right now."

Inhale.

Exhale.

Mirari waited, but nothing came to her.

"Sorry," she fumed, shoulders slumping.

Salathiel shook his head. "That's all right. We have time to practice."

CHAPTER TEN

Gaven followed Eoin down a lonely dirt road that cut through the countryside. They traveled through the night with their hoods up on nondescript mares purchased by Erel.

"Let's stop here," Eoin said. "Give the horses a rest. We're about halfway there."

Gaven dismounted and looked around. Even picturing a map of the area, he couldn't imagine where Eoin was leading him. He didn't think there were any cities in this direction. Off the road, Eoin led him to a small watering hole for the horses.

Eoin crouched on the balls of his feet with unusual grace and balance for one so large. He blew on his hands, rubbing them together. Tucking his hands under his arms, Gaven stomped his feet against the cold and walked a circuit around the pond. By unspoken agreement, they lit no fire. Even though winter had a firm grasp on Althaea, a campfire was too risky.

"Your Honor," Eoin said, still looking at his fingers.

"What?"

"I've been thinking." Eoin got to his feet and brushed his hands on his pants. "It'll be safer if my comrades didn't know who you are." Gaven glanced at him but didn't argue. "If any of them are captured, the less they know, the better."

Gaven had thought of this, but he hadn't expected Eoin would agree to lie to his comrades. Though he was their leader, how he spoke about members of the Blessed made the hierarchy seem a bit arbitrary. It was always comrades and compatriots, never subordinates.

"That's fine," Gaven said. "Secrecy is better for me."

Eoin headed for his horse and fiddled with the straps for a moment. "Try not to take offense if they say something negative about you. That is, you, the region leader."

"Ah."

That was the real problem, wasn't it? He had no doubt made enemies of his own people and across the empires. It was nothing new, but the thought still pained him.

His eyes darted away when he said, "I couldn't care less what they say about me."

Gaven had mounted his horse when the moonlight reflected off a splash of purple below him. Swearing, he jumped back down and grabbed the necklace where it had fallen on the frozen ground. He ran his thumb over the purple gem. He couldn't lose this.

"Your Honor?"

"I'm fine," he said. Carefully, he looped the necklace around his wrist twice and tucked it into his glove. The metal was cold against his skin, but it was good that he could feel it. "I'm fine," he said again and lifted himself atop his horse once more.

They returned to the road. A few hours later, an isolated farm came into view. There was a wooden fence around the property, broken and falling apart. Farm equipment was lying in the dirt and the barn door was left open with no sign of any animals. A ripped cloth waved in the chilled wind and Eoin sighed when he saw it.

"Good. They're here."

They headed down the worn path toward the abandoned farmhouse. They tied the horses behind the house so that they couldn't be seen from the road and to shield them from the wind. At the back door, Eoin knocked in a distinctive pattern. Gaven heard a sudden rustling inside though it took a moment for someone to respond.

"Who's there?" a woman demanded.

"It's Eoin."

"E-Eoin!" The creaking door swung open. She stared at Eoin as he pushed his cloak down. "Eoin. It is you." Reaching out, she grabbed Eoin's arm. "Inside, inside. Come inside." She pulled him in and Gaven followed, making sure his hood covered most of his face as he closed the door behind him.

Gaven was shocked finding only a handful of them. Less than he thought, but perhaps that was to be expected. He and the Council had been thorough. Now, they were only a ragtag group of six, including Eoin.

"Eoin? I can't believe you're alive," said the woman. Evidently a former beauty, she was now older with sun-weathered skin and piercing eyes. Her clothes were well-worn and covered in patches. "I thought they executed you."

A woman leaning against the wall, snorted. "No wonder the Council is scrambling." She had a cruel scar across her face that twisted when she spoke. It looked bold and recent. A survivor from Aias?

"Myrana?" Eoin smiled when he saw her. "You made it."

"Yeah. I didn't think the same of you. How did you escape the Council's brutality?"

Though Gaven tried to stay out of the way, Eoin motioned toward him. No one said anything about his cloak, but they looked at him with curiosity just shy of suspicion.

"I had help from my friend here," Eoin said. Gaven grunted a welcome under their gaze. "Please forgive his hood. He's worried about the Council finding him."

"Understandable," an unassuming man said from the corner. He had a shaved head and wore a simple brown robe. "We don't ask questions. If you need sanctuary, you'll find it here."

"Yeah!" A lean, young man with a dirty face got to his feet. His eagerness reminded Gaven of Dorain. "I get that. Uh, wait. What should we call you?"

Gaven shifted on his feet, silently motioning Eoin to take charge.

"Just call him… Spirited Cat," Eoin said. Gaven frowned at him, but Eoin only smiled.

"Spiritel will do," Gaven said.

"Welcome, Spiritel," another woman said. She was tall and lanky with a crossbow attached to her hip. "Anyone who can stick one up the Council is a friend in my book. I'm Brigid. That's Aitken." Brigid pointed at the robed man in the corner. "The one who needs to wipe his face is Sven."

The young man's hand flew to his face and he hastily scrubbed his reddening cheeks. "It-it's soot," he said. "I'm an apprentice blacksmith."

The sun-worn beauty who'd let them in was Isemay and the woman against the wall was, of course, Myrana, a brawler and an Aias refugee.

Myrana was quiet and observant and unlike the others looked at Gaven with no small amount of wariness.

"Who are you?" she demanded.

"Myrana," Isemay said. "Isn't it enough that he helped Eoin?"

Based on Myrana's scowl, it wasn't. So much for no questions. Eoin stepped forward, and Myrana backed down at his insistence.

"Spiritel not only helped me get away, but he also wants to aid our cause and hunt down the Defiants," he said. "He's a powerful warrior. We're lucky to call him our ally."

"You know the Defiants?" Myrana asked Gaven, her curiosity

wiping the grimace off her face. Her intimidating stance seconds ago had greatly diminished.

While Gaven pondered how to answer, Eoin spoke. "It's true that not many outside this room even acknowledge the Defiants as different from the Blessed, but Spiritel has personally encountered them."

Myrana pushed away from the wall, intrigued. She nodded a few times. Gaven braced himself for more questions, but it seemed Eoin's explanation was enough. Was it that easy to be welcomed here? Simply out of common hatred of the Defiants?

With the introductions out of the way, Eoin and Gaven were invited to break bread with the rest of them. Eoin followed Isemay farther into the farmhouse where they were keeping their supplies.

"Have you been traveling all night?" she asked. Her voice faded as they got further into the house.

But Myrana paused in the doorway and placed her hand on the frame. She spun around and leaned on her arm. Gaven tugged on his hood, though he didn't think Myrana would recognize him.

"Don't look so dour," she said. "Look, man, I didn't mean to grill you. All of us here, we've lost someone too. If not to the Defiants, then to the Council's crusade against them." Reaching out, she clapped Gaven on the shoulder. "Just remember, you're not alone. When you're with the Blessed, we take care of each other."

"Thanks," Gaven managed to say.

Nodding, Myrana led him to the other room. Inside, the others were already discussing the Defiants and any rumors they'd heard about them. These six weren't the last of the Blessed. They existed in many small pockets around the country where they collected and shared information.

Gaven learned more in ten minutes than he'd gathered in all his time following the Council's lead. A conversation he had with

Mirari came to mind. After he had the man who attacked her in the plaza executed, she'd argued that mercy would have been better. She'd wanted to question him more.

He twisted his hand, feeling the gem of the necklace slide against his wrist. She'd been right, hadn't she? Killing everyone connected to the Blessed wouldn't get them answers and it wouldn't resolve the chaos blanketing Althaea Main.

The group discussion came to a close when a direction was decided.

"Spiritel? Are you ready?" Eoin asked Gaven who was standing in the doorway.

Gaven nodded. "Lead the way."

CHAPTER ELEVEN

Gaven tugged on his hood and bit back a curse. It was a windy, cloudless night and the moon shone down on them like a particularly large lumastōne. It was fortunate for Gaven that they didn't have to use lumastōnes – he was fretting over his hood like a washerwoman over the clothesline. And the last thing he wanted was to worry about keeping his hood down during a fight.

It was bad enough that Eoin wanted him to use a sword. A sword of all things! How close would he need to get to his target before making so much of a scratch? Gaven could use his own weapon that was hidden in his back pocket, but that was off limits as long as he was Spiritel. Everyone would recognize his spear, even if he didn't channel kore into it. So many limitations. He fiddled with the rusted handle of the second-hand sword they had given him. How far would it get him before it broke? This thing should've been smelted years ago.

He sighed silently in relief when he caught sight of Brigid loping back where they were hunched behind a line of barrels. She was moving toward them swiftly, faster than when she'd left to scout out the warehouse.

This was the second warehouse where there had been reports of possible Defiant activity. The first had been a bust with no Defiants. But the crates had been labeled with the sigil of House Tepis and Gaven had gleefully put the information aside to be conveyed to Erel at an opportune moment. Still, it wasn't what he was here for.

"It's definitely them." Brigid ducked down with a soft huff. She reported that, unlike last time, this warehouse wasn't empty. "I couldn't get a good look from the window, but it appears there were only six or seven people inside. Minimal weapons that I could see. I don't think the leader is there." The others cursed their misfortune and wondered what to do next.

The Blessed weren't fighters and lacked instinct. Brigid had an eye for detail, but it had to be coaxed out.

"Where were they standing?" Gaven asked.

"Two by the door. The others were sort of bunched together to the right of the entrance."

Gaven rubbed his chin, humming to himself. That was a strange pattern. Was this the place?

"Were they facing toward each other or away?" Eoin asked, catching on.

"Uh, away," she responded, seeming startled by the question.

"With their weapons out?" Gaven asked. She nodded. Gaven glanced at Eoin before turning to address the others. "We're going to hit this warehouse," he ordered.

"Why?" Aitken asked. "Won't we lose our advantage?"

"Yeah," Sven piped in. "I thought we were supposed to keep a low profile until we found their leader." He glanced between Eoin and Gaven, looking for answers.

"The Defiants are guarding something in there," Eoin said. He spoke patiently, giving them time to figure it out. It reminded Gaven of his time training the Knights at the Estate. They had grown so much since, but now he didn't even know if they were on the same side.

"It could be weaponry," Gaven continued, "and destroying it would be a blow to their combat strengths. It could also be something as simple as supplies."

Or it could be something much worse.

"Right," Sven said with a nod. "And they still got to eat."

"Exactly," Eoin said.

"Come," Gaven said now that the others understood a little about what was at stake. "Let's not waste any more time." Before they left, he added one last thing. "Don't let any of them escape so we can still keep our advantage. We cannot allow them to report to their leader."

"Understood."

They moved swiftly across the empty field. The warehouse they were aiming for was one of three and situated along the Althaean Sea coast. It was a drop point for passing ships and, they had hoped, Soteria's hiding place. The warehouse was made of two materials, stone on the bottom-half and wood on the top. The front double doors were made from reinforced wood and were large enough for entire wagons to drive through. Brigid directed them to the apertures located in the back.

Eoin bent down and cupped his hands. Isemay stepped into his hands and Eoin boosted her up to the opening in the wall. They waited with bated breath before she finally stuck her head out the window and tossed down the secured rope. They ascended slowly with Gaven taking up the rear.

Inside the warehouse, they assessed the Defiants. The warehouse was just as Brigid had reported. Besides two guards by the door, the rest were clumped up around the crates just underneath where Gaven and the others had come in. Though guarding supplies, they weren't a disciplined army, lounging around the crates, alert but not on guard.

Gaven motioned for Brigid to stay where she was while the others crept toward the stairs. With the Defiants' lax attitude, they would have one clean shot to take them by surprise before the enemy realized they were under attack. Keeping low, they stalked forward until they were as close as Gaven deemed to be safe. He held his hand up in a fist and waited.

There looked to be two swordsmen, a spearwoman, and a brawler. When the brawler shifted his weight Gaven caught a glimpse of a smaller woman behind him. She didn't have any obvious weapons but she wore the robes of a celta.

He waited a moment longer, just in case, but he had seen what needed to be seen. There were five enemies here. When they attacked, the two by the door would advance and it would be on Brigid to stop them. He glanced over to Eoin who nodded.

Gaven motioned the others forward. Myrana surged ahead, moving swiftly across the floor. Without a hint of hesitation, Gaven followed after her. There were cries of alarm as the Defiants noticed they were under attack.

One of the men swung his sword at Myrana, focusing intently on the woman coming toward him. She jumped, using his shoulder as a springboard to launch herself at the brawler behind him. While the first swordsman was distracted, Gaven jammed his sword under his breastplate and impaled him. He bit back a curse.

With a kick to the swordsman's stomach, Gaven jerked the weapon out, just as the other swordsman came at him with a wild swing. Gaven ducked under the blade and jabbed his sword forward. This one was tougher than the first. His ugly mug was set in a snarling grimace and he was built like a stone wall. Even when Gaven landed a solid hit on his side, the man brushed it off and hammered his elbow into Gaven's chest. They both staggered back to catch their breath.

"Watch out!" Brigid called from her vantage point.

Ice was forming overhead – decent-sized chunks of hail that could cause some damage if they hit just right. Gaven took a risk and ducked behind one of the crates to block the hail from reaching him.

"I got her!" Sven shouted, rushing toward the hiding woman. He was swinging a well-maintained hatchet, and a puff of wind under his feet boosted him over the crates. The hail changed direction, and shortly all signs of the celta disappeared.

"Found you," the swordsman said through bloody teeth, whipping around the corner of the crate.

Gaven spun just in time and rolled out of the way as a blade struck down where he'd been sitting. The blow was strong enough that the blade sunk into the crate. The attacker abandoned his weapon, preparing to jump at Gaven.

Gaven ducked and thrusted his shoulder into the swordsman's stomach, using his own momentum to toss him onto his back. Before he could recover, Gaven pointed his rusted sword downward and thrusted it through the swordsman... and the ground. There was no way he would waste his efforts pulling that one out.

To Gaven's surprise, the fight was winding down and victory was in clear sight. Perhaps this small crew would be enough to take down the Defiants. With success in mind, Gaven searched for any survivors. He saw Eoin with his back turned, hovering over Isemay and Aitken. Aitken was casting healing kore on the renastōnes placed over their cuts and scrapes.

Gaven realized he had his guard low when he heard the slightest scraping sound – metal sliding across the stone flooring. Others continued their winners' banter, and it was clear that they hadn't noticed the sound.

An injured swordsman jump to his feet with vigor that shouldn't have been possible. His sword was inching toward Eoin's exposed back.

Gaven quickly grabbed the spear at his feet, and with a spin, launched the weapon with deadly force and pinpoint accuracy. *Thud!*

The swordsman arched forward and slammed to the ground

with the spear through his back. Eoin stared at the dead man at his feet, shocked as the sword clattered out of the Defiant's hand.

"That was amazing!" Sven said, breaking the silence. He ran up to the skewered man and examined him with intrigue. "I've never seen anyone turn their feet like that."

"That was… impressive," Eoin said. He met Gaven's gaze and gave a nod of appreciation.

Gaven deflected the appreciation away in his stare. He mumbled, "I told you I'm better with a spear."

Eoin laughed, as did the others.

"Did any of the Defiants survive?" Gaven asked.

"Over here," Myrana said, waving.

Myrana had bested the enemy brawler and his eyes were closed and his body was already forming bruises. Blood trickled from his nose to blend in with the red staining the left side of his face.

"Are you sure?" Gaven asked dryly, kicking the brawler's booted foot.

Myrana flushed. "He's alive." She reached down to strike his face, which Gaven didn't think was helping.

Gaven examined the crates the Defiants had been guarding. With Brigid's help, he pried the lid off of one of the crates. As he feared, it was stacked with spears. The next one had broadswords.

"This is great," Brigid said. "A significant blow to the Defiants."

"Perhaps," Gaven said.

"You don't agree?"

Eoin approached them. "This was a fairly small guard unit," he said. "Perhaps Soteria let her guard down, but it's just as likely that this was only a small shipment and there are bigger out there." Eoin didn't mention that with these many weapons, there were likely that many Defiants too. Many more than they anticipated.

"Oh." Her shoulders slumped and her disappointment was echoed on the faces of her comrades.

"This wasn't nothing," Eoin said, clapping her on the back. "We've kept these out of the hands of the Defiants and that's something to be proud of."

"It's true," Gaven said. "This was a good start, but this is just one of many."

"You should listen to Spiritel," Eoin said. "He has a lot of experience." It was strange that it didn't come off as mockery, strange enough that Gaven chose to ignore Eoin's remark as he continued to rummage through the rest of the crates.

By the time he examined the last crate, the fallen Defiant in Myrana's custody had been revived.

All except Eoin approached Gaven and spoke in a low voice. "You're worried about something."

"Yeah." He patted the crate behind him. Eoin didn't say anything and Gaven elaborated. "I heard a rumor that a box of weapons had gone missing."

"What kind?"

"Hāstal."

Eoin sucked in a breath. He understood. Such advanced weaponry in the hands of a single person could be devastating. Most peasants would never have seen weapons like that, but they didn't need to be educated to use them.

"And you think Soteria has them?"

"That's what I fear."

"It's better to hope for the best but to expect the worst," Eoin murmured.

"Exactly."

"Where did you hear this rumor? Can you ask this person for more information about the missing shipment?"

"He told me all he could." And he wasn't happy about that. "We won't get any more from him."

"Hey, Eoin, Spiritel, he's awake," Myrana announced.

"Well, maybe we'll get something from him," Eoin said, motioning.

Nodding, Gaven followed him. Calling the man "awake" was a little optimistic. He was semi-conscious, but perhaps they could get answers out of him anyway.

Crouching down in front of the brawler, Gaven tapped him on the cheek until he opened his hazy eyes.

"Where were you shipping the weapons?" he asked. The man's head started to lull to the side and Gaven gripped his chin, forcing his head upright. "Where were you shipping the weapons?"

"Y-you'll… never stop… us," he slurred.

"Stop you? Why would we? We're on the same side." Nothing was stopping Gaven from using Erel's tricks.

Concussed and nearly unconscious, the brawler didn't need to be convinced much of Gaven's acting skills. "We… are?"

"Of course. The rest of our brethren were dead when we arrived. You have to tell us. Where were the weapons meant to be shipped. We have to deliver them to Soteria, don't we?"

"Y-yes." He was fading fast.

"Where?" Gaven said urgently. He leaned in when the man started whispering.

"The p-port," the brawler said. "They… have to make it… to… the… port." His head slumped forward, insensate or dead.

Sighing, Gaven sat back on his heels.

"What did he say?" Eoin asked.

"Unfortunately, it was nothing specific. The weapons were supposed to go to a port."

"No idea where they were shipping them?"

Gaven shook his head. It wasn't a dead end, but there were so many ports in the empires that it felt a little hopeless. Not that he could share his doubts with the others. "We'll just travel along the coast and look for signs of the Defiants or any ships that may be suspicious."

"What about Oulfa?" Isemay said.

Oulfa? It was a port town near the border of Althaea Main and Ophallen. "What about it?" Gaven asked.

Eoin nodded at her. "That's a good idea." He looked at Gaven. "I have a contact in Oulfa. He'll know of any unusual activity happening in the area."

"Very well."

"What will we do about this?" Sven asked, motioning toward the carnage.

"We'll have to report it," Gaven said.

"Report it? To the region leader?" There were cries of alarm from the others and Eoin had to step forward to calm them.

"He's right," Eoin said.

"You can't be serious. We can't trust the region leader," Myrana spat.

Gaven stayed quiet, hiding his clenched fist behind him. They wouldn't want to hear any defense he might have for himself.

Eoin stepped up. "We can't take these weapons with us and we can't just leave them either. What if more Defiants find them? All of our hard work will have been for nothing."

They were silent for a beat before Isemay spoke up.

"T-then, can't we just burn them?" she asked.

"Besides the fact that I'm against needlessly smelting good weapons?" Eoin said dryly. She flushed but he only smiled good-naturedly. "These weapons came from somewhere. We don't have the resources to track them back to their source and make sure they aren't supplying others with more."

Aitken nodded in understanding. "We can only treat the symptoms, but they can find the root cause."

Myrana's shoulders slumped. "I understand, but… the region leader. He's a lackey of the Council. They won't care that we stopped the Defiants. They'll see this as another red flag from the Blessed, and hunt us down."

Eoin reached out and clapped Gaven on the back. "I wouldn't worry about that. We've got Spiritel on our side." Gaven eyed him sideways, unsure where Eoin was going with his speech. "Did you not see him fight? I'd say his battle prowess could give even the Valiant Tiger a run for his money."

"Oh yeah," Sven said, raising his fist. "The way you threw that spear. Not even the region leader would have been able to catch that."

Gaven could see how Eoin's words managed to relieve some of the tension as they joked about who would win in a duel between the Valiant Tiger and himself. He wanted to believe that the words were said only to reassure, but from the way Eoin looked at him, it was a camaraderie he hadn't expected to find among the Blessed. Eoin grinned at Gaven like he was in on the joke. It was the sort of lighthearted jab he would have expected of Haynes or Erel.

Clearing his throat, Gaven moved away from the others.

"Enough," he said. "I appreciate your vote of confidence, but I for one wouldn't want to face the Valiant Tiger, which I might have to if we don't stop standing around chatting."

There was some laughter and Myrana even jostled him as they made their way out of the warehouse. The Defiants and their leader were still out there and they had only a vague idea where to start looking for her. There was still much to be done, but Gaven was alleviated of that hopeless feeling.

This – what he was doing with the Blessed – felt good. It felt right. He tugged on his hood and followed the others out.

CHAPTER TWELVE

Mirari thrusted her palm toward a large stone. Nothing. She raised her other hand and did the same. Morning birds greeted her and filled the still air. A few landed in front of her, taking sips of water from the rills running between her and the boulder. Mirari sighed and dropped her hands.

"No luck?" Salathiel said as he approached her. He gazed at her makeshift training ground – a giant boulder enclosed by smaller stones, all precisely aligned. She must've spent more time constructing the area than actually training. Her frustrations showed, and she likely had given up a long time ago.

"Fangbane thought I could control it," she said with a huff. "Everyone thinks I can just summon fire on command. Well, I can't!"

"Okay, well, I'm not Fangbane." Salathiel took her hand and curled it into a fist. He pointed it to the rock. "Imagine a jar with a lid. Your rage is inside. The fire is inside. Can you picture it?"

She nodded slowly. If she did it right, she would see an object in the darkness of her mind, possibly white. When Salathiel did this, he saw a white jar, more like a vase. It was half his height.

The lid fit snugly into the lip of the vase and the handle was shaped like a tear-drop.

"Do you see it?" Salathiel whispered, making sure her mind was still in the moment.

"Yeah."

"Now, lift the lid. Take a peek and see what's inside."

Mirari, no doubt, had more baggage than he did. She would see every hurt, from her parents to her shattered relationship with Gaven, and everything stuffed in between. Her eyes tightened as she imagined disembodied hands reaching out to the vase and slowly tipping the lid.

She threw down her fist and opened her eyes.

"There's nothing," Mirari huffed. "There's nothing inside."

Salathiel frowned. "Even if you don't see it, I believe you're making progress."

"That doesn't make me feel any better."

"I mean it. The jar works." Salathiel twisted his fist and fell silent. "Julie taught this to me when… I went through the same thing."

She searched in his eyes for an answer, and kept her gaze on his scar.

"You can't keep hiding yourself from me," she said, placing her hand over his. "Will you tell me what happened? Why did you leave me?"

Salathiel gave her a forced smile. Her unwavering gaze told him that he didn't have a choice. Perhaps the truth would inspire her, but it could just as easily make her hate him. Ignorance was a bliss that Mirari couldn't see, but how long could he protect her? He huffed, lowering his gaze to the ground.

"Five years ago…"

SALATHIEL SIGHED as he left the house after saying farewell to Mirari. Shaking his head, he straightened his back and shook off the worry he had after their conversation. His job may not be as glamorous as a region leader, but it put food on the table and that was enough.

As a retinue, his job was somewhat of a cross between a courier and a bodyguard. He delivered things if they needed delivering and protected things if they needed protecting. It didn't usually pay much, but this job in particular was unique. He couldn't help but jump at the opportunity to make *real* money. Mirari seemed to like the hairpin he'd given her, but he imagined what he could really give her with this job's pay.

As Salathiel forged his way toward the outskirts of town, a palpable weight of ominous stillness enveloped him in the cool, misty air. The locals had whispered cautionary tales about Smuggler's Dell, a forested realm with nothing but scant remnants of a bygone era. It wasn't merely the wandering unde-sirables that cast a foreboding aura, but also the unsettling fog that clung to the atmosphere like the lingering spirits of those who had once traversed its mysterious depths. Salathiel pushed these tales from his mind as he arrived at a neglected depot and slipped through a narrow opening between two weathered planks of wood.

He was surprised by the tall rows of crates that made its way into Smuggler's Dell. Solarin was nothing, a pitstop for most trav-elers – trades this large were usually dealt with in other cities. He assumed the pay for this job was in proportion to the size of the shipment, but deep down he knew there was a reason it was happening in Solarin. He was directed to stand guard by the crates stacked in the corner, and the mystery quickly left his mind.

Salathiel looked in both directions and saw three traders. He was standing hidden in the shadow of the mazed crates. The shipment was too large for only one person.

He turned to one of them and asked, "Is there anyone else coming to help?"

"What? You want to share the pay?" the boss, a tall, scrawny man with a cigar hanging over his stubble, asked with a chuckle.

"Oh, no, sir."

"It's fine," his associate said. "We only need one guard."

He was a bit plump and squat compared to his partner, and his accent told Salathiel that he was not from these parts. The man tipped his hat and lowered his voice like he was letting Salathiel in on a secret.

"There's only supposed to be three of us, so you best stay out of sight. Just make sure those Althaean bastards don't try anything."

Salathiel grimaced and the man laughed again.

"Yeah, exactly. They'll have guards too, no doubt. Once we get paid, we bail. They'll have to take all this stuff back to Rhue? Rhia? Ah, I don't remember." He patted the wooden crate. Salathiel could hear something delicate tinkling from inside it. "Not my problem, right?"

"Yes, sir."

"Good man." The man patted Salathiel's shoulder and wandered back to one of his companions. He yelled, "Hey, do you remember where this stuff is supposed to go?"

The third trader, a woman fashioning a pair of high heels that complemented her burgundy-filled lips, spun around to look at him with a sharply raised eyebrow. "How should I know?"

"Don't look at me like that. It's just bothering me. I swear it's on the tip of my tongue. Rhua?

The woman scoffed and rolled her eyes. "Rhea?"

He snapped his fingers. "That's it. Rhea."

"Why do you care? Planning on visiting?"

The boss huffed a laugh. "Yeah, right. Rhea can drown with rest of them Althaean towns by the sweat of my balls!"

"I don't know," the tall man said, taking a puff of his cigar.

"Didn't they finally abolish the Separation Laws? Things are about to change."

They all laughed.

The short partner struggled over to Salathiel's corner. He patted a large crate, then eyed Salathiel. "You there. Don't just lurk about. Help me with this."

Salathiel glanced at the client who nodded with a roll of his eyes. Stepping forward, Salalthiel held his hands out. "Yes, sir. Sorry."

The man harrumphed and let Salathiel take the crate. The cargo clinked dangerously during the switch, probably something made of glass.

"Careful!" the man snapped. His face was pale and he stepped back hastily. Nobody moved for a moment while Salathiel tightened his grip. When the glass settled down the man sighed. "Careful. It's delicate."

He backed away and Salathiel realized it was more than just delicate.

Under their watchful eyes, he carefully transported the box the rest of the way to the other crates. The three clients stood stiffly until he'd gently placed the wooden container and returned to his corner.

The woman shuddered. "Even if I wanted to, I'd never visit Althaea knowing what's in store." Her eyes glanced meaningfully toward the crates. Salathiel followed her gaze, a heavy pit forming in his stomach. Just what were they selling?

"Hey, don't worry about it," the boss said, patting her shoulder. "Those Althaean bastards are going to tear up their own country. It's got nothing to do with us."

"'Cept we're the ones risking our lives transporting their goods," the short one said with a sneer.

"They're paying, aren't they? Althaeans don't have much and I'm willing to take what they do have. Aren't you?"

With their backs to him as they talked, Salathiel took a step to the side, bringing him closer to the crates. He cracked the top of the box he'd carried over. It was filled tightly with rows and rows of little glass vials with cork stoppers. The blue liquid inside was bubbling lightly. He lowered the cover and stepped away. Based on how it looked and the way the clients had reacted, it was likely a dangerous poison.

Turning to another crate, he lifted the wooden cover. The box was stacked with short swords, their sharp edges glistened in the low light. He looked through a few more crates; it was all weapons.

He tuned back into the clients' conversation.

"Truly, Althaeans are so brutal," the boss said, as if the three of them were blameless. "All that backbiting and power-grabbing and they accidentally get themselves a region leader with a brain."

"Can't have that!" the woman snorted.

"Oh, they won't." He thumbed his hands toward the crates. "Althaea Main will be the proving ground for why Althaeans will always be backward barbarians. That Tiger fellow wants to be like a Minettan? He'll see just what that gets him." They laughed again. "Althaeans will always have exactly what they deserve, which is nothing!"

Salathiel frowned, scrutinizing the crates he was surrounded by. He was stuck, with an awful twist in his stomach, unsure what to do. If they were going to Rhea, it would be affecting Althaea Main, Gaven's region. What if these weapons were meant to take him down?

Salathiel scoffed. Gaven discarded them like trash to go play warrior. He never looked back. He never wrote. The only reason Salathiel knew he wasn't dead in a ditch was because he'd made a name for himself as a region leader. And now that name was going to get him killed.

Salathiel crossed his arms. He always kept up on the news coming out of Althaea, with an obsession he refused to admit. It was because Gaven was still his cousin, and he knew better than anyone that his irrational arrogance was likely creating enemies.

Salathiel's gaze flickered over to the boxes of weapons and his thoughts turned to Mirari. He'd never be able to look her in the eye if he just left Gaven to his fate. Besides, if he abandoned Gaven, wouldn't he be just as bad as him?

But then getting involved with things that were none of his business was just the sort of thing he usually chastised Mirari for. Sighing, Salathiel lowered his arms and edged closer to one of the boxes. He didn't have to run out there and start throwing punches. He had to be smart.

He inspected his surroundings and found a sharpened stone on the ground. He rolled it in his palm, feeling the jagged edge. *That'll do.* Keeping an ear out for the clients, he opened the box again. He tossed the rock and a few more stones inside. By the time they got transported to Althaea Main, the rocks would do some damage to the swords inside, dulling their edges. It wasn't much, but any more could get him killed.

In one of the smaller crates, he noticed something different. Glowing lines on the hilt marked the daggers as some sort of hāstal weapon. There were other gadgets below them, separated by a soft folded cloth. He felt helpless, staring at them. He had no idea how these hāstal weapons worked, but didn't want to imagine the amount of damage they could do if he left them as is.

Carefully lifting a mechanical glove out of the crate, he turned it over. It was heavy and surprisingly warm in his hands. After turning it a few times, he found small metal rods on the side. He loosened them with his fingers, returned the glove to the box, and hastily did the same to the others. He hoped that during travel, they would fall out and become useless by the time they reached their destination. It was the best he could do. He hoped it was enough. He could be saving lives, and the thought eased him a bit.

The three traders were still in animated discussion. He sighed in relief that they hadn't caught him.

The last thing to take care of was the poison. When he lifted the lid, he couldn't help being intimidated by the vials. He could toss a rock in there too, but if the vials broke, whoever was carrying them would die a gruesome death. Scowling, he ran his hand through his hair. He had to think of something else.

The vials were tightly stoppered. He didn't know a lot about poisons, but he was pretty sure they had to be transported in a certain way not only to keep them from breaking but to keep them potent as well. He drew one of his daggers and leaned down. He silently cursed himself as he pierced the top of the stopper, exposing the poison to the air. He held his breath, but nothing seemed to happen. Did the rolling bubble inside look a little less…volatile? Maybe. Salathiel wasn't sure if it was working, but it was the only thing he could think of. Resolved, Salathiel did the same to the other vials before replacing the top.

He quickly got back into place just as the boss walked over and pulled out his pocket watch. He looked over to Salathiel's corner, nodded to him and said, "They'll be here soon."

Not long after, Salathiel heard footsteps coming from the far end of the depot. He peered through a stack of crates and saw three tall, rough-looking men in homespun clothing. The scowls etched on their faces spoke volumes, with each furrowed brow and hardened jawline reflecting the harsh experiences that had shaped them. Their eyes, sharp and keen, scanned the surroundings with unsettling focus.

Salathiel's three clients stood in front of the crates, assuming an almost predatory stance with squared shoulders and unyielding expressions directed at their natural enemies – the Althaeans. The boss gruffly demanded the money, and the Althaeans scanned the crates once more.

Salathiel's eyes widened at the sound of the large bag hitting the ground. The lady started forward her loud heels hitting the ground, but one of the Althaeans intercepted her. "Not so fast, little lady." She scowled but stepped back. "It's all there. We need to check the weapons first."

The boss fretted, peeking in Salathiel's direction. "It's all there. We're the ones taking the risk. We should get to count the money."

"By all means," the Althaean leader said, waving his hand toward the bag even as he moved unerringly toward the back of the dwelling. The second accompanied him while the third stayed with the bag. Salathiel ducked out of sight, hiding behind one of the larger crates in the back. Did the Althaean intend to check all of them? If they caught him, he was doomed and so were his clients.

Keeping his head down, Salathiel heard the crates opening and closing. The footsteps were getting closer. His hand went to his belt, but he decided against drawing his dagger.

"All clear over here, Boss," the second man said.

"Seems the damn Minettans got something right. Let's get out of…"

"Boss?"

"What?" the Althaean leader walked over to his comrade and jerked a crate. Salathiel heard the telltale sound of glass rattling before the Althaean turned to the Minettan traders and fumed, "Do you think we're fools? You're trying to trick us!"

"We are doing no such thing," the boss said. Salathiel winced when he heard swords being drawn. He palmed his daggers. This was going south, and fast.

"Look at these." The Althaean threw a box heavily onto the ground to the alarmed objections of the clients. Salathiel flinched, hoping that crate didn't contain the poison vials. He peeked out and found the other Althaean still standing by the crates. He cursed to himself.

"These are not what we ordered," the Althaean leader snarled. "Look and tell me if these could kill anybody. You were trying to pass water off to us like we wouldn't know the difference."

There were slow footsteps and then Salathiel heard his boss speak. "If those poison vials were faulty, that's no fault of ours. We just deliver them as promised."

Their silence told Salathiel that it wasn't what they wanted to hear. He slipped around the crates, trying to make it to his clients, just in time to see one of the Althaeans slip his hand into his back pocket. With a flick of his wrist, Salathiel nailed a dagger on the Althaean's hip. His scream sent the room into full alarm, and he staggered to reach and pull out the blade.

With no more time to waste, Salathiel rushed out from behind the crate. The Althaean leader was about to take a swing at his boss. Salathiel tackled and grappled him, pulling him away.

He heard his short partner shouting, "Get the money! Get the money!"

Salathiel twisted away from his boss and lifted his dagger just in time to block a swing overhead. The Althaean leader forced his short sword down toward Salathiel's head. Rotating his wrist, Salathiel shoved the blade away and kicked the man in the chest. He fumbled back into a stack of crates.

One of the Althaean henchmen was joined by two guards that stepped out from the maze of crates, daggers in both hands.

Salathiel began to back away, and the three men took their positions, circling him. The Minettan woman was behind him, bent over the bag of money. The scuffle had left Salathiel separated from his two male clients. He had been cornered by the Althaean holding a bloody dagger that came from his hip.

Salathiel held a dagger in each hand, spinning them between his fingers, looking more confident than he felt. Inexorably, the guards were enraged, but he could tell it made the Althaeans wary. They turned to their boss.

"Deceptive scum," the Althaean leader snarled, spitting

blood onto the floor as he got to his feet. "What are you waiting for? Slit their throats!"

The first guard darted forward, faster than Salathiel expected. He swung his sword in a wide arc that Salathiel barely dodged. Twisting on his heels, he swiped his dagger across his back, the swordsman returned the blow with a brush against his ear.

Ear ringing, Salathiel returned to his stance. He resisted the urge to check his wound, but the pain was enough to distract him from a blow to his chest. He peered down, gripping the man's arm. He pivoted, pulled the man forward, then struck his elbow down on his back. It was a critical point, one that would render him paralyzed for some time.

The man dropped to the ground, and the Althaean trader followed through with a swipe of his sword. Salathiel leaned backward into a somersault, pressing his weight onto the ground and delivering a full-forced kick to the man's chin. When Salathiel landed back on his feet, he felt a pull in his chest. He seethed, tearing his mind away from anything but the battle before him. Whatever he received, he would return tenfold. His knuckles turned white as he clawed at the ground. Salathiel channeled his kore into the earth and a large stone shot up, protruding from the ground, with a force strong enough to knock the swordsman high in the air, falling out of sight behind a row of crates.

For the last one…

He was spinning a mace, his heels dug deep into the ground as he beckoned his challenger. Salathiel charged forward with a fierce yell. It was careless of him, but Salathiel never had to fend for his life more than now. The guard's mace swung toward Salathiel's face. Salathiel ducked under the attack but he wasn't fast enough. One of the spikes sliced across his eye.

Spinning to the side, Salathiel delivered a swift kick to the man's midsection. The man doubled over in pain, and Salathiel pointed both his arms downward. Vines erupted from the cement ground and cascaded across like a tsunami. The guard was trapped under the roots before he saw what had happened. He was alive and struggling, but barely. The weight of the roots would crush him soon enough. Salathiel stumbled backward, blood trickling down the side of his face.

"Help!" he heard someone cry right before the sound of a blade meeting flesh.

Salathiel turned, cursing himself. The chubby Minettan collapsed to the ground as his assailant removed his sword from his guts. Salathiel's boss was only steps away from becoming the next victim, scrabbling across the ground, trying to get away from his impending doom.

Salathiel reached in his coat for another dagger and threw it. It cut through the air with a whistle and found a home in the Althaean's eye. His distraction nearly cost him as the Althaean leader came swinging his sword as though Salathiel's leg was a block of wood to be chopped.

Salathiel fell backward in a roll, but the blade cut deep into his leg. He cried out, wildly throwing his second dagger toward his attacker. He was startled when it landed, but not more than the leader who crashed to the ground with the blade in his throat.

Gasping, Salathiel staggered to his feet. There was one left, but unfortunately, Salathiel was just about tapped out. He scanned his surroundings, twice. Where did he go? He checked behind the crates where he had landed. There was no body. And where was the woman? Had she fled?

He limped over to his boss as blood gushed from the wound in his leg. He could barely see through the cut dripping into his eye, and his body began to feel heavy.

"We should go," Salathiel said, trying to help his client up.

The man batted his hand away but staggered to his feet.

"Grab the money," he wheezed, bracing himself against the wall. "I'm not leaving without it."

Salathiel looked around and found the bag had been kicked halfway across the room toward the other wall. He took a few steps forward, then froze when he came to his senses. Why would anyone leave without the money?

"Don't move," a voice called from his right.

Salathiel pivoted in place and froze. Two paces away stood the Althaean with a mechanical glove on his hand, pointed directly at Salathiel. The other was gripping the throat of the terrified woman. The Althaean's rugged face was lit gruesomely by the glowing marks on the side of the glove. The palm had a pulsing, circular gem, likely the most powerful form of hāstal Salathiel has ever seen, and he didn't want to find out what it did. Smirking, the Althaean caressed the gem.

"This, this is the exact problem," he muttered, half to himself. "Damned featherpits involving themselves in the affairs of Althaea."

"We want nothing to do with your rebellion," the boss said. He pointed a shaking finger toward the Althaean. "If you leave now, we'll spare your pathetic life."

The Althaean's smirk widened and he swung his gloved hand pointing at the woman. A humming noise was coming from the powered gem, growing louder as it illuminated brighter. "You think I care about my life? My life is meaningless compared to my cause. My people will reclaim our land from the vermin infestation."

Salathiel mentally measured the distance between him and the Althaean. If his leg wasn't messed up, he could have tackled the weapon out of the man's hand. The woman's eyes were pleading for him to do it.

"Don't bother," the Althaean said, glancing at Salathiel as if he read his mind too. "Even if you kill all of us, the rebellion will come for you, vermin. We have an army, a strong one." He laughed. "No one's going to help you. Not even the region leaders."

Salathiel gritted his teeth. He couldn't refrain himself from shouting, "Oh yeah? You think you can beat the Valiant Tiger? The Council? Your rebellion means nothing!"

What was he saying? Since when did those wealthy snobs care about what happened to the peasants? They weren't going to save his life. If they were here, they would've killed him with the Althaeans. He lowered his head. His life wouldn't mean anything to Gaven.

Salathiel seethed. Right now, he didn't care about the rebellion or the Althaeans. He only wanted to get out of the situation with his life intact.

"Don't just stand there," the boss snapped. "Get the money!"

Salathiel furrowed his brows, darting his eyes between the money and the woman. "But—"

"I said—"

The Althaean jerked the weapon at him. With a surge of adrenaline, Salathiel darted forward, seizing the weapon in the blink of an eye and redirecting its ominous light toward the ground. Wrestling against the might of the Althaean, Salathiel vowed to keep fighting no matter what. He steeled himself as the weapon's glow intensified. But in the back of his mind, he knew his fate was more or less the same with the weapon's lethal power at close range.

To his luck, smoke began trickling out from the glove. He quickly let go and jumped behind a crate for cover. The Althaean yelped, desperately trying to take it off. Salathiel heard the metal object clang on the ground, then all sound was lost as a bright light encompassed the depot.

For a moment, there was peace and clarity. He didn't know how long he was in that state, but he didn't want it to end. Time seemed eternal... until the light vanished and he opened his eyes.

Salathiel's first thoughts when he woke were confused. He was surrounded by darkness. Not much time had passed because the sun had yet to rise. Salathiel sat up. He had fallen quite a distance from the crumbling depot, which had been destroyed by… whatever had happened. He couldn't remember anything after the blinding light. He rubbed his head and stared down in shock. He turned his hands over, but where he'd thought he'd seen burns on his hands there was only clear skin. Shaking his head, he stood up. He'd thought he'd died when he'd been blown outside. The shock must have rattled him. Gingerly, he put weight on his left leg but found that not even that injury was bothering him. For a second, he wondered if he was alive. He looked back at the dwelling – there was a small chance anyone else was, but should he check?

He ravaged through the debris, searching for… anything. The crates were destroyed, his daggers still nailed to a few of them. He placed them back in his pocket and continued searching the rest of what remained. The weaponry was untouched, but something was off. He couldn't find any bodies. There were pools of blood where they should've been. And, the money was missing.

Soft footsteps alerted him. In the blink of an eye, he had his daggers out and took cover. Warily, he watched a woman emerge from the shadows. She had a stack of timber in her arms and she carried it proudly. He stared at her, feeling drawn to this woman. She had a powerful aura around her. Then, he recognized her.

"Councilor," he said, stepping out from the foliage. It had been three years, maybe more, since she saved him and Mirari from the assassins at their home. Now draped in a simple garment, she seemed like an average noble. "What are you doing here?"

She dropped the wood into a larger pile, then threw a red

stone in it. Steam rose from the pile and the wood began to wither into ash.

"Getting rid of the evidence," she said.

Did she also move the bodies? And the money? Salathiel didn't want to pry. He knew better than to question the actions of a councilor, especially Councilor Julie, who had a reputation for carrying a personal agenda.

He simply asked, "Why?"

"You're the only one alive. How are you going to explain that?" She broke another piece of wood in half with the stomp of her foot and added it to the steaming pile. Most of the wood had withered, and with a kick from the wind, the ashes vanished into the air. At the rate she was going, no one would've guessed anything had existed there. "And you're right. Death will follow wherever these weapons go. You did a good thing."

Salathiel tilted his head. Was she watching the entire time?

Then she rested her sapphire gaze on him. Her usual stern demeanor was absent, dissolved like the timber under her feet. Instead, Salathiel was met with pity.

"You look lost," she said. "Do you need help?"

Salathiel shook his head. He didn't know what to make of what had just happened. He assumed that she wanted him to walk away and pretend to have not seen her, that none of it happened. He was about to, until he caught a shimmer in the corner of his eye.

A silver tag engraved with the name of one of the Althaean traders was peeking out from behind a crate. His mind drifted to the conversation between his clients. A rebellion was breaking out in Althaea Main, and Gaven would be caught in the middle of it. Such a talented warrior as Gaven wouldn't need Salathiel's help. Salathiel scoffed at the idea. But his heart sank when he analyzed the havoc that was caused by one hāstal weapon. How many more weapons were making their way to Althaea?

He stared at the tag again, knowing he couldn't go home just yet.

CHAPTER THIRTEEN

"So you went to Althaea?" Mirari asked. Salathiel nodded as she brought her hand up to her chin. "During the Siege?"

"I had to warn Gaven," he said, rubbing his thumbs together. "With all those weapons, I was so sure that they were planning on assassinating him."

"You did the right thing."

A smile lit her face, but it only made him feel sick. A detail was missing in his story and he knew Mirari would be able to put the pieces together. Out of shame or disbelief – likely both – he chose not to tell her the truth. Would she look at him differently if she knew? Could she still see him as her brother?

"Did I?" He shook his head. "Or did I make it worse?"

Salathiel looked her in the eye and waited. At first, she was puzzled, furrowing her brows. She pondered for a while, only staring back at him wondering what she missed. Then her mouth opened. She hesitated and failed to make out any words, and before she could say anything, Salathiel held up his palm.

He nodded. "Let me explain."

FINDING a way into the grand Althaean city was an easy task with the dead man's identity. Salathiel had discovered that the Althaean was a high-class trader, with a history of selling thousands of weapons to armies across the empire. Luckily, he was not yet known for his treachery, and Salathiel was able to slip into Althaea Main with his clearance as far as the inner fortress. He now needed to find Gaven's room without raising suspicion.

Slipping past the guards was easy. He hurried down the hallways, searching rooms along the way. Hearing approaching footsteps, he ducked into a dark corner. He didn't think he was hidden well enough though and debated drawing his dagger. Attacking Gaven's soldiers wasn't likely to convince anyone he was here to warn the region leader. If he was caught, he'd be lucky if these Althaeans only threw him out.

In the end, the debate was pointless because the soldiers' gaze swept past him without so much as a second glance. He sighed silently and waited for them to turn the corner. But another soldier coming from the opposite direction intercepted them.

"Where are you headed?" one of them asked.

"Upstairs," she responded. "One of the grunts moved a shipment of shield tanks and can't remember where he put them. I got to report it to the region leader before tomorrow's battle."

"You better not," the other guard said.

"Yeah," the first one said. "Just grab that grunt and shake him 'til the memory falls out. The second in command said that whoever disturbs them will be skinned and turned into armor for the new recruits." All three shivered.

"Is it that serious?" the woman asked. "Isn't it just a bunch of peasants we're up against?"

"They're not taking any chances," the second guard said with a nod. "They've even dismissed all the guards from that floor. No one's allowed up there until the commander, the second in command, or the region leader says so."

"Ah, okay," the woman said. "I better go find that crate

then." They separated. The woman passed by Salathiel's hiding place, but she, like the others, didn't notice him.

When they were out of sight, Salathiel stepped out. He had to get upstairs, but the stairs were likely guarded. He approached a window and peeked out. There were no guards in sight. He found another window directly above.

Stepping onto the window ledge, Salathiel grabbed the rough stone frame. He braced himself but found hoisting himself up didn't take nearly as much effort as he expected. He scraped away some of the mortar with his dagger and made handholds for him to grab. The wall wasn't exactly scalable, but he managed to make it to the next floor. He knew there would be no one there, but had to be sure and scanned the hallway before swinging his leg over the windowsill and landed on silent feet.

He walked the quiet hallway, hearing muffled voices only from one room. He hesitated reaching for the knob. Changing his mind, he knocked. An enemy wouldn't knock on the door.

The door was thick and heavy and the murmurs inside didn't so much as pause. Perhaps they couldn't hear him. Raising his hand, he knocked again. Louder and louder he knocked until he was pounding frantically at the door. Finally, his attempts yielded results.

Not only was the door yanked open, but it was Gaven himself standing in the doorway. A part of him was relieved to finally see his face. His cousin had grown well in the years since Salathiel had seen him, though Salathiel was still slightly taller. Gaven was thickly muscled and unshaven, but Salathiel could still recognize the features they shared underneath all that hair.

"How did you get in here?" Gaven scowled.

Salathiel chose to ignore his tone. He was here to save Gaven, not get into an argument. He looked around, glad that Gaven's tenor hadn't attracted the attention of whoever was in the room beyond.

Lowering his voice, he said, "Gav, we need to talk."

Gaven's brow furrowed. A slow recognition dawned on him. "Sal?"

"May I come in?"

He was relieved when Gaven stepped back and gestured for him to enter, closing the door behind him. Gaven glanced past Salathiel. They were in a small, personal library. The walls were lined with bookshelves and comfortable couches. Beyond the room they occupied, there was a curtained-off area. A woman's muffled voice was rising and falling.

"What are you doing here?" Gaven asked, staring hard at him.

Salathiel shook his head. There really was no time to explain the strange sequence of events that led to him standing before Gaven. He was here for a more urgent reason. "That battle you're planning in Rhea. You need to stop."

Gaven raised an eyebrow. "How do you know about Rhea?"

Salathiel stepped forward. "You need to let it go. It's a trap. They know you're coming."

"Gods, slow down." The corner of Gaven's mouth ticked up like he was fighting a smile. Salathiel could tell he wasn't taking this seriously. "It's been ten years and the first thing you say to me is about politics?" He crossed his arms and shook his head. "Are you going to explain how you know about the mission? Or why you're in my region?" He threw his hands down, sounding conciliatory. "Talk to me. I'm afraid I'm going to need more details."

Salathiel bit back his frustration. "There's only so much I can say. You just have to believe me."

"You know you sound like a spy, right? I sure hope you're not because I can't make any exceptions for you."

Salathiel's mouth snapped closed and he realized that even though this was still his cousin, Gaven was a different person. He was an Althaean, and he certainly acted the role. Those soldiers had said that Gaven's operation was intended to wipe out peasants. People who were just trying to get by. People like their parents.

Gaven smiled like he was trying to lighten the mood. "You okay?"

Salathiel shook his head, feeling the weight of his realization like a stone. "What you are doing, it isn't right. People are dying on both sides. Is this truly the way you want to rule Althaea Main?"

"With all due respect, you have no idea what's going on. And I suggest you stay out of it."

Salathiel felt disgusted. Gaven had turned into one of the Althaean thugs. What would Mirari think, knowing what Gaven had become?

"Gaven, look me in the eye and tell me you're going to end the raids. Do you really want to be a murderer? Is this how you want Roselyn to think of you?"

Gaven's jaw flexed as he gritted his teeth. He paused for a moment before raising his hands. "Okay, I'm afraid you have to leave. I—"

Salathiel grabbed Gaven, lifting him off his feet. There was no point. He never listened. He always just did whatever he wanted, damn the consequences. But not this time – lives were at stake.

"You have to call this mission off," he shouted, shaking his infuriating cousin.

"Let go of—"

"You have to!"

Gaven grabbed Salathiel's wrist and yanked backward. Salathiel was caught off balance. He lost his footing. The world tilted and he slammed onto the floor. Dazed, he gripped Gaven by the wrist while he tried to get his bearings.

A dark, hazy mist enveloped his hands. It was cool and soothing. It coiled like a ribbon, twining through Salathiel's fingers, and he gasped when it moved toward Gaven's arm.

All the color drained from Gaven's face. His eyes widened even as they gazed through Salathiel, seeing something beyond him. Gaven jerked back, pulling his arm from Salathiel's grip but the mist stayed with him, sliding up his arm. It spread, faster and faster. Before Salathiel knew it, Gaven's whole body was consumed by the mist.

Gaven started swaying where he was crouched and Salathiel scrambled upright. He could just make out Gaven's face through the mist. To his horror, the light in Gaven's eyes died. But he knew Gaven was still alive because of the weak movement of his hands, reaching out for help.

"W-what?" Salathiel said, barely able to speak. "Gaven, what's happening?" he called, grabbing Gaven's hand, desperate to help.

Gaven only grunted and started twitching. He opened his mouth and out poured a soul-crushing yell, as if he was being skinned alive. Salathiel jerked back as Gaven collapsed. This wasn't what he wanted. He reached out, but stopped before he touched Gaven.

He didn't know how to help if trying would only make things worse. All he knew for certain was that the Althaeans in the other room would be on their way to investigate Gaven's cries. Gritting his teeth and squeezing his eyes closed, he hurried to his feet and ran for the door.

He looked ahead, skidded to a stop, lips parting in shock. The way ahead was blocked. By Gaven. He looked as well as he had when he'd first opened the door and pissed to all Inferna.

"Gaven… How did you…"

"Who are you?"

Salathiel fell silent. Warily, he glanced back and found Gaven where he had left him insensate on the floor. He reached for his daggers, but when he turned back the vision of Gaven was gone. He didn't get a chance to guess what happened before a petite woman popped up in his field of view.

She rammed her shoulder into his abdomen, using surprising force to shove him into a bookshelf. They hit the ground amidst a hailstorm of heavy tomes. The woman grabbed his daggers, pulling them free before he could stop her.

He snarled when the blades bit into his flesh. The daggers dug deeper into his chest and shoulders when she leaned against them to leverage herself up. She froze halfway off of him, looking down at the damage she'd caused. Her brows furrowed with revulsion.

Salathiel wasted no more time. He grabbed her wrist and squeezed. She writhed in his grip, twisting and punching, but only really panicked when the mist returned. She leaned forward and sank her teeth into his hand like a rabid animal. Hauling his fist back, he punched her. Her head snapped to the side and she tumbled away from him.

Salathiel jumped to his feet, lifting his hands to ward off her next attack. It didn't come. She was on her hands and knees, staring at the mist that was spreading from where Salathiel had touched her. Her breathing was choked as the mist wrapped around her and she collapsed next to Gaven.

Without looking, Salathiel yanked the daggers from his chest and raced toward the door. He skidded down the hallway and swung his legs over the side of the window. Soon, the whole fort would be out looking for him.

The ground seemed far away. He didn't have a choice though. As long as he didn't break both legs, he'd be fine. He jumped, hitting the ground hard. However, when he stood up, there wasn't so much as a twinge in his legs. He didn't feel any pain at all.

He looked down and gasped. Black sludge was oozing from the wounds from his daggers.

"What's happening?" he said, holding his hands up. He didn't have an answer and until he knew, he couldn't go back home.

With one last glance back at the fort, Salathiel slipped into the night. He trudged on, picking a seemingly meaningless direction. When he believed he had reached far enough, he rested.

Salathiel sat around a campfire with his back hunched, wondering what he was going to do next. The troubles in Althaea would only get worse and if he returned to Minetta, he'd be tempted to check in on Mirari. He looked at his trembling hands, cursing himself for whatever he had become. If there was one thing he knew, he had to stay as far away from Mirari as he could.

The bushes to his left began to rustle, but he didn't care. If he was caught, death would be mercy.

To his surprise, it was Councilor Julie who emerged from the bushes. This time, she was decorated in armor, firm and gallant. A light went off in his head and Salathiel got to his feet. Of course. She must have the answers.

"Councilor." He stepped forward. "Can you… help me?"

She stared at him as if she had been looking for him this whole time, waiting for him. It was the first time he'd seen the corner of her lip rise slightly, and it was a smile he knew he could trust.

With her head lowered, Mirari shrunk into herself. When she didn't react, Salathiel continued.

"It was an accident," Salathiel said, biting his lip. "But it didn't matter. I saw the true side of Gaven. He would've done far worse things if I wasn't there."

"That means," Mirari paused, "you have dark aura."

"But I can control it." Salathiel showed her his empty hand. "And I'll never use it again, ever."

"How do you know that?" Mirari said. "What if you become desperate… like Soteria?"

"Dark aura only consumes those who are conflicted within their own minds. If you are at peace with yourself, you cannot harm others." He waved his hand in the air. "Soteria didn't learn to control dark aura, nor did she feel the need to. Her life was spared, but her master's was not, and she couldn't understand why. She was stricken with so much grief that the only thing on her mind was to finish what he started." He nodded to her with a plea. "Julie and I couldn't get through to her, and now she's running out of control. That's why I must stop her. *We* must stop her."

Mirari stared at her hands in silence. He had expected some uproar from her, or at least a scolding, but he could tell there was something else troubling her mind.

Clenching her hands into a fist, she asked, "Why would you force me to learn something that could kill you?"

"Because I know you can control it." He reached his hand out, stroking her back.

"Does that mean… I have to use the flames on you too?"

The corner of his lips perked into a smile, and he did his best to hide the thought of an alternative reality he had feared. But according to Julie's story, the flames and dark aura worked hand-in-hand. They needed each other to achieve balance, and Salathiel saw a future where he and Mirari could live peacefully regardless of their abilities. A simple life in Solarin – he was sure Mirari wanted the same.

But for now, all he could tell her was, "Let's hope it never comes to that."

CHAPTER FOURTEEN

"Well, that's it for me," Aitken said, getting to his feet and dusting his robes off. "Sleep well, my friends."

"You too. Rest well," Eoin said with a wave of his hand. Aitken chuckled like he didn't quite believe it. He arched his back with a groan and shuffled off to the tent they had set up against a large tree. With Aitken safely ensconced in his tent, Eoin motioned to Gaven. "Food's still warm."

Gaven grunted and leaned forward to fix himself a bowl of the slop they had charitably called soup. The group was on the way to Racca, a city along the coast of the Gulf of Oris – just Gaven, Eoin, their small group of Blessed members, and a couple of tents shared between the seven of them. For Gaven, this was nothing compared to traveling with his soldiers. To avoid detection, they had to hunker down in abandoned buildings or sleep under the stars if there were no other options.

Aitken was the last to go to sleep for the night, allowing Gaven to finally take his mask off. He put it on the ground, resting it against his pack so that he could see it from where he was sitting. He still wasn't quite used to his new accessory – in the shape of a tiger. Eoin must have thought himself very clever.

Eoin softly rapped his knuckles against the door while Gaven leaned nonchalantly against the stone wall, keeping a lookout. A squad was patrolling the streets and they had decided that it was safer for most of their group to hang back while Eoin and Gaven slipped into Oulfa. Eoin's contact was another blacksmith who did repairs for the soldiers stationed nearby.

Eoin knocked again and sighed. "Maybe he's not here."

Gaven didn't know if that meant his friend had stepped out or gotten caught in one of the Council's searches. If he had to guess, Gaven would pick the latter. There had been a larger presence of soldiers than they had previously seen. Fortunately, his speculation was proved wrong when the door was jerked open.

A lanky man stuck his head out, his thin face pinched with fear. He glanced in both directions before hastily beckoning them inside.

They stood in his kitchen. He jerked his hands through his hair and nervously paced in front of them. "Eoin, what are you doing here?" Though his words were sharp and angry, he kept his voice low as though someone could be listening.

"Checking on you. We haven't heard from you in—"

"For good reason." The man sighed and slumped down in a worn chair. "Surely you've seen the army, haven't you? They're grabbing anyone they even suspect of being a rebel sympathizer."

"We've seen them." Eoin motioned toward Gaven's hooded figure and it only increased the other man's visible anxiety. Tugging down his hood, Gaven turned to stare out the window. So far, they remained undetected but the man's fear kept Gaven on edge. "We hadn't thought the Council's raids had come this far South."

"They haven't," the man admitted. "Not yet, at least. It's only a matter of time though. One of the patrols happened upon a cache of weapons they think belonged to the Blessed. It's only a matter of time before they start knocking down our doors and taking us away."

In the window's reflection, Gaven watched Eoin grip the other man's shoulder in silence. It was the only comfort he could offer. No one could curb the Council's crusade.

"The weapons were found in Oulfa?" Gaven asked, still watching the reflection.

"Uh, no. Not here exactly, but it was just off the coast."

"Was it docking here?" Gaven asked.

"No, it…" The man turned to Eoin. "Who is this?"

"He's an ally," Eoin said. "We call him Spiritel."

"Spiritel…? I've heard of you." Disturbed, Gaven glanced at Eoin who only shrugged. Whatever he'd heard, it seemed to calm the man down because he decided to answer Gaven's question. "The shipment was heading to another city, farther down the coast. I'm not sure where exactly. The manifest was destroyed when the soldiers were investigating and I asked around the docks, but no one knew anything about the ships. Not that the Council will care about that."

"True enough," Eoin said. He took a step toward the door. "We really appreciate your help, but we'll take our leave now. We won't put your family in danger any longer."

Gaven nodded his agreement, but the man got to his feet, holding out his hand. "Wait."

"Was there something else?" Eoin asked.

"No, it's…" He took a breath. "It might be more suspicious if you're caught wandering around so late." He pointed to another door, hidden in the shadow of the cupboard. "That's the forge. You can spend the night there."

He wasn't wrong and Gaven was happy to spend the night inside and away from the winter's chill. He went inside to set up a place to sleep while Eoin spoke to his friend a little longer. In the middle of the night, Gaven's sleep was disturbed when the two blacksmiths woke the forge. They opened the door and between the heat from the forge and the winter's bite, Gaven was comfortable enough to fall back asleep.

Next morning, he was presented with a mask. Eoin's face was carefully neutral while the other man was practically bouncing with undisguised glee.

"Your name is becoming well-known," Eoin said. "It's best if your face doesn't become famous as well."

"I'm honored to help Spiritel rid us of the Defiants," the man said. "I'm at your disposal."

Given the man's enthusiasm, Gaven had to accept the mask with dignity and grace. "Thank you."

HIDING BEHIND A MASK LIKE FANGBANE? Like the Defiants? Gaven was no coward… but he knew it was for the best. What he was doing wasn't the Valiant Tiger's work at all. He might as well be a different person.

Gaven turned the mask away and returned to eating.

They sat in silence for a moment and Gaven looked up when he could feel Eoin's eyes on him. The blacksmith had lost his look of mirth and his gaze had turned contemplative. Eoin glanced down at the fire when Gaven met his eyes, but as soon as Gaven returned to eating, he sensed he had Eoin's attention again.

"Speak," Gaven said. "You want to say something?"

"I'm sure it's nothing you want to hear."

Gaven grunted. "That hasn't stopped you before." He braced himself and said, "Just say it." He wasn't a coward that couldn't hear some unpleasant words.

Eoin chuckled. "It's only that I was struck by how familiar this is. The two of us have sat around a campfire before, sharing a meal. It's funny, is all."

He didn't sound like he thought it was very amusing, but

neither did Gaven. It was the circumstances. All that lost time with no way to retrieve his memories. To know what he did. To remember who he killed.

"You're right. I didn't want to hear that." Gaven had no idea what he had missed, how he had acted during the lost time. He set his bowl aside and scrubbed his hand over his lip. "Go on." Eoin raised his head, surprised. "Tell me more. We used to eat together like this?"

Eoin was slow to answer but eventually he gave a short nod. "On occasion. More during the early days. As more people joined our cause, you patrolled more often. But when we did sit around the campfire, it was much like this." He snorted a laugh. "Of course, now, you don't wander off in the middle of the conversation."

"How…" He felt like he was worrying at a wound, preventing it from healing and yet he had to know. "What was I like?"

Eoin crossed his arms, tapping his shoulder as he thought. "It's hard to describe." Gaven stared down at the fire while he waited. "You weren't so different from how you are now."

"Really? How can that be?"

"You were… intense. I suppose that's the only way to explain it. You were single-minded to the point of obsession. You wouldn't let anyone deter you from the task. In some cases that was good, and in some cases, bad." Eoin fell silent as he seemed to think about one of those bad cases in particular.

Gaven let the sounds of the night fill the air between them, but there was one last question burning in his mind. They were battling a powerful enemy with an almost endless number of followers. There was no guarantee either one of them would see tomorrow. If he did not ask now, he might not get a chance later. There was no one else to ask. Gaven knew there were many factions in the Blessed, but Eoin's was the only one he could trust.

"While I was possessed, I said… that I regretted leaving my family, right? Who d-did I mention anyone?"

Gaven was unsure how to put his question into words. His mind drifted to faint memories of his mother; he couldn't even remember her face. Salathiel and Roselyn were there for a couple years in his life, then he was on his own, climbing his way past scum like Inigo to make it to the top. Even at the top – when he could have everything his way – it was lonely. Grimacing, he glared hard at the fire to avoid looking at Eoin.

"Why would I bring up something… I don't even have?"

Eoin sighed. "I wouldn't know the answer to that, but surely there must be someone dear to you." Eoin rubbed the back of his neck. "Soteria's power – it seems to follow the eye of the beholder. She can't tell you what to think, only force you to act on your deepest desires. Maybe you've locked out the people you care about from your mind for so long that you've forgotten about them." He tapped his chest. "But deep down they are still there in your heart."

Gaven averted his eyes, taking interest in the last drop of slop in his bowl. He simply said, "I see."

"May I ask a question now?"

Gaven exhaled slowly, setting down the bowl. "Sure."

Just because he heard Eoin's question did not mean he had to answer. If Eoin wanted to know about Gaven's past, then he would have to keep waiting. Gaven would not speak of it.

"While Sven and I were gathering supplies, he asked around about the Council's movements. Don't worry. He may not be particularly stealthy, but everyone's eager to talk about the Council these days. People were clamoring to tell him the latest news."

Gaven was surprised that Eoin switched topics, but he didn't mind it.

"What did they say?"

Eoin rubbed his thumb against his knuckles and replied, "It

wasn't the news of the Council that intrigued me. While they were talking about them, somebody mentioned our glorious Region Leader Gaven." Crossing his arms, Gaven leaned against the log behind him. "It seems the region leader has been seen on patrol around Althaea Main. It's fairly innocuous, but strange all the same."

"Perhaps they made a mistake," Gaven said. "Or lied so as to seem more interesting."

"Why lie that they saw the region leader do something so mundane as to patrol his own region?"

Gaven waited, but Eoin didn't continue. His heart sounded loud in his ears. He knew where this was going.

"Ask what you're asking."

"Now that I think about it, it's not so much a question. I'm sure I'm correct." Eoin lifted his head to boldly claim, "The soldier that helped me escape is a shapeshifter."

Gaven didn't answer, neither confirming nor denying the truth. It didn't matter. Eoin nodded as though Gaven had spoken.

"I always thought there was a strange familiarity among all the soldiers that had followed your path of betrayal, and I never met the same person twice." He sounded amused, and his mouth quirked up into a smile. "Here I was worrying over how you were playing your cards, but you have an ace up your sleeve. No one even knows you're gone, do they?"

"You're quite confident in your speculation, aren't you?"

"I am. Because I've seen them, even worked with them at some point." Eoin chuckled, then let out a sigh of relief. "Thank the Gods there's at least one of them still out there. They're talented. Please send my compliments to them." He nodded his head a few times, then turned to Gaven. "It takes a certain kind of bravery to lose everything and still keep fighting."

Gaven knew he was lucky to have Erel. At first, she had tried to dissuade him from investigating the Blessed, from meeting the same fate her family did. Ultimately, she chose to help him. Even through her trauma, she had stood by his side. Truly, Erel was the best second in command he could ever hope for. She hadn't explained everything about the loss of her tribe. Gaven would never doubt Erel's courage, but he wasn't sure if she couldn't find any information about what happened to her people or she simply hadn't wanted to know.

"They told me that it was the Blessed who attacked their tribe," Gaven said.

"Laikos the Acolyte," Eoin spat. His smile quickly faded. "The Blessed used to be about peace and equality, but Laikos, Soteria, and other leaders like them have given us a bad name, making people cower whenever they hear 'the Blessed'. He loved that." He nodded to Gaven. "You know why? He's a coward. He feared failures. So when he wanted something, he would go to the extremes for it, made sure he always won. He attacked the Belligmn Tribe, no doubt. He made sure everyone in the Blessed knew that was the punishment for disobedience."

"Why did he kill them?" Gaven asked.

"Laikos wouldn't dare exchange information with us poor peasants." He bit his lip. "However, I did hear that it was some kind of, let's say, a difference of opinions. Are you sure you want to hear it?"

Gaven frowned. "You, more than anyone else, make sure I hear unpleasant truths. What is it?"

"The shapeshifters originally worked with Laikos. They were essentially assassins that worked with the Blessed."

Assassins? Gaven thought of Erel's skill with a blade. She must have been trained from birth. "If they worked together, what happened? Why did he turn on them?"

Eoin shook his head. "I don't know the details, only that the shapeshifters chose to sever their agreement with Laikos. They disagreed on the targets of their assassination."

"So he wiped out the tribe," Gaven said, and Eoin nodded.

"I agree with the shapeshifters. If Laikos was truly the Goddesses' messenger, shouldn't he direct them on the paths of love, not murder?" Eoin shook his head and continued, "Unless that's what Fate's Fable was really about."

Gaven furrowed his brow. "Fate's Fable? How does that one go?"

"It's about two goddesses who determine the fate of humans." Eoin squinted as if he was trying to recall a distant memory. He turned his palms, facing each other. "Fate and devotion go hand-in-hand. You turn on devotion, you will meet fate." He dropped his hands with a scoff and mumbled, "Something like that. If you believe in gods."

Gaven scoffed. "We control our own fate," he said. "And we would be weak to think otherwise."

Turning his head toward the dark forest, Gaven began to imagine the battles he'd fought. He couldn't begin to count how many wars had begun over a conflict in religion. How many minds he couldn't change because people were told how to act and believe.

Eoin frowned and said, "Your courage is admirable but..." He bit his lip. He had never looked at Gaven with such intensity, and Gaven felt the gravity of his words. "There are some things we cannot control, and we'd be weak to deny it."

CHAPTER FIFTEEN

Outside his father's office, Dorain took a breath and bumped his head against the door. It was uncomfortable enough to be back at home in Falum. Every green tapestry, every painting hung along the long corridor, gave him a bitter reminder of his suppressed past. But Dorain was stronger now. He could endure it.

Kea trilled softly and flicked her beak through his hair. Lifting his hand, he ran his finger over the soft feathers. He could do this. He had to do this. It was his choice to come back, after all.

"Dorain?" his father called. Dorain hated that room – *his* room.

Straightening his back, he swung the door open and greeted his father, Councilor Dareh. His father was staring darkly at the reports on his long, mahogany desk, glancing up only long enough to glare at Dorain.

"What are you doing lurking in the hallway?" he huffed. "Come inside already."

Dorain stepped through, balking when he glanced to the side. His father's large, striped beast companion was stretched elegantly on the floor by the door, watching Dorain through glowering eyes. Nodding awkwardly to the saberlion, he shut the door and stepped to his father's desk.

"You wanted to speak to me?"

His father grabbed a stack of papers and shoved them into Dorain's arms. Kea squawked and fluttered over to the plush chair set against the wall.

"Have you heard of Spiritel?" he said while Dorain fumbled with the sheets.

"I, no, I haven't." He tried to twist the papers around to read them. "What is that?"

"It's a person, of course." He snarled, "An Althaean."

Dorain didn't sigh, but it was a close thing. Moving to the chair with Kea, Dorain sat down and hunched over the reports. He scanned them quickly and soon got the gist of it. Spiritel was something of a folk hero to the Althaean people. He showed up when they needed him, taking out ruffians and thugs terrorizing the cities he passed through. No one knew what he looked like or where he would appear next. He never asked for payment or favors. He seemed to exist only to help.

"This is good, isn't it?" Besides the fact the man was an Althaean, Dorain didn't know why his father was even talking to him about it. As far as the reports went, he never even crossed the border.

His father sighed, a gusty exhale. "Have I taught you nothing?"

Dorain's gaze escaped to the window and away from the disappointment on his father's face. He mourned for his youth when he'd simply run off to join the Knights to escape from his father. The problems he faced now were too big to run from.

His father continued, "Just what do you think Spiritel's goal is?"

Dorain didn't dare answer "to help people" because that was obviously incorrect.

"He's another rebel," Dorain said.

"Correct. Althaea is our enemy barely held at bay by the alliance. It's to our benefit to keep an eye on such powerful enemies." Getting to his feet, his father gathered some papers and tucked them underneath his arm. Even as he disparaged "Spiritel", his derision for Dorain was evident. "This "Spiritel" is a dangerous animal for the same reason I don't trust those Knights. Fighters with the support of the people and not beholden to the Council have too much power."

Appropriately chided, Dorain said, "I understand. You are right. The Knights have been brought to heel but Spiritel is a growing force. We must find out more about him."

His father's lips curled into a smile. Walking around his desk, he placed his hand on Dorain's shoulder. Surprised, Dorain raised his head to meet his father's scrutiny.

"Study those reports. Maybe you'll actually be able to learn something from them." Turning sharply on his heels, he headed toward the door. "Come on, Pierce," he said, opening the door and letting the saberlion out first. He glanced back at Dorain. "I'll expect a report by the end of the week." The door shut behind him.

Stretching out along the chair, Dorain let his legs dangle over the side and covered his face with his arm. That had been one of the more positive interactions he'd had with his father. Leaving the Knights had given his father a positive impression of him for once. But Dorain still didn't agree with his mindset. He only told him what he wanted to hear. Cawing, Kea hopped on the back of the chair until she was standing over him.

"Yes, I suppose you're right." Dorain read the papers more thoroughly. He had to come up with some clever observation. If nothing, his father would know he'd read the papers.

For a while, it was quiet except for the shuffle of papers. Everything seemed as he first stated, just a masked man traveling around doing good. It reminded him of Fangbane, except this guy wasn't hiding in his office all day. He laughed to himself.

What if they were the same person, or at least after the same thing? Would it be a crazy idea to suggest recruiting Spiritel into the Knights?

Rising, Dorain studied the map framed behind his father's desk. He found the towns Spiritel had visited. Nehum, Oulfa, Lundar. They were mostly clustered around the Gulf of Oris.

"Wait a minute," he muttered to himself. Using his father's desk, he spread the papers out and arranged them in the order of the incidents. When he glanced back at the map, he could see Spiritel was moving unerringly down the coast, specifically in towns with ports, though he couldn't be sure where the man was heading.

He started stacking the papers back together. When they were grouped together in his hand, he flipped through them one last time to make sure he had everything, and his eyes caught on a word.

Hale.

Brow furrowing, he sank down into his father's chair and ran his eyes over the stray paper he'd inadvertently picked up from the desk. He heard a noise from outside and hastily put the paper down. He needed to examine the paper more closely. He didn't want vital information to slip away.

The door opened and his father stepped through. He hastily vacated the chair at his father's frown.

"Yes, yes. I'll get back to you." He was speaking into his clōve. He signed off, closing the door behind him. "Slacking off as soon as I turn my back?"

"I was just looking at the map," Dorain said, stepping back against the wall as his father approached.

His father didn't take his seat, but instead crossed his arms to stare at the map.

"Very well," he said to Dorain's surprise.

"Did something happen?"

"Yes," he said, beckoning. Dorain stood next to him. His

father wasn't as tall as he remembered. There was a time he used to tower over Dorain. "Are you listening?"

"Yes, I am, Father."

"Reports have been coming in from the scouts the Council sent out. There's been some unusual activity around this area." He circled the area inland between Ophallen and Axillaire on the map, northeast from the town of Xeran. "Here, and here. Our raids have turned up a number of sympathizers in this area. We intercepted a weapons shipment coming from one of their ports. The armies from Ophallen and Axillaire will catch them in a pincer."

He pointed to the small village that was going to be destroyed if they implemented their plan.

"What about the weapons?"

"We'll send the Knights to the port to confiscate the weapons," his father said with a dismissive shrug. "Give them something they can't fail at." Dorain watched his attention drift away from the weapons and back to the planned massacre. If the town was in Minetta, would his father be more conservative with his actions?

Dorain glanced at his father out of the corner of his eye as an idea struck him. "I think the Blessed are holed up in Racca, closer to Gulf of Oris," he said, pointing to the city between the intercepted weapons and where Spiritel was last spotted.

"There's no indication," his father dismissed.

"The weapons—"

"One shipment. Compare that to the numerous dissidents found along the Ophallen–Axillaire border."

"Why would they ship weapons by sea if their headquarters is landlocked?" His father took a breath, practically swelling with his retort. Dorain continued before he could speak. "What if I'm right? What will happen?"

"What? You want a pat on the back and a job well done? Aren't you too old for that?"

Dorain kept his gaze steady though he wanted to wilt under his father's sneer. "I mean, if I'm right, and the Knights run into the Blessed, won't they get the credit for defeating the Blessed? After all, the Council were the ones who found the weapons."

His father's nose wrinkled and he scowled at the map. "You might be right." He nodded slowly as he pondered Dorain's words. "It wouldn't hurt to err on the side of caution. We can provide them with support. If, *if*, you're correct, it'll be the Council who claims credit for the Blessed's defeat."

Dorain was just glad he was able to prevent another massacre. He watched a smile alight on his father's face.

"And if you're wrong or it goes badly, they'll only have the Knights to blame. Good job. This was well thought out."

Dorain was shocked by the approving look he was graced with. Ducking his head, he rubbed the back of his neck.

"Thanks." He cleared his throat and his father turned away. Kea returned to his side. She hopped up his arm to rest on his shoulder. "I'll, uh, I'll inform the Knights of their new assignment."

"You can leave." Dareh said with an absent wave.

Outside of his father's office, he slumped tiredly against the door. He brushed his fingers over Kea's feathers. Eyes shut, she trilled with delight.

"We did it," he said softly.

THE KNIGHTS WEREN'T at the Knights' Estate, not since Fangbane announced that they were now under the servitude of the Council. One may argue that it was no different from being disbanded. That was perfect for Dorain. After all, he didn't want to risk running into Fangbane.

Dorain learned that Lucan was on his way to do business in Namani, the fruitful capital city of Nanaka just northeast of

Althaea Main. He would deliver the message to Lucan there, but it was more of an excuse to stop by the nearby village of Aias. They said there was nothing left to be found in the village, but Dorain thought it warranted another look.

The village was hard to find. It was a tiny, obscure hamlet hidden in a dense thicket. Dorain only knew the general location based on the reports, but with Kea's help, he managed to stumble through the tightly packed trees and onto an ill-maintained dirt road. It was quiet, until he heard a voice.

"I thought I recognized that kestrel."

Startled, Dorain straightened to warily look at the one person he hadn't expected to find in Aias.

Lucan.

He looked much better than the last time Dorain had seen him. No longer did his pale appearance make him look like a ghost haunted by the loss of their teammate. It seemed Hime was right, and he just needed some time.

"Lucan," Dorain said, cheerfully dusting his clothes off. "I'm glad I was able to find you."

"Oh? Were you looking for me?" Lucan folded his hands, hiding them behind his back, and looked at Dorain. Well, Dorain *thought* he was looking at him. He often couldn't see Lucan's eyes were behind his tinted glasses. "What can I help you with? Or should I say, what can I help *Councilor Dareh* with?"

There was truth to his words. Dorain wanted to relay the Knights' assignment to Lucan instead of directly to Fangbane. On the other hand, that wasn't why he wanted to see Lucan. Honesty might beget honesty, and that's what he was hoping to get from Lucan.

"I wanted to investigate Aias," Dorain said. "Something about this whole situation just doesn't seem right, don't you think?"

Lucan's shoulders dropped a little as though that wasn't what he expected Dorain to say, but also that the words weren't unwelcome.

"You're not wrong," Lucan said. He held his hand out to his side. "Shall we walk?"

As Dorain looked around, he tried not to gape at the remains of a place where people used to live and thrive. It soured his stomach. Aias was small. Standing in the center of the road, they could see almost the entire village or what remained of it. It had been decimated. The buildings were in ruins with broken windows and shattered doors. Debris and dried blood littered the ground and the forest was quick to reclaim the land. Vegetation was overgrown, giving the village the feeling of a haunted field.

Dorain kept his voice low and respectful as he said, "So this is Aias?"

"What's left of it," Lucan said, then sighed. "Unfortunately, there doesn't appear to be any evidence left. The secrets of what happened here faded along with Mirari."

He sounded disappointed, so Dorain patted him on the back and said, "Please don't take it so hard."

"Of course." Though he didn't move, Dorain could see him withdraw. "I'm only disappointed that I wasted my time. To think, I could be in my library having tea right now."

Dorain seized on the excuse. "I wouldn't call it a waste. Though I wanted to stop by Aias, I was on my way to you."

"Ah, so you are here on behalf of the Council." Before Dorain could respond, Lucan took a step back. "Out with it. What is it that they want?"

"We have a common interest," Dorain said, then paused. He had to tread carefully. Lucan was shrewd and this conversation could definitely be considered a battle of words. "We can still work together, despite the differences in our alliance. Even if I am no longer a Knight, I hope that we can keep a positive rela-tionship."

"How well you speak," Lucan said with a disbelieving smile.

"Can you clarify exactly on what matter the interest of the Knights aligns with the Council?"

Dorain did not remind Lucan that the Knights worked for the Council now. He wasn't his father and it wouldn't do anything to endear himself to the Hales.

"The Blessed," Dorain answered. "We can agree that they pose a threat to the three empires."

"We've tried everything we can to find Eoin."

"That's what I wanted to talk to you about," Dorain said, leaning forward. "We have a probable lead on his location." Lucan's eyebrows rose. Dorain reached into his bag to pull out the map he'd used to navigate toward Aias.

Crouching down, he spread it out across the ground and pretended this was completely normal. He ran his finger along the coastline.

"Many weapons have been confiscated in these areas and there's a chance the Blessed are congregating here in anticipation of another large-scale attack on par with the Althaean Siege."

Lucan drummed his fingers against his knees and hummed. "Were you able to find any information about the weapons?" Dorain looked at him in confusion and he clarified. "Where they came from? Who's supplying them?"

"No." Dorain hadn't even thought of that! "Not yet," he said to hide his ignorance. "The Council wants the Knights to investigate the weapons and intercept any more shipments."

After a moment of contemplative silence, Lucan asked, "And the Blessed are at this location?"

"Here," Dorain said. He tapped Racca. "It's only speculation, but we believe that this is where the weapons were being shipped to."

"The Council will let *us* handle this investigation?"

Dorain nodded. "Even if the Blessed aren't there, if you can stop the shipment of weapons, it will be a great step toward stopping the Blessed once and for all."

Lucan narrowed his eyes. Dorain wasn't sure if he believed him. Lucan pondered for a moment before straightening himself.

"Then you can trust us to take care of it."

Dorain nodded and folded his map. A sharp avian cry drew their attention to the air. Kea was circling overhead. She swooped down, rustling their hair as she rushed by.

"She seems to be enjoying herself," Lucan said.

"Actually…"

Kea glided back down and Dorain lifted his gloved hand for her to settle on. She cooed at him with an inquisitive tilt of her head. She didn't use anything as explicit as words with him, but he could understand her all the same.

"All right," he said with a firm nod. "Show the way."

"Something wrong?" Lucan asked, arching an elegant eyebrow.

"Kea found something. You're welcome to join us," Dorain said, loping after the kestrel. Without a word, Lucan fell into step behind Dorain.

Kea was circling an area near the edge of the village center. It was a little out of the way, tucked near the treeline, and not immediately noticeable from where they had walked through the village.

"What happened here?" Dorain wondered as he approached the area Kea was perched over. There was a dark scar in a spiral pattern on the ground as if the very ground had been burned away. "What could have caused this?" He glanced over to Lucan. "A hāstal wea—"

"No," he said firmly. "Not in that pattern. It'd have to be someone's kore." Lucan crouched down next to the odd mark. "Yet, fire kore…"

Lucan kept the rest of his thoughts to himself.

Dorain recalled his father's warning that it was prudent to know about all powerful fighters. What was someone with that much kore doing in a small backwoods village? Was it the Blessed? Was it Spiritel?

That triggered the memory of the report he'd found in his father's office. For some reason, he was looking into the Hale's kōnvoy accident that happened nearly two decades ago. Dorain darted his eyes between Lucan and the burnt ground.

"Is it familiar?" Dorain asked.

Lucan looked at him over his shoulder. "No, I don't think so." He turned back and rubbed his fingers through the soot.

Dorain braced himself. It felt awkward to ask, standing over the deep burn scar. It might be overstepping propriety, but if it wasn't a coincidence someone should look into it.

"Dorain," Lucan said. He got to his feet and without facing him, continued, "Whatever you're going to ask, please do."

Dorain flushed at being so easily found out. "It's delicate," he confessed. "Kind of personal."

"Well now I'm curious," Lucan said lightly. "What is this personal matter involving me?"

"I was hoping you could tell me about the kōnvoy fire that happened eighteen years ago." The gentle smile faded from Lucan's face and he grew stiff as if he had been carved from stone. Dorain continued anyway. "In the fire, your uncle was killed along with his wife and daughter. Is that correct?"

"It is." Lucan unclenched his jaw to say, "Why are you bringing this up?"

"I don't mean to dredge up troubling memories," Dorain said. "I wanted to know if your own investigation into the accident had uncovered anything?"

"No," Lucan said with a stiff shake of his head.

"So, you have no idea what caused it?" Dorain pressed. He pictured the report, trying to remember everything he had seen in the brief moment he had been able to examine the paper. "Your cousin's body was never found. Is that correct?"

"That's true. Though I don't know why it's relevant."

Dorain racked his brain. If he poked at an unhealed wound in Lucan's past, there had to be a reason for it. Otherwise, it was just cruel and not what he wanted. An inexplicable fire. A young girl unaccounted for. What did it mean? His gaze once again drifted to the darkened ground.

"I just noticed the similarities between these two events. An unexplained cause. A missing body. A lack of evidence…"

"And what would you know about it?" Lucan cut in with a voice iced over.

"I found information about it in my father's office and—"

"Councilor Dareh is investigating my family's tragedy?"

"It was a report he acquired." That knowledge wasn't any better received by Lucan. Dorain had to admit that it was odd his father had information about the kōnvoy accident, but it also didn't feel right jumping to conclusions before asking Lucan himself.

"Is this why you've sought me out? On behalf of your father?"

"No, no," Dorain said with a quick shake of his head. "Look, Lucan, I'm sorry that I brought it up, but considering this here," he waved his hand toward the blackened earth, "I'd wondered, if this was truly kore in the works. What if both incidents were caused by the same person?"

That seemed to convince him. Lucan's anger faded when he looked at the mark again, and his eyes widened.

"You think…?"

"Could someone in the Blessed be involved in the accident?"

Lucan's body language shuttered and he turned away. "No, I doubt it."

"There must be—"

"Dorain," he said stiffly. "I appreciate your concern but you're mistaken. This has nothing to do with the Hales. The kōnvoy incident was an accident, and nothing else. Please tell your father that he has nothing to worry about." Lucan stepped forward and began making his way out of town. "If he dares to pry anymore into my family's tragedy, I will gladly see him in court."

Dorain opened his mouth, but the words froze in his throat. It still felt like he was missing something, but he didn't think Lucan would be open to any further conversation. He would have to try to solve this another way.

CHAPTER SIXTEEN

Mirari took a second to admire the bright lights illuminating the large, stained-glass windows at the Twin Cod. It was a charming tavern in Racca at the end of the Yountilla River. The round, wooden beams that supported the upper floors were draped in a colorful flag. Salathiel was looking for evidence of the Defiants, but Mirari could do some scouting of her own while she waited.

With her hood pulled securely over her head, Mirari stepped across the threshold into the tavern. She crossed the hard wooden floors to a flight of stairs. On the second floor, she found a small, out-of-the-way table that overlooked the first floor. It was early enough that the regulars who came for their midday meal were yet to arrive. She ordered the local specialty, twice-baked cod with hazelnut bread, and waited.

She didn't want to tell Salathiel that she'd learned all about gathering intel during her time in Althaea. That used to be her contribution to stopping the rebels that plagued Althaea Main, back before everything fell apart.

They had to be careful about investigating. Racca was much bigger than Aias and the other outlying villages in

Althaea Main. If Soteria caught wind that people were looking for her here, she could disappear without them ever crossing paths.

Soon the tavern was packed, both upstairs and downstairs. The clientele was mostly local workers and everyone seemed to know each other. They exchanged subdued but friendly greetings with each other. Conversations merged into a dull roar. With so many people around, Mirari expected the place to be livelier. Before he had left, Salathiel had attributed the morose pall over the town to Soteria's influence. She was definitely in the city and now they just had to find her.

"Here you go," the harried barmaid said, placing the steaming plate in front of Mirari. It was piled too high for one person to possibly finish, unless it was Neo. No wonder this place was popular. "Just give me a yell if you need anything else." Mirari agreed and the woman hurried off to tend to the next customer.

Keeping her head lowered, Mirari tucked into the cod and strained her hearing to listen to the conversations around her – an unreasonable customer that needed managing, a large order that was going to take all night to fulfill, an important shipment arriving later that night. It was mostly work-related chatter that brought back memories of her time as a merchant in Solarin.

"You can't go!" a woman whispered. "Are you mad?"

Without pivoting, Mirari slightly turned her head to listen to the young couple to her left. The woman looked on furiously while the man seemed troubled and overwhelmed. He ran his hand through his hair and braced his elbow on the table.

"What else am I supposed to do?" he said. "I need that shipment."

"Hire someone. A courier, retinue." Mirari felt a pang of unease. "A street urchin. Who cares? Just don't go yourself." The woman reached out to grab her companion's wrist. "Please, I couldn't bear it if anything happened to you."

He turned his hand so he was clasping hers. "I know, but there's no one to hire. No one will go down to the docks."

"For good reason," she added. "If anyone were found out, they could be arrested by the Council for being a dissident, or sympathizer, or whatever. This is not the time."

"Then when is the time? The Council will only continue to arrest people, and the region leaders are too scared to stand up to them."

They seemed more concerned about catching the Council's attention than whatever danger lurked at the docks. Not that Mirari could blame them. On their way to Racca, Mirari and Salathiel had heard many stories of towns and villages that had been ransacked and raided under the Council's orders as they tried to flush out the Defiants and anyone connected to them.

There was even news that the Knights had joined the Council, but Mirari didn't believe *that* was true. Fangbane had always made a point that the Knights should be a separate entity from the Council and other petty political squabbles.

But there was hope. There was a new and rising fighter – Spiritel – a warrior so talented that those who had watched him in battle believed that he would become the next region leader. He had been chasing after members of the Blessed, perhaps even the Defiants, but Mirari wasn't sure whether he was friend or foe. The last thing she wanted was another fighter joining their complex feud.

"Do you think having a "reason" will be enough for the Council?" the woman said. The man blew out a frustrated breath and sat back in his chair, pulling his hand away. "Fine. You want to go. Go. In fact, I'll join you."

"Absolutely not."

"Why not? Hmm. 'Cause it's dangerous?"

At a stalemate, they stewed in silence. The barmaid hesitantly approached and refilled the mugs. She didn't immediately leave. She glanced around, then whispered to them. Mirari peeped over the railing so they didn't think she was listening in on their conversation.

"Sorry, but I didn't mean to overhear," the barmaid said. "You weren't talking about going to the docks, were you?"

The man groaned. "Not you, too."

"Yes, please," the woman said. "Can you help him see reason?"

"Oh, I don't want to get involved," she hemmed, clearly wary. "I was just wondering if you'd heard of Spiritel? He and his team go around getting rid of *those* people." Her voice had taken on a self-important lecturing tone. "Your best bet is to wait on him, if you ask my opinion."

"I've heard of Spiritel," the woman said. "He's here? How do you know?"

"It's what the folks around here have been talking about all day."

The man got to his feet. "I've got a business to run. I can't just wait around for a phantom to deal with those ruffians."

"It's better than getting the Council involved, isn't it?" the woman said.

"How do you even know he's real?"

"My sister saw him herself," the barmaid said. "I know what he looks like."

Mirari was curious to know if she knew more. She heard that the man hid his face behind a mask – much like someone else she knew – and no one knew his true identity.

Down below, the door had been routinely opening and closing as patrons came and went. This time, when the door opened a familiar hooded figure stepped inside and looked around. His gaze unerringly looked up and Mirari waved down. Salathiel nodded and headed toward the stairs.

"All right, all right," the man said. The barmaid, now finished gossiping, went back to her duties while the young couple grabbed their cloaks. The man continued grumbling as they left. "I'll wait. Gods help me. I'll wait."

The man and woman passed Salathiel on the stairs and shuffled out of his way.

"I found her," Salathiel said, sliding into the chair across from her.

"The docks, right?" She slid the rest of the cod over to him.

"Yeah?" He tilted his head to the side, looking at her curiously. "How did you know?"

She shrugged while he finished off her plate. "It's just something I overheard."

Salathiel scraped the plate clean. "Ready?"

"Yeah, let's go."

In contrast to the Twin Cod Tavern, the tavern down by the docks was cheerless, dirty, and cold. It looked like the sort of place sailors would take their shore leave, but now there wasn't anybody outside and the sounds from inside were muted and dull. It was impossible to see anything more than vague, shadowy figures through the dirt-smudged windows, but they didn't dare enter. They decided to make their move only when night had fallen, crouched in the alley across from the tavern. The street was narrow and it would only take a few steps to run across.

Squinting, Mirari tried to focus on Salathiel as he spoke. Her head was pounding and she lifted her hand to rub her eye.

"Mirari?" Salathiel squeezed her shoulder, grounding her in the moment. "Are you all right?"

She cleared her throat and nodded. "Yeah, yes. Say again?"

He looked at her for a moment but didn't argue. "The place is crawling with Defiants, too many for us to handle on our own. There's a drainage pipe over there." Turning back, he pointed to the right side of the building. "We should be able to scale the side. Soteria is in one of the rooms on the upper floor." He looked at her one last time. "Ready?"

To be honest, Mirari didn't think she was. She still couldn't summon fire on command, but knowing she was the only one who could defeat Soteria, she had to be ready. Smiling lightly, she nodded. Her only fear was that she might hurt Salathiel, but it wouldn't be an issue if she could control her fire like she needed. She thought about the jar of anger Salathiel had taught her about. Her hand clenched into a fist.

Nodding again, she got to her feet. "Let's do it."

Salathiel peeked out of the alley and motioned to her when the coast was clear. They darted across the street, heading straight for the side of the building. They found the drainage pipe right where Salathiel had said.

"Wait for me down here," he said, starting the ascent. "I'll let you know when it's safe to come up."

He climbed easily, scaling the wall as though it were a simple flight of stairs. At the window, he held himself up with one arm on the sill and one leg braced on the pipe. Drawing his dagger, he pried the window open and slithered inside.

Mirari climbed up after him as soon as he motioned. It wasn't as easy as he made it look. She had to fight for every handhold and she feared slipping down and attracting attention when she was in a vulnerable position. Finally, she made it to the window and was grateful to take Salathiel's hand and let him help her over the edge.

With her feet firmly on the ground, Mirari inspected the quiet hallway. It had three doors. An open doorway stood directly across from them that led to a flight of stairs and the barroom downstairs. Mirari took a step forward and cringed when the floor creaked underneath her feet. The walls were half-rotten from the strong sea winds and the floor was warped. Hopefully, no one downstairs noticed or cared.

"Do you know which room she's in?" Mirari asked.

He shook his head and approached the first room. Seeing him in action for the first time in years reminded her that Salathiel was stealthy, better than before. His steps were light and quiet as if he was performing a pavane dance across the floor. Pressing his ear against the door, he listened. After a moment, he shook his head and walked to the next room. She followed closely, keeping her hand on her sword.

He started to turn away but froze halfway there. Narrowing his eyes, he leaned in again.

"Is that her?" Mirari whispered.

"Maybe. Let me check. Wait here."

"Why? Aren't I the only one who can stop her? Why should I stand out here?"

Salathiel was hesitant before turning to face her fully. He placed his hands on her shoulders and backed her up, away from the door. Squeezing her shoulders gently, he crouched so he was meeting her gaze fully.

"I'm not trying to sideline you," he said. "I'm going to try to reason with her first. And if that doesn't work, yes, you are the only one who can defeat her. I have to make sure you have that opportunity. Just wait and watch. If she turns violent and you have the chance to take her out, do it."

Mirari wasn't exactly pleased with the plan, but it made sense. She nodded, turning back to the door, and Salathiel slid it open with his dagger. He slipped through the door, leaving it just cracked behind him. Mirari's hand tightened around the hilt of her sword while she listened in.

Soon enough, Mirari could hear an oddly familiar voice speak.

"How did you get in here?"

"I've been looking for you for a long time," Salathiel said.

"To what end?"

"To stop you. This, what you're doing, isn't right. You have to understand that."

"I'm carrying out my destiny," she said, voice rising. "As should you."

"This is not what Lachess wanted."

"Why would the goddess choose me if not to avenge the fallen? You of all people should understand."

Mirari recoiled. Soteria didn't sound evil. She spoke candidly, sincerely. But it was clear that she had no intention of stopping.

"You were blessed with a second chance, but it doesn't mean you go back to doing what you were doing before. It's exactly the opposite. You can use it to take another path."

"There's only one path for me. I must finish what Laikos started."

"I won't let you continue."

Shink! Somebody drew their weapon.

"I won't let you stop me!" Soteria let out a yell and Mirari heard the sound of two blades clashing. She pushed the door open, staying low to the ground as she crept inside.

The noise was coming from farther inside. Mirari straightened and looked around. She was standing in a small sitting area with a long, low table and a threadbare couch against the far wall. Doors stood on either side of the chair. The one closest to her was barely cracked while the other was wide open.

She rushed toward the room. Just as she entered, she heard glass breaking and watched Soteria shove Salathiel through the broken window. Salathiel kept his grip on her tunic and they both tumbled out.

"Sal!" Mirari yelled. Rushing to the window, she saw them plunge to the ground. Salathiel rolled to his feet, holding his fists up. He looked uninjured, but, unfortunately, so did Soteria. She'd managed to keep her daggers, but Salathiel lost his during the fall.

Rifling through the room, Mirari found two daggers buried deep into the wall by the bed. Mirari jerked them out and ran back to the window.

Soteria was speaking again. She had a silver mask over her face and two daggers pointed at Salathiel. Mirari couldn't hear what they were saying, but Salathiel shook his head. Soteria tilted her head, finding Mirari at the window, then turned on her heels to flee.

"Wait!" Mirari shouted, and she tossed the daggers to Salathiel. He snatched them out of the air and chased after Soteria.

Mirari bit her lip at the fall. Too high. Cursing, she headed back to the drainage pipe, and prayed that Salathiel wouldn't get too far ahead.

CHAPTER SEVENTEEN

I t was late at night when Gaven, Eoin and the rest of their group arrived in Racca. They entered along a small side street dressed as simple travelers, and though there weren't many people out, they garnered a lot of attention from the locals. They stopped outside of a local tavern while they decided who would be sent in to gather information –

Isemay and Sven. Gaven didn't dare say that of the six of them, they looked the least threatening.

He was about to settle down in the shadow of the alley when he took notice of a young couple heading their way. The man looked stubborn yet resigned as he was pulled along by the woman. Her eyes darted up and down along the street, looking for something. Perhaps they had lost something the man found insignificant.

Gaven settled down on a barrel in the alley next to the tavern while Eoin leaned against the opposite wall with his arms crossed. Eoin hadn't worn his bandages for a while, but for some reason the talla on his arm was more prominent tonight than ever. Gaven couldn't help but stare at the markings of a dragon.

For a second, his shoulders felt heavy as he reminisced about his region.

The others were on the opposite side of the tavern, keeping an eye out for soldiers and an ear out for the two inside in case they got into any trouble.

"There!"

Gaven looked over sharply to the couple and found the woman pointing at him and Eoin. He straightened his back, glancing over to Eoin. Even as the couple moved in on them, they chose to stay where they were. They didn't look like a threat and they didn't look antagonistic. The man's face had slackened after the initial surprise as he let himself be towed along with no resistance.

The woman ran up to the two of them, admiring Gaven's mask in awe. She touched her own face and said, "It's true. You're Spiritel, right?"

Embarrassed, Gaven was glad his face was hidden. "Can I help you?" he asked gruffly. Eoin coughed to barely mask his snigger and Gaven glared at him.

She lowered her voice and glanced around like she was just now realizing they could be overheard. "They say you're the one who takes care of… certain types of people."

"What kind of people?" Gaven asked warily.

"The people… the Council is looking for?"

Gaven straightened and motioned for her to continue. She tugged on the man's arm, pulling him to stand next to her. "Tell him," she ordered.

The man looked uncomfortable, but did as she asked. "Down by the docks, some people are congregating." The man spoke in a hushed tone about the thugs and ruffians who had taken over the docks and filled it with crates no one else was allowed to know about. Anyone who probed too deeply into what they were doing disappeared.

"I had an apprentice who was supposed to meet my dealer at

the Salty Loch. I'm expecting a very important shipment. My business is—" The woman jabbed her elbow into his side and he redirected. "Anyway, my apprentice got roughed up by the thugs that have taken over the Salty Loch and couldn't even get past the door. If that's not enough, he quit because some woman scared him."

"Did he say what she looked like?" Gaven asked.

The man looked at him warily. "Not her face, but she was wearing a…" He motioned toward Gaven.

"A mask?" Eoin said, pushing away from the wall. "A silver one?"

"Yeah, that's right."

The woman stepped forward. "Are you going to get rid of her and her gang? We're good people, just trying to make a living. We don't want the Council to think we have anything to do with them."

"We understand," Gaven said. "We'll do what we can." A look of relief lit up both of their faces. "Go home and don't tell anyone about this."

They departed, clutching at each other. When they were out of earshot, Gaven turned to Eoin and said, "Soteria."

He nodded. "We found her."

UNDER THE COVER OF DARKNESS, Gaven and Eoin's team observed people moving boxes into warehouses while guards held their gazes over them. Gaven was grim as he recced the number of people the Defiants had amassed. His small group was vastly outnumbered. Gaven hadn't realized how many people were caught up in the Defiants' madness. If they got into a battle with any of these groups, defeat was inevitable. Even with Gaven's strength and experience, he would still be overwhelmed by their sheer numbers. And now, it seemed Soteria was fully outfitting her dissidents with supplies for a proper army.

"Do you think those are all weapons?" Isemay asked, looking nervous.

"It's likely," Eoin said.

Gaven agreed. It was similar to the weapons cache they had found in that second warehouse. Gaven couldn't imagine the damage Althaea would suffer if Soteria managed another large-scale attack like the Siege. Not just Althaea – all the empires, and the regions beyond.

"Someone has to destroy them," Gaven said.

"We can't lose this opportunity to find Soteria," Eoin said.

Gaven reached up to run his hand over his stubble and found the mask in the way. He still wasn't used to it. He thumbed over the sharp edges.

"We'll have to split up," he decided. It was the only way to accomplish both tasks.

"We can take out the weapons," Myrana said. "You two should find Soteria."

Eoin nodded, thoughtful. "You five should stick together. Take out the warehouses one at a time."

Gaven left Eoin to give out the instructions while he ran his thumb over his knuckles. If Soteria was here, could Mirari be nearby? If she wasn't and he defeated Soteria, where did that leave him? He would have no other clues to find her.

"Eoin, Spiritel, take care," Brigid said.

Eoin clasped her shoulder and crouched down with Gaven while the five members took off toward the first warehouse. They kept low and moved fast to avoid the attention of the Defiants. They were a better force than when Gaven had first met them, but they were still a small group.

"Do you think they'll be alright?" Gaven asked.

Eoin shrugged. "I pray that they are, but there's nothing more we can do for them now."

"Except cut the head off the snake."

"Well said."

Gaven didn't know what would happen to the Defiants once Soteria was dead. Would they be released from their corruption or lose their morale? At the very least, losing their leader would disrupt the Defiants enough that Erel, or even the Council, could round up the last of them and put the whole thing down for good. Althaea and all of the alliance needed to be free of this dark threat.

"Come on," he said. They were heading in the opposite direction toward the tavern. They darted down the street, keeping to the shadows. They paused to get their bearings in an alley next to a shop that stank of fish, a block away from the tavern according to the directions.

"Nervous?" Eoin asked.

Gaven shot him a look and refused to answer. He couldn't afford to be nervous. All these months on the road, away from Althaea Main and his duties as region leader, led up to this. He couldn't say that he was nervous. He couldn't say that he feared what would happen if they encountered Soteria and he couldn't say that he feared what would happen if they didn't. There was no way to put into words how he felt about it – about confronting a woman capable of warping minds to her own will.

"You?" he asked.

Eoin chuckled. "I leave my fate up to the gods."

Somehow, the words settled Gaven. Not because he believed in the gods but because of the opposite. His fate wasn't at the mercy of a whim – it was in his own hands. He was in control of his own actions.

It felt like he was just now emerging from underwater, making a difference and making amends for not only his actions during the Althaean Siege, but also what he'd done under the Council's orders.

His zeal for justice was a double-edged sword, but no longer would just anyone pick him up and point it toward their enemies. The Valiant Tiger was infamous, not because he was an easily manipulated pawn, but because of the strength of his spear and the strength of his will.

It mattered not if he was anxious or fearful of facing this woman and what would come after. He would do it anyway. He had to seize this opportunity while he had it.

Averting his gaze, Gaven looked into the distance with his lips pressed tightly together. He didn't know how he would formulate a response that would encompass all that he wanted to say and there was no time for it either. He tensed and watched two people, unbelievably fast, chasing each other down the street opposite from them. He gripped Eoin's shoulder to get his attention.

"There. Did you see that?" he asked.

Eoin shook his head. "I didn't, but there's a commotion coming from that tavern." Where he pointed, Gaven could see the door opening and people spilling out, hands on their weapons. Something told Gaven to pursue the two figures.

"Should we split up?" Eoin asked, reading the look on his face.

"Whatever it takes to find Soteria."

"I can handle her," Eoin said with a confidence that Gaven was not certain of. "I know her," he said, amending the doubt on Gaven's face. "I'll try to talk to her. I won't fight her unless I have to."

The figures were getting farther away, and Gaven had no choice but to accept Eoin's assertion. Nodding, he clasped Eoin on the shoulder and darted off after the figures he had seen.

Something about the two combatants made Gaven uneasy, as if his shadows had taken form in the real world. He was drawn to them with curiosity he couldn't discount.

Gaven raced down the street, peering down the numerous

alleys and darkened corners for them. He was greeted with the muted roar of moving water as he got closer to the ocean.

At an intersection, Gaven came to a stop. He had lost them. He spun in a circle, but there was no sign in which direction they had gone. He wouldn't have thought they'd been able to make it as far as they had, but their speed had been incredible. If they knew their way around…

His head perked up when he heard the sound of metal clashing. Holding his breath, he strained his ears. There. Just over the sound of the ocean, he could hear someone fighting. He slipped into a small alley between two buildings. It was an enclosed space with barely enough space to swing his weapon, but he had to stay cautious. He didn't want to be discovered until he had ascertained what was going on.

On the other side of the alley, he found himself at the pier. It was rundown and nearly abandoned. The wooden pier that extended into the ocean was half-rotted through and the sparse crates along the side looked lonely and forgotten under the clouded moon. Gaven swept his gaze left and right.

Clash!

He jerked back, ducking behind an old crate. On the far side of the pier, he saw two figures in black, blending into the very night like the shadows were clinging to their legs. One was tall with broad shoulders while the other was shorter and wiry. Gaven observed them for a moment. The moon peeked out from its cover and flickered briefly over the two fighters.

A flash of silver caught his eye and his heart skipped a beat. With his hand on his spear, he watched, carefully inching closer. He kept his eyes glued to the two figures dancing in the dark, specially the one with a mask. He might only have one chance to strike and he had to make it count.

Gaven was ready to pounce when the hair on the back of his neck stood up. He turned, lifting his spear to intercept the blade aimed for his legs. His attacker – a woman by the looks of her delicate lips peeking from under her hood – stumbled back but kept her footing.

Gaven took a swing. Had it been anyone else, they would've been dead before they saw the point coming. But this woman had caught and blocked his spear with her sword. From the way she held her stance, he could tell she had mastery over her weapon. He felt her blade pivot, and he quickly jumped back before she could launch a counter strike.

She lunged forward. Gaven rotated his chest, and now she was in front of him, her torso perfectly exposed. He struck under with his fist, but her hand nudged his wrist just enough for him to miss. She had a tight grip on his arm now, and she brought him down in a backdrop with a force he didn't expect from her petite figure. Gaven's weapon slid farther into the alley away from him.

He quickly got to his feet, but she did too. He pointed to the ground and a slab of stone rose between them. It was the first time he had to use his kore while playing the role of Spiritel, but this was no regular enemy, and it gave him enough time to pick up his spear.

It didn't take long before he saw her leap above the wall with a burst of air under her feet. She dropped to the ground and it only took two strides for her to reach him, sword raised with a loud cry.

Gaven barely dodged the bite of her blade. He took a few more steps back, and she took his bait, striking under his feet.

Another slab rose under his feet, pushing him over her height, and he brought his spear straight down at the attacker. She lifted her sword, angling exactly forty-five degrees. With a twist of her wrist, she deflected the blow.

There were few people who moved in ways he couldn't predict, and even fewer people who could counter him. Two times may have been a coincidence, but three times was not. There was no way he wouldn't recognize that maneuver.

He had taught it to her.

He repelled her sword again. This time he lowered his spear. "Stop. Enough!" he said.

She didn't yield.

"You're Spiritel, aren't you?" she hissed, her blade still turned up. "What are you doing here? Whose side are you on?"

"You—" He stopped, realizing his voice was distorted by the mask. "I… know I have a lot to explain, but now is not the time." Lifting his hand, he jerked it from his face. "Lower your hood."

She gasped. They stood there in silence before she lowered her sword.

"You're… Spiritel?

Gaven knew how strange it looked. Spiritel was the commoner people whispered about with reverence and awe, the hero they turned to when they lost faith in their region leaders. But Spiritel was a region leader.

Her trembling hands were slow. She hesitated before flinging her hood back and met his gaze.

Mirari's lips were pressed together and her back was firm, but there was something fragile about her wide eyes.

Under her disheveled hair, she looked worn out, as if she hadn't had proper sleep for days. He couldn't imagine what she had been through since he abandoned her. The fragile look disappeared from her eyes when he took a step forward as she retreated.

Many emotions filled Gaven. Relief. Sorrow. Anger, at himself. She had every right to be skeptical. He had wronged her, but Mirari was possibly the only person in the world he didn't want to be afraid of him. They shared a bond, and she knew every bit of good and bad in him. Beyond that – they shared a childhood.

Mirari looked like she was ready to run. He saw her take another step back, and it twisted his heart.

"Roselyn, please!" Gaven said, reaching out his hand. "I'm not your enemy."

Mirari froze, her eyes widened. Out of fear? Uncertainty? Were those tears welling in her eyes?

She took a deep breath and asked, "How long have you known?"

"Not long enough," Gaven shook his head. "Why didn't you tell me?"

Before she could answer, another voice called her name and she turned.

Gaven hadn't seen him arrive. A man stood in the mouth of the alley, directly behind them. His familiar, silvery voice derailed any other thoughts Gaven had. Though scuffed and ruffled, he was drawn to his dark-hair and clean-shaven chin. It tingled an odd feeling in Gaven, especially when the man looked fondly at Mirari.

"There you are," he said as he placed his hands on her shoulder.

Then, it clicked. Was it really him? Salathiel? Gaven was frozen in shock as his mind began to spiral. For the first time in a while, he felt vulnerable as his locked memories began to overwhelm him. If there had been any other assailants hiding in the alley, he would've been dead. But maybe he deserved it.

Salathiel glanced at Gaven coolly and tugged on Mirari's arm. "Come on, we have to go."

She gripped his sleeve, but didn't move. "Sal, it's—"

"Soteria fell into the water. We have to catch her." He tugged again, a bit more insistently. Gaven knew Salathiel was ignoring him. He tried to hide his scowl, though he probably didn't do a good job of it.

"But..." She glanced at Gaven, and blanched at his expression.

Gaven knew Mirari had lied about her identity. He may not have known why, but he had come to accept it. But this? She lied about this too? His hand clenched into a fist.

"I thought you said your *brother* was dead." He snorted. He felt like a fool. "I guess that was a lie too?"

She shifted to her back foot and her gaze flickered down. He could tell she was tense and wary, but he held onto his anger. It was something familiar for him to cling to instead of being swept away by his hurt. He'd been searching for her for months, hoping to get answers to the questions that plagued him. Now, he'd only found more questions. More lies. How many more did she have?

CHAPTER EIGHTEEN

At the dark look on Gaven's face, Mirari took an unwitting step backward. They hadn't parted well and now they once again stood on opposite sides. She wasn't sure if Gaven would listen to her any better than he had in the past. She would try, anyway. She parted her lips to speak but her view of Gaven was obscured by Salathiel's broad back.

"Don't talk to her like that," he said.

She could hear Gaven growl, "Get out of my way. I'm not talking to *you*. I'll have her answer. Now!"

"And what gives you that privilege?"

Mirari sighed, pressing her hand to her face. Salathiel was always overprotective, but in this case it wasn't necessary. She was shocked to see him so hostile toward Gaven. They were family.

She wasn't scared of Gaven. She'd never been scared of what he'd do to her, but about what he'd do to their relationship. Even if he pushed her away, she wanted to be a part of his life. That had been her wish when she joined their family, as it was now. Straightening her back, she refused to wilt under another accusation of deception.

"Why do you think you deserve the truth?" Salathiel said.

"You've done nothing but push us away. You may have gotten bigger, but you still act like a child, Gaven."

Gaven gritted his teeth and said, "You'll show me respect."

"Maybe when you've earned it, you'll—" Grounding herself, Mirari grabbed Salathiel's arm and forced him behind her.

"What's wrong with both of you?" She scowled at them, but they were still speaking with intense glares. She sighed and turned to Salathiel. "Give us a moment."

"What?" Salathiel leaned forward, but she raised her hand at him. "He's going to kill you. Those are his orders," Salathiel said.

Mirari thought of that possibility. She had betrayed Gaven, and he had every right to end her life. She was friends with the Blessed, and that made her an enemy of the empires. Still, she owed him answers. It was time. "I'll be fine. Trust me." Salathiel didn't back away until she nudged him and said, "Go find Soteria. I'll be right with you."

Salathiel sighed and glowered at Gaven one last time. "If you do *anything* to her…"

"We're not kids anymore," Gaven said, narrowing his eyes at him. "Your authority is nothing to me."

Scoffing, Salathiel ran toward the ocean.

Mirari watched until he was out of sight. She approached Gaven, rubbing her arm and softening her eyes that met Gaven's. She was within arm's reach from him when she noticed Gaven's gaze flicker over the wound. She stopped.

"I really thought he was dead. I sat through five years thinking the Blessed took him."

"I know you don't believe in the good in the Blessed, but they have helped me in many ways. We're going to stop the Defiants together. We know how to do it."

Crossing his arms, Gaven scanned the street and asked, "And your name?"

Of course. That was what was really bothering him.

"Did you really expect Roselyn Hale to live forever as a peasant? I'm sorry. I kept it from you because—"

"I've heard enough for now."

"But—"

Faster than she'd ever seen him move, Gaven drew his sword and lunged forward. She could read his direction in the shift of his weight. Flinching, she dodged to the left while he swung to his right. The sharp whistle of his blade through the air was cut short when it bit into flesh not her own.

Shocked, she turned to see Gaven hadn't been aiming for her at all. A man armed with an axe had been sneaking up on her and she hadn't noticed.

"Pay attention," he said sharply, pulling his blade free. The assailant stumbled back, injured but not fatally. "There are still enemies around."

"R-right." She shook her head to reorient herself. Her heart was pounding from the close call and the sound was reverberating in her head. She readied her sword.

Before the man in front of them could gather himself, another sturdy warrior confronted them from the opposite side of the street. Mirari glowed when she immediately recognized Eoin.

The assailant dodged Eoin's first blow, but then caught a meaty fist in his stomach. He crumpled forward, and Eoin finished him off with a swift blow to the face.

Mirari's shock at his arrival was compounded when Eoin saw Gaven and wasn't on his guard. Instead, Eoin lifted his hand to greet Gaven like he was an old friend and Gaven stepped forward in response.

"How's it looking?" Gaven asked.

"We took care of the warehouse," Eoin said. "No sign of Soteria."

"I believe she may have escaped into the waters."

But instead of the ocean, Eoin searched behind Gaven and

his face lit up. "What do you know? You found her, and she's alive." He nodded at her. "It's nice to see you, Miss."

Mirari tilted her head. What was happening? How much time had actually passed while she'd been in that cabin?

Gaven's cheeks turned a light pink. "Yeah, well…" He swung around to face the ocean. "Let's go. We need to find Soteria."

<hr>

Mirari, Gaven, and Eoin ran down the street, hugging the shore in search of Salathiel, Soteria, or footprints to indicate that they were on the right path. The waves roared as their feet kicked up loose gravel and dirt. Soon enough, they caught sight of a group of men assembled on the shore behind a warehouse. Salathiel was standing against a dripping Soteria, but he was also surrounded by at least eight other Defiants, more incoming.

Gaven rushed forward, striking the closest Defiant before he had time to react. Twisting around, he dodged another blade, and swiped the assailant's tendons. In rhythm by his side was the blacksmith, who charged at an incoming Defiant and knocked him with the upswing of his axe. They fought well together, Mirari thought as she tried to make sense of this strange, new camaraderie.

The Defiants may have thought her distracted, but from the corner of her eye, she sighted a man charging at her from the right. She feigned ignorance until he was close enough to take a swing. She ducked and lunged forward, her sword gliding through his stomach. Kicking him away, she noted that the ground was growing slick with blood. But also, among the fallen Defiants, an open path to her brother.

Mirari weaved through blades and bodies to reach Salathiel. In no time, she was shoulder-to-shoulder with him. He glanced over at her and smiled. Taking a step back, he turned so that the two of them were back-to-back.

"Use your flames," Salathiel said. "I'll watch your back."

She glanced at him out of the corner of her eye, keeping most of her attention on the woman across from her. "H-here? Now?"

"You can do it," he said with a firm nod. "I believe in you. Now's your chance to take care of this threat once and for all."

"Right." But there was a problem – Mirari still couldn't summon the flames on command. She would be of more use if she fought with the rest of them. To pray for a miracle? She thought it was a waste of time.

She caught sight of Gaven working his way toward Soteria from behind. She couldn't help remembering how he had looked when they were kids and her fire had gone out of control in the forest. She didn't want to see that look on his face ever again.

But if what Salathiel and Julie said was true, this fight would not end until her flames put an end to Soteria and her army. They would fight until exhaustion. She didn't have a choice.

Scowling, Mirari raised her sword and took a step toward Soteria. She wasn't a child anymore. She wouldn't lose control and she wouldn't harm any of her friends. Not again. She darted forward, swinging her sword. Soteria caught the blade in the "v" of two black steel daggers and forced Mirari away, dancing out of reach of another attack. Mirari cautiously stepped closer. The blades appeared to be carved from the night sky and she didn't want to misjudge the length and end up gutted.

In a swift motion, Mirari slashed at Soteria and grazed her arm. It was deep enough to seep blood, only…

"W-What is that?" Mirari's eyes widened, as did those around her. The only one who didn't seem surprised was Salathiel. A thick, dark substance dripped from the wound. If Mirari didn't know any better, she would've thought she wasn't seeing properly. The Defiants didn't bleed like her; Mirari concluded such an effect was only granted to those who were directly touched by Lachess. Soteria wiped the substance away with her other arm, and Mirari saw that the wound had been sealed with a faint scar.

"A regular blade can't hurt her, Mirari," Salathiel reminded her. She knew *that*, but didn't realize it took on a literal meaning. "You have to use the flame."

Staring at the eerie substance smudged on Soteria's arm, Mirari began to feel lightheaded. An uneasy feeling rushed through her body and, like a spike shoved through her eye, pain lanced through her head. She involuntarily lifted her hand to her head, but simply ran it through her hair to hide her pain.

"Minds are such fragile things, aren't they?" Soteria said in a voice that was vaguely familiar to Mirari. Though Soteria remained masked, Mirari could sense the mirth in her voice.

Mirari ducked and dodged two more strikes. She struck out her foot, catching Soteria's wrist and spinning one of the daggers out of her hand. The masked woman spun around, kicking wildly. Mirari caught the sole of her boot with the hilt of her blade, knocking her down. Lowering her sword, she lifted her left hand and held it up with her palm facing Soteria.

Nothing happened.

Soteria lifted her dagger and tilted her head at an arrogant angle. She said, "Did they make you believe you could stop me with those flames?"

"I know I can." Mirari kept her surprise from her face, briefly envying the other woman's mask.

"But they didn't tell you *what* you are, did they?"

Mirari furrowed her brows. "What are you talking about?"

"You wouldn't want to kill me if you knew."

Soteria charged forward, and Mirari blocked her swing. She shook off Soteria's words, focusing on her mission. They exchanged another flurry of blows before Mirari retreated a few steps and tried again.

Breathing deeply, she closed her eyes. She reached deep inside of her and tried to find that fire that burned within. None of her practice had borne fruit, but she had hoped the fire would appear when she needed it most. Now was that time.

Clang!

Her eyes flew open. Gaven was standing next to her, blocking the dagger flying toward her face. It swung away then twisted at an unnatural angle to fly back to Soteria's hand. Gaven grabbed Mirari's shoulder and jostled her.

"What are you doing just standing there?" he said. He took his place next to her. "Did you forget she can control weapons?"

It seemed Mirari had forgotten a lot of things. Most importantly, she didn't need fire. She had a partner. Regardless of the paragon's bond, she could still rely on Gaven.

"I'm here." She lifted her sword again to confront Soteria. "I'm here," she repeated softly, speaking more to herself. How foolish to rely on something she had not mastered. If Gaven knew he might just throw her off the battlefield himself.

Soteria rushed forward, swinging her two blades down in an arc. Mirari met her in the middle. She caught one of the daggers with her blade and ducked under the swing of the other. She spun and jabbed her elbow into Soteria's chest.

Gaven lunged, extending his spear. Soteria dodged the deadly end, but Gaven twisted the weapon to sweep her leg out from under her with the blunt shaft.

Releasing her daggers, Soteria caught herself with her hands and flipped past them. One by one, the two blades spun around, heading straight for them.

Spinning his spear, Gaven batted them out of the air. But the daggers pivoted and, in the blink of an eye, gravitated back toward him. He batted them away again, but barely in time. One of the edges grazed his shoulder. They returned, and Gaven swiped them away. He could hold his own, but for how long?

Mirari knew he was at a checkmate. She took a step forward, ready to lunge at Soteria while she was distracted. But her body stopped on its own. The sounds – clashes of metal, battle cries, ocean waves – muted for a second. Her mind went blank as if she had jumped forward a few seconds in time. When she blinked, everything resumed.

Only now, she was looking at the battle as if it were a dream, fully aware of her surroundings but disconnected from her senses. She questioned whether what she saw was truly happening.

She ran up to Soteria – yes, this is what she wanted to do – and struck her in the face. Soteria stumbled back with her hand to her cheek. She looked at her wide-eyed, seemingly in fear, and hesitated for a second. Seething, her anger returned and she threw a punch back. Mirari caught it in her palm. She had enough strength to push her back, farther and farther, until Soteria released her hand with the turn of her body. Mirari lost her balance and, with her body pulled forward, Soteria struck her.

Mirari crashed to the ground – she didn't physically feel that, but she imagined it felt like hitting a stone wall. She rolled away before Soteria could stomp on her chest, then grabbed a handful of dirt and tossed it at Soteria before she could attempt another stomp.

Shielding her eyes, Soteria choked on the dust, and it was enough time for Mirari to push herself off the ground in a forward flip – she couldn't do that before. She was impressed with herself and her newfound flexibility.

"I'm not afraid of you," Soteria said, wiping the dirt from her face. She readied her fists in front of her face. She said something else that Mirari couldn't make out, Soteria's voice fading in and out, but she caught the words, "…you're barely in control."

"Ending you only takes a fraction of my strength," Mirari said, or did she? Despite hearing them, it didn't feel as though the words came out of her mouth. It was stern, commanding, and full of more confidence than she actually had.

Mirari jumped Soteria, shoving her shoulder into Soteria's

stomach and forcing her to the ground. Bucking like a wildcat, Soteria struck out at Mirari's face. Mirari blocked her blow with her forearms and countered with a punch to her arm, then her chest. When Soteria lashed out again, Mirari grabbed her wrists and forced them down.

A shadow fell over them. Gaven's spear thrust past Mirari's shoulder to press against Soteria's throat.

"Give up," he snapped. "You lose."

"Not until my last breath!"

Folding her knees against Mirari's chest, Soteria catapulted her in the air. Mirari's body slammed on the ground. Before Gaven could react, Soteria kicked his spear away with one foot and landed a blow to his chest with the other. Spinning, she cradled her legs over Mirari and pressed a dagger to her neck.

A drop of blood escaped Mirari's neck, and it stung more than it should.

Mirari definitely felt that – liquor poured over a cut, a branding iron pressed against her neck – but no matter how loud she screamed, no sound came out of her mouth. From the edge of her vision, she saw something black rising into the air from the dagger, a dark mist, at Soteria's command. It adorned her like a weighted vest, an ugly one.

Mirari was sinking, her vision escaping the more she drifted away. She wasn't sure if her heavy eyelids gave out first or if she had sunk beyond the ground, but soon enough she was surrounded by nothing but black – lost, all alone.

A reddish light seeped out of Mirari's palm in waves like a gentle mist. She gripped the hilt of Soteria's blade, her flame growing, interlacing and expelling Soteria's dark power until it was no more.

With her other hand, Mirari grabbed Soteria's mask and forced her to the side. She slammed her head into the ground, then again. Her fingers held a tight grip on Soteria's mask as she continued pounding her into the ground until a crack slithered up the side of the mask.

"You don't fear me," Mirari said, forcing her up by her mask. A reddish light glowed between the mask and Mirari's palm. "You fear that your fate will come true. And it will."

The light erupted into a roar of flames, lighting up the dark night and engulfing Soteria's body. She was barely visible to the onlookers, but they could see that her body quavered under the pressure of the flames.

"W-What is that?" Gaven said, unable to turn his eyes away from the light. He had seen those flames before, unfortunately, many times, but this was different. No heat was emitting from Mirari's hand, only a discomforting aura. Though he stood strong, his feet looked ready to retreat. He must've known that no weapon could counter the force before him.

Eoin wrinkled his forehead. He seemed to have figured something out, but whatever it was, he kept it to himself. He called out to Gaven, "Quick, I need a rope."

Gaven's eyebrows furrowed. "For who?"

"Whoever you want to lose."

Before Gaven could respond, the ground below began to open, and vines began to mold around Soteria's body. Her legs were locked in place and her wrists were interlaced with the earth. With Soteria confined, Mirari released her grip and the flames disappeared into thin air.

Salathiel breathed a sigh of relief and lowered his hands. The vines detached themselves from the earth and Soteria's confined body tumbled into the ground.

Eoin was impressed. "That will do."

Mirari smiled, pleased. It only lasted for a second before her legs gave in and she collapsed.

"Mirari!" Gaven could only take a single step before Salathiel blocked him with his arm.

"She's fine," he said. "She will wake up soon."

Gaven gritted his teeth. "How do you know?"

"I know so much more than you."

They glared at each other. Eoin darted his head between the two men.

"Do you two know each other?" he asked.

Salathiel scoffed, turning away. He walked up to Soteria, arms crossed. Her chest was heaving. He frowned, not looking at all pleased with their success.

"We should kill her," he said.

"She's captured," Gaven said. "There's no need."

"She'll keep going until she's dead."

"She deserves a trial," Gaven said. He stood up so that he was squared off with Salathiel. "That's what Mirari would want."

"You don't know what she wants," Salathiel said, narrowing his eyes. "That's what *you* want, to please the Council."

Eoin stepped forward, the only one with a level head.

"Let's calm down," he said, standing between the two hotheads. "We can discuss this."

Mirari's eyes fluttered open. She pushed herself up and sat on the ground. Rubbing her eyes, she mumbled, "What happened?"

"You did it," Salathiel said, crouching next to her with a smile. "It worked."

Mirari's face brightened, but only for a second before she was distracted by Soteria's cries. Soteria began to writhe like a Narvian queensnake. Her movements became crazed and frantic as she tried to escape the vine's grip. She slammed her head into the ground, cracking more of her mask.

The memories came back to Mirari now – they were fighting Soteria – but how did they catch her? Why had she passed out on the ground? She could not recall.

Gaven was staring at Soteria with a strange look on his face.

"What is it?" Eoin asked.

He strode forward and grabbed Soteria's chin, tilting her head back. Grasping the remains of the mask, he tore the metal away and tossed it aside. His eyes widened.

"That's impossible," he whispered, loosening his grip on Soteria.

The woman jerked her head out of his grasp, turning away from him with a snarl. Mirari's mouth opened when she caught sight of the face hidden underneath the mask.

"Erel?"

Familiar, deep, brown eyes glared at her where normally they sparkled with mirth. Indeed, it was Erel's face twisted in a vicious sneer. The face faltered for a brief moment, but when she leveled her dark look at Mirari there was no recognition in her eyes.

"No," Gaven said. He had shaken off his hesitation and calculated with a contemplative frown. "It's not Erel. Her aura is different."

"Then… who is she?"

He opened his mouth, but then closed it. That shocked look of betrayal had faded. "I can't say for sure."

She could tell he had an idea, but he didn't want to say it. Why not?

The sound of metal clashing cut her off. Frowning, she glanced over her shoulder at the swords exchanging blows near the town center, and the voices raised in battle cries.

"We need to end her now or get her out of here," Salathiel reminded them. "We don't know who else is here."

It could be the royal army for all they knew, and they would surely not be greeted with mercy. Over Soteria's head, the three of them exchanged a look. Finally, Eoin stepped forward.

"I'll check," he said. Without waiting for them to respond, he headed down the street, sticking close to the side of the buildings. Eoin peeked out of the alley to consider the state of things. He'd barely stuck his head beyond the stone walls before he jerked back. He jogged back to them with a concerned pinch to his eyebrows. "It's the Knights."

Mirari's heart pounded. How did they know to be here? It didn't matter. They were here now and she didn't know what to do or how the Knights would react when they saw her.

"You need to go," Gaven said to Eoin. Reaching into his pocket, he pulled out Spiritel's mask and pushed it into Eoin's hand. "Find the others and get out of here. I'll make sure this mess gets cleaned up."

"What should I tell the others?"

"Whatever you have to." He motioned toward the mask. "Just make sure Spiritel carries on. The people need him."

Eoin nodded and reached out his arm. Gaven clasped his forearm right over the dragon talla. "You're a good man. Good luck."

As she was watching them, Salathiel came up behind her and grabbed her wrist in a gentle but firm grip. "You too, Mirari. We can't let them find you here."

"For once, we're in agreement," Gaven said, turning around.

Salathiel started to pull her away, but she dug her heels in, pulling her wrist from his grasp.

"You two may be in agreement, but I'm not," Mirari said, crossing her arms with her head held high. "I'm going to stay."

"You can't," Gaven said. "Both of you are supposed to be dead. How are you going to explain that?" Gaven looked over his shoulder. The clashes were getting closer. "I'll handle the clean-up, but for now, you two need to leave."

Mirari frowned at Soteria straining against the bindings trapping her. Mirari's forehead had worried lines. "What if she does something to you again?"

"And you can do something about that?"

She glanced at Salathiel, but couldn't think of what to say. She was the *only* one who could do something about it, but would she be able to unleash it again?

Mirari could hear the Knights – Shiba's commands, Neo's grunts – and she made up her mind.

"You need me," she said. She knew Salathiel was fine on his own, and had been fine on his own for a while. But Gaven, regardless of the status of their partnership, couldn't face the Knights or the Council on his own.

"Mirari—" Salathiel started, but she cut him off with a fierce hug.

Even if Gaven managed to hide the fact that he had been running around the empire as Spiritel, the vigilante hero, she couldn't imagine how he was going to explain why he was fighting the Blessed alone, or how he captured Soteria alone. She was sure that Gaven would be accused of conspiring with the Blessed. She would take the blame with him, in hopes that it would soften whatever punishment he would face. As much as she wished she could run away with Salathiel, she had still hoped the three of them could be together again. That meant they all had to be alive.

"Go! Quickly," she said. "I'll find you when this is over."

Salathiel was hesitant, but he returned her hug.

"Be safe," Salathiel said. Leaning into her ear, he whispered, "Don't tell them about your power, not even about Councilor Julie. No one can be trusted."

As he started to back away, he gave Gaven a rough look. Mirari didn't know if Gaven would say anything; there was no time.

A man came flying from around the corner, chestplate caved in from a well-placed punch. Neo followed, jogging around the corner. The ferocity on his face was comically wiped clean by his surprise.

"Your Honor? What are you—" And then he saw Mirari and his mouth dropped open. "M?"

A Defiant yelled as he came at Neo from behind with a sword

above his head. Before Neo could strike, he fell to three shurikens in his back.

"Neo, what are you gawking at?" Shiba said, scolding him from behind. He peered over Neo's shoulder and realized what had held up his partner. Shiba glared at Gaven with a scowl. He looked ready to unleash a string of profanities until he saw Mirari behind him, and by her feet, a woman bounded on the ground. Shiba stood still for a moment before rubbing his temples. "What is going on?"

One by one, the Knights appeared before Mirari – Hime, Lucan, Kylah. To her surprise, they greeted Mirari like she'd been away on a trip instead of turned traitor and presumed dead. Even Shiba didn't carry his usual scowl underneath his bitter frown. His crimson eyes, normally fierce and commanding, held a depth that seemed to reach into the recesses of her soul.

Lucan strode to the front and embraced her, squeezing her tightly to make sure he wasn't dreaming. Scanning through the crowd of faces, Mirari realized there was one missing.

"Where's Dorain?" she asked. They deflected, avoiding her eyes. "What happened to him?"

"He left the Knights," Hime said.

"He joined his father," Shiba corrected.

That didn't make sense. Dorain and Dareh were like oil and water. They didn't mix. What could have spurred Dorain to work with his father?

"Don't jump to conclusions now," Lucan said. "He was the one who told us to come here."

Shiba said, "Are you saying he knew Mirari was alive?"

"I'm simply saying he gave us an opportunity." He nodded to Mirari. "The best there was."

"Oh," Hime said, jumping slightly. Her pale eyebrows pinched together with consternation. "That reminds me. Dorain said his father will send troops after we secured the port."

"See," Shiba scoffed. "He doesn't trust us."

"The real question is why are you working for them," Gaven said with a hostile twist of his lips. "The Knights are supposed to be independent."

Kylah inched in front of Shiba and held her gaze on Gaven. She had stayed silent up until now.

"Do you think we had a choice?" she said, folding her arms across her chest. "Unlike you, we don't enjoy killing, but you left us to fend for ourselves." Her attention was drawn to something else, and she pointed it out. "I think the better question is what are you doing here, and who is that?" She pointed to the tied woman at their feet.

"Is it just me or does she look familiar?" Neo said, scratching his head. He crouched lightly on the balls of his feet and stared at Soteria like that would make her face make sense. "What's her name? Erel? Your second in command?"

Shiba must've had the same thought. He raised his brows at Gaven.

"This doesn't look good for you, Kitten," he said. "Running around in that cloak, lying about your location, about Mirari, and now, your commander under arrest?"

"This isn't Erel," Gaven said. Despite the accusations, he remained confident. His eyes didn't waver from Shiba. "You'll find that my second in command is still in Althaea Main."

"Then, who is she?" Hime asked. Mirari stepped in.

"That's Soteria," she said. "She's the leader of the Def— the Blessed."

The Knights didn't know how to respond. Eoin, the escaped leader they had been hunting for weeks, wasn't the leader of the Blessed? They had never even heard of Soteria. Kylah furrowed her brows.

"The one you've been looking for?" she asked.

Mirari nodded. "She's the real person responsible for all this, the attack at the Grand Ball, even the Althaean Siege. The Council should be happy with this gift."

An understanding smile crossed Kylah's face. She was the only one Mirari had talked about the Defiants, and Mirari was glad that Kylah seemed to believe her now.

"And what about you?" Shiba asked. "Did we finally catch you?"

"Shiba," Lucan hissed.

"I'm just asking." He turned his nose up. It wasn't a hostile question, she knew, and it came with good intentions. A blanket of silence settled upon them. Mirari didn't have a response for him. They had every right to not trust her. Were the Knights still on her side? With their alliance with the Council, could they be?

"Can't we just say we didn't see her?" Hime said softly with a pleading glance.

Before anyone could object, Kylah stepped forward and said, "I'm willing."

"Me too," Lucan said.

Shiba sighed. "We can't guarantee your safety from the Council," he said. He turned away and mumbled just loud enough for everyone to hear. "But you're still one of us. We'll back you up as much as we can."

The rest nodded in agreement.

Mirari was filled with a fondness for these people who were willing to help her escape. At the same time, she was tired of running. She didn't know what would happen to her or if she would be able to clear her name, but she didn't want to spend the rest of her life looking over her shoulder, wondering if someone would recognize her and report her to the Council. Their words motivated her to stand her ground, and she would prove her innocence, and Gaven's.

"There's no point in my running anymore," Mirari said, shaking her head. She nudged her head toward Soteria. "We have what the Council wants. The war is over."

"Catching her might help your case," Lucan said. "But Eoin

is still missing, and some of the Councilors believe you aided his escape. This would look like a trade-off."

Mirari's forehead crinkled as she thought of that day. She could barely remember the details. She didn't even know Eoin was arrested. Gaven must've read the look.

"Her ignorance will aid her," Gaven said. "Besides, she truly escaped death." He gently touched her shoulder, slowly tugging the garment under his fingers. Mirari's heart skipped a beat. She quickly grasped his hand to a halt, but before she could scold him, he said, "She has proof."

Mirari looked down at her exposed shoulder and saw a line across her skin. Though the wound had healed, the scar was prominent. How did he know that was there? Mirari was about to ask, until…

She heard a synchronized march coming from the other side of the port. She had to make her decision, now.

Tearing away from Mirari's scar, Lucan shook his head. "I don't know if that will be enough."

"Once you're brought in, you won't be able to change your mind," Shiba said in agreement. "Are you sure the Council will believe you?"

Mirari lifted her chin with confidence she didn't fully feel. She sighed and said, "I accept what happens next."

CHAPTER NINETEEN

There hadn't been time to talk before Mirari and Soteria were whisked back to the Hearth to stand before the Council. Mirari was detained and isolated from the others for the duration of the trip. No doubt intentionally, so she couldn't make plans with Gaven or the Knights. Her mind was occupied with trying to craft a strong case for herself. She couldn't do it, not without talking about her flames or dark aura, or revealing Salathiel and Councilor Julie's involvement.

At the Hearth, she was treated no different from any other prisoner. She had been sequestered in a cold, dark room, but it didn't last long. Gaven had come for her, and with her hands tied behind her back, he escorted her down the hall in silence.

Mirari glanced over at Gaven. She wanted to ask him for help, ask him what he was going to say to the Council, but he had avoided her gaze during the entire walk. She knew that meant she should keep to herself. Perhaps he was still upset that she had lied to him, or maybe there were hidden guards watching them. She couldn't read the expression on his face.

They reached the golden doors of the courtroom, and Gaven let out a heavy sigh.

"Ready?" he asked.

Not really, but she nodded anyway. There was no point in delaying. He pushed the doors open and they stepped through.

Gaven held his hand out with a slight bow to the councilors. He stood close by while Mirari took the center stand. She was a trapped bug under the scrutiny of the six councilors, suspicion and distrust clear in their gazes. At the stand, she saw Fangbane and the Knights, and Dorain watched discreetly from the door behind the Council's thrones.

Mirari resisted the urge to wither under the Council's unfriendly stares. She felt a little more at ease with Gaven by her side, but she didn't know what he could say to save her. She had no status, no political power or money to defend herself. Unless he revealed her to be Roselyn Hale. He wouldn't, would he?

"There are… several questions for you Miss Zanette," Tarek began. He looked up from the paper in his hand and scanned her as if he was examining every thread in her garment and every hair on her head for the slightest impurity. His eyes narrowed. "I heard you had died. I see that was a mistake."

Mirari glanced at Gaven, but he kept his gaze on the ground.

"I… was unaware I had been declared dead, Your Grace," Mirari said, lying. She lowered her head so that she didn't have to look into their skeptical eyes. Was that the right answer? Tarek kept his judgmental gaze on her.

Novinha turned her nose up and said, "Region Leader Gaven, when you were last here, you told us that your partner, Mirari Zanette, had been killed in the battle at Aias."

"That is correct," Gaven said. He didn't look up from the ground. He too kept his response short, and Mirari realized that was the game she had to play.

"And yet, here she is." Novinha gestured to Mirari. "Have you taken to lying to the Council now?"

Dareh scoffed and leaned back on his chair. He said, "He has never respected the Council's authority."

"I have great respect for the Council," Gaven said, laying his hand over his chest. His mouth twitched under his stubble and Mirari didn't know if he was hiding a smile or a frown. She felt like she didn't know this version of Gaven at all. He said, "But there is a traitor among us."

Murmurs crescendoed through the room.

"Silence," Suzan ordered. She swept her gaze across the room like a watchful hawk until they obeyed her, then returned her downward scrutiny upon Gaven. "Elaborate, will you? Who is the traitor?"

"Someone wanted Mirari dead." Mirari furrowed her brows. What game was he playing? "Mirari and I suspected that Eoin the Blacksmith was not the mastermind." Gaven paused and nodded at Mirari. "She did a thorough investigation at Aias and confirmed he couldn't have targeted the Grand Ball. It went against his beliefs, and he didn't have the resources to launch such an attack. We knew there was someone else responsible. After all, it was Soteria who Mirari encountered at the Grand Ball."

Suzan asked Mirari, "Is that true?"

Mirari took a deep breath and said, "That is correct. The memory came back to me at a later time."

"Someone didn't want her knowing this," Gaven continued. "They took advantage of the battle at Aias to silence her. I didn't know she survived until now."

"This still does not clear Mirari of her involvement with Eoin," Dareh said. His voice echoed slightly louder than the rest as he waved his hand around. "What is there to prove that she did not form an alliance with the Blessed? Perhaps she even freed Eoin in exchange for Soteria?"

Gaven's brow furrowed, but he stood strong in light of the scowling faces of the Council. He was unconcerned with the vitriol directed his way and Mirari tried to follow his lead. He glanced at her, quickly, before anyone noticed. She recalled what he had said before she was arrested, and tilted her head to the scar on shoulder. It was peeking out from under her garment.

"I could not have freed him," she said. "I narrowly survived my injury, and I was still recovering in Althaea Main during Eoin's trial."

Gaven continued, "Despite her injury, Mirari was committed to catching Soteria. With a mark on her head, she was only able to catch Soteria while faking her death."

"Either way, you have all failed to return Eoin to us," Dareh continued. "The Knights included. We cannot rule out your involvement in his escape."

Mirari watched Gaven bite his lip. She didn't have a counter for this accusation, and clearly, neither did he.

"I object!" a voice called from behind the councilors. The attention in the room shifted to Dorain, who had stepped forward and positioned himself at the end of the row of councilors, a place he clearly shouldn't be in. He kept his attention to the wall across the courtyard instead of facing his father like a good soldier.

"Who gave you permission to speak?" Dareh scowled, about to burst a vein.

Ignoring him, Dorain continued, "Councilors, you must understand that while all members of the Blessed are dangerous, some are far worse than others."

"Under whose judgment?" Dareh's bark grazed their ears.

"Silence, Dareh!" Tarek said. There was a snap to his voice no one had heard before. He frowned at Dareh and in his usual, gentle tone, he continued, "Was he not the one who discovered the Blessed's hideout? Surely your son has proved his competence, if not superiority." He gestured for Dorain to continue.

Ignoring the fumes coming out of his father's ears, Dorain bowed his head and continued, "Eoin was a feather in the wind. He was an idealist, but nothing more than a gentle giant. Soteria, on the other hand, had the ability to control others.

Mirari has found the person responsible for the attack at the Grand Ball," he paused. "As well as the Althaean Siege. She found the culprit behind all the terror that has reigned over the last five years. Not just found, caught." He glanced at Mirari, and she could make out his smirk. "We should be proud of her."

Mirari couldn't hold back a smile of her own. For a second, she was lost in his kind words, thankful that she still had a place in his heart.

"That will be all," Dorain stepped back into the shadows behind the Councilors. Some of the councilors were impressed, nodding at each other. Locking his eyes on the table in front of him, Dareh shrugged his shoulders back and slumped in his seat.

"The boy speaks truth," Novinha said, nodding her head. "Soteria's capture should be enough to omit any suspicion toward Mirari."

"Very well," Suzan said, sounding disappointed and skeptical at the same time. "However, Region Leader Gaven. You still haven't answered the golden question. Who is the traitor?"

Gaven blinked twice. He kept the answer to himself, if not to tease them. Finally, he cleared his throat and said, "Someone on the Council is working with the Blessed."

In the uproar that followed Gaven's words, Mirari watched him with wide eyes. Did he know about Councilor Julie? What evidence did he have? She flinched when Dareh slammed his hands on the table and rose from his seat. Suzan extended her arm in front of him, but before any words could come out, Julie shouted.

"Halt," she said, raising her hand at them. "I would like to hear his explanation." Leaning in, she brought her elbow to the table and laced her fingers together.

"As do I," Adder said. "This is a big accusation. I trust you have a reason?"

Mirari glanced at Julie, who stared back with a cold gaze.

Mirari didn't know what Julie would do if Gaven pointed his finger at her.

"The Council has known of the Blessed's existence for years, yet chose to do nothing," Gaven said, focusing on Tarek. "We were discouraged from taking down our greatest threat, even uttering their name." His eyes shifted to Suzan, who sat next to him. He continued going down the line. "There is someone on the Council who disagrees with eradicating the Blessed, and to get rid of the threat, they're using this opportunity to force us into a state of divergence." He smiled at Adder, then to Novinha. "Who on the Council is most likely to be the traitor?"

"Outrageous!" Dareh said, fumes coming out of his ears.

"Is it?" Gaven pinned him down with his words. "Who wishes to watch us fail? Who has the power to sweep all of this under the rug?" His final gaze landed on Julie. While most of the other councilors were outraged, she didn't seem disturbed by the accusation at all. It was as if she was daring him to say her name.

"Spit it out," Novinha scowled, waving her hand. "Who do you declare the traitor?"

"I don't know," Gaven smiled. He clearly enjoyed listening to the uproar that followed. With that smirk on his face, Mirari realized he was beginning to sound like Erel. "But I'm sure Soteria has the answer for us."

The room went silent once again. Dareh sank down in his seat and started looking around at his fellow council members. Mirari could tell Gaven's words were getting to him.

"It *is* outrageous," Novinha said as she began rubbing her temples. "However, I can't say that some of my fellow council members haven't acted in a way that speaks to a personal agenda."

"I could say the same," Adder said, glaring at her. "For now, should we just be satisfied that the Blessed has been defeated? Whomever the traitor is, they won't take any more actions now that Soteria has been captured."

Narrowing his eyes, Dareh looked at Adder, "What an odd thing to say."

Adder bristled at the insinuation.

"Is he not correct?" Suzan asked. "Why are you so eager to accuse him?"

"Don't try to turn this around on us," Novinha said. "Wasn't it your protege who first became possessed by this woman? You were so quick to absolve him of any guilt for his actions."

"Because he *had* no guilt for his actions. Don't rehash problems that have already been resolved, Novinha."

"Resolved? The burden runs deep in Minettan veins." Novinha got to her feet. "Our problems will never be resolved as long as an alliance exists with your corrupt nation."

"This accusation will not get us anywhere," Tarek said, lifting his hands to order peace between the warring sides. "We can't accept such words easily and we can't dismiss them either." Novinha sank back into her seat while Suzan crossed her arms, minorly appeased.

"Surely, we can agree that a proper investigation is called for," Julie said. It took a while, but eventually, the others agreed with a spoken word or a begrudging nod. She stared down at Mirari with harsh eyes, and it took all of Mirari's willpower not to turn away from her intense look. "There's one other issue to address."

"What other issue?" Adder asked, irritation clear in his voice.

"The woman," Julie said. "The accused leader of the Blessed, the one we call Soteria."

Suzan's eyebrows pinched together and she leaned forward. "That's right."

Mirari's heart skipped a beat. What game was Julie playing? What if Soteria told the Council about dark aura?

"Let's not play coy," Dareh said, with a smug look on his face. "She has more than a passing resemblance to your very own second in command, don't you agree, Region Leader Gaven?"

"Let's not jump to conclusions." Gaven gestured tox the door. "You can hear Commander Erel's testimony for yourself."

"You brought her here?" Suzan asked and Gaven nodded.

"I did. I will send someone for her with the Council's permission."

"Yes, please do so," Tarek said, running his hand over his long beard. He gestured to the guard, and the guard opened the doors.

The court remained silent as the doors creaked open and footsteps echoed down the hall. Murmurs rose through the room as Erel joined Gaven's side.

It was gratifying that even the self-possessed Erel looked a little nervous standing in front of the Council. Mirari had stepped to the side so she could see the nervous twist of Erel's fingers as she held her hands behind her.

"Greetings, Councilors," Erel said, with a perfect bow.

"Raise your head," Novinha ordered.

She did. Mirari didn't have much cause to analyze Erel's face beforehand, but looking closely now she could say that while Erel and Soteria looked alike, they weren't identical. If they were standing side by side, Mirari might think Erel was looking to the future rather than looking into a mirror. Where Soteria had fine lines around her eyes and mouth and weather-roughened skin, Erel's features were smoother, younger by as much as a decade.

Mirari could tell by the pinched look on Dareh's face that others had also noticed. There was no way they were the same person. That didn't stop him from trying though.

"Can we confirm that Soteria is still located within her cell?" Dareh said.

Adder scoffed. "Aren't you trying too hard?" he said. "Have you forgotten that she came to us for help during the Siege? That she bravely led Gaven's army against their own leader?"

Tarek nodded. "That's right. Her loyalty to Althaea surpasses none."

"Fine then," Dareh said bitterly. "Lady Erel, make this simple for us. Why does our prisoner, the leader of the dissidents that have caused much death among the three empires, look so remarkably similar to you?"

Adder shook his head. "This is a waste of time."

"But it is a question on everyone's minds, is it not?" Novinha said, gesturing to Erel. "Please, speak."

Erel bowed again, hiding her face. "I'm afraid I don't have an answer. Before I was old enough to remember, my family left our village to try for a better life in the city. That is all I know. If I had other family in Althaea, my parents did not live long enough to tell me about them. I could be related to Soteria…" She lifted her head and spread her hands. "It's only speculation. That's all I know."

Adder drummed his hand against the arm of his chair. "Orphans are unfortunately common in Althaea." He turned to Dareh. "Are you satisfied or do you plan to have her arrested based on her looks?"

Dareh's face was flushed with anger. "I suppose we'll have to trust that this woman has no familial obligation then?"

Erel nodded. "Councilors, I assure you my loyalty cannot be swayed by some supposed blood ties to a woman I've never met before."

"And how can we trust your word?"

"Enough," Suzan said. "Erel has done nothing to warrant this scrutiny. It's time to move on."

"Councilors, I will gladly be under your watchful eyes until I've proven my loyalty." Erel must've known that was the best possible outcome.

"Well said," Tarek said with a nod. "If it's agreed, we should focus on what should be done to Soteria."

"What's there to discuss?" Julie said. "She'll be executed."

Mirari stared at Julie, but she did not waver. Did she really mean that? Was she not friends with Soteria?

"It should be a public execution," Dareh said. "This is nothing short of a celebration."

"I can agree with that," Adder nodded.

A spectacle. It sounded morbid and inappropriate, but Mirari knew better than to voice those thoughts. The councilors were finally in agreement. They were talking over each other only in their excitement that the death of a woman was something to be celebrated, and Soteria would be forced to stay within the walls of Althaea Main until her execution.

Mirari caught sight of Erel who was staring straight ahead. Her face was oddly blank, a great play against the Council, but Mirari could tell that her mind was lost.

Out of the corner of her eye, Mirari could see the Knights didn't look happy, but, of course, no one could say anything. To stand up for their enemy, or to argue for a more dignified death, would put a target on their back. There could be no hint of corruption or betrayal. They just had to accept the Council's word, and let this finally be over with.

A guard hustled over to Mirari to release her aulāce. She breathed a sigh of relief, wiggling her newly freed hands. The councilors began to make their way out of the courtroom. On the way out, Julie called two guards to the lower level.

"Don't let the prisoner out of your sight until she has been properly consigned to Inferna where she belongs," she said.

They nodded. Mirari watched the guards hustle toward the cells. So did Erel – watching the guards, she tightened her hands into fists behind her back.

"If that's all," Suzan said dryly, turning to Gaven, "you're dismissed."

Mirari, Gaven, and Erel bowed and walked out of the courtroom. Anything to get out from the scrutiny of the Council.

Once she was out of the doors, Mirari released a heavy sigh of relief. It went better than she expected, but of course not without the help of her allies, which, at first, she wasn't sure she still had. Smiling softly, Mirari decided to thank Gaven. She turned to him, but Erel was standing between them with a dark look in her eyes. The way she was worrying her bottom lip with her teeth made her look deeply unhappy, and Mirari's smile faded.

"Erel?" Mirari asked. "Is everything alright?"

The unhappiness slipped from Erel's face, evaporating away as easily as water. For a moment, she looked completely blank, just for a flicker, before a smile spread across her face too exuberant to be real.

"Look at you," she said, nudging Mirari's shoulder until she leaned away. "You're like a puppy. Will you wander back to Althaea Main with us?"

Was she invited? Mirari looked past her to Gaven, but she still didn't know what to make of his expression. He didn't say anything, his eyes unreadable. He reached down to touch his wrist where she could see something underneath his sleeve. Even if Gaven supported her during the trial, it didn't mean he forgave her for all her lies.

"I don't think so," Mirari said, looking away.

"Really?" Erel said. She sounded surprised, but Mirari nodded anyway.

"Not yet, at least. There are some things I need to take care of." She was hoping Gaven would give her an answer, but he was already walking to the main doors.

"Even if he doesn't say it, he wants you back," Erel said." You're welcome to visit any time." Erel bowed to her before joining her leader on the journey home.

"Mirari?" Overwhelmed by all the attention, Mirari sighed and turned around. Fangbane had descended from the spectator's stand and was approaching her. She didn't know what he was going to say. Was he happy? Angry? The mask didn't help, and she was tired of trying to read people's expressions. She would listen to what he had to say, anyway. It was better to face it sooner than later.

Mirari gave a small bow when he approached. Standing in front of her, he held out something shiny in his hand. She gasped and reached a hesitant hand toward him.

"I believe this is yours, isn't it?" he said. She could hear the beam in his voice. With an encouraging nod, she took it out of his hand. "Welcome back."

Her fingers curled around it. She didn't realize how much she missed the sight of the golden phoenix, if not the feeling of it in her palm.

"You're giving this back to me? But…" Words failed her and she stared speechlessly at the badge.

Fangbane nodded again. "The sacrifices you made for the three empires will not be forgotten," he said. "I want it known that no matter what happens, you are a member of the Knights. We will stand by you."

She smiled to herself. Surviving the trial was a luxury, but to have her old life back, her brother alive, and the Defiants defeated? What more could she ask for?

PART III

CHAPTER TWENTY

Mirari's room at the Knights' Estate was just as she left it. Even though there were no servants, someone – Starlight, no doubt – had dusted and cleaned in anticipation of her return. She ran her hands over her badge. In that cabin with Salathiel, she never imagined she'd be back here. Back and welcomed. She was smiling softly to herself when there was a knock at her door. She turned, expecting Starlight or Fangbane.

Lucan was leaning against the door frame. She couldn't tell what look his eyes held behind his white glasses and she stood, frozen.

"Can I come in?" he asked.

"Y-yes, of course," she said. She took a step back, and shut the door behind him. She didn't know what to say. He must have been devastated when Gaven reported her death. She felt guilty that she hadn't been able to reassure him, but it was too dangerous to do so.

"Mirari…"

She took a breath and gathered her courage. "Lucan, I'm sorry," she said. "I know I should have – but I couldn't—" She shook her head. "There's no excuse—"

He wrapped his arms around her, cutting off the unintelligible flow of words. He didn't say anything, just held her. She gripped his soft shirt. "Lucan, I'm sorry," she muttered. "I didn't mean to hurt you again."

"It's okay," he said, his whispers inviting her to his safe haven. "You don't have to apologize. I understand. I know why you did it."

She frowned and pulled back. She didn't know if she should just let him live with his misconceptions.

"Lucan, there's a lot you don't know."

"Ah, let's sit?" He motioned toward the settee and they sat down on opposite ends. He lifted his hand to fiddle with his glasses. "You may be right that I don't know everything that happened, but there's a lot you don't know either."

"What do you mean?"

He smiled at her. "You think you're the only one who had an adventure these past few months?" He smiled. "I meant what I said. I am proud of you. I spent these few months trying to make *you* proud."

"Lucan...?"

"When Gaven first told everyone that you were," he took a breath, "dead, I was in denial. I didn't want to believe it. I had to know what happened... and I found the truth."

Mirari thought about it and guessed, "Gaven?"

He shook his head. "Inigo."

Mirari blinked in surprise and he laughed.

"Don't worry, I took care of him. He won't bother you anymore."

"What do you mean? You confronted him?" she asked.

He smiled, a little melancholy. "I have an idea. I understand what happened and why you had to go into hiding for your own safety." He ran his hand over her hair. "What will you do now?"

Mirari bit her lip. "I need to go to Solarin."

"A little trip home? You deserve it."

Mirari chuckled. Home? She couldn't call it that exactly. She had yet to decide whether to return to her life as a Knight, or as a merchant of Solarin.

Crouching down, Mirari used her hand to wipe the dead leaves off the grave. Only a few months ago, she'd thought she'd never return to Solarin but here she was. All that was missing now was Salathiel. He was likely back at Julie's cabin, but at least she knew he was in safe hands. Smiling lightly, she traced her fingers over the words engraved on the tombstones.

"I found him," she said. "Joachim, I found Sal." Spring was arriving and small mortwort buds were starting to sprout on the grave site. Wrapping her cloak around her shoulders, she settled down against the tree Joachim had been buried underneath. Closing her eyes, she tilted her head up toward the sun. "And Gaven… he knows who I am now."

"That's good to hear."

Mirari's eyes shot open. It wasn't Joachim. It didn't even sound like him. Kylah stood in front of her, amusement lurking in her bright, red eyes. Still stunningly beautiful, Kylah looked more like a goddess. Placing her hand over her chest, Mirari slumped back against the tree, exhaling loudly. "You just about scared me to death."

"I hope not." Kylah closed the distance and sat on the other side of Joachim's grave. "Not after you just came back." Her raised eyebrow spoke louder than her words.

Blushing, Mirari tightened her grip on her cloak. "Aha, yeah. Sorry."

Kylah let the words sit before she leaned in and said, "I'm not mad."

Mirari examined her more closely and, to her surprise, she really didn't seem angry. She was more settled than the last time she'd been at Mirari's house. Her shoulders were looser and she no longer had that pinched, haunted look in her eye. Kylah glanced at her and quickly looked away. To Mirari's shock, she actually blushed, a light dusting of red that brought out her natural beauty even more.

"Kylah?"

She fidgeted and if she didn't look so happy Mirari would actually have been worried. Elegantly tucking her legs under herself, Kylah fully met Mirari's gaze. Tossing her hair back like she was declaring war, Kylah announced, "Neo and I are getting married."

"Really?" A series of nods. "Kylah! That's great! That's wonderful." Mirari pulled her into a hug. "I'm so happy for you. When is it? And where?"

"Starlight has offered the Knights' Estate. It seems fitting since it's because of the Knights that we met. And it'll be in two weeks, plenty of time after the execution."

They grimaced. It's not that they didn't want the leader of the Defiants dealt with, it just felt in bad taste for the Council to glorify her death.

"Everyone's going to be there?" Mirari asked to spin the conversation away from the grim topic.

"Yes and…" Kylah appeared shy again. "I was hoping you would stand with me during the ceremony. My siblings won't be there and I don't really have any other—"

Mirari reached out and grabbed her hands. Kylah snapped her mouth closed.

"I'd be honored."

"Thanks, that's… that's really nice to hear."

Mirari grinned. For the most part, everything was going well.

"Oh," Mirari said, remembering. "Did you hear what I was saying earlier?"

"Some of it."

"About Sal?"

"Sal?" She tilted her head.

"He's alive," Mirari said with a bright smile. "I found him, and he's… well." Mirari didn't know how else to put it.

"Invite him to the wedding," Kylah said.

"Really?"

"Yes, of course." Reaching into her bag, she pulled out a thick paper and held it on her lap. "It'll be good to see him again. And I want everyone there. *Everyone*." She stared Mirari down, running her hand over her bag. She reached out and Mirari accepted the thick paper that Kylah pushed into her hand.

"What's this?"

"Gaven's invitation."

Mirari tried to give it back but Kylah primly folded her hands on her lap.

"Why are you giving this to me?"

"Because someone has to deliver it to him."

"But I'm—"

"Avoiding him?"

Caught, Mirari pressed her lips together. "You finally have no secrets with him, and yet, you're here, hiding." She flicked her fingers toward the invitation held gingerly in Mirari's hand. "Take that to him and talk to him."

Mirari's shoulders slumped and she nodded. She would have to face him sooner or later.

CHAPTER TWENTY-ONE

The wedding invitation felt like it was burning a hole in her pocket. Back in Althaea Main, Mirari was slow to approach the fort. Keeping her hood up, she wandered through the plaza. Soldiers marched the streets, as they always did, but it was vastly different than the last time she had been there. The soldiers were doing simple patrols and people neither fled at the sight of them nor roused each other to rebellion. It was calm.

Mirari stopped at one of the stalls in the plaza. She pretended to look over the wares while she listened for any rumors.

"I recognize you!"

She snapped her head up. The merchant was vaguely familiar but she wasn't sure she knew him. Uneasy, she started to draw back, but he reached a meaty hand out to grab her wrist.

"Or rather I recognize that bracelet," he said.

She followed his gaze down at the feathered bracelet adorning her wrist. She'd almost forgotten it. She glanced at his stall, and saw more bracelets like hers, each a unique variation.

"Let's see now." He held her wrist up to his eye and examined the piece. He hastily let go, likely remembering exactly who had brought it for her. "Oh. Sorry, Miss. I mean… Milady." He bowed.

She shook her head. "Please, none of that." The last thing she needed was to attract attention.

"I mean no harm to the region leader's partner. Please forgive me." He bowed twice more.

She kept her composure, but felt unsettled. "You're forgiven. Please stop bowing. I'm not even— I'm not—"

"Oh, I get it." The merchant lifted his head and winked at her. "I understand."

Mirari didn't know what he "understood", but at least he'd stopped groveling. She fidgeted, searching for something to change the conversation.

"How has everything been?" she asked.

"Much better," he said with a bobbing nod. "Thanks to you and His Honor."

"Me?"

"Of course. Everyone's heard about what you did for Althaea Main. I admit, not many people expected much from a, uh, Minettan—" He waved his hands in front of him. "Not me, course… I always loved Minettans, and Valenians. Everyone!" He scratched the back of his head. "But people here, they've certainly changed their tunes now. People are telling me, "You were right. Minettans are good"." He gestured to the jewelry in his stall. "Finally, they see the beauty."

Mirari smiled. "That is good to hear."

"Slow and steady." He nodded with glee. "Spiritel and the Spirit Soldiers are helping too, no doubt."

She didn't know who the Spirit Soldiers were but she could guess. "Why don't you tell me about them?" she said.

"Oh, of course, of course." He winked at her and she had to resist the urge to smile at his enthusiasm. He told her there had been quite a few sightings. "They keep us safe from the wicked, unlike the Council. No offense, Miss. The Council likes to turn the other way."

It sounded like her friends from the Blessed were continuing their fight against the dregs of the Defiants. She was glad they were able to shake off the stigma the Blessed had acquired from leaders like Laikos and Soteria. She wished them well.

She thanked him for the stories. Smiling, she waved and walked away.

It was nice to feel warmth in a neighborhood that once drove her out. She doubted she would get the same treatment when she headed into the fort. What exactly did Gaven say about her? Did people still assume she was his partner? Either way, she wasn't looking forward to finding out.

<hr>

Mirari was able to pass through the fortress gates with ease. With her chest out and chin held high, she wandered into the courtyard. She was met with a few curious eyes, but for the most part, she did not recognize anyone. Gaven must've hired more soldiers since her departure.

"Lady Mirari!" Mirari jumped as Haynes approached her at a gangly run. Behind him, Erel approached, much more sedately. That was her only warning before Haynes swept her up in a crushing hug.

"It's good to see you," he said.

She patted him on the shoulder and rocked back when he finally set her down.

"You too," she chuckled.

"Don't look so nervous." He wrapped his arm around her shoulder and jostled her some more. "We knew you'd come back, but it would've been nice to be let in on the plan." He scowled, but the playful twitch of his lips let her know he didn't really mean it.

"Can you blame her?" Erel said, coming to a stop in front of them. "Taking part in a secret mission? I'm not sure you've ever heard of the concept of whispering." Haynes tried to protest, but she just pushed him aside and took his place at Mirari's side.

"Did you know?" Mirari asked.

"Of course," Erel said. She raised her eyebrows. Had Gaven told her *everything*? Erel started dragging her toward the fort. "Come on."

"Where are we going?" Mirari asked.

"I thought you came here to see him. He's been in quite the mood since he returned from the Hearth. I think he was missing somebody. Hmm, what do you think?" Erel smirked, leaning in and pressing her cheek against Mirari's. Mirari felt her face heat up, and she pushed her away.

"Wait till you see what we've done to the West Wing," Haynes said, blooming with excitement. He pointed to the building across the courtyard. "You must visit the outpost. The guards have dubbed it the vacation house."

They let Haynes babble on until they reached Gaven's study. Whatever he was saying, Mirari wasn't listening. She was frozen with indecision. Of course, Erel couldn't just let her take her time. The woman reached over Mirari's shoulder and rapped loudly on the wood.

"Go on," she said, slapping Mirari on the back. "I know you're not a coward."

Erel grabbed Haynes by his collar and walked away before Mirari could say anything.

"Enter."

She tensed, but opened the door anyway. Gaven did a double take when he saw her standing in the doorway. He got to his feet slowly. "Come in."

Shutting the door behind her, she walked in and sat in the chair he motioned toward. She wrung her hands together and stared down at his desk to avoid his gaze. This was the first time they could talk properly and she didn't know what to say. They had worked well together in the battle, but now that their blood had cooled, Mirari didn't know what was left of them.

"Gav—"

"Mir—"

They fell silent and looked at each other.

"You go—"

"You can—"

Mirari chuckled – but Gaven did not – and she covered her mouth. She motioned for Gaven to go first.

"Why didn't you tell me?" Gaven asked and the smile fell from her face.

That was the crux of the matter. The lies. She didn't know how to describe their relationship now. It was intimate, at least before she betrayed him and built a brick wall between them. No, that wall had stood from the day they reunited on the battlefield of the Althaean Siege. His eyes held such disdain that she had lost her nerve. She had realized it was naive to think he'd even care who she was. They chose to hide their true selves from each other. She wanted to tear down that wall, and she believed Gaven felt the same.

"I thought…" Mirari paused, "you wanted nothing to do with us." Gaven had a pinched look on his face. She couldn't tell what it meant. She continued, "Sal warned me that you wouldn't care."

"You believe in everything he says?" Mirari was taken aback by his sharp words. He must've realized this and shook his head. "Nevermind. This isn't about him." He gestured to her. "Please, elaborate."

Mirari looked down at her hands. Rubbing the bracelet on her wrist, she reassured herself that Gaven always meant well underneath whatever he said. He was different from the Gaven of her childhood, but it was also her fault that she didn't accept the person he had become. The corner of her mouth ticked up in a somber smile.

"You were… different," she said. "I expected Gaven Zanette, but I met the Valiant Tiger." He looked hurt, and that wasn't what she wanted. She waved her hands around to show she was talking about all he had accomplished. "You have made a name for yourself. I thought bringing up Roselyn would be…"

"Pointless?"

"That you wanted to forget her."

"Bah!" She jumped at the harsh sound. Gaven stood up and walked around the desk. Stopping in front of her, he leaned back against the desk. "I never forgot Roselyn." She watched him rub his thumb over something on his wrist under his sleeve. "I *never* forgot my promise to Roselyn."

"Promise?"

He snorted and pulled up his sleeve. She gasped and reached out her hand, stopping before she touched the necklace wrapped around his wrist.

"Is that…?"

"I was supposed to return this, remember?"

She curled her hand to her chest. "I remember."

He pushed away from the desk and walked behind her. She brushed her hair over her shoulder so that he could reach around and settle the necklace around her throat.

"The kirinvā stone," he said, clipping the gem around her neck. "Infused with the power of the Gods, it protects the bearer." He placed his hands on her shoulder. "Even if I don't believe in Gods, it certainly worked for me. You protected me all these years. Not just as Roselyn, but as Mirari." He paused. "You've given so much to me."

Mirari hesitated, lifting her hand to fiddle with her newly returned necklace. Though it had been forever since she laid hands on it, the edges felt familiar. She clenched her fist around it.

He stepped away, returning to his side of the desk and pretended to be fixated on the soldiers drilling outside the window. He pursed his lips and asked, "Would you want to be partners again?"

She held her breath. *Did* she want to be partners with him again? Yes, of course. More than anything. However, she wasn't sure if that was wise. There was so much baggage between them. Could they really go back to how things were before?

"It's fine," Gaven said. "Forget I said anything."

She jumped to her feet. "No, wait. It's not that I don't want to, it's…" She hugged herself, turning away from him. "I lied to you."

Gaven sat back down and folded his hands in front of him. "We were both hiding who we were. Things will be different this time. I know it."

Mirari curled her lip. There was something else.

"And… I have yet to tell you about my ability."

"I don't care."

"W-what?"

"You heard me." He motioned toward her eyes, "none of that changes my mind."

"You don't even know—"

"And I don't need to. All I know is that…" He cleared his throat and averted his gaze. "I'm not myself without you. Whatever you're going through, we'll face it together. No matter what happens, I'll be by your side."

Mirari swallowed her breath. With a skip in her step, she pounced on him, wrapping him in her arms. He tightly embraced her back, his fingers playing with the end of her curls.

"Mirari Zanette," he paused, "no, Roselyn Hale, give me the honor of serving you till my dying breath."

He pulled her away, squeezing her shoulders tightly before letting go. Gaven lowered to the ground on one knee. He took his compact spear from his belt and extended it, laying it out before her.

"I hereby request your alliance to become my eyes and ears in the time of uncertainty."

The spear illuminated and it made her feel safe. She nodded, her lips curling into a smile. Touching the spear, she felt a wave of energy surge through her, and she felt Gaven's familiar warmth.

"Gaven Zanette, by my blood, I swear to be your sword and shield in the battles to come."

Their breaths aligned like their souls and a feeling of calm washed over Mirari. She felt no sense of regret, just rightness. She grinned, laying her hand over her chest.

"That's it then." He smiled. "You'll be sticking around now, won't you?"

Before coming to Althaea Main, she didn't have an answer. She realized that she made her decision by coming here, but she wasn't sure if she was entirely happy with it. What about Salathiel? Could he accept the fact that she had chosen to be partners with Gaven again? Would he be alright if she chose being a Knight over the life she had with him?

Just then, Mirari remembered the reason she was in Althaea Main.

"I have this for you," she said, reaching into her pocket and producing the crisp invitation. "Kylah and Neo are getting married. It's being held at the Knights' Estate and Kylah wanted me to deliver this to you." He accepted the paper. "You'll be there, won't you?"

"Sure."

"Kylah also said I could invite Sal." His face soured and she could feel his dissatisfaction. She touched her chest. She'd forgotten how it felt to have his feelings with her. "Don't be like that," she admonished. "Sal is Kylah's friend too."

Gaven furrowed his brow. "Really?"

His gaze briefly shifted to the ground. He may have realized that there was lost time to catch up on, and the many things he didn't know about Mirari before she became a Knight.

"Could you tell me everything that happened while I was gone?" he said, his eyes sincere. "I mean it. I want to know what you and Sal have been up to all these years."

Mirari smiled. "Of course."

CHAPTER TWENTY-TWO

Erel was back at the Hearth, but for the first time, it was her own desire. Confinement to the fortress meant nothing to her. She could slip out and back before anyone noticed. It was an urgent matter. She needed to see the leader of the Defiants for herself.

The security around the Hearth had increased but it was no trouble for Erel to navigate. She molded herself into one of the guards. She'd been doing it for so long and so often, she had a solid routine to get herself exactly where she needed to be. Erel made her way through, heading down into the dungeons once again. It was easy to exchange pleasantries with the guard on duty while he packed up his things and left.

She stood with her back to the door, long enough for the guards to settle after the shift changes. Erel silently sifted through the keys and opened the door. She counted down the seconds – ten minutes before the next guard took her place.

She swung the door closed behind her and held the lumas-tōne up toward the woman chained to the wall. To Erel's ears, her slow steps sounded loud in the enclosed room.

Erel took in the face she'd thought she'd only see in the mirror. It was just like Gaven had said.

Crouching down, Erel shifted back into her disguise, a twin to the prisoner. She positioned herself at eye-level.

Erel curled her hand against her back to keep from reaching out. "Eir?"

Soteria went still like prey that caught the scent of a predator. Her familiar brown eyes widened in shock. Eyebrows pinched together, she searched Erel's identical face.

Eir shifted in high alert and scowled, "You're one of them, aren't you? Shapeshifter!"

It was her. Her childhood friend who she had loved and thought she had lost. How could it be?

"Eir…"

Squeezing her eyes closed, Soteria shook her head. "Don't call me that. Do *not* call me that." When she opened her eyes, her gaze was cold and strict. "I rejected that name decades ago. I've discarded that name like I've discarded the heathens that called me it. I am Soteria."

"You are Eir," Erel said, managing to keep her voice down. Rising, she started pacing the few steps from one end to the next. "What have you done to yourself?"

"I did what the gods wanted."

Erel dropped her gaze to the floor. Eir confirmed a theory she didn't want to believe.

"Laikos took you that night, didn't he?"

"He *saved* me."

With Erel's hand down by her side, her face was obscured by shadows. That didn't stop Soteria from squinting at Erel's face. The chains creaked as Soteria pushed herself up on her knees. Her face twisted in a sneer that warped her features harshly.

"The Belligmn Tribe lost their way," Soteria continued. "They were supposed to continue providing the goddesses with sacrifices. You were cowards. You ran from your duty and you brought on the curse!"

"There is no curse," Erel said. "Laikos lied to you. Our Gods would never ask us to kill others."

"You all deserved to die!"

Erel was stoic under Soteria's onslaught of cruel words while inwardly, she cursed what had happened. Eir had been a kind-hearted girl. Gentle and brave. She'd gone back to their burning homes in a desperate attempt to save Erel's family. It broke Erel's heart to see how much Eir had changed.

Soteria's clothes were ripped and her injuries untreated, but she drew herself up as much as she could, still so brave.

"Do not cower behind false skins," she said. "Show me your true form and face judgment!"

Erel lifted her hand to her face. Indeed, now was not the time for a facade. If she hoped to reach Eir, even a little, she would have to show herself as she truly was. The sorrow on her face faded in an instant, and Erel mirrored Soteria's stance so that she could see Erel fully in the light of the lumastōne. Her hair grew long and lightened to a pale green. She stood to her tall, willowy height and looked on the woman whose form she had used for years.

"You… you're one of the royals?" Her gaze was running over Erel's hair like she had never seen anything more disgusting. "You, more than anyone, must face death as is the will of the gods."

Erel kept a straight face, but her heart was anything but calm.

"Is that what Laikos told you when he murdered my family?" Erel asked with grace.

"Master…" Soteria shook her head, rattling the chains. She looked pained, gazing the distance. "He… he showed me the truth. He had so much left to do. Why? Why did she take him?"

"Eir," Erel continued, wanting to reach her. "Do you

remember me? I'm Erel." Soteria continued to shake. "When we parted, you were going to save my family. Do you remember? What happened? Eir, what happened to you?"

THE WAY back felt infinitely shorter. Eir forced herself to keep going forward even as the heat grew thicker and she began stumbling upon bodies of those that hadn't made it far. She skulked around the edge of the clearing, heading toward the tent of the prince and princess. She had her own dagger, a gift from Erel, and she began cutting her way through the thick material just as when she and Erel had escaped.

Her shaking hands felt clumsy as she carved a back entrance into the hut. Forcing the burlap aside, she crawled through the tiny opening. Something wet touched her hand.

She yelped, slapping her hand over her mouth. Small bodies were discarded on the ground. They were still in bed and she prayed that they hadn't felt the hand of death descend.

A strong hand gripped her ankles. She screamed as she was pulled from the hut with force, banging her elbow on the side of the hole and dropping her dagger. A grim-faced man grabbed her wrist when she tried to fight her way loose. His other hand released her leg to grab her brown hair and haul her to her feet.

"Let me go! Let me—" He hit her in the face. Ears ringing and head spinning, she didn't come back to herself until he dropped her like a sack of dirty laundry on the ground. Blinking dizzily, she met the blank gaze of one of the elders. The blood that spilled from the gaping wound at his throat was already drying at the edges.

Crying, she scrambled upright and looked around. She was in the center of the village with the heat from the burning huts bearing down on her. The man who had grabbed her was retreating, searching for more survivors, but she wasn't alone. Aside from the bodies of the elders, she was captured alongside Rauf and Elysande, Erel's parents. They both had their arms bound behind their back. They were on their knees and held in place by two brutish men. Bruised and bloodied, they looked like they had fought valiantly before being subdued. Rauf was listing to the side but he perked up with muted horror when he saw Eir.

A man stalked into view, stopping to tower over her. Tall and graceful, he jeered at her with smug disdain. He grabbed her hair, tilting her head back. He was tall and imposing and he spoke in a confident and commanding voice.

"Who's this, little bird?" he asked, glancing over to the king and queen. His navy hair fell loosely down his back and over his monk's robes.

Elysande was glancing around like she feared Erel would be the next dragged out. After all, they were always together. Pressing her lips together, Eir met the gaze of Elysande and tried to project an aura of calm. There was no way to tell Erel's parents that she was safe without revealing it to this priest who stood coldly over the murdered elders.

"Let her go, Laikos," Rauf hissed. "She's nothing. Have some honor."

Laikos raised an arrogant eyebrow. She whimpered when he dragged her closer to the royal couple. "Nothing, you say? Then what was she doing skulking about in your children's tent?" Laikos ridiculed her with dispassionate curiosity. "Thieving?"

"No, no," Eir said, tugging uselessly at her hair. "I'm just a servant. Please, please let me go. I just do the laundry. I don't know anything."

"A servant?"

"Only a servant," Elysande said. The young serving girl had never seen such disappointment in Elysande before. "She's a servant with no abilities. All she's good for is doing laundry."

Laikos eyes gleamed with satisfaction. Eir started crying when he raised a blood-stained dagger. "If she's good for nothing else, she'll make a worthy sacrifice."

"Laikos!" Rauf roared. He jerked forward, almost breaking free from the grip of his guard. "You're a monster. You say you're working for the Goddesses, but you're only following your own evil doings. The Goddesses would not want you to murder a child."

Eir cringed away from the darkness that crossed Laikos' face. He released her abruptly to turn on Rauf. He approached slowly, walking with a coiled grace like a briar snake ready to strike.

"I am a messenger for the Goddesses," he said, speaking in a low, almost soothing voice. Rauf straightened his back and lifted his chin, meeting Laikos gaze without fear. "I have received their word. You and the rest of your tribe have turned your back on your duties. For your disobedience…" He raised the dagger diagonally over his head. "The Goddesses have deemed the Belligmn Tribe to be wiped out." He brought the blade down and across.

Blood spurted out of Elysande, arcing far enough that it splashed across Eir's legs.

"Elysande!" Rauf screamed. He lunged forward, trying to catch his wife as she collapsed on the ground, choking and gasping. He bent over her body until she stopped convulsing and went still.

Eir was shaking. She tried backing up but ran into the legs of the man who had captured her. Arms crossed, he barely spared her a look.

Snarling, Rauf jumped to attack Laikos, aiming to ram into his legs. The two guards grabbed him and forced him to the ground. He was almost rabid.

Laikos was only amused as the king's face was ground into the dirt. He started pacing easily between Eir and Rauf. Sighing, his voice took on a fatherly tone.

"Honestly, Headmaster, what did you think was going to happen? The Belligmn Tribe used to be good and devout, dutifully bringing sacrifices to our Goddesses. What happened?"

"These sacrifices do not align with true Moranity," Rauf said. "You should be ashamed of yourself. The shapeshifters will no longer be assassins for some twisted understanding of the Goddesses' will."

Laikos stopped and slowly turned to face him. He motioned with his hand and the guards jerked Rauf back to his knees. Eir could see their muscles bulging as they struggled to keep him in place. Laikos walked forward, each step measured and purposeful.

"Such blasphemous words." He flicked the blood from the dagger and held the blade up to his eye. "I see now why I was granted a divine revelation." He nodded toward the guards and settled his hand on Rauf's shoulder, ignoring the curses that poured from his lips. "You should be grateful that despite your disobedience the Goddesses will take your life as a sacrifice."

"To Inferna with—" Laikos jabbed the dagger into Rauf's chest, twisting it with cruelty.

Eir slapped her hands over her mouth as she watched the life drain from Rauf's eyes. Laikos pulled the dagger free and the Blessed let Rauf collapse next to Elysande.

"No, no please!" Eir begged, weeping and shaking. She was caged between the guards and the monk with nowhere to run. She didn't want to die.

Laikos crouched in front of her. She could only fear the dagger held in his hand until he grabbed her chin and forced her gaze up. His hand was cold and dry as he tilted her head, examining her. A dark feeling crawled through her mind.

"The Goddesses' word was that no shapeshifter should live because of their disobedience. If you're truly not one of the shapeshifters then you are one of the Blessed." His words echoed through her mind like tremors of a sandworm as he burrowed deep within her very being. "Reject the Belligmn Tribe, for now you can serve the Goddesses as I do."

She screamed, but it did nothing to drown out his voice.

"The only will is the Goddesses' will. Your only reason is for the Goddesses. Think of nothing else and you will have salvation."

Eir jerked and wailed, trying to escape to no avail. She could feel her memories eroding under the onslaught. Memories of her kind-hearted lady and the tribe she had loyally served, all eaten away like termites in a barbed yucca. Gone. All gone.

When she opened her eyes, Laikos was smiling gently at her. "There you are."

A BROAD SMILE formed on Soteria's face.

"Laikos taught me the truth and opened my eyes to the world as it is," she said, tilting her chin up and meeting Erel's gaze boldly. "It was the will of the Goddesses that all of the shapeshifters should die. They failed in their duties and have been consigned to death." She looked at the dagger in Erel's boot and her gaze faltered. "You should fall on your blade and give yourself over to the Goddesses as I have done."

Erel lowered her head in mourning and dropped her hand to her dagger, running her fingers over the hilt. The realization of what had happened to Eir was a heavy truth. She must have been in torment all these years.

"Don't look down on me," Soteria spat. "I am the fortunate. I am the Blessed." Her lashes fluttered as she blinked rapidly. "Lachess rewarded me with her gift." Soteria raised her palms at Erel as if she expected something to be there. "She speaks through me and it is by her will that I follow the true path."

Mind warped, she could only preach what Laikos had put into her head. He had killed Erel's family and burned her tribe to the ground. Erel had lost her security and status. She had lost her friend. Erel was grateful that Laikos was already dead. She only wished she had been the one to take his life. But there was one last thing she could do.

She shrank back, sad for her lost friend. Erel pictured the gallows being erected in the public square. Soon it would fill with people coming from all over to observe the execution. They would trot her out like a show horse and kill her in some messed up, gruesome show.

Wrapping her hand around the hilt of her dagger, she bowed her head.

"For my friend who sacrificed everything for me and for my family," Erel drew her dagger, "I won't let them make a mockery of your death. You were my best friend and I'll never forget you."

Blinking through the tears forming in her eyes, she took a breath and held the blade steady. She met her dull eyes, faded from the shine that once gave her the courage to live.

Leaning forward, she placed the tip of the blade against Eir's chest. Eir closed her eyes, unafraid and unresisting. Erel ached for her living features one last time. The form she had chosen hadn't been exactly Eir but Erel's interpretation of what she would look like as an adult. There were some differences, but Erel still thought the beauty of Eir's noble spirit shone through.

"This is the last thing I can do for you." She thrust the dagger forward, piercing her heart. With a sigh, Eir slumped forward into Erel's waiting arms.

Erel pulled the dagger from Eir's body and started arranging her shirt to cover the wound. She unlocked the chains and drew a cut across her neck with a spare dagger that she left in Eir's hand. Her body was arranged neatly, and for the last time, she was at peace.

Pausing, Erel frowned and leaned over to inspect her neck more closely. Black sludge oozed from the wound and she found it mirrored on the dagger. She had seen the unsettling sight once before when she had fought the man right before the battle in Rhea.

"The curse," she muttered. "It's real."

Now, she realized, she couldn't keep that secret to herself any longer.

CHAPTER TWENTY-THREE

The Knights' Estate was decorated with streams of white banners and pink and yellow florals. Fangbane wrapped his arms around Starlight's shoulders as he watched the normally stoic Kylah express her heart. She was nearly in tears as she recited the vows she had prepared.

The gathering for the wedding was small; just the Knights and their families. Mirari's eyes were bright, even though her thoughts were bitter from Salathiel's lack of presence. Even Shiba's face was more sweet than bitter. He was, no doubt, thinking of Mecate and what could have been. Fangbane didn't need to read his mind to know that.

Starlight had outdone herself decorating the Estate. With Lucan's help, elaborate floral arrangements had been brought in. The Knights were standing outside, eyes fixed on the beaming couple standing underneath an arch draped with ailolia and goldenglow flowers. The backs of the two rows of chairs were covered with sugarbloom to match the color scheme of soft pink and forest green.

Fangbane glanced to his right at Dorain, who had his full attention on the newlyweds, genuinely happy for them.

He leaned in, whispering to Dorain, "It's good to have you back."

Dorain awkwardly grinned, nodding once to Fangbane, then quickly turning away. Something pained him inside. There was no doubt that some of the Knights, particularly Shiba, were still giving him trouble for leaving the Knights. He hadn't quite been welcomed back yet, and certainly not as the hero he deserved to be seen as.

Just a few weeks prior, Dorain stood by his father's side. It was no surprise that he was back with the Knights after his bold stance against Dareh during Mirari's trial. The Council may have praised his insight, but Dareh could never stand to be made a fool. Fangbane could tell that Dorain had no regrets. In fact, Dorain never truly wanted to leave the Knights. He took advantage of his family ties to influence the Council from the inside, but he never intended to work for his father. Fangbane was happy to return Dorain's badge, but he wouldn't be able to predict what trick Dorain would try to pull next.

"I'm sure it would have taken longer without your aid," Fangbane continued. "A lot of lives were saved thanks to your sacrifice." He inclined his head. "Thank you."

Dorain's face cleared and he looked bashful again. "Oh, yeah. I— I just wanted to do my part."

Fangbane smiled. He wanted his Knights to get along. He was looking forward to things returning to normal.

Starlight reached out to tug on Sarkan's shirt. He'd been well-behaved during the majority of the ceremony but his patience was waning and he was playing with the flowers on the back of his chair.

Gaven's clove lit up and he slipped away from the group with a grimace. He wasn't gone long, returning just before Neo and Kylah made their first walk as a married couple. Fangbane didn't think even Mirari had noticed he was missing. Fangbane approached Gaven as they prepared to move inside for the continued festivities after the ceremony was over.

"Is everything all right?" he asked.

"It's fine," Gaven said and his thoughts mirrored his words. Raising an eyebrow, Fangbane glanced at his clōve. "Fang, relax." He patted Fangbane roughly on his shoulder. "It's a celebration."

Fangbane sighed. Just as he was about to agree, his own clōve lit up. He glanced between it and Gaven who only shrugged and headed inside.

Fangbane was surprised to have Suzan's voice filter through the clōve. "Suzan," he said. "What's happened?"

She laughed. "I'm sure Gaven's already told you, but I'm just making sure you know." Fangbane remained silent as Suzan spoke about the death of their prisoner. No wonder Gaven hadn't been upset to hear it. "We've conducted our investigation and believe Soteria killed herself."

Fangbane frowned, doubting the results of the investigation. "How?"

"A hidden blade," Suzan responded promptly. "A clean cut to the neck." Fangbane's lips parted to question her more, but she blew out a frustrated sigh. "Fang, I know what you're about to say. There's no greater conspiracy or plot. She was crazed and probably giddy at the idea of reuniting with Laikos. That's it."

His shoulders slumped and he was glad the others had already gone inside. "Very well. Thank you for telling me."

"I'll leave it up to you when to tell Shiba," she said.

"Me?" He was incredulous. "Isn't it the Councilor's job to inform their respective region leaders?"

She scoffed. "Considering his partner is getting married, I thought it was prudent for you to inform him when you thought the time was right and it wouldn't interrupt the ceremony. Can I count on you?"

Fangbane had to be satisfied with that. It was a shock that the councilors from Minetta had managed any type of compromise with the ones from Althaea. "Yes. I'll inform the others at the end of the reception."

"Good." They exchanged a few more pleasantries before Suzan hung up.

Curling his hand into his fist, Fangbane took a calming breath and pressed his hand to his chest. He needed to stop rummaging for something to rattle this peace that was slowly settling. The Blessed had been silenced. Kylah and Neo were married. Gaven and Mirari had repaired their relationship. Things were… good. He should be happy that things were returning to normal.

"Not quite," a voice called.

He whirled around. Only this one could consistently manage to surprise him. "Sorren."

"Sorry, Father," Sorren said, not appearing sorry at all. Fangbane didn't expect him to come to the wedding, especially since he didn't want others to know that he was Fangbane's son. "I just spoke with Mother and Sarkan. They seem to be doing well."

"We enjoy seeing you. You should visit more often," Fangbane said in the sincerest way he could. He paused. "But you're not here for the wedding, are you?"

A small frown was curling around his lips. Then Fangbane registered what Sorren said, or rather thought. A warning from him had to be considered carefully.

"Sorren, what do you mean things are getting worse?"

He shook his head. "I heard about Soteria, but, unfortunately, it doesn't end with her."

"Have the Blessed not been defeated?"

Sorren looked off into the distance, seeing something beyond them. "You didn't kill the root of the issue. I don't know for certain what will happen, but…"

"But?"

"Six years ago, remember how I told you to let Mirari cross

the border with us? To fight the Althaean Siege? It was on the condition that she would not fight." His eyebrow arched. "Sure, she helped end the siege, but the path she chose... has consequences."

Scanning his son's mind, Fangbane lurched forward in shock.

He shook his head. "Haven't you learned better by now than to read my mind?"

"Is that all true?" Fangbane stuttered. Shaking his head, he calmed his breathing and focused on the present. Sorren lowered his gaze. He didn't need to answer. "And it's inevitable?"

Fangbane wasn't sure why he asked. Sorren's visions were never wrong. He saw the world consumed in fire, violence, and death. There was no one left. Not the Council, not the Knights. Fangbane even saw his own corpse skewered in front of the burning estate. His death wasn't what concerned him, however. No one would be left to stop these forces. He didn't know the cause or how such destruction came to be, but he was sure that if he continued reading Sorren's mind, he would see all three empires in ashes.

Clearing his throat, Sorren spoke, "That's the worst case scenario. If you do exactly as I say, we can drastically mitigate the damage."

Laughter floated from inside the building, taunting them to return to the festivities. But how could Fangbane celebrate knowing what he just saw?

Sorren continued, "I've thought about this a lot, Father, and there is no alternative. Do you know of Fate's Fable? The Goddesses Cygnus and Lachess?"

He shook his head. "Can't say I do."

"You should." Sorren glanced over his shoulder at the celebrations before turning his attention back on Fangbane. "You need to return to the reception. Act like you didn't hear any of this. I'll be in touch."

Sorren fixed his tie – not that it mattered – and proceeded down the arch that led out of the estate.

"Sorren, wait," Fangbane said, reaching out his hand. The Althaean Siege was bad, and they had just barely stopped the Blessed. But this? He swallowed his breath before continuing, "What is the best case scenario?"

Sorren narrowed his eyes. He didn't give his father the pleasure of digging into his mind this time. Turning around, Sorren left Fangbane with a final message.

"If you knew, you wouldn't be able to do it."

CHAPTER TWENTY-FOUR

A few weeks had passed since Kylah and Neo's wedding. Fangbane had been feeling a pressing sense of urgency, but he knew he had to tread carefully before pushing the Knights about Sorren's warning.

Sorren's instructions were delivered later through a carrier pigeon to ensure the message was clear and discreet. He was right, Fangbane didn't like the plan. But to prevent what he saw in Sorren's mind, he was left with no choice. He had to put away his selfishness to ensure everyone else's safety.

Fangbane waited for days, maintaining an air of happiness and peace until he finally saw the opportunity to execute the plan. Starlight, Hime, and Mirari were having supper when he caught wind of Mirari's passing thoughts. She was sulking at her soup, scooping up a spoonful and letting it trail off her spoon over and over again until it was cool enough to drink. He would seize this opportunity.

"Have you heard from Kylah or Neo?" Fangbane asked.

"Yes, they'll be returning soon," Starlight said with a smile on her gentle face.

"It's nice to spend some time away after all that's happened," Hime said, nodding in conversation with Starlight.

"That's good," Mirari said. She had her hand on her chin, paying little attention to the conversation around her. Her spoon circled her soup more times than necessary as she thought, *Sal hasn't talked to me since I invited him to the wedding. Is he ignoring me?*

She showed nothing of her inner turmoil on her face as Fangbane listened on.

"It's been quiet lately," Fangbane said. "If you would like to spend some time away as well, Hime, you are more than welcome to."

"I'll consider it," Hime said, smiling. "I think Father would appreciate my return."

Should I go visit him? Mirari thought, but she quickly shook off that idea.

Conversation drifted on the way he wanted, except, his wife had probably noticed. Without turning her head, she flashed him a questioning look, then resumed her meal.

Sorren had warned him that Starlight would catch wind of it – that it wouldn't hinder the mission as long as she remained ignorant of the situation and followed along. Sorren didn't have to question Starlight's loyalty. If he asked anything from her and argued that it was for the good of the world, she would listen to him unconditionally.

Fangbane was still brooding over the plan when Starlight climbed into bed next to him that night.

"What's wrong?" she asked, facing him.

"What?" He attempted innocence, but she wasn't buying it.

"You were reading throughout dinner, and you've been brooding ever since. What's wrong?"

He hesitated. "If I asked you to do something odd, would you do it without explanation?"

She blinked. "Did Sorren say something?" Fangbane nodded,

and she bit her lip. She closed her eyes and released a heavy sigh. "Of course. What is it?"

FANGBANE INTERCEPTED Mirari in the afternoon the next day. He didn't need to read her mind to see the lightness of her steps. Starlight had succeeded in her part of the plan.

"Ah, Mirari, there you are," he called as she headed toward the courtyard. "Do you have a moment?"

"Sure," she said, stopping. "Is everything all right?"

He peered into her eyes, but they remained clear and pure – no sign of what lurked beyond.

"Yes, everything's fine. I just wanted to let you know that when Neo and Kylah return, I'll be calling a meeting with the Knights to discuss the events of the last few months." He pretended he didn't see the disappointment on her face. "That's all I wanted to say. I'll let you get back to it."

She didn't move.

"Mirari? Is everything all right?"

She smiled, but it was brittle. "It's fine. I'll be there."

He settled his hand on her shoulder before she could leave. "I can tell something's bothering you. What is it?"

"Oh, yeah? Can't you just read my mind?"

He didn't need to. "Your brother?" he said.

She exhaled. "Yeah. I was going to— It's fine. I can see him later."

"Mirari, if you want to see your brother, you can go. I'm fine with it."

She touched her badge. *I just got this back. I want to be someone they can rely on.*

"I don't plan on giving out any missions," he said with a laugh. "I just want to check in with the Knights to see if there are any updates, any underlying issues we should be taking care of."

He patted her shoulder and she wavered. "I'll debrief you once you return."

"Okay." Her face was beginning to light up when she remembered, "And His Honor, I was planning on asking him to come with me." She paused. "Would that be—"

"Completely acceptable," he said. "He's returning to Althaean Main tomorrow, so I'm sure he wouldn't object to travelling with you."

A bright smile spread across her face and she bowed. "I'll return soon."

Fangbane returned the smile, not that she could see. He nodded and waved her goodbye. "Take your time."

FANGBANE'S MACHINATIONS BORE FRUIT. Mirari had gone to meet her brother, and no doubt, chastise him for not attending the wedding. Gaven and her, they would take some time travelling through Althaea Main before heading to Valenia. It was more than enough time for Fangbane to work on the Knights.

With Kylah and Neo back, the Knights assembled. Fangbane was sitting on his desk, waiting for the others to arrive. He had a steaming pot of tea ready and he poured himself a cup as the Knights trickled in one by one. Kylah and Neo were together, of course, and Shiba followed closely behind. He was debriefing Neo on what had happened in Avon while he was away. Hime arrived and greeted Kylah with enthusiasm. Lucan was much calmer since Mirari's return. Fangbane would need to keep an eye on him, Sorren had warned.

Dorain was the last to arrive, slipping in with a sheepish slump of his shoulders. Even though a few weeks had passed, tensions with Dorain and some Knights were still high. They had mostly avoided each other until now. Forced into a room together, Shiba had some things to say. He puffed up his chest and strode up to Dorain.

"Look who decided to join," Shiba said.

"Be nice," Neo said with a hearty laugh.

"He did it for us," Hime chimed in. "He was always one of us."

"He's just mad Dorain managed to fool him," Kylah said, covering her smirk with a sip of tea.

Lucan shook his head, "It doesn't matter if the whole scheme was a giant waste of time."

Dorain flushed and he exchanged an odd look with Lucan. Rubbing the back of his head, he argued, "It wasn't a waste of time. I found out where the Blessed were hiding, didn't I?"

"The point was for us to work as a team," Shiba said, crossing his arms. He nodded toward Fangbane, looking for approval. "But you thought the Knights were useless."

"I didn't say that," Dorain said, lurching forward.

"How can we trust that you won't leave again?"

Fangbane held his hands up. "Let's all calm down now," he said. "What matters is that we took down the Blessed. I'm confident that no one else could've accomplished what we've done." Shiba's eyebrows rose like he didn't quite believe him. That was fine. Fangbane didn't need his approval.

Shiba's eyes shrewdly gazed at Fangbane. "Why have you called us here?"

Fangbane cleared his throat. "We have to continue doing our part to bring peace and comfort to the people."

"Why? We don't have any enemies left. We don't work for the Council anymore." Shiba snorted. "I'm not going all the way to Narvi to transport grain again. I have more important things to do."

"I agree," Kylah said. "Individual regions can call on us if they have problems, but there's no need for us to overreach and unnecessarily interfere with other region leaders."

"Of course," Fangbane said. "That makes sense."

"Oh, I know," Dorain jumped in, raising his hands with excitement. "We're going to catch the Spirit Soldiers."

Fangbane shook his head. "No, no, nothing like that."

He didn't know much about the Spirit Soldiers and Fangbane didn't think they *should* do anything about them. For one, the reports about them had been largely positive. They weren't randomly attacking people or destroying property. The second reason was that their targets were mainly the Blessed stragglers. Those remaining pockets of rebels were being rounded up along with any missing weapons or poisons. Fangbane was happy to let them continue operating without bringing them to the Council's attention. They gave him time to discuss more important things.

Fangbane sighed. Getting to the point, he said, "This has to do with the Blessed." The room fell silent and all eyes turned to him. Fangbane steepled his fingers together. He continued, "Soteria's abilities. They weren't normal, and they didn't just come from nowhere."

"What are you saying?" Shiba scowled. "Whatever power she possessed died with her."

"His Lord may have a point," Lucan said with his hand pressed to his lip. "Whatever she had, it wasn't kore, and we'd be foolish to not investigate it more."

"Is this a fact or theory?"

Lucan maintained his calm composure. "All I'm saying is that we should be thorough. We've come this far to defeat the Blessed. We should make sure that they never have the power to rise up again."

Fangbane nodded. He had the Knights on his side now. This was what Sorren wanted, but parts of his vision were still missing. He needed the Knights to fill in those gaps.

"I have a theory I need you all to investigate," Fangbane said. "Have you heard of Fate's Fable?"

Hime tilted her head and pursed her lips. "I believe I have," she said. "That's from Moranity, right? The one with the Goddess of Fate and Goddess of Devotion?"

"It is."

"I'm not too familiar with it. After all, no one worships those Goddesses anymore, not that I know of."

"Not since Laikos," Kylah said, reminding everyone. Their eyes widened as if a light went on in their heads.

"Oh," Hime gasped, bringing her hands to her lip. "I nearly forgot."

Fangbane continued, "The way Soteria's ability worked had a lot of similarities to the story. I believe there is a connection."

"You have something more tangible than a myth?" Shiba asked, skeptically.

"You saw the destruction." Fangbane gestured out the window. "The Althaean Siege, the war with the Blessed. At every instance, we've encountered some uncontrollable, possessive force. We must go back to the beginning and look into the legend that started Moranity."

His warning managed to blunt Shiba's sharp interrogation, and his silence convinced the rest of the Knights of the same.

"All I can say is someone reached out to me to warn of an upcoming threat. I trust this source implicitly. They have insight that has helped me in the past and they've yet to steer me wrong." Fangbane had so much to thank his son for. Getting to his feet, Fangbane gestured for the Knights to do the same. "Let's reconvene. Find out what you can about this legend."

CHAPTER TWENTY-FIVE

Gaven took a deep breath as he rode with Mirari through the gates into the fortress of Althaea Main. Their trip through Althaea had been uneventful, almost peaceful. That was, no doubt, thanks to the Spirit Soldiers. There were still some sightings of the Defiants, but without their leader, they were disorganized and ineffectual like an army of ants kicked off their path. The streets were peaceful, the guards had more free time on their hands, and for once, Gaven didn't find himself scrambling to tend to some emergency.

The sight of his luscious, green courtyard put him at peace. Even though he had made a home at the Knights' Estate, it was a relief to be back in his territory. Unfortunately, his stay at Althaea Main would only last a few days. He agreed to accompany Mirari on her trip to visit Salathiel. Gaven would rather submerge himself in a swamp full of pomeralian slugmires, however, he would do it for Mirari.

"Your Honor, Lady Mirari!" Haynes said, approaching them at a light jog. He waved his hand wildly as if they couldn't see him. "Welcome back!"

Gaven rolled his eyes as he dismounted from his horse.

"Calm down," he said. Haynes straightened his back and stood at attention, and yet, Gaven could see the energy thrumming just underneath his skin. Some things never changed and there was no point in chastising him when he was a competent commander.

Gaven absently handed the reins over to the waiting stablehand and Mirari hopped down from her mount, keeping her reins in her hand.

"I can handle it, thank you," she said when the stablehand tried to grab her reins. She glanced back at Gaven and he gave her a nod.

"Go ahead. I'll catch up with you later," he said.

She smiled and waved to Haynes as she followed the servant to the stables. Without turning around, Gaven asked, "Where's Erel? She's here, isn't she?"

The Council had ordered her to stay in Althaea Main for a reason. The death of Soteria had Erel written all over it, but he could only claim plausible deniability if she wasn't seen sneaking off.

"Uh, yes," Haynes said. "She's…"

"Here, Your Honor," Erel said. Gaven stepped around and saw Erel approaching. She seemed normal – not that her blank face was any different – and she carried herself a little more loosely. He hoped she had found some closure. Smirking, she shooed Haynes away. "Don't you have recruits to train?"

He laughed. "Alright, I'm going." He saluted Gaven and right before he ran off, he said, "Oh, and if she says I broke anything, I definitely didn't."

Gaven grimaced, covering his face with his hands. "Did he?"

She tilted her head instead of answering. Sighing, he headed into the fort, leading the way to his office. They talked about trivial things. She had kept him informed while he was away so there weren't any issues with Althaea Main to discuss.

"How was the wedding?" she asked.

"Good, good."

"Wow," Erel drawled. "You sound like you had a great time."

He held the door to his office open for Erel and closed it once she stepped through. Erel dropped into the chair across the desk and he moved on from the wedding conversation.

"You heard, right?"

"Heard what?" Erel asked. She was leaning back in the chair, watching him with a knowing smile.

He sank into his chair, rolling his eyes again. "Soteria took her own life."

"What?" Erel theatrically lifted her hand to her mouth. "That's crazy."

"That's the official report," he said. Erel dropped the act so he continued. "That means you're no longer bound here."

She frowned, leaning forward like she was listening to something that wasn't Gaven's voice. Stilling, Gaven quieted his breathing until he heard it as well. Haynes booming laugh accompanied by lighter, feminine laughter. Mirari.

"Do you still not trust her?" he asked.

"I told you I *do* trust her. It's just…" She wrinkled her nose.

"Right." Her inability to shift into Mirari. "You're wary." She nodded. He didn't want to dismiss her suspicions, but at the same time… "You know Mirari and I reestablished our partnership, right?"

Erel un-tensed long enough to give him a sardonic look. "You think I couldn't smell that?"

He rubbed the back of his neck and sighed. "That means I need you to be on board, Erel." She pressed her lips together and didn't say anything. "Mirari and I are going to… visit someone. You'll be in charge while I'm away."

She exhaled roughly. "Of course. Who else could you trust? Haynes?" They shared a grimace. "There's something I need to show you first." She reached into her pocket and pulled out something wrapped in a cloth. She placed it on the desk and unfolded it. A dagger sat between them, unremarkable, except the blade was covered in a dry, black tar. Gaven repulsed.

"What in Inferna is this?" he asked. There was no doubt it was Erel's – it had her golden signature on the hilt – but what did she murder with it? He shook away that thought – he knew exactly who she murdered, but what was the substance he was withering from? Grabbing the dagger by the hilt, he tilted it toward his face.

"This isn't the first time I've seen this," she said, speaking slowly. "The man who attacked you before Rhea bled the same way."

He put the dagger down with a thump. "Well, I can assure you, Mirari bleeds red. There's no worries there."

Erel nodded slowly, only looking slightly relieved. "There is a connection," she warned. "Between the three of them."

"So you've said." He got to his feet. "Erel, I appreciate your concern, but I'm not going to doubt my partner. I don't believe I have anything to fear with her and to treat her otherwise would be to disrespect our bond."

"I'm not worried about her, or you, to be frank," she said. He waited, sure there was more she wanted to say. She kept her gaze forward, staring at his bookshelf. "Have you heard of dark aura?"

Gaven furrowed his brow. "I've heard of it, sure." The way Gaven saw it, it was a strong type of spiritual energy, and extremely rare, so rare that no one he knew had ever encountered it. No one knew what its power truly held, or how to describe it. It was no more than a myth. He darted his eyes to the dagger, then back to her. "There's no evidence that dark aura exists, Erel."

"Because most people don't live to tell the tale." She flashed a smile, but it wasn't quite as filled with amusement as it usually was. "I can't believe I didn't see it before."

Gaven scratched the back of his head. He leaned forward,

taking a good look at the substance. Staring at it gave him an uncanny feeling. He thought back to what Eoin said about Soteria's unusually powerful influence over people's minds. If dark aura could subvert will and elude memory, it all made sense – the rise in support for the rebellion, the reason behind his memory loss.

"Our elders told us stories of it all the time," Erel said, "to discipline us, of course, a warning for those prone to disobey orders." Erel shook her head. Folding the cloth, she said, "I'll discard this. Just… keep it in mind."

"Will you look into it?"

Erel looked up, surprised. "I… I will."

He wouldn't easily forget her words of warning, especially not if it was Mirari's life on the line.

BACK AT THE ESTATE, Fangbane and Starlight were presented with a thick book. Kylah found it in Shiba's fortress library. It was worn and dusty, and was ready to fall apart from its leather binding if the rope was untied.

Fangbane didn't want to touch it. It would only confirm the truth he didn't want to hear. He let the Knights present him with the information they found from reading Fate's Fable.

"This is a copy of what is inscribed at the Belligmn Tribe," Neo said, miraculously opening the book to the passage with such delicacy that not a single page fell out. "If your theory is true, then we know the source of Soteria's power."

Neo passed the book to Hime, who read each line to Fangbane and the Knights. She knew a thing or two about gods, but it was Kylah and Starlight who truly decrypted the message in the cautionary tale.

She described two goddesses, Cygnus and Lachess, companions since the day of creation, inseparable until they encountered a moral disagreement over the life of a boy who drowned in a river. The villagers prayed to Lachess, the Goddess of Devotion, to bring him back to life, and she restored his life with *ning-ürip*.

"By the cursed feet of Behama, what is *ning-ürip*?" Shiba said, interrupting her.

Hime and Starlight were wary to answer. Those who were proficient in medical studies were well aware of the "concept" of *ning-ürip*, but it was nothing more than speculation, a medical alternative that, without proof, didn't exist. Such controversial topics were often banned from discussion.

"Some people call it dark aura," Lucan said, not wasting a moment to show off in front of Shiba.

"Right," Kylah said. "It's a strong type of spiritual energy, like… voola, necromancy—"

"I know what dark aura is," Shiba scoffed. "It's what lunatics search for when they're upset about how weak their aura is. But it's not real, and neither are goddesses."

Dorain groaned. "Just let her continue."

Fangbane nodded, and Starlight gestured to the book.

"Well, the boy was brought back to life," she said. "But ning-ürip lived with him like a curse, and everyone he touched became corrupted. They started killing each other, nearly destroying the entire village."

"And then comes Cygnus, the Goddess of Fate," Hime continued, and recited, *"she cleansed the boy, bless akü-kene, with the touch of her plays."*

Fangbane didn't need to look at Shiba to know that he was rolling his eyes.

"And what is akü-kene," Shiba asked?

"We… don't really know."

Starlight piped in. "In some translations, it's said to "flutter and dance", something like fire."

She went on to explain that Cygnus killed the boy, and Lachess was furious. The goddesses struck against each other in a blazing feud that cost many mortal lives. Finally, the other gods separated the goddesses, banished them from Nagama, and imprisoned them into mortal bodies to be reincarnated every one-hundred years.

Shiba was sulking in his chair. He refused to accept that this was the most important thing on their agenda. His legs were bouncing with a need to act, his thoughts moving quickly. Fangbane understood he didn't care for all the sitting around and talking – he wanted action and he wasn't opposed to crossing blades with a goddess.

"Why now?" Lucan asked. Though he seemed just as skeptical as Shiba, he was at least intrigued at the theory. He played on the idea a little more. "If they reincarnate every hundred years, why are we only seeing dark aura now?"

"The vessel has to be right," Kylah said, showing off her gem bracelet. "Anyone can hold the stones of Aten, but only the best of the best can wield their power. It's the same with Cygnus and Lachess."

"And with such rarity, the likelihood of them both resurfacing at the same time is extremely low," Starlight said.

Low, but not impossible. If one goddess revived without her rival, she may choose to live a quiet, humble life, but Fangbane saw a level of unprecedented apocalyptic destruction that couldn't have been caused by dark aura alone. The message was clear. They had to find the goddesses before they found each other.

Hime set the book aside, her movements cautious and entrenched in worry that may have helped convince the others that the threat was real.

"Assuming your supposition is correct," Lucan said, addressing Fangbane, "dark aura is real and Soteria used it to lead the Defiants. What then? What do we do?"

"We can't fight a goddess," Hime said, shaking her head.

Fangbane nodded. "That's why we have to find Cygnus. As

the myth goes, Lachess can only be defeated by Cygnus. While we may not stand a chance, Cygnus is our only hope."

"We don't even know what they look like," Dorain said, pinching his brows. "They could be anyone."

"We will find them," Fangbane said. "We find someone like Soteria, who uses dark aura to possess others, or we find her rival…"

"Someone who uses flames," Dorain said, raising his head to the front of the room. Kylah scowled at him.

"Don't look at me," she hissed. "I think I would've known by now if I was a Goddess."

Raising his hands, Dorain took a step back. "I'm just saying…"

Shiba barked. "The kid is right."

"Hey," Neo said, holding his hand out in front of him. "None of that now. A lot of people have fire kore."

Fangbane clapped his hands, bringing their attention back to him. The last thing he wanted was for them to fight amongst each other.

"Neo is correct," he said. "There's no correlation between a person's kore and whether or not they are the vessel. It's the same with Laikos. He was a powerful empath, but he didn't have dark aura."

"Then…" Lucan trailed off, frowning behind his glasses.

Fangbane narrowed his eyes. Whatever Lucan was about to say, he couldn't read his mind.

"Then how are we meant to find them?" Neo asked. At least, that's what he thought Lucan was about to say.

"Right." Shiba got to his feet. "What lead do we have?"

"This won't be easy," Fangbane said. "But we must find the vessels. Make Lachess your priority. We need to stop her before she infects another person."

There were a couple nods, even if they didn't agree. For what else could they do?

The only one who wasn't all in, at least mentally, was Lucan. He seemed lost in thought. His mind was running in an odd pattern and Fangbane couldn't quite read.

Shiba sighed. "And if we find Cygnus, how can we guarantee that she will be on our side?"

"I wouldn't want to challenge her," Fangbane said, with a chuckle. "Not the very person who controls fate."

"So, once we find the two vessels, you will let them fight," Lucan clarified. "Whatever happens will be out of our control."

"That is correct."

Shiba scowled. "That's not like you, Fang."

Fangbane tried to not be offended by Shiba's words. He was always an advocate for change, helping people see the light in impossible situation, however, he felt that this situation was out of his control. Sorren said it himself. This was the best case scenario.

"He's right," Starlight said, shaking her head. Her gaze shifted to her folded hands. "What can we do but let them fight?"

Kylah added, "And pray that they don't destroy humanity in the process."

Fangbane could tell that the Knights were beginning to see the same horrific future that Sorren had shown him. It was the motivation they needed.

"Regardless," Lucan said, brushing away the tension. "I will be leaving tomorrow. I have business to take care of in Althaea Main, and I'll search for the goddesses along the way." He bowed and adjusted his glasses. Turning to Fangbane, he nodded, "I'll be happy to relay the information to Gaven."

Fangbane thought about it. He didn't want this getting back to Gaven for as long as he could hold off on it.

Gripping his masked chin, Fangbane said, "No need. He and Mirari will return to the estate. I will tell them then."

Lucan kept a cold frown on his face, but Fangbane couldn't

read any of his thoughts. Lucan simply nodded, hiding his discomfort.

Fangbane got to his feet and stood by the book. Did he dare touch it? Acknowledge that the whole thing was true? He didn't have a contingency plan for a deity battle. All he had was Sorren's vision, and, if he were to follow through with his plan, all his thoughts – his beliefs, his morals – had to be locked out. There would no doubt be regretful decisions in the near future. For the greater good, Fangbane would do it.

"Let's find the Goddesses."

CHAPTER TWENTY-SIX

Gaven and Mirari entered the city of Wildemire, a charming civilization located at the base of a mountain. There was no shortage of visitors and locals crawling into the shops and houses etched into large trees. Gaven observed every entrance and the jar that hung over each door, each containing a shard of lumastōne. It lit the city in an atmosphere of a soothing green glow; a beauty that couldn't be obtained in Althaea.

Gaven focused on that instead of the imminent meeting with Salathiel. He was only here to accompany Mirari, but from the way she was acting, she seemed to think he and Salathiel were going to have a long overdue talk. If Salathiel had something to say, Gaven would hear him out, but otherwise, there was nothing left between them. He kept his mouth closed, not wanting to upset the delicate balance of nerves and happiness Mirari was exuding.

As Mirari led him through the city, she kept checking street signs as if she wasn't familiar with the city. Hadn't she said she spent the winter with Salathiel here? As they neared what looked to be the outskirts of the city, Gaven pointed at a cabin. Mirari had called Salathiel's cabin oddly rustic and this was the only one that fit the description for miles.

"Is that it?"

It was folksy and snug with a stone fireplace emitting smoke to ward off the crisp spring morning. The outer structure was made from logs and twine, and the steps leading up to the building were carved into a massive oakwood tree trunk.

"Huh?" she asked. "You want to go there?"

He looked at it more closely and realized it wasn't a cabin, but a small tavern called the Shepherd and Blade. Gaven *did* want to go in there.

"I could use a drink," he said.

Her nose wrinkled in exasperation as she spoke, "You're just trying to get out of seeing Sal."

He nudged her shoulder. "Can't I do both?" He took a few steps forward, but stopped when she didn't move. "Mirari?"

"Maybe you should stay here," she said.

He faced her fully. "I said I'd come with you, didn't I?" Even if he didn't want to.

"You two clearly have unresolved business." She frowned. "But maybe I should talk to him first. That might ease the tension."

Gaven hesitated. "Are you sure?" She nodded and he sensed worry from her heart. Regardless, he admired the brave face she put on. "All right." He raised his finger. "But if you take too long, I'm coming after you."

She rolled her eyes. "What do you think is going to happen? It's just Sal." She left with a little wave and Gaven went into the tavern.

He found a seat at the bar, isolated from the few other patrons. He was barely halfway through his second ale when he began to feel guilty. Despite Erel's warning, he knew Mirari could take care of herself, but she didn't have to. This went beyond his obligation as Mirari's partner — she and Salathiel were family — and here he was, drinking to avoid slight discomfort.

Sighing, he tossed back the rest of his ale and dropped a few coins onto the table. Outside, he headed in the direction Mirari had left in. As he was already on the outskirts of town, the road in front of him disappeared into the forest.

He scanned the vicinity. The houses were nothing like the cabin Mirari had described, but maybe it was outside of the city? Shrugging, he followed the road, stepping over broken twigs and disturbed bushes, evidence that someone had passed through the forest.

Gaven stopped for a moment, wondering if it truly was the right direction, but when he took a deep breath, anger and confusion shot through him. He brought his hand to his chest.

As soon as he realized what was happening, Gaven bolted into a run.

***

MIRARI COULDN'T SAY she wasn't a little disappointed that Gaven had agreed to stay behind. She wasn't surprised either. Neither Gaven nor Salathiel had expressed an interest in talking. They'd always butted heads, even when they were younger. Securing her travel pack more snuggly on her back, she headed off toward the cabin.

Under the cool shade of the trees, Mirari's good cheer returned. Maybe this was for the best. It would be easier to convince Salathiel to come into the city. If he didn't want to talk to Gaven, she could always ask Salathiel to only walk her back. She wasn't very familiar with the area having spent most of her time in the cabin. Salathiel would agree to that. Between him and Gaven, Salathiel was always the more reasonable one.

She sighed in relief when the mountain cabin came into view.

She left the tree line and ascended the carved mountain steps up to the cabin. It seemed larger than her memory and she was slightly out of breath when she made it to the final step. She knocked, leaning against the side of the mountain to look down at the forest below.

The silence stretched out and she knocked again, rapping her knuckles against the door by her hip. Maybe he wasn't here. It was a bit of a risk just showing up with no warning, but she didn't know how else to find him.

She heard footsteps approaching the door and she straightened. There was a moment of panic – what if it was Julie – before the door opened to Salathiel's scowling face. A smile broke across when he saw her standing there and he quickly pulled her into a hug.

"Mirari!" he greeted. She laughed into his shoulder as he squeezed her tightly. His hair was slightly disheveled and since she last saw him, his chin had grown a light peach fuzz. "Come in. Don't just stand out there." He took her pack from her shoulder and directed her inside. Placing the bag next to the door, he peeked his head through the doorway. "I was beginning to worry."

"About what?" she said with a chuckle.

"That the Knights weren't letting you go. Any longer and I would've stormed to Minetta myself."

"What are you talking about? I'm free to go anytime. They don't control me." She waited until the door closed and then hit him gently with the back of her hand. "I'm here to yell at you," she said. She crossed her arms to frown at him. "Why didn't you come to the wedding? Kylah was expecting you."

Snorting, he glanced out the window but from where she was standing, she didn't see anything. He didn't respond. She was waiting for him to say something witty, but he wasn't playing around – no, she recognized that look of disappointment.

"Sal? What's going on?"

"Did you come by yourself?" he asked.

"Yes." Only then did he turn back to look at her. He took a seat on the plush couch with a heavy sigh. Perching next to him, she asked, "Is everything all right?"

"I'll be blunt, Mirari," he said. He ran his hand through his hair. "You can't be around the Knights. It's not safe."

"Safe? With the Knights—"

"The Knights *are* the problem. You can't trust them."

She wanted to laugh. It had to be a joke, but Salathiel was serious. "I don't understand. What do you mean?"

Reaching out, he touched her feathered hairpin – the last gift she had received from him.

"You made a mistake going back to them," he said. "They were going to kill you for treason."

Mirari brushed his hand off so that she could twist around to face him.

"Sal," she said, crossing her arms. "The Knights didn't know anything about what happened in Aias. They still don't know anything about Soteria, or you, or Councilor Julie. You're being overprotective over nothing."

Salathiel glanced at the badge on her chest. She shielded it from his gaze, forcing him to meet her eyes once again.

"Am I? Does Fangbane know about your ability?"

Mirari started to protest, but she didn't know the answer herself. Sure, he had *seen* it, but he didn't know about Soteria, dark aura, or anything else in between. Heck, so many years had passed, he may have already forgotten about it.

Salathiel took her silence as an answer and continued, "Why do you think Fangbane wanted you to be a Knight? Why you, out of hundreds of top tier fighters?" He didn't wait for a response. "It's because he knows you're a great threat, and he wants to keep you locked up."

"You're delusional," Mirari scoffed. "I haven't threatened a thing."

"That'll change when—" Salathiel pursed his lips. "Exactly," he said instead, rubbing his fingers against his temples. "You're not a threat." His voice was softer now and he shifted toward her. "I know you, Mirari. I know the good in you. But people like Fangbane and the Knights? You have something they don't know about, and that's scary to them."

A dark scowl crossed Salathiel's face and he pointed to a stack of papers on Julie's desk.

"You've seen what they did to the Defiants, or anyone they thought was a Defiant; entire villages, slaughtered. No trial. No justice. Your fate will be the same. Sooner or later, it won't matter who Mirari is. The instant you lose control over your flame—" Salathiel paused, rubbing his hand over his chin. "You know how it'll end."

Mirari shook her head, her hands curling into a fist.

"No," she said. She shifted forward too and her voice cracked as she yelled, "Say it. Tell me how this ends."

Tears began to swirl in her eyes, and she quickly wiped them again. He tried to reach out to her, but she slapped his hand away.

"They will kill you, Mirari. Trust me."

"The Knights don't act on fear like that. They're—they're resilient. They're the strongest people I know."

It was about time she spoke up about the injustice. The side of the Knights that no one saw – that they only wanted to do good, and they made sacrifices in the name of justice.

Shiba and Neo, rulers of Avon. They had enough to worry about in their region. Why bother helping other regions? Rival regions?

Dorain and Hime, those dynamic youths Mirari always admired, practically disowned their heritage in pursuit of justice. She believed they made the biggest sacrifices of them all. After all, where would they go if Fangbane hadn't taken them in?

Her cousin, Lucan, had no business doing business outside of the Hales. He stuck his nose out in peasant problems that their family, no doubt, disapproved of. Had he continued along the course of what was expected of him, he may have been no different from Inigo. He could be living easy, wealthy. Was selflessness a crime?

And the Witch of Aten? Forced out of hiding? Risking assassination to help her friends? Kylah did not need a reminder of what murder and wrongful blame looked like.

Mirari believed Fangbane and Starlight had no shortage of sacrifices either. Though she knew little of their past, she knew for certain that they dedicated their entire life to bringing peace across the empires.

"I know the Knights," she said through clenched teeth. She pointed to her chest. "I *am* a Knight, Sal. I have drawn blood just as much as any other Knight. You have no idea how difficult it is to do good and be shamed, to be called a murderer, just for trying!"

That's right. What right did Salathiel have to judge any of them?

To her surprise, Salathiel was calm. He kept his gaze on her, waiting for her to calm down.

Salathiel took a deep breath and said, "You can choose to be with the Knights, or with me, but I'm sorry, Mirari. You can't have both." She shook her head. She couldn't believe he would even suggest such a thing. "You need to wake up. Fangbane, the Knights, even Gaven—"

"What does Gaven have to do with this?" Mirari's voice rose again, her chest ached with every word. "He's your cousin!"

"Not since he left us. Admit it, Mirari. Is he the same person you thought he would be? Did he welcome you back with open arms?"

She fumed with a rage she had never expressed toward him before. "He's been through a lot, just like everyone else."

"He used us and never looked back, and now he slaughters

villages for a living. Face it, Mirari. He turned Althaean. He doesn't care about you or anyone else."

Bang!

They both startled at the sound. Mirari whipped around to see Gaven glowering in the doorway. He put his foot down, the door kicked open. A crack ran through the thick wood where it had slammed into the wall.

"Don't put words in my mouth," Gaven said, scowling at his cousin. He barged into the cabin.

"He followed you," Salathiel said, laying his hand against the hilt of his dagger.

"A good thing, too. What lies are you feeding her?"

"Only the truths you don't want to admit." Salathiel took an aggressive step forward and Gaven matched him. "While you've been off killing out of pride, I've been taking care of her. I've been her brother. You became Althaean. The day you walked out the door, you left this family."

Gaven's shoulders coiled, the way they always did right before he was about to punch someone. Mirari stepped in between them.

"That's enough," Mirari snapped. Hands on Gaven's shoulders, she nudged him out the door. He took a few steps down.

Glancing over her shoulder, she winced at the disgust on Salathiel's face. "I choose the path where all of us can live peacefully together. I won't choose between the two of you."

Salathiel shook his head. "Then you're the delusional one, Mirari."

Her eyes drifted to the floor. Was there nothing she could say to make them stop fighting? The more she tried to think of a response, the more her head began to hurt. She was surprised to hear Gaven respond.

"I know Mirari. You tried to tame a wild card," he said, looking his cousin in the eye. "But she's a fighter. Freed from your control, she will achieve greatness and she deserves nothing less."

Gaven took Mirari's hand and guided her down the steps. "We'll be taking our leave."

They had only descended a few steps when Salathiel yelled, "I know the truth. Tell them! Will they accept you as I have?"

With no energy left in her scuffed throat, she ignored him, not daring to look back, and followed Gaven down.

CHAPTER TWENTY-SEVEN

Once they were out of sight of the cabin, Mirari groaned and brought her hand to her head. She looked defeated and Gaven cursed Salathiel for causing this.

"Where's your cloak?" he asked. Her bag was gone too. "Is it still—"

"Just leave it," Mirari said, rubbing her temples. Her shoulder slumped and she released a tired sigh.

Gaven shrugged his cloak off and draped it over her shoulders. With her head bowed, he doubted she even noticed. He didn't know what to say. He gritted his teeth and shoved his hands into his pockets.

Mirari came to an abrupt halt. She flicked her fingers and inhaled sharply like she was coming awake. Gaven felt the tides of grief and uncertainty wash away with a single wave, leaving behind a sense of calm like stagnant water, still and undisturbed.

He grabbed her hand, but she flicked it away. She took a few steps forward and pivoted with a little whirl, light on her feet.

Gaven recoiled at the twinkle in her eyes – they were glowing a bright magenta. Her intense gaze held him captive, and for a moment Gaven forgot to breathe.

"Mirari?" he asked. With all his courage, he slowly raised his hand toward her. His other hand slid closer to his back pocket. She was still as a doll, until her eyes flickered between his eyes and his hand.

"It'd be a pity to kill you," she said.

Her voice cut through him as if words had teeth. That this entity could put words in her mouth angered him. In a blink, Gaven drew his spear, and he held the blade inches from her neck. Mirari didn't flinch in the slightest. She tilted her head up, beckoning him to continue.

"You don't have the guts," she said.

Gaven scowled, the cold blade now touching her neck. "Release her."

"If you know what's good for you, you'll do as I say."

"I will only listen to Mirari."

Whatever, or whoever he was speaking to, he would fear those eyes no longer. He would free her from this possession at all costs, as she had done for him.

But instead of fighting him, she narrowed her eyes at him. She scanned him once more, then turned around and started walking back to the city. Confused, Gaven followed her.

"Hey," he called, trailing close behind. "I'm not done with you!"

She ignored him. In his heart, he couldn't sense anything different − she was still there − but he knew for certain that *something* had taken over Mirari's body. He could see it in the regal precision of her steps and the twist of her face. She held her head high with a kind of pride that Mirari never showed. Was this what Erel was trying to warn him about?

If she turned out like Soteria…

He glanced at the dagger in his belt. Could he do it? Could he do as Erel did? He shook his head. It was too early for that. He exhaled deeply, turning his focus to his heart. He searched for a feeling… anything… and there it was – a twinkle of light, hiding, slumbering in a cave during a winter's storm.

Gaven looked ahead and found they were rapidly approaching the city. Running, he intercepted Mirari and forced her to stop.

"Enough. Release your control over Mirari," he said. She scoffed and twirled around him to keep walking. "I said stop!"

He grabbed her arm. She looked from his hand to his face and her eyebrows lowered over those glowing eyes. "Just what do you think will happen if I *stop*?"

He thought about it, but realized he had no idea what was binding this person to Mirari's body. What conditions forced them together? Could they even be separated?

She snatched her hand away from his with a strength Mirari did not possess.

"The battle does not end until all of ning-ürip is purged from this world," she said.

He curled his eyebrow. "All of what?"

"You humans call it dark aura."

His face must have contorted in shock for her to release that cruel laugh, and begin walking again. He rushed to keep up.

"I know what you're thinking. No such thing? Much like how you don't believe in gods? You yourself have been corrupted by dark aura, and you refuse to believe its existence?"

Those words left Gaven in silence. Erel was right and now he understood what force was at hand. What was her relation to Soteria?

"Who… are you?" Gaven asked. Part of him was afraid of the answer.

She released a heavy sigh and turned to him. He felt like a fly caught under the woman's piercing gaze.

"Your people call me Cygnus." Cygnus? Where did he hear that name before? "I am the Goddess of Fate."

Gaven took a deep breath, recalling Eoin's story of Fate's

Fable. He still didn't quite believe it, but what if what she claimed was true, what did she want with him? What was she doing with Mirari?

"I'll make this easy for you," she said with a dismissive wave of her hand. "History is doomed to repeat itself and only I can dispel dark aura." Cygnus flicked her wrist, and a reddish blaze emerged in her palm – the soul flame. "As long as Lachess continues to roam this earth, she will spread dark aura. You need to bring her to me."

Gaven furrowed his brows. That meant there was another goddess on the loose, and she was also occupying a human vessel. He shook his head, crossing his arms. The destruction was done. What choice did he have but to believe her?

"Who else has dark aura?" he asked.

She turned her head and he followed her gaze to the mountain they had just descended. He couldn't see it, but he pictured the cabin up there. Gaven's eyes widened.

"No."

"It all started with him, just as it did with the boy." She clicked her tongue, mumbling to herself. "Lachess, you poor thing. So predictable." She waved a dismissive hand at Gaven. "Surely he will lead you to her."

Gaven shook his head. The events of that day when he lost his memory replayed in his head, only now Salathiel's image replaced the blurred face of his assailant. He and Salathiel may have had their differences, but he refused to accept what she was saying. "I don't believe you. Salathiel wouldn't…"

But did he really know anything about the cousin he hadn't seen since he was a child? If anything, Salathiel was right – the three of them were no longer children allied by innocence and ignorance. Salathiel may have well been a stranger to him.

She shrugged. "Not on purpose, perhaps, but it happened all the same, didn't it? Do you now understand the urgency of this matter?" Sighing, she closed her eyes and tilted her face toward the sun. "Don't you feel some responsibility for your actions, even if they were not entirely your own? Don't you want to prevent Lachess from infecting more people with her dark aura?"

"I…" He roughly ran his hand through his hair. "Yes, of course."

"Then help me."

She continued walking, heedless of Gaven's reaction. She didn't need to make sure he followed her. She had him like a moth chasing after a flame.

Gaven could hear the murmurs of the village from afar, and soon the bustling plaza came into view. Few would notice them in this crowd.

Rooting his feet on the ground, he shook free from her insidious words.

"I won't," he said.

Her face went cold even as her eyes lit with a spark of fury. "Do you think it's wise to deny a Goddess?"

"Maybe not." He looked around. "But how do I know you're better than Lachess? How do I know you're not hurting Mirari?"

The woman blinked and her face softened. For a moment, Gaven thought that he had gotten through to her, or even Mirari. Then she lifted her hand, fingers uncurling to reveal a small flame cradled in her palm.

"You sense her, don't you? She's safe, sleeping, and for the better. Mirari cannot control akü-kene. After all, it's not simply fire."

She smiled at the flickering flame. A smile that sent a chill down Gaven's spine. He reached for his spear, but kept it compact.

She extended her hand toward him. He felt frozen in place. Something cold was touching his soul even as he felt the fire warm his skin. "Fire feeds on air and wind. The soul flame devours something else entirely." She whispered, "Life."

Without looking, she flicked her hand sideways and the flame landed at a man's feet. He screamed as the fire spread, climbing up his legs and stomach, his chest and shoulders. Right before he was completely consumed by the flames, Gaven caught a glimpse of his terrified eyes. The life in his eyes faded and dulled. He collapsed to his knees and fell forward, growing silent.

Screams erupted from passersby as they rushed to bring water in a futile attempt to save the man. He was dead before he even hit the ground, and not from being burned alive.

Shaking, he stared at the creature inhabiting Mirari's body. Nowhere did he detect a hint of Mirari in her cruel gaze. Mirari would be horrified, but this wasn't her. This was Cygnus. More fire curled around her hand and she smirked at the assembling crowd.

"What Lachess is doing is much worse. She tortures her souls. I put them out of their misery. What do you think?" she asked. "Do you need another demonstration?"

Gaven shook off his stupor and grabbed her arm. Cygnus seemed shocked, long enough that he was able to drag her into an alley and away from the crowd of innocent bystanders.

"Enough of this," he said. "Return Mirari."

The corner of her mouth perked into a smile, and she laughed, "I know your weakness."

Gaven slammed her into the brick wall, crushing her wrist. He drew a dagger and braced the blade against her throat. She tilted her head back, taunting him again. He pressed his body forward, leaning into her space. The dagger remained steady and unmoving.

He searched her face. Those glowing magenta eyes, the inhuman smile on her lips. He knew it was only Cygnus looking back at him, but he couldn't help seeing Mirari's face either – not just Mirari, Roselyn.

Shuddering, he stepped back. His shoulders slumped and his blade hit the ground with a light clink.

Cygnus chuckled. "That's what I thought."

"If I deliver Lachess, will you disappear as well?"

"Do you think I enjoy being in this mortal world?"

"Swear an oath."

Standing tall, she roared, "No, you swear *to* me. If you wish to see her again, you will devote yourself to me."

Unheeding, Gaven huffed and repeated. "Once Lachess is gone, you will never possess Mirari again. Do we have a deal?"

Cygnus scowled. Though her eyes still radiated, he noticed that her gaze was not as intense as before and her fingers were trembling. She seemed to have grown tired, and as scared as he was of facing fate herself, he knew she would not be raising another flame at him.

She covered her face with her shaking hands. "Very well. Bring her to me."

"Who is Lachess? Who is her vessel?"

"*She* will know." Cygnus released a heavy sigh and rested her eyes. When she didn't open them, Gaven thought she had fallen asleep. She slumped heavily against the wall, and he caught her before she fell.

He grabbed her shoulders and pulled her into a hug, resting his chin on her head. Gaven could hear her breathe peacefully, and that feeling of peace echoed in his heart. Squeezing her tightly, he closed his eyes and followed her rhythm.

CHAPTER TWENTY-EIGHT

Mirari awakened inside a carriage. She didn't recognize the interior, but knew she was safe seeing Gaven sitting across from her, asleep against the wall. She peaked out the window. There was nothing but dry land. They must be heading back to Althaea Main.

"Mirari…"

Gaven rubbed his eyes and sat up straight. A smile appeared on his face. For some reason, he wouldn't stop looking at her. She would've thought he was mocking her, but behind that smile, something was deeply troubling him – for the first time, she felt his sorrow in her heart. She scanned his face for an answer.

"What happened?" she asked. "Did Sal…" Then it occurred to her that she couldn't recall what had happened before she fell asleep. Did he say something that upset Gaven? Did they end up fighting?

"Did Salathiel tell you that he has dark aura?" he asked. His smile disappeared and he lowered his gaze. Mirari sat up, carrying the same frown on her face. She wasn't sure how he found out, but he must've known the truth about his possession.

"I'm sorry," she said. "I didn't know how to tell you."

"And it's not your duty to tell me," he said, clenching his hands into a fist. "He lied to me."

"It was an accident."

"If it was, why didn't he do something about it?" Gaven raised his voice. "Why did he run and put the blame on me?"

Mirari shook her head and said, "It's not his fault."

Gaven hissed. "I can't believe you'd still defend him."

"I'm not defending him. I just want us to get along."

"And when will you see that will never happen?" Mirari bit her lip. Gaven had every right to be angry, but she could tell that even he didn't blame Salathiel. It was a different kind of rage she felt kindling in his heart. "Admit it, he's gone. He's just like everyone else with dark aura – delusional. A pawn of Lachess."

Mirari furrowed her brows. "Who?"

Gaven paused and scanned her eyes. He was hesitant, "You... don't know?"

"Know about what?"

"The Goddesses." Mirari shook her head. Salathiel never mentioned anything of that sort to her. Gaven groaned. "This is why we can't trust Sal. He didn't even tell you."

"What are you going on about?"

"The source of your soul flame. The source of his dark aura." He ruffled his hair. "We're caught in a battle between Goddesses."

Soul flame? Goddesses? Her forehead crinkled as she recalled the inscription on the stone at the abandoned village. "The fable."

Gaven nodded. "That village had been long destroyed, but the Belligmn Tribe built their civilization on top of it." He showed her his clōve. "Erel knows the story well. I'm sure she can help us."

Mirari shook her head. She still couldn't recall the conversation they had with Salathiel and how Gaven got all this information. She couldn't have simply fallen asleep. It left her with one other possibility. Mirari brought her hand to the edge of her eye.

Gaven frowned. "I spoke to her. She calls herself Cygnus, and she promised to go away once Lachess is defeated."

"*A reincarnation of one-hundred years' immortals,*" Mirari recited, then lowered her head. "I am a vessel."

She didn't know how to feel about it. On one hand, she was relieved that there was a reason why she failed to control her ability all these years – her actions, the destruction she had caused, were not her fault. At the same time, what was her duty as a vessel? Was she supposed to just let Cygnus roam free, or was she obligated to contain her?

"If Salathiel isn't Lachess," Gaven asked, "then who is the other vessel?"

Mirari bit her lip. There was only one other possibility. She had saved Salathiel, and he was loyal to her. Salathiel was crazed because he was listening to the lies that she was feeding him. "Councilor Julie."

Gaven's eyes widened. "Councilor Julie? Why her?"

Mirari hissed, "Why *me*?"

Gaven shook his head. "Are you certain?"

"I don't know who else it could be." Mirari released a heavy sigh as she glanced out the window. She could see the fortress of Althaea Main peeking from the horizon. She wasn't worried about Julie, but her relationship with Salathiel had changed.

They entered the fortress and Mirari cringed away from Haynes' enthusiastic greeting. She didn't feel like pretending everything was all right. It was almost better when her fire had been uncontrollable. Now it was in expert control, but the expert was a goddess who was willing to kill to prove her point.

Mirari snuck a glance at Gaven and was glad he hadn't abandoned her after encountering Cygnus. It must have been frightening to face the very person who controlled fate and had tried to kill him on multiple occasions.

"Has there been anything to report?" Gaven asked, standing between her and Haynes. The commander was enthusiastic, but not pushy.

Mirari listened while Haynes gave a brief report though there was nothing amiss in Althaea Main. Everything was just fine. It felt like there should have been something. Her world had turned upside down and yet, just as she had hoped, peace was slowly making its way through the empires.

"…And one of the Knights arrived yesterday," Haynes said.

Mirari zoned back into the conversation. Leaning around Gaven, she asked, "One of the Knights? Who?"

"Uh… pale guy. Fancy clothes."

"Lucan," Gaven scowled. "And where is he now?"

"He's been staying at an inn in the upper city. Erel's been keeping an eye on him."

"Why?" Mirari asked.

Haynes shrugged. "He said he was here on business, but, no disrespect, Milady, but he seemed kind of… squirrelly? He wanted to see you. Wouldn't say what for."

If it was weird to Haynes then Lucan must have been acting very strangely.

"We'll take care of it," Gaven said. Mirari shared a determined look with Gaven and they headed back into the city. "Which inn do you think he's staying in?" Gaven asked. "The most expensive one?"

Mirari huffed a laugh. "Yes, probably."

The inn was located a little ways away from the plaza. A large stone-walled building, understated and elegant, it looked more like a manor than an inn. The only reason they knew for sure that it was the correct location was because of Erel, who materialized out of the shadows toward them. She had a good view of Lucan's room from a nearby alley.

"What's he up to?" Gaven asked.

"Nothing," she said. Gaven shot her a dubious look, and she lifted her hands. "I mean it. Nothing. He's contacted a few merchants in town, but I investigated, there's nothing shady about it. He just refuses to leave until he sees you, in private."

"You didn't try to... speak as me?" Gaven asked. There was something odd about how he said that, but Erel shook her head.

"It seems that you two previously discussed something I wasn't aware of. I wouldn't know how to act."

"What are you talking about?" Mirari asked.

A moment of unease passed between Erel and Gaven.

"Not important," Gaven said.

"I... I can explain later," Erel said to Gaven's obvious shock.

Mirari's gaze flickered between the two of them. Finally, Gaven spoke. "We need to talk about the "other thing" too." He shuffled toward the inn. "But later. We should see what Lucan is here for."

They headed inside, just Gaven and Mirari. They bypassed the counter and headed straight for the stairs. They knew exactly which room Lucan would be in based on Erel's observation.

As they trudged up the steps, Mirari said aloud, "I wonder what Lucan wants."

"As his cousin, you probably have a better idea than I do."

He didn't sound upset that Lucan knew her real identity before he did. She wanted to be happy about that, but she was still worried about Cygnus. She was only just now learning what that meant – how dangerous it was for the people around her.

They stopped outside Lucan's door and knocked. Belatedly, she realized Lucan had said he wanted to speak to Gaven. They had just assumed that meant Mirari too. The door opened.

Even with his glasses hiding his eyes, Mirari could see Lucan's expression sour when he saw Gaven. Mirari almost laughed for lack of anything better to do. Why would he insist on seeing Gaven if he was going to be so upset at the sight of him? She must have made a sound because Lucan's face lit up.

"I'm glad to see that you two have made amends," Lucan said. He glanced between the two of them and stepped back. "Please, come in."

The interior was exactly the type of place her parents used to stay in when they weren't moving between the many Hale estates. Her eyes were drawn to the elaborate rugs hanging down the walls to keep the interior warm.

Lucan offered them tea and fussed around a bit until Gaven demanded to know what Lucan wanted.

"You got us both out here," Gaven said. "What is it?"

Lucan sighed, bracing his elbows on his knees and leaning forward.

"Did you know that Fangbane called a meeting while you were away?" he asked, stiff and serious.

"Yes," Mirari said. "I told him to fill me in when I got back."

Gaven raised a brow. "I wasn't informed."

That didn't seem to surprise Lucan. "There was an agreement to keep the matter quiet, and it seems both of you were left out of the picture on purpose. I'd be interested to know why." He glanced at Mirari to her surprise. "And it goes without saying that I wasn't here. Whatever Fangbane is up to, we should be wary."

"We need details, Lucan." Gaven said. "What happened at the meeting?" Instead of answering, Lucan pressed his thin lips together, reluctant or unsure how to continue. Gaven continued, "Look, I know we've had our differences in the past, but we both want what's best for Mirari."

"Yes, I suppose that's true." He blew out a breath and turned to Mirari. "Is it alright to bring up your "theory" about what happened to your parents?"

Mirari tilted her head. She couldn't piece together why that had anything to do with the Knights.

"I don't see why not," she said.

"For reasons unknown, Fangbane had us investigating an old fable." Lucan paused. He scrubbed his hands through his hair, leaning back in his seat. "Fate's Fable, the story of Cygnus and Lachess."

Mirari felt as if her soul left her body. She lowered her teacup, not trusting her shaking hands to hold the delicate porcelain. It clanged loudly on the table. Lucan nodded.

"Judging by your demeanor, you've heard of it."

Mirari nodded woodenly. "Only recently."

What were the chances that they had all discovered this story at the same time? Gaven had an equally confused look on his face, but his confusion quickly turned into a scowl.

"Should we be offended that we missed an opportunity to be told a bedtime story?" Gaven asked, crossing his arms. He knew, perhaps better than Mirari, that Cygnus was no fairytale, and he'd experienced the effect of Lachess' dark aura. What game was Lucan playing?

"Fangbane believes that the myth is real," Lucan said. "He has full trust in his source, whoever that may be. More so, he believes that the story is a warning."

Mirari didn't know where to begin. She decided to ask the direct question first. "A warning for what?"

"According to the legend, the goddesses were in a feud, and many lives were taken along the way. The only reason they stopped fighting was because the other gods punished them and confined them into mortal bodies. They don't awaken if the vessel is not suitable to wield their divine power, but..." Lucan lowered his gaze. He was deeply troubled by some thought. "Allegedly, there is proof that, for the first time, both goddesses have been reborn at the same time. And unfortunately for us, the Goddesses will fight until the other is defeated."

"And you believe this?" Gaven asked.

"I have reason to," Lucan said, almost ashamed to admit it. His eyes shifted to Mirari. "Do you understand?"

Mirari had told him that she believed she started the fire on the kōnvoy that killed her parents. He called it absurd and brushed it off at the time. Did he change his mind?

Before Mirari could respond, Gaven said, "Regardless of whether or not gods are real, why is this relevant?"

"Fangbane is taking this warning as fact. He believes that Lachess has aligned herself with the Blessed, explaining their recent uprising. If this is true, then we need to ask for Cygnus' help in defeating her. He is hunting for both vessels."

Gaven snorted and ran his hand over scruffy face. "He wants to eschew the safety of the people and to simply leave it up to the gods?"

"That does appear to be the case," Lucan said, his voice as dry as a sand dune. "Unfortunately, there doesn't seem to be any other way to defeat a goddess besides pitting her against another goddess, at least according to Fangbane. It is not an absurd idea, but I expected him to take some responsibility." His attention alternated between the two, as if tracking the currents of an unspoken conversation. "I have a good idea why he chose to let the Gods battle. We've been talking around it, but I believe you understand my point, Mirari?"

Mirari concealed her trembling hands between her legs. She had avoided his gaze this entire time, for she couldn't think of a lie or any alternative explanation to his story. His reasoning was thorough, as usual. Why hunting a goddess had suddenly become the focus of the Knights bewildered her, but how much longer could she hide it from them?

She understood now why Salathiel chose to go into hiding. How terrified he must've been to wield a divine power he couldn't control. But he looked well now, perhaps even better than their days in Solarin. If he could learn to control his new power, so could she. Pretending that the goddesses weren't real wasn't going to make it go away. She had to work with Cygnus – she didn't know how, but she had to – and she knew she needed help.

She took a deep breath and said, "I am Cygnus' vessel."

Lucan frowned. "I was hoping you were going to disprove my theory."

With a contemplative gaze, Gaven leaned forward. There was no point in trying to cover it up. Whether or not he believed in gods, Mirari didn't know, but he remained skeptical of the true nature they were dealing with. She knew he saw hope where she couldn't. If anyone had the courage to face a power so divine as it was ambiguous, it was Gaven.

He asked Lucan, "How did you find out? How did *Fangbane* find out?"

"I don't know if Fangbane *knows*," Lucan said. He sighed and stretched his legs out like he was exhausted. "He said we need to find the vessels. He didn't say anything about Mirari. However," he addressed her, "if I recall correctly, you used fire during the battle at the Althaean Siege. It'll only be a matter of time before he connects the pieces. As for me, I didn't believe it at first, but —" His forehead contorted. "It's been happening more often, hasn't it? You've been leaving quite a trail."

Mirari bit her lip and nodded. She recalled the battle in Aias, then the port where she fought Soteria. Even just yesterday, after speaking to Salathiel. She said, "Cygnus seems to react whenever I am close to someone with dark aura."

Lucan held his hand by his lip and nodded. He adjusted his glasses and asked, "Do you know who Lachess' vessel is?" Gaven and Mirari glanced at each other as if they didn't want to admit it, and Lucan's brows furrowed. "Is it bad?"

Mirari nudged Gaven to deliver the bad news. He sighed and said, "It's Councilor Julie."

"Councilor Julie? Are you sure?" Lucan was leaning forward,

his hand braced against the small table. "If you are wrong, this is a huge accusation."

Mirari's gaze was focused on her teacup, but she brought her attention back to Lucan. She said, "I am almost certain it's her."

Lucan pondered for a moment. "Is that who you were trying to accuse during Mirari's trial?"

Gaven chuckled. "I had no idea at the time. I was bluffing." He shook his head as if he regretted not knowing sooner.

"Should I tell the Knights this?"

"No," Gaven said, bringing his hand to his chin. "I don't know what Fang is up to, but I don't like the sound of it. We can direct them if we stay ahead of them. Until then, let them conduct their own investigation. I doubt they'll find anything if their target is a councilor."

And a Valenian one at that – they were more reclusive than the others. Mirari wondered if they would even consider investigating the Council. Had the others believed Gaven's accusation against the Council to be a ploy as well?

Lucan nodded and got to his feet. "I should head back. I don't want them to become suspicious."

Gaven stepped outside to give Mirari a chance to say goodbye to Lucan. She would join him back at the Knights' Estate soon. She didn't know what to do, but she agreed with Gaven and Lucan that it was best to play ignorant.

She fell into step next to Gaven as they headed back into the street.

"Gaven?"

"Hmm?"

"Do you think Sal was right?" Her gaze was on the floor, waiting for his answer. "Are the Knights… using me?"

He stopped and grabbed her arms, forcing her to look at him.

"You can't trust what Sal says. He doesn't know anything. He's never met the Knights."

That was true, but the more she thought about it, the more she realized that if this was Fangbane's plan all along, she was playing right into it. At the same time, she agreed with Fangbane – perhaps the best play was to let Cygnus fight Lachess.

She worried her lip. "What if Fangbane is right?" He scowled and she had to hurry to continue. "I meant about defeating Lachess. We both know how dangerous she is. Don't I have a responsibility to try?"

What didn't make sense was why would Julie, or Lachess, encourage her to control Cygnus if it was designed to end her?

She was pulled out of her thoughts as Gaven forced her chin up.

"Not at the cost of your own life," he said. "If it were anyone else, would you be so cavalier with their life? If it were me, would I be an acceptable sacrifice?"

She shook her head. Every step up till now was had been about saving Gaven's life.

"If you wouldn't sacrifice me, don't sacrifice yourself," he said, and it soothed her.

"I won't," she promised. "I'll live. I swear."

PART IV

CHAPTER TWENTY-NINE

Crossing the bridge onto the Knights' Estate, Mirari and Gaven were greeted by Shiba and Neo in the courtyard. Mirari couldn't believe her eyes when she saw them planting fresh goldenglow flowers along the side of the estate, decorating the earth in brilliant reds and yellows. The estate grounds were clean and refreshing, welcoming spring with a new look, and Mirari felt at home. Mirari was impressed by how delicately Neo held a dainty goldenglow in his large palms. He set the flower in a hole and brushed soil around the edges.

Gaven glanced around and noticed something missing.

"Where is everyone else?" he asked.

"While you were on vacation, the rest of us were put to work," Shiba said with a huff. "I'm sure Fang will debrief you."

Gaven raised a brow. "And he left you two on gardening duty?"

"We did our part," Neo said with a big grin on his face. He whispered to Mirari, "Can you believe it? Shiba volunteered to stay back. We're just taking a little break."

Shiba omitting himself from the action? That was truly an oddity.

Gaven told Mirari, "I'll go see him then." He nodded to Shiba and Neo before making his way inside. Mirari could feel that Gaven was calm. That was no surprise. If anyone could conceal a plan, it was Gaven. He would face Fangbane alone, knowing Mirari wouldn't be able to handle it – her mind was not in the right place, and that was dangerous against a mind reader. Still, she couldn't help but worry if he would be able to pry information out of Fangbane without revealing what they knew about the vessels of the Goddesses. For Mirari, hiding the truth from Shiba, Neo, and the rest of the Knights would be a challenge of its own.

Neo brushed his face with the back of his hand, smearing dirt along the way. He got to his feet and waited until Gaven was out of sight.

"How is your brother?" he asked. "What's his name again? Salathiel?"

Forcing a smile, Mirari shrugged. "Good. The usual. We just had a lot to catch up on." Mirari kept a bright smile on her face as she stepped past Neo. It was frankly the last thing she wanted to talk about. "Please excuse me. It's been a long journey."

Neo didn't stop her and picked up his shovel as Mirari went inside. On her way up the stairs, a voice called to her.

"You don't want to talk about it?" Shiba said. His stern gaze bore into her as he shut the courtyard door behind him.

"The journey was fine. Informative," she replied with a practiced smile that quickly wavered.

He stood still, crossed his arms, and waited. His silent intensity, more effective than his physical outbursts, created a discomfort she struggled to navigate. There was an unspoken understanding in his actions. He wanted details.

"What?" she huffed.

Shiba sighed and unfolded his arms. "I can see that's not true. Your negative energy is suffocating the estate."

He advanced until he stood mere inches away, a little too close for comfort.

"I— I don't know what more you want me to say," she said, climbing a few more steps.

"Something has happened, and you're trying to face it alone. You're about to go to your room and cry yourself to sleep over it, aren't you?" He raised his hand and continued before she could protest, "You always forget that we're here, Mirari. The Knights. Lean on us for once. I'm tired of watching you stumble on your own."

This was not the Shiba she thought she knew – the stoic and aggressive leader she had grown accustomed to. Mirari's chest tightened with unexpected warmth.

She was left speechless, grappling with conflicting emotions that tore her between her bond with her brother to the loyalty she shared with the Knights. She couldn't reveal Salathiel's warnings against the Knights or the doubt that lingered in her mind. But Shiba was right – the Knights had always supported her and she had no reason to doubt them.

Her eyes stung, a single tear escaping – she blamed it on the scent of fresh soil and goldenglow flowers on his clothes. The thought of it made her chuckle.

Shiba sighed and reached his hand out, his thumb brushing away the stray tear. "Look, there's always a solution to every problem. It just may not be the solution you want. Do you understand?"

Ducking her head, Mirari nodded.

Like an alert hound, Shiba fixed his attention to the end of the hall. Mirari followed his gaze, finding nothing, but moments later she could hear heels clicking against the marble floor.

"Don't talk to her," Shiba said.

"What—"

Mirari's response died in her throat as Shiba pulled her in. It wasn't quite a hug, but she was close enough to feel the beat of his heart.

He whispered into her ear, "Lord Fangbane and Starlight have been keeping secrets from us. I just don't know what. Don't try to tell me that you don't see it too." Shiba pulled back and gazed at her with intense gravity. "Mirari, I may not know everything but I'm not daft. Go to your room, now. I'll keep Starlight busy."

Shiba gave her a gentle shove, and Mirari ascended the remaining steps. She darted her eyes between the hall and Shiba. He nodded and encouraged her to move faster. Mirari shook off her thoughts and hurried to her room.

She closed the door and leaned heavily against it. What did Shiba mean? How much did he know? And what if he knew something that she didn't?

That simple interaction drained her, and now she was left with more questions than she had moments ago. She wouldn't take his warning lightly – there was something Shiba learned from the Knights' meeting while she was away. Hopefully, Gaven would learn the same in his current meeting with Fangbane.

***

"AND THEN, and then the frog got away," Sarkan said, waving his hand around to encompass his entire story. Fangbane had his head braced on his chin while he stared at his youngest – six-years-old and already perceptive. Sarkan was on his lap, but as he got more excited about his story, Fangbane suspected it was only a matter of time before his energy became too much to be contained. He would soon burst into a run.

There were two quick knocks at the door and it swung open, startling father and son. Gaven was much the same as the last time Fangbane had seen him, though there was a tightness around his eyes. The region leader hesitated when he saw Sarkan.

"I can come back later."

"No need," Fangbane said. Sarkan jumped down from his lap.

Lifting his hands in the air, Sarkan said, "I'll go find Mr. Hoppy okay?"

"Okay, Sharky," Fangbane said with a laugh. "Be gentle."

"I will," Sarkan said with a wave. He ran out of the room, forgetting to greet Gaven as he left.

"Ah, sorry about that," Fangbane said, waving his hand toward the unoccupied chair.

"It's fine," Gaven said. "I interrupted you."

Fangbane folded his hands together as Gaven sat down.

"Welcome back. What can I do for you?"

Gaven's thick, dark eyebrows lowered over his sharp eyes. "Wasn't there a Knights meeting? I wanted to stay apprised of any new... missions we might have."

Gaven's mind was in turmoil, but Fangbane caught a whisper of a name in the maelstrom of thoughts.

...Lucan...

The name was coated in anger like sticky multart.

It made sense. Since that Council meeting where Gaven had announced Mirari's death, Lucan had been, understandably, upset. Fangbane had hoped the two would eventually come to an understanding, especially now that Mirari had been found alive.

But Fangbane knew that there was another possibility. Lucan had been hiding his thoughts for an unknown reason, and he wouldn't be surprised if he had already delivered Gaven the news.

Were they working together or against each other?

He wouldn't stir this pot, Fangbane concluded. Either way, it was in his favor to tell Gaven about the goddesses himself, according to Sorren's plan. After all, Gaven was integral to keeping Mirari close.

"The meeting?" Gaven prompted.

"Right." Fangbane moved some papers around as he carefully chose his words. "I have reason to believe that Soteria obtained her power from someone. Our next target is finding that source and making sure more people don't have access to that ability."

"You said Mirari didn't need to be at the meeting," Gaven said, crossing his arms. "Yet you've assigned a new mission to the Knights?"

"During the discussion, the conversation changed." Fangbane hesitated but continued, "I did consider tabling the discussion until you and Mirari returned, but I ultimately decided against it. This threat will not wait for us. Time is of essence."

He caught Gaven's thoughts as if he wanted them heard.

What are you playing at, Fang?

"It was for your benefit." Gaven seemed on edge, but still willing to listen. Fangbane could work with that. Leaning forward, Fangbane said, "I suspected you would not have been pleased when the question of your memories inevitably came up." Gaven tensed. "*Have* you recovered any part of your mem—"

"No," he said, as if his glare could prickle Fangbane's skin. Gaven had no thoughts following his stern dismissal.

Fangbane shrugged and settled back in his chair. "That's all right. It was only a question." Gaven crossed his arms and did the same. "As it stands, the other Knights are doing what they can to find out more about Soteria's past, to see when and where she might have encountered the source of this ability."

"Do you have any leads?"

This time Fangbane's hesitation was not an affectation. He couldn't predict how Gaven would respond when he said, "Yes. A higher power." Fangbane pointed to the roof. "Gods at play. Soteria's abilities were consistent with a myth about..." Gaven rolled his eyes. "Problem?"

"Gods? Really?"

"You did ask me what the source was."

"I thought you'd have something concrete. Something based on facts and logic."

They were at an impasse. Fangbane didn't have the where-withal or desire to convince an atheist of the danger Lachess posed.

Although Fangbane couldn't hear Gaven's mind clearly, he caught unusual thoughts from Gaven – murmurs that resonated with feelings of disappointment. It was as if Gaven knew what Fangbane would say and had hoped it would be different.

His thoughts remained elusive, veiled in ambiguity. Over time, Fangbane noticed that Gaven had grown clever around Fangbane's ability. While he respected Gaven's desire for privacy, the flow of understanding they once shared now faced obstacles. A growing sense of distance threatened to pull them apart.

"If you have nothing of importance to say..." Gaven started to rise. "I'll inform Mirari of the situation."

"Wait."

"What is it?" Gaven said, annoyed.

"You believe, don't you? Even you have considered the possi-bility that this had all been the work of the gods."

Fangbane watched the muscle in Gaven's jaw flex, in his moment of anger or confusion. Gaven lifted his hand and squeezed the bridge of his nose.

"Laikos, Soteria," Gaven said, shaking his head. "There must be a reason why they all talk about the gods. That's all there is to it. Were they right?" Gaven scoffed. "I wouldn't believe the words of lunatics."

Fangbane nodded. Gaven stared at him before heading for

the door. His mind was clouded and obscured like a thundercloud had rolled over his thoughts, and there would be no point stopping him from leaving. Whatever information he had, Fangbane knew it would be hard to obtain it from him.

CHAPTER THIRTY

Mirari took a wary step toward a gilded mirror hanging from the wall in her room, staring at the shroud that covered her reflection. Pulling a corner of the shroud, she peeked at her reflection.

Long, wavy hair. Bright, purple eyes – Mirari had always been somewhat concerned over her appearance. First, it was because she looked like her parents, a Hale, and she hated it. Once she was able to put that aside, her paranoia dragged her into her eyes of chaos.

Staring deep into them, she frowned. She was herself, for now. But was there no way to communicate with Cygnus on her own? Was there no way to be in control?

According to Gaven, she couldn't control the soul flame. She was stuck at the mercy of the goddess within her. Yet Mirari rejected that idea. She refused to be a pawn in a war between two deities. She was a person. She existed. She lived.

"Hello?" Mirari called. She felt ridiculous talking to her reflection.

Reaching out, she placed her hand on the mirror and

blocked her view of half her face. She felt silly but didn't know what else to do. In the past, there had been whispers in her mind. She had always ignored them, but maybe that had been Cygnus trying to communicate with her. Maybe there was a way for them to work together. Before, Mirari had tried to take control of the flames. Now, she would try to listen and reach out to the goddess within her. She cleared her throat and tried again.

"We need to talk." When still there was no response, she scowled and leaned forward. "Don't hide from me. Answer me."

Hide? You think I'm hiding?

Mirari gasped and jerked her hand back. She could see it — her face in shock, her own face the way it was supposed to be. But there was a sparkle in one of her eyes, a wavering glow. One of her irises, that was once a familiar purple, was evolving into a bright magenta and it kindled like a fire.

Mirari took a breath. Her hands were shaking, dreading the sight of her greatest fear. She exhaled. She had to be brave. It wasn't just about her, but Salathiel, Gaven, the Knights – they all depended on her to be in control. She steadied her hands and leaned forward, gaping at her wide-eyed gaze. Her shocked expression began to relax, her eyes now steady and calm.

You can hear me.

Mirari watched her lips. They weren't moving when she heard her own voice, but they felt numb as if she had lost control of it. Mirari couldn't tell if she was frozen with fear or if Cygnus was controlling her body but she knew that sense of calm was not from her.

She parted her lips and responded, "I can."

The voice sighed. *Finally.*

Her voice was faded as if she was struggling to keep up.

Mirari shook from her daze. Taking a deep breath, she spoke louder. "Who are you?"

You already know the answer. You already know everything.

"Then why me? What do you want from me?"

You? You think this is about you? She sounded amused. *Don't be foolish. You were just unlucky to be born into this mess. You and your friends.*

Mirari wet her lips. If what Gaven said was true then Cygnus would stay for as long as Lachess lived. The two of them would leap into a battle, heedless of the lives around them, until one rose victorious.

Mirari's hands would take more lives. She shook away that thought.

"You want to end Lachess, right?" Mirari said. "I'll help you, on the condition that I get to stay in control."

That's not possible. You cannot bear the flames. She paused. *You are strong-willed, child, but that won't be enough to stop Lachess. You mortals are chained by your emotions. Lachess will not hesitate to act on your weakness.*

"Do you have to kill her? Lachess?"

That is what we are fated to do. The gods will not allow us to return until one of us is gone.

"And can you not rewrite fate?"

Cygnus didn't speak, but her eye remained a blazing magenta.

No, I cannot.

Mirari shook her head. "Then are you a real Goddess? No. I refuse to believe that."

Your ignorance is more reason you cannot fight Lachess. You will lose. Even your so-called brother knows this. He does not pick a fight he cannot win. He knows to fear me, to fear you.

Salathiel? Mirari's hands tightened into fists. "You keep him out of this."

I'm afraid that's not possible. He was gone the moment Lachess chose to give him dark aura. Everyone who has met her touch will end with the same fate.

"He's harmless. He doesn't use dark aura at all."

Even if he can control it, do you deny that dark aura has not changed him?

Mirari lowered her gaze, thinking back on her last interaction with Salathiel. She was sure that Salathiel was being influenced by Lachess only because he felt beholden to her. If Salathiel was freed from Lachess' influence, he would be able to think clearly again. No longer would he blindly follow Lachess. He would accept the Knights' help once he understood how dangerous Lachess was.

"You saved Soteria," Mirari said, eyes widening as she met her reflection again. "And Gaven. You took away their dark aura."

Such power doesn't belong in the hands of mortals. After all these years, I see that Lachess has failed to understand this.

Mirari pondered. Maybe Cygnus wasn't so bad after all. She seemed to only wish to undo the damage that Lachess caused. Mirari braced her hands on either side of the mirror. "Then do it for Sal."

Immediately, she replied, *He does not desire to be saved.*

"I'll make a deal with you."

She recalled the mythology books she read in Julie's cabin. If she learned anything, it was that the divine spoke a different language. If one wanted to be heard, they had to make an offering, or a deal.

Cygnus was silent, listening. Mirari didn't trust Cygnus – not just her, but any entity that had control over her body – but for Salathiel sake, she would take the risk.

"I won't resist you anymore," she said. "Do what you must, but first, you have to save Sal."

There was a pause as Cygnus considered Mirari's proposition.

He will resist.

"Please, you know he's better than this."

More silence. Finally, Cygnus sighed.

Very well.

Mirari nodded at her reflection. The glow in her eye began to fade, and Mirari released her breath. Was that it? She didn't even know if she was truly alone or if Cygnus could see everything even outside of consciousness. She would have to take precautions.

She pulled the curtain back over the mirror. She knew it wouldn't stop Cygnus from coming out as she pleased, but it made her feel safer. Taking a step back, she fell onto her bed, her hands clasped lightly over her stomach. She tapped her finger against her knuckles, reducing her anxiety to the tapping.

She was still Mirari. She was still in control.

It was almost a relief when someone knocked on her door. She rolled off the bed, landing agilely on her feet.

She hoped everything went well with Gaven's conversation with Fangbane. She threw open the door and reared back in surprise.

Not Gaven.

"I'm sorry. Did I surprise you?" Starlight said, tilting her head to the side.

"A-a little," she said, taking a step back. "I— thought you were someone else."

Starlight gracefully invited herself in, stepping across the threshold with an air of harmless curiosity. She took a quick glimpse of everything in her room, and her gaze lingered on the cloth-covered mirror. To Mirari's surprise, she made no comment.

"I ran into Shiba in the hallway and he told me what happened," she said, her tone filled with genuine concern.

"He did?" But what, Mirari wondered. Was he not the one who told her not to talk to Starlight? Starlight stood in the center of the room, her hands tucked innocently behind her back. As Mirari carefully closed the door, she couldn't help but feel a certain wariness. "What did he say?"

"Well." Starlight bit her lip and pivoted from the mirror. "He said you were tired and needed time alone, but I figured it was more than that. After all, a trip to visit family should be a happy one."

Mirari acknowledged Starlight's thoughtfulness but couldn't shake off the conflicting emotions. Shiba's warnings and Salathiel's ultimatum echoed in her mind, and Starlight's calm presence clashed with their cautionary words.

"I wanted to lend you my ear, so to speak, if you wanted to talk."

Mirari shook her head. "It's just something Sal said."

"He doesn't like us?" When her delicate voice peaked, it felt like heartbreak. Mirari must've looked startled when Starlight chuckled and said, "I've surprised you again."

Mirari laughed lightly. "Sometimes I wonder if you're a mind reader too."

"I don't need to be a mind reader to read the worry on your face." Starlight stepped in front of her and rested her hands on her shoulders. "Hate often stems from misunderstanding. Judgment, clouded by anger and fueled by ignorance."

Starlight's unwavering belief in understanding and unity felt like a lifeline. She refocused her gaze to the ground for a brief moment, and when she returned, the twinkle in her eyes grew brighter.

"Why don't you invite him here?" she said. Her face beamed as she gave Mirari's shoulders a gentle squeeze.

"Here?" Mirari scanned the room. "Why?"

"Maybe if he saw that the Knights were friendly, that there was nothing to worry about, it would assuage some of his fears." Mirari hesitated, her eyes flickering between the room's shadows and the compassion in Starlight. The idea was plausible, and, more than anything, she didn't want to fight with Salathiel.

"Do you think it will work?" she asked.

Starlight shrugged. "Doesn't hurt to try."

Closing her eyes briefly, Mirari exhaled deeply. "Alright, I'll invite him."

Starlight's smile brightened, and she gave Mirari's shoulders a final, affirming squeeze. Her firm grip stirred hope within her. "You'll see. Sometimes, all it takes is a chance for understanding to bloom."

CHAPTER THIRTY-ONE

Gaven guided his mount down the familiar dirt path. The trail through Malino stretched for acres, farther than his eyes could see.

The trees touched the sky and towered over him on this sunny day, just as they did when he was a child. He crossed a stream and made a turn at a large tree. No traveler would take this path – it was hidden and unmarked – but for him it was second nature. The air was calm, nothing but a bird's lullaby in cadence with the rustle of leaves. A kick of fresh air was what he needed, and time away from the nonsense about gods. Nothing had changed about these woods, but part of him wished it had.

He had promised Mirari to deliver a message to Salathiel – an invitation to visit them and the Knights at the Estate. He wasn't happy about being the messenger, but Mirari insisted that he and Salathiel had amends to make. How would inviting Salathiel to the Estate help rebuild their broken family ties? Gaven could not see it.

The real reason why Gaven accepted the task was because he saw it as an opportunity to finish what he started. Salathiel had lied to him, hurt him. Why should Gaven arrive with a peace offering?

Instead, Gaven chose a detour – to the origin. For some crazy reason he thought it would grant him clarity for the situation that they were in.

Riding through the forest, Gaven saw a clearing to his right – his old favorite hunting spot – and turned the corner. Not long after, the forest opened into a large field. There was soil where plants used to be grown, and an abandoned cottage where there used to be life.

His heart skipped a beat as memories flooded. He had run through these fields every day, taking a sturdy stick from the pile of branches he collected on the side of the cottage, and sparred in front of the porch until dusk. Salathiel's mother practically had to drag him back inside for supper. He chuckled at the thought.

Gaven got off his horse and stepped onto the porch. He heard the familiar creaks of the board under his feet every time Salathiel's father came home after tending the fields.

Gaven was almost at the front door when he froze – the rhythm was off and he could tell that sound was coming from more than one direction. He stood erect, feeling an unsettling aura from inside. The only reason he hadn't drawn his weapon yet was because the aura felt familiar, and a part of him believed that the feeling should be welcomed.

He heard a whistle through the air and stepped to his right.

Thunk!

A dagger nailed the support beam to his left. The message was clear, and Gaven cursed at himself for going against his instincts.

Reaching for the weapon in his belt, he pulled forward his spear – extending it a bright glow – just in time to deflect a second dagger.

Recognizing the dagger now lodged into the support beam, he seethed.

"You're not welcome here," the familiar voice called from inside.

Gaven scowled, holding his spear at the ready. "What are you doing here?"

"This is my home." Salathiel appeared into view. He had a similar scowl on his face and a dagger in each hand.

"You're not the only one who lived here." Gaven corrected him. "Besides, shouldn't you be in Valenia? With Councilor Julie?"

Salathiel scoffed. "You think I was dumb enough to wait for you to return?"

Gaven's knuckles turned white. He charged forward with a cry. "Then you know why I'm going to kill you!"

His spear crashed down on the fragile porch where Salathiel stood. Salathiel kicked his wrist, forcing Gaven to flex his fingers and loosen his grip and his weapon thumped onto the deck. It was a smart move, but Gaven didn't need his weapon to best Salathiel. Gaven pivoted his body and returned a kick. It was strong enough to make Salathiel stumble back into the wall.

"You were dead to us the day you left these grounds," Salathiel said, planting his feet. He chuckled, taunting with his hands for Gaven to approach. "You wanted to be a proud Althaean. You got your wish."

Was this what it was all about? Jealousy? He would kill his cousin over that? Gaven shouted, "Is it so hard for you to be happy for me?"

Salathiel's face softened for a moment. But his scowl returned and he shook his head. "I *am* happy for you. I always was. But I can't ignore the fact that you're a danger to everyone, especially Mirari. How many lives did you take during the Althaean Siege?"

"The Siege?" Gaven pointed his finger at him. "You did that

to me. To think you were so weak-minded to resort to making deals with gods."

Salathiel came forward, twirling the dagger with his fingers. "Dark aura shows our true selves. You couldn't control it because it was what you wanted. You kill. Is that not what you plan to do to me now?"

Salathiel no doubt also came with this intent, but before Gaven could argue, a dagger lodged into the ground inches from his foot. He followed the dagger with his head, then back up at Salathiel.

"Last warning. Get out."

It wasn't just about Salathiel using dark aura on him, it was the way he degraded Gaven and judged his worth. The audacity, calling him a traitor to his people and his family. The wrath in his spear was fueled by decades of animosity.

Gaven kicked the dagger away. "You couldn't finish me off the first time. What makes you so sure you can this time?"

Salathiel lunged forward with his dagger.

Gaven turned his feet, dodging one violent swipe after another, each step moving closer toward his fallen spear. He ducked and pulled his spear up in time to block another swing. They were both aggressive fighters, desperate to dominate. As children, they had grappled with each other in the same way. That was their fun, but what was once bashful playtime was now a bloodthirsty brawl.

Salathiel was stronger now, and terrifyingly agile. Gaven couldn't catch him before he elbowed him in the chest, then crouched and kicked his ankle. Gaven lurched forward and stumbled. Salathiel was a bull charging against a stone wall, but not one strong enough to knock him off his feet. Gaven held a beat, leaning on his spear for support when he saw an opening. He shifted his weight onto his spear, forcing it down deeper into the earth. The ground under Salathiel's feet sank and he fell backward.

Fuming, Gaven raised his spear. For all the pain that Salathiel caused, death would be mercy. But in this moment, there was nothing he wanted more than for this nightmare to end. His anger fueled his kore, channeling his energy into the weapon and it illuminated brighter.

Nothing could hold him back, not even the gentle tug he felt in his right ankle. But by the time he looked down, his entire body below his lower torso was wrapped in vines, confined to the ground. They compressed his body, crushing him under their grip. He felt his breath slipping away.

Gaven hastily struck down on the vines. He didn't have time to react when Salathiel lunged forward and lodged a blade into his shoulder, forcing him to release the breath he was holding.

He didn't want to admit that he had underestimated his opponent. Had Gaven not hardened his body with some of his kore, he would've broken a few ribs. How did Salathiel become such an adept fighter, or was it dark aura that was giving him strength?

His eyes wandered to the hilt still in Salathiel's hand – an opening. Gaven reached for his arm and pulled him forward.

Salathiel stumbled, and his body met the sharp end of Gaven's spear. Where there would normally be blood was a black substance spilling from his wound.

Gaven was sure of it now, and though it may have been cruel to end his cousin's life, he needed it for his own peace. Wasn't Salathiel doing the same to him? Gaven almost felt sorry that their relationship had to end this way, but surely Salathiel understood.

Gaven pushed him back, freeing him from the point of his blade. Salathiel faltered backward and pressed his hand against his waist. The bleeding didn't last long. Salathiel lifted his hand, and in a matter of seconds, the wound was sealed.

Dark aura. Of course, he had nearly forgotten that Salathiel was a victim of dark aura no less than Gaven was himself.

Except, he had it worse – dark aura was Salathiel's lifeline. Gaven understood now that it took on a literal definition. As long as he had dark aura, he was invincible, and there was only one thing that could dispel it – the soul flame, in Mirari's hands.

Gaven lowered his spear, realizing that it was futile for him to fight Salathiel.

"Are you proud of this?" Gaven said. He reached for the dagger in his shoulder and yanked it out, flinching. He tossed the dagger at Salathiel's feet so that he could see what real blood looked like. To his surprise, Salathiel refused to meet his gaze. He kept his hand pressed against the wound even though it had stopped bleeding.

"I was dead, Gaven," Salathiel said, a bite to his words. "I didn't want *any* of this."

"You're both wasting your time."

Recognizing the voice, Gaven didn't rush to find Julie standing on the porch, arms crossed and sneering at both of them with disgust. Gaven took a wary step back.

How long had she been there, and why hadn't he sensed her? Judging by her discontent, she must've known that Gaven knew her true identity. He bit his lip and addressed her by her real name.

"Lachess."

If the councilor was in control, he would've bowed, but instead, he held his chin high. This was the supposed Goddess of Devotion. Gaven, while entertaining the idea, remained skeptical about the existence of gods. Yet, he decided to exercise caution, questioning the reliability of his senses when it came to deities.

Slowly descending the steps, Lachess approached Gaven with grace. She reached forward, and Gaven took another step back.

"You're tarnishing the ground with your blood," she said. Her palm opened up to reveal a folded cloth. Gaven stared at the cloth, and hesitating, he took it.

"Thank... you?" he said, pressing it against his wound. She

doubled back to Salathiel and tugged on his arm, forcing him to rise.

"You both want the same thing," she said. "I don't see why you're fighting."

"It's clear that we don't," Salathiel said. He darted his hate-filled eyes to Gaven for a moment, then back to Lachess. Lachess arched an eyebrow. Sardonic or surprised, it was hard to tell.

"Tell me, Valiant Tiger, do you find Cygnus… delightful?" Gaven wrinkled his forehead. Before he could respond, she continued, "Then tell me, why work with her?"

Gaven didn't know how much she knew, or how she obtained her information. Perhaps she was all-seeing. He had learned his lesson after facing Cygnus. They could see through deception. He should have expected this from the Goddess of Devotion.

"I'm only doing it to free Mirari," Gaven said. "Cygnus said she'll leave forever once you're gone."

Lachess turned to Salathiel and kept her focus on him as if she was waiting for him to speak, and he did in a heartbeat.

"Do you think she'll uphold that promise?" he asked with a roll of his eyes.

"I trust her over a bunch of mind-controlling demons."

Lachess held her wrists out in front of Gaven. "Then go on. Take me to her."

"What?"

"Is that not what she wanted? If it will free the woman, then so be it." She lowered her hands and turned away, making her way back to the porch. "But we all know that won't happen."

Gaven narrowed his eyes. He turned to Salathiel, then back to Lachess. "What game are you playing?"

Salathiel shook his head. "As long as Cygnus leaves us alone, Lachess won't fight back."

"I never wanted a fight," Lachess said. She descended onto the porch steps like a falling leaf, her legs crossing with the fluidity of a winding river. "It is Cygnus who initiates these wars.

But even so…" Lachess lowered her head as if a memory had struck her.

"Cygnus is her *friend*," Salathiel said, with a sigh that seemed to carry the weight of his emotion. "She's tired of fighting. Don't you see?" He turned to Cygnus. "But Cygnus won't stop and you know that. How much longer will you wait?"

Lachess turned her gaze to Gaven, no doubt avoiding Salathiel's question.

Gaven wasn't sure. He bit his lip. Sure, it made sense that after centuries of fighting, Lachess was ready to surrender. Then why was she spreading dark aura? Why hadn't she faced Cygnus yet? It sounded too good to be true.

"We are here against our will," Lachess said, as if she had read his thoughts. Gaven's head shot up. "No, we're not mind readers. I can just tell by the look on your face." She closed her eyes for a moment, and when they opened, they twinkled with a sapphire glow more intense than before. "Reincarnation is our punishment. The cycle continues until one of us kills the other in this state. All I wanted was the best for humanity, to bless those who deserved a second life, like Salathiel. If Cygnus still fails to understand my intentions, if she would sacrifice me to return to Nagama, then so be it. Let us involve mortals no more."

Gaven could sense sincerity in her words. What he understood was that she was tired of living as a mortal, so she did what she believed in – blessing the devoted with a second chance in life. She wasn't spreading evil; she was doing it out of kindness, defying the rules of the divine to follow her heart. In a way, she had become human, and she was ready to die for her beliefs, knowing that, even if she defeated Cygnus, the gods would not accept her back.

"And Julie?" Gaven asked. "What happens to her once you die?"

She stood motionless and Gaven wasn't sure if she had heard him.

She blinked and spoke, "Julie is gone. That is the fate of the vessel."

Gaven opened his mouth, but he realized he had nothing to say. Lachess was implying that Cygnus had lied. About Mirari. About saving her.

"It's time for you to decide," Salathiel said, crossing his arms. "Who will you side with?"

Gaven frowned. He knew how much Mirari feared Cygnus, but could he really trust the deal that he made with the Goddess? Could he trust Salathiel or Lachess? Gaven released his breath. It wasn't about who he believed, but what would help free Mirari from Cygnus.

"Well?" Gaven sighed. "What was your plan?"

"Only dark aura can kill Cygnus," Salathiel said. He held up his hand and a faint, black mist began to flow out of his palm. "I can do it, but only when Cygnus is active."

Gaven narrowed his eyes. "That's dangerous for you. If you're too close to her—"

"But it's what I'll do, if it means Mirari will be freed."

Lachess glared at him and scowled, "Salathiel, I told you. Don't you even consider—"

"I have to try. And I'm going to do it whether you're coming or not." Salathiel dispelled the dark aura from his hand and, without looking at Lachess, made his way inside the house. He picked up his bag along with a few items on the table. "Now we just need a way for me to get inside the Knights' Estate."

Gaven sighed, recalling Mirari's invitation. Salathiel already had Fangbane's permission to enter.

"Lucky for you, that won't be a problem."

CHAPTER THIRTY-TWO

There was a knock on one of the doors at the Hale's Estate in Valenia. It was quite late – hours after supper when most had retreated to their quarters – but the guards, standing with their backs to the main door, trained to react to every sound, remained alert and attentive. One of them twisted and peered through the looking glass. At the sight of the dragon crest of Althaea Main residing on the visitor's chest, he opened the door immediately.

"We've been expecting you, Milady," he said with a bow. He raised his head and took Erel's coat. Erel scanned the vast, marble hallway, then the spiral staircase in front of her.

At the top of the staircase stood the master of the estate, Lucan Hale. His arms were crossed, chin high as he stood behind life-sized portraits of his parents. Her arrival was expected, but not this soon. She must've come rushing from Althaea Main as soon as Gaven gave the order. For some reason, he said Erel could help them.

Lucan examined the woman. Seeing her up close for the first time, he could see why she had been mistaken for Soteria. But

Soteria had a menacing aura that complemented the twisted look on her face. Erel was calm, almost lifeless.

She began ascending the staircase with a blank expression, and without greeting Lucan, she passed him. He followed closely behind up the rest of the stairs.

"Where are you now?" she asked.

"The Knights are finding the vessels," Lucan said.

Before reaching the top, she asked, "Do *you* know who the vessels are?"

Lucan dabbed his eyes, and his silence seemed to be enough for her. She nodded, then continued up the stairs.

Stunned, Lucan pulled his glasses off and rubbed his eyes. He needed a moment to recollect his thoughts. Did she know as well? Gaven had told him that no one knew of Fate's Fable better than Erel. He didn't explain why, but Lucan assumed that it was because she was old enough to remember the annihilation of the Belligmn Tribe and may have had some ties to it.

But if Erel knew Cygnus' vessel, that meant she came with the intention of protecting Mirari. Perhaps that was what she meant when she questioned Lucan's trust. It was a plausible assumption considering she was Gaven's second in command. Lucan was relieved to have another person on Mirari's side.

"I got word from His Honor on the way here," Erel said. Lucan placed his glasses back on his face returning to his professional demeanor. "Lord Fangbane invited Salathiel to the estate, and he accepted."

Lucan furrowed his brows. "Why?"

"Beats me, but that means we don't have much time. We'll just have to do our part." She nudged her head down the hall at an open door. "You're in charge here. What's the *real* task?"

For now, Lucan could only lead the Knights in one direction without jeopardizing the identity of Cygnus' vessel, to focus their search on Lachess' vessel first. Gaven and Lucan were hoping to find evidence to prove that Julie was affiliated with Soteria, or even better, the one responsible for spreading dark aura. If the Council found out about Julie's betrayal, she would be put away. They wouldn't have to fight Lachess and Cygnus would remain slumbering.

Lucan kept his voice steady as he pressed his hands to his lips. He couldn't help but feel as if they had missed something.

"Look deeper into the fable," he said. "We need to know exactly what we're dealing with if we want a chance of stopping her before a deity war breaks out."

Erel nodded. "Let's see what you've found so far."

They entered the Hale library and closed the door behind them. It was a humble room that was only a fraction of the library at the Knights' Estate. Lucan had decided to do his research here because of its proximity to the Tribe of Paragons. If he wanted more information about Julie, that was where they had to go to obtain it. However, Lucan didn't tell the Knights it was specifically Julie he was suspicious of. Rather, he encouraged the Knights to think about Gaven's accusation at the trial.

All was quiet in the library, just the sounds of pages turning and Kylah grumbling. She didn't even look up from the stack of papers in front of her when Erel came in. It was just the three of them. Shiba and Neo were back at the Knights' Estate – no doubt where she wished she was – and Dorain and Hime had set off to the Tribe of Paragons to find any reason to suggest that either Tarek or Julie was the traitor. Kylah had combed through the Council's records of recent spendings, court rulings, even recreational trips, anything to suggest that they had collaborated with the Blessed. She had nothing on Suzan, Adder, Dareh, or Novinha. Lucan didn't dare tell her it was just to keep her busy, not that Kylah would thoroughly go through the paperwork anyway.

It eventually came to a head when Kylah tossed the paper in her hand and rose. She started pacing around the table.

"This is madness," she said. "How can we accuse a councilor of being an evil goddess?"

"You just have to trust me, Kylah," Lucan said. Reaching across the table, he grabbed one of the discarded books and dusted it. He resisted the urge to sigh. "Besides, I have a credible source."

"Your "credible source" is political suicide."

Kylah crossed her arms and glared at Lucan, but he tried to ignore her. Not looking away from his own piece of literature, Lucan asked in a mild voice, "What's really bothering you?"

Kylah scoffed, crossing her arms. "Obviously, the fact that we've spent days trying to find something based on your "credible source" and we are getting nowhere with this theory. Isn't it time to search in another direction?"

Kylah was interrupted when Lucan's valet knocked on the door. The door slightly crept open, and a young man came into view. His soft cheeks and blue curls poked through the small opening.

"My liege," Shire said. "The Knights have returned."

Nodding, Lucan gestured at him. "Bring them in."

The door creaked wider. Shire bowed as Dorain and Hime walked into the room with books and scrolls in hand.

"Were you able to find the "something"?" Lucan asked.

"Nothing, unfortunately," Dorain said. "Their records are clean." He laid out the scrolls one by one as Hime set down her books next to them. Erel had her eye on one of the scrolls, bearing the crest of House Kouki, Julie's family. She reached for it and opened it.

"What of Councilor Julie's history?" Erel asked.

"Oh, right," Dorain peered over her shoulder, skimming over the text. "Kylah said something about a big fire at Julie's residence when she was a child, so I brought this. It's tragic, but I don't think it will prove anything."

Lucan walked over and skimmed through Julie's history

himself. If Erel had taken an interest in it, surely it was important.

"If I recall correctly, the celta and paragon tribes were at war at that time," Hime said.

"The leaders from two of the three houses that rule the Tribe of Paragons were assassinated," Kylah said. She swallowed a breath and exhaled deeply. Lucan could tell she didn't want to talk about it, but she mustered on. "It was what arguably started the war. The tribe was left in the leadership of a few kids. With an uncertain fate, it was why many people, including Neo's family, left Valenia."

Studying the paper, Erel recited, "There's no evidence of what caused the fire that killed the Koukis, or if it was deliberate or accidental. All that is recorded about it is that there was one survivor."

"Julie, we know," Kylah said, taking the scroll from her and skimming it for herself. "But how will this help us?"

Erel blinked once at Lucan. It was as if she was asking permission to reveal her thoughts.

"What is it, Erel?" Lucan asked.

"It's only a hunch," she said, humming to herself. "Surrendering to emotions unveils the vulnerability within."

Kylah raised a brow. "What are you implying?"

Erel sighed. "People change after a traumatic event, that's all. This must've been Julie's turning point, the reason why she became such a ruthless councilor."

Lucan was quiet while they discussed what this meant. He understood what Erel was implying. It was just like Mirari and the kōnvoy accident – stricken by grief, and weak after she witnessed her family's death, Julie would have become easy for Lachess to take over. But it wasn't evidence they could use to prove that Julie was Lachess' vessel.

"Perhaps we could say her family's tragedy is what led her to support rebels like the Blessed," Dorain said.

Kylah sighed. Gesturing to the scrambled papers on the table, she said, "Julie is clean. They all are. We don't have any solid evidence that they conspired with the Blessed, and certainly nothing that links her to being a vessel for a goddess."

Kylah was right. They had made no progress. Pinching his forehead, Lucan paced around the table. He couldn't give up now. It was this or letting Mirari fight Julie. He wasn't just worried about Mirari getting hurt, but also the amount of destruction two goddesses could cause. It certainly was enough to worry Fangbane and send him scrambling into researching an old fable.

The room grew loud with Dorain throwing obscure ideas off the top of his head and Erel yelling back. She sighed, giving up on Julie's scroll and shuffling through the other books on the table. Hime was hunched over an ancient-looking scroll. It had a much darker tint than the rest, worn from the ages. Lucan recognized the pattern of text — it was an old copy of the fable.

"Can I see that?" Lucan asked. With a nod, Hime stepped to the side. He had already memorized every word the first time, but for some reason he hoped that reading it again would spark an idea. Half-listening to Dorain, Lucan skimmed over the words in front of him. He was taken aback by the last paragraph. He started at the beginning and reread it again, then again.

"It can't be," Lucan said to himself. But it was loud enough for Hime to hear despite the roars of the other two in the room. He rubbed his fingers against his temple.

"What's wrong?" Hime asked.

Lucan let out a small chuckle. "My memory may be souring. This is not how I remembered it."

He drew Erel's attention, who walked over and read the scroll quietly to herself while Hime explained that the scroll was the earliest copy of the fable she could find, and that some words may have muddled over time.

"Is this right?" Erel asked, cutting Hime off.

Startled, Hime widened her eyes. "I think so, yes. As I said, legends may vary with time, but I believe this is the oldest version."

"This part is different." Erel pointed her finger to a specific line near the end of the page. It was the same line that caught Lucan's attention. She said, "This… is not how history remembers it."

If the original text was accurate, Mirari was in trouble. The heavy thumping in his chest overpowered any attempt to conceal his sense of urgency. Ducking his head, he hasted for the door. "I apologize. I'll be right back."

He didn't go far, only stepping out into the hallway. Using his clōve, first, he reached out to Mirari. There was no answer. He wasn't worried. Yet.

Next, he tried Gaven. This time when he didn't get a response, he let out a guttural groan. He tried again and then once more.

"Come on. Answer, damn it." He pinched the bridge of his nose and sighed again. Now he was desperate.

He contacted Fangbane.

Still nothing.

"All right, that's enough."

He whirled around. Kylah was standing behind him, arms crossed and leaning against the wall.

"You can't fool me, Lucan," she said. "I know when you're up to something. For months now, you've been acting strangely, running away for all these super-secret "business deals." You know something. Don't you think the rest of us deserve to know?"

It came as no surprise that Kylah had caught wind of his secrecy. She was clever, perceptive, and had spent enough time with him and his parents in the past to know when there was an oddity in the Hale business. Lucan tightened his hold on his clōve and considered lying – he had all the evidence to support it.

But Kylah wasn't mad, as far as he could tell, and lying to her didn't sit right with him. They had a trusting relationship that extended long before the Knights, and he couldn't betray that trust.

Kylah sighed and frowned. "I get the feeling that Lord Fangbane just wanted the rest of us off the Estate. Why are you helping him?"

"I'm not *helping* him," Lucan sighed. "It's... not easy to explain."

"Try me," she huffed. Lucan could tell that she wasn't going to budge. She continued, "What Erel found made you realize something. You might as well just tell us since I just heard you trying to contact the others."

Lucan knew there wasn't much time left, and that perhaps his mistake was keeping the others in the dark. To advance further, he needed the help of the Knights. Gaven and Mirari would have to forgive him – to Lucan, this was the best course of action.

He motioned toward the door. "I only want to explain this once. We should rejoin the others."

She nodded and followed him back into the library. The room grew silent, all eyes turned to Lucan. He frowned but took his place at the front of the room. The stares of his fellow Knights were unnerving, but he wasn't unfamiliar with presenting to a crowd. The difference now was that he was presenting someone else's secret, and that didn't sit right with him. There were things that could remain a secret, like his relation to Mirari. He took a breath and thought about how to explain the situation strategically.

"It began after Eoin's trial," Lucan said. That was a good place to start. "I couldn't accept that Mirari was labeled a traitor any more than Dorain could, so I started doing some investigating on my own. I didn't mention it because by Fangbane's order, the Knights were meant to implicitly agree with the Council's order."

"You were working with Dorain?" Hime asked.

Dorain shook his head. "I knew we couldn't get anywhere from our current position," he said. "I didn't know Lucan was doing the same."

Lucan continued, "Though we went separate ways, Dorain found a piece of the puzzle I didn't see before."

"I did?"

Lucan bit his lip and nodded. "Councilor Dareh was looking into my family's history. There *was* a reason, something I should've caught much earlier." Dorain tilted his head. "There was a fire on the kōnvoy that killed the Hale family in Minetta. There was also a fire that broke out in Aias when Gaven's army captured Eoin. The nature of both disasters was fire, but not quite."

"What do you mean not quite?" Hime tilted her head.

"Fire leaves burn marks and residue from ashes." Lucan paused. "In both cases there are burn marks, but no ashes. The marks were of the same pattern, a spiral, controlled, as if it were kore. But fire kore is not strong enough to leave behind the damage it did."

"And you thought it was more than a coincidence?" Kylah asked.

"I knew it." Lucan pinched the bridge of his nose. "You see… I know what caused the explosion on the Hale's kōnvoy. *She* told me. I… just didn't believe her at the time."

"She?"

Lucan braved himself. "It's Mirari. She's Cygnus' vessel."

To his surprise, the Knights were skeptical.

"But Mirari has wind kore," Hime said.

Kylah simply frowned. Lucan expected her to have more of an outburst, but she dug into herself like she had realized something she didn't want to admit.

"Are you sure, Lucan?" Kylah asked. "That conclusion seems like quite a jump."

"He's right," Erel said, jumping in. "I've seen the flames, and it's not kore." All eyes shifted to her as she paced to one of the open books. It had an illustration of the goddesses – elegant in long gowns, gracefully flowing with time. "When the goddess reincarnates, she walks the earth in a mortal body as if it were her own. Her divine powers are awakened and the host is placed in slumber."

Hime rubbed her thumbs together. Her eyebrows pinched when she lifted her gaze from the illustration to everyone in the room.

"Does Mirari know?" she asked. "Does Lord Fangbane know?"

"Of course they know," Kylah said, eyeing Lucan. "But if they already know, why were you in such a rush to contact them?"

Sighing, Lucan gestured to the scroll Hime had found. "Mirari has come face-to-face with Lachess' vessel, Councilor Julie. In fact, she was trying to help Mirari control Cygnus."

"So, it is Julie?" Dorain shouted, getting to his feet. "I knew it!" The others were not so surprised, or rather they didn't care now that they knew Mirari was involved.

"That makes no sense," Hime shook her head. "Are they not enemies?"

"Cygnus and Lachess were inseparable, working hand-in-hand," Erel said. "The best of friends, until Lachess saved the drowning boy. It is possible that after centuries of imprisonment, that resentment is no more."

"It was that passage that troubled me," Lucan said. "Modern inscriptions say that Cygnus saved the town by purifying dark aura."

"And this scroll says she purified *the town*. She killed every one of them," Erel said, pointing to the line of text. "We have always known dark aura to be the evil force of nature. It has given us nothing but trouble over recent years, however, we can't assume that Cygnus is all-good either."

"So, we can't trust deities," Dorain said. "What was so urgent about that?"

Lucan responded, "Lord Fangbane invited Mirari's brother to the Estate. He was the one who put her in touch with Lachess."

"He *what?*" Erel hissed. "So, it was *him?*" She was practically fuming when Lucan raised his hand to calm her down.

"At first I didn't think much of it but…" He furrowed his brows. "He disappeared right before the Althaean Siege, and reappeared now of all times. What was he doing all this time, what's his affiliation with Lachess, and is it a coincidence that we are not there now?"

"*He* started the Siege," Erel seethed. She grunted and released her frustration with a stomp to the ground. "Why didn't I see this?"

"Don't blame yourself," Lucan said. "None of us could've foreseen this. Perhaps, not even Fangbane. But if he did, then…"

Hime's ocean-blue eyes widened as she was the first to understand what he was implying. She glanced toward the scroll. "Lord Fangbane thinks Salathiel is Lachess," she said with gentle horror. "He wants them to fight."

Kylah shook her head. "Sal wouldn't do that. He cares about Mirari."

"Enough to do what?" Lucan prompted. Kylah closed her eyes and shook her head again. He could tell she was suffering just imagining it. "That's why I was trying to contact them. To warn them."

"You couldn't get through?" Erel asked. Lucan shook his head.

Gritting his teeth, Dorain grabbed his coat and headed for

the door. "Then we have to get back to the estate as quickly as possible."

CHAPTER THIRTY-THREE

Salathiel barely kept the sneer from his face as he crossed the bridge leading to the massive, sprawling estate. He knew Mirari was in there, trapped inside the gilded cage. He glanced to his right. Gaven kept his head high by his side. He didn't know if his words had got through to Gaven, but he knew he could count on his support to help defeat Cygnus.

Salathiel had been furious with himself about how his last conversation with Mirari had gone. He shouldn't have shouted. He hadn't known how to reach out to her after their disastrous argument, but he did want to make things right.

As for the Knights, he still didn't trust them. Mirari was brave and relentless, and the Knights would take advantage of that. They would put her in dangerous situations, sacrifice her for the greater good, and Mirari wouldn't bat an eye. She wouldn't know better. All she ever cared about was helping others.

He was here now, in this viper's nest, to make Mirari see reason. She would come to understand exactly who the Knights were, one way or another.

Mirari was waiting at the end of the bridge. She ran up to them and greeted them.

"Sal," she smiled. "Thank you for coming."

"Of course," he said, trying to hide his discomfort.

She looked at Gaven for a brief moment, and he returned a nod. Salathiel wanted to grab her hand and run away from this place. But for her sake, he had to pretend to get along with her new friends, and when the right time came, he would expel Cygnus.

"You two made up?" Mirari asked Gaven.

Gaven rolled his eyes. "Sure."

That was enough to light her face.

Gaven took the lead, opening the doors to the estate and guiding them down the hall. Even though the hall sparkled with a dazzling brilliance, its pristine marble walls – the sheer grandeur of the place, from the spotless floors to the entire majestic structure – only fueled Salathiel's unease.

Strolling between Gaven and Mirari was a mix of emotions for Salathiel, tinged with both sweetness and awkwardness. The reunion wasn't unfolding as he had imagined. The air was filled with unspoken tension, and Salathiel couldn't shake the feeling that their paths had diverged more than he had realized. Instead of reconnecting with his two siblings, it felt more like he was navigating the company of two strangers.

Gaven, with his unwavering strength and focused determination, seemed almost unchanged since their childhood. Yet his muscles had grown alongside his ego, and his once empty threats now carried real weight.

On the other hand, Mirari, though only five years had passed, had matured in ways that Salathiel hesitated to acknowledge. She had transformed into a skilled warrior, exuding confidence and carrying herself with a newfound pride that was absent in their Solarin days. While she might not require physical protection anymore, Salathiel couldn't help but notice that she remained somewhat naive about the complexities of the world around her.

Mirari attempted to bridge the quiet with small talk – the weather, the animals in the forest surrounding the estate, and the materials used to construct the estate.

"It is nice," Salathiel admitted. He gave her a gentle smile. "But I just want us to go home."

"You'll see," she said. "I know you have a bad opinion of the Knights, but they're really nice people."

Salathiel couldn't think of a response that wouldn't lead to another argument, so he remained silent. Mirari must've seen through him, and said nothing more.

Five people were waiting in the ostentatious foyer, animated in conversation with a cup of buzzbean in their hands. As soon as he saw them enter, a tall man, big with muscles thicker than his head, set down his cup and stepped forward. He greeted Salathiel warmly. Salathiel noticed that he bore the crest of Avon on his shoulder, as did the haughty fighter next to him who was staring him down.

"You must be Salathiel," he said, extending his huge hand. "Mirari has told us so much about you."

Salathiel had always regarded himself as tall, but next to this man, not quite so. He had seen him before, but now, standing close to the giant he was slightly more intimidated than he wanted to admit.

Salathiel's gaze traced the marble floor beneath his feet. Putting his hand in his would be no different than sticking his finger in a carnivorous plant trap. The smile faded from Neo's lips and he patted Salathiel's back instead, laughing with a deep bellow.

"I see the resemblance between you two," he said. "I'm Neo, and this is His Honor, Region Leader Shiba Zabato." He swept his hand toward Shiba who said nothing and kept an intimidating glare on him.

"Right," Salathiel said. His eyes, cold and calculating, locked onto Neo. "You and Kylah tied the knot. Congratulations."

His words were delivered like stale bread, but Neo savored it like forbidden fruit.

Neo smiled, "Oh, we wished you could've been there."

Salathiel didn't. He knew Kylah needed space. With a bounty on her head, it couldn't have been easy for her to be out in the open – to roam around as a Knight. That wasn't the Kylah he remembered. Was she forced to become a Knight? Forced to marry this strange man?

The brawler before him was no ally from the past, no comrade with shared memories; he was a stranger who had wedged himself into Salathiel's life simply because of his relationship with Kylah.

Salathiel turned to the puppet master. The one with a mask was Fangbane, no doubt. He was as people described him – scrawny, odd, and mysterious. He was a mind reader, and Salathiel was prepared for that. He took a deep breath and kept his mind focused.

"Welcome," Fangbane said, with open arms. "I hope your trip was uneventful."

Salathiel didn't respond verbally, but he sent a blistering response in his mind.

Fangbane paused, then turned, unfazed by Salathiel's thoughts, and indicated the woman and child next to him.

"This is my wife, Starlight, and our son, Sarkan. We like to call him Sharky. He'll put just about anything in his mouth."

"Hello and welcome," Starlight said with a gentle smile. "Mirari has told me so much about you." She tugged on the child's shoulder, drawing him forward. "Say hello."

Sarkan, the wide-eyed six-year-old, gazed up at Salathiel as though hungry dragons were circling overhead. His tiny mouth hung agape, frozen in fear, resisting even Starlight's comforting presence. Salathiel couldn't help but question if this pint-sized bundle of fear before him knew how to move.

Mirari nudged Salathiel with her elbow. "Salathiel," she hissed. "Be nice."

Salathiel unclenched and stiffly said, "Hello."

Sarkan cringed and ducked behind his mother's leg. Flustered, Starlight tried to pull him out. "I-I'm sorry, I don't know what's gotten into him. Sarkan, what's wrong? You were so eager to meet Mirari's brother. Come say hello."

Sarkan was cowering as if the monster under his bed had come to life. He whispered something to his mother that might have been a greeting or a complaint. It was impossible to hear when he spoke into Starlight's dress. She cast a worried look at Fangbane. Salathiel could tell that she was sending him a message, and it put him on edge.

Shrugging, Fangbane clapped his hands. "That's all right. Why don't you and Sharky take Salathiel's bags to his room. We'll be in my study if he changes his mind. How does that sound?" he asked, crouching down. "Do you mind helping out?"

Sarkan nodded and Mirari passed Salathiel's bags over to Starlight.

When Mirari returned to Salathiel's side, she smiled and explained, "We don't have servants here. It isn't anything like you'd expect."

She must've remembered when Salathiel called the Knights spoiled and privileged. It was odd, Salathiel admitted, but it didn't change his perception of them.

"We pride ourselves on being self-sufficient," Fangbane added. "Come on," he said, motioning. "I'll show you to my study."

The study was fairly large with a desk against the wall. A long couch, flanked by two chairs, sat directly across from the desk. Fangbane sat at his desk while Mirari and Salathiel took the couch. Shiba and Neo took the remaining seats while Gaven chose to lurk in the corner by the window, like a sulky child.

"You are welcome to stay here at the estate," Neo said. "A change in scenery is nice. Plus, you can talk to Mirari every day."

"I can do the same in Solarin," Salathiel said, glancing at Mirari. "If she chooses to do so."

Neo let out a big laugh, dispelling the tension. "You won't be able to say no after you've tasted Starlight's cooking."

Gaven jumped in. "I imagine there's not a lot of trouble out in that nothing town," he said.

Salathiel's eyes narrowed. "Some of us are satisfied with simple things."

Neo looked between Gaven and Salathiel. He had a little awkward smile playing at the corner of his mouth. "Do you two know each other?" he asked.

Salathiel bore holes into Gaven's eyes and watched his jaw flex under that Althaean stubble.

"I believe Gaven and Salathiel had a misunderstanding earlier," Fangbane said. Salathiel could practically hear the smirk in his voice. "But that's why we're here, correct? We just want to show you that the Knights don't mean any harm."

"Yeah," Neo said, rocking forward with too much energy. "There's nothing to worry about."

"And I suppose I should just take your word for it?"

"Salathiel," Mirari admonished, but he shook his head.

He didn't think much of the Knights before he arrived, and now, his opinion had only soured. If they were so close, why hadn't Gaven told them the truth about Cygnus? Why did Mirari act like they were family when she didn't trust them with her birth name?

"You don't have to take our word for it," Fangbane said. "Please, let our actions speak for us."

Salathiel hissed at himself for letting his thoughts trickle out.

"We stopped bandits from attacking caravans," Fangbane continued. "We stopped riots, we defeated Laikos—"

Salathiel snorted. "What about Byham?" He arched an

eyebrow when they didn't immediately respond. "Didn't I hear that the Knights killed dozens of civilians there?"

Shiba furrowed his brow. Adjusting himself to sit up straight, he dug a glare into Salathiel. "They attacked us first."

"Who is more likely to win? Defenseless peasants or the Shadow Soldier?" He glanced briefly at him but didn't linger on the intimidating scowl in his eyes.

"And what qualifications do you have to justify your opinion?" Shiba said, his words clipped and raw.

"Now, now," Neo said, humming. His eyes executed a deliberate dance across the room before settling on Salathiel. "They were driven by an unnatural power. We didn't have a choice."

"You always have a choice." Salathiel shot a piercing glare at Fangbane. "And you chose to become the Council's lackeys."

Fangbane spread his hands and shrugged. "It was my failing, I admit. I went to discuss the Council's patrols to reduce the collateral damage, but by the end I had to agree to join the Council or risk having the Knights disbanded entirely." He got to his feet and tucked his hands behind his back. "You see, here, we are all just human. We make mistakes and all we can do is try to rectify those mistakes. I hope you won't hold my mistakes against the Knights as a whole."

"Please, Sal," Mirari said, reaching out to him. "It was a difficult time. Don't let a few bad instances dismiss all the good the Knights have done."

He shook her hand off to get to his feet. He paced in front of Fangbane's desk and looked him in the eye. "You act like the blood on your hands was put there by someone else. Wake up, Mirari. You can't trust them."

"Salathiel, please," Fangbane said, holding his hands up, placating. "Nothing needs to be resolved today. We brought you here to discuss this. Perhaps it would be wise to talk more on this after you've rested."

"I don't need to rest and I don't need to talk anymore."

Mirari tugged on the end of his shirt, a silent plea for restraint. It reminded him of when she was younger.

"Salathiel," she said. "I thought you came to meet the Knights, to hear them out and understand them."

No, that wasn't why he was there. Every second he spent at the estate was suffocating. Breathing in deeply, he wrapped his hand around Mirari's wrist.

"I already understand them," he said. "I came to help *you* understand them." She shook her head, but he kept talking. "Don't you see? There's always an excuse. Nothing was their fault. They were only following orders. It was a mistake. They had no choice."

"Salathiel, can't you see we're on the same side here?" Fangbane said.

"No, we're not," he huffed at Fangbane. His eyes blazed with an intensity that could rival the fiery pits of Inferna. "If we are, then tell her. Tell Mirari why you really wanted her to join the Knights." Salathiel waved his hand to her. "Tell her what you plan to do about Cygnus."

A tense stillness enveloped the room, broken only by the anxious exchange of glances among the assembled. To him, it was a clear sign of where they stood in this cold war.

The room erupted in hushed murmurs, a cacophony of uncertainty. Shiba and Neo engaged in furtive whispers, their eyes betraying shared concern. Gaven's hiss cut through the tension, a venomous undercurrent directed at Salathiel, who stood at the epicenter of the storm. Mirari, sensing the imminent tempest, got to her feet and at clutched Salathiel's shirt.

"Sal," she said. "He doesn't need to—"

"Answer the damn question," Salathiel snapped.

Fangbane chuckled, raising his hands in a futile attempt to pacify the brewing storm. Pacing toward the door, he said, "I fear that this discussion is no longer—"

With a flick of his hands, Salathiel slid two gleaming blades into the palm of his hand and flung them directly at Fangbane. In that fleeting moment, he imagined the look of terror hiding behind that silver mask.

The blades shot through the air with a sharp whistle. Before they could find their home in Fangbane's chest, they clattered against Gaven's spear as he twirled the shaft and batted them out of the air.

Silence descended in the study. Fangbane had lurched backward, pressing his back against the wall while Gaven stepped in front of him. He glowered at Salathiel, holding his spear aloft as he defended the snake.

"What was that?" Gaven scowled.

"If you get out of my way, you'll see exactly what that was."

Salathiel surged forward like a tempest unleashed. The blades danced in his hands, a deadly symphony of steel. He tossed one of the blades with a sinister trajectory that would have skimmed past Gaven and embedded into the masked man. He knew Gaven would intercept it, and he did, deflecting the dagger left his body exposed.

Like a phantom materializing from the shadows, Salathiel seized the moment, swiftly closing the distance. His boot met Gaven's chest with a resounding impact. The warrior tumbled across the room, and the room echoed with the clash of shattered glass and tumbled furniture as he took a side table and a ceramic vase down with him.

Rolling up his sleeves, Salathiel approached Fangbane with determination etched across his face. He cared not for the fact that Gaven, should he choose to stand in his way, had greater strength. There was only one outcome, and he knew it – Salathiel would be victorious as long as Mirari was on his side.

Just as the challenge danced on his mind, a force collided into him, a blitz of power that sent him hurtling against the wall. Shaking off his daze, he saw Shiba and Neo standing resolute in defense of Gaven. The Shadow Soldier, Iron Fist, and Valiant Tiger. Fighting the three of them would be no easy feat.

"Choose wisely," Shiba said, his eyes growing cold. He played with a dagger in his right hand, twirling it with immense speed and precision.

"There's nothing we can't talk about," Neo said in the most serious demeanor Salathiel had ever seen from the giant. He had his silver gauntlets on now and offered peace with them. "Lower your weapon."

Salathiel scanned the wrecked room, and his gaze stopped on the horrified look on Mirari's face. Her eyes were wide as she staggered back a step.

"Mirari, you have to understand." He held his hand out, but she stepped back enough for Fangbane to grab her hand and pull her behind the desk.

"Was this your plan all along?" she asked with a tremor in her voice. When he didn't say anything, she covered her mouth. "Y-you changed. The Salathiel I knew wouldn't have—"

"I am that Salathiel. I…"

He dropped his plea seeing the fear on her face and Fangbane's hand on her wrist. She wouldn't listen to reason. Not now, not with the Knights whispering in her ears. He hardened his heart and pulled forth two more daggers, one in each hand. He had no choice. If he wanted to save Mirari, he would have to get rid of the Knights.

And he knew that if he did this, there would be no turning back.

CHAPTER THIRTY-FOUR

Salathiel's eyes had a manic gleam in them when he lunged forward. He ran straight for Neo, who was ready to meet him with his fists. With the twist of his body, Salathiel launched one dagger at Shiba and another at Neo. It caught Shiba off guard and grazed his shoulder. The second dagger bounced off Neo's gauntlet, but by the time he lowered his fist, Salathiel had grabbed his hand and pulled him forward into a back toss. The ground shook with a loud thud.

Behind the desk, Mirari stood frozen, her eyes wide. Likely, Fangbane was shocked too. How often did they see someone capable of sweeping Neo off his feet? Dark aura gave Salathiel a fighting chance against three of the best fighters in the alliance. Could they still win? Mirari clenched her fists, the gravity of the situation settling upon her like a heavy cloak.

"Sal!" Gaven's voice thundered through the air. Shards of ceramic fell to the ground as he got to his feet and took a step forward. "Leave them alone. Your fight is with me."

Salathiel scoffed, "I thought you wanted to save Mirari. Whose side are you on?"

Gaven opened his mouth but no words came out. He froze in

place and Salathiel could imagine the turmoil and conflicting thoughts running through his mind. Would Gaven live up to their alliance? They had always butted heads, but regardless of how they grated on each other's nerves, they both loved Mirari. They wanted the best for her.

Shiba glanced at Gaven with eyes thirsting for blood. He scoffed at him, then focused on Salathiel. "He wants a piece of the Knights. We'll give it to him."

Neo ran his fingers up his right arm, drawing his kore in arcane patterns. Disks of light conjured over his arm. Whoever was doomed to meet his fist would surely feel pain. He waited for his lord's command.

Salathiel raised a dagger at his eyeline and positioned himself in a defensive stance. The anticipation was thick in the air.

"Mirari will come back with me," he said, his voice laced with determination. "She'll see reason just as soon as the rest of you are dead!"

Before he could take a step forward, he was lifted and thrown off his feet, his daggers slipping from his grip. Helpless in mid-air, he tumbled. From the corner of his eye, he saw a dark figure grasping his leg. He slashed at it, dispersing the shadow and freeing his body. But time betrayed him, and two deadly daggers hurled toward his chest. Salathiel twisted his body and dodged one of them, but the other lodged into his shoulder.

Rolling behind a tipped chair, Salathiel deftly wrenched the dagger out of his shoulder. He ignored the pain and the black, spilling substance that came with it. With his good hand, he motioned to the ground. An eerie stillness gripped the air for a heartbeat, but then the room began to shake. Rising from the floor were weaves of vines as thick as hundred-year-old tree trunks. They had risen enough to block the view from every direction; only Salathiel knew exactly where everyone was in his entwined labyrinth.

He could hear Neo pounding on the foliage, a pitch of determination from the right. But where was his partner? He felt a brush of wind grazing him from above. The Shadow Soldier was flying with grace in a perfect arch over his head. He landed behind Salathiel, jerking him down by his wrists; they were practically glued to the floor by two dark hands.

Neo made his way to the scene with a grand entrance, tearing a hole through a thick root as if it were but a puff of cloud. He didn't stop, charging straight at Salathiel, fists radiating with an azure glow. The chance of escaping was close to none, but Salathiel noticed that the floorboard beneath him had begun to crack. By now, Neo had vaulted skyward. It took another second before the ground shot up – a colossal dirt pillar collided into the brawler.

But as it crumbled, Salathiel could see that Neo emerged unscathed. The two hands confining Salathiel to the ground flung him into the air – not what he was expecting. Salathiel couldn't control his momentum when his chest met Neo's fist. He felt like he was hit by a kōnvoy, and to make matters worse, his body crashed into an invisible barrier that shimmered upon impact. A punch to his shoulder threw him off, but Salathiel wouldn't go down alone. He secured his legs around Neo's torso and they both crashed hard, trembling the earth.

Mirari let out a loud gasp when they landed. Freeing herself from Fangbane's grip, she ran up to Salathiel, who had Neo's neck in a firm grip.

"Stop this!" she commanded, attempting to tear him away from Neo. After some effort, she managed to pry them apart.

"They will kill you, Mirari," Salathiel said, trying to catch his breath. "Will you let them sacrifice you to the goddess?"

Before Mirari could answer, Starlight paced into the room and her cry pierced through the air. She was calling Neo's name with urgency. All eyes followed her path as she ran up to Neo and knelt at his body. He was groaning with pain and hardly moving. Starlight was frantic, on the verge of crying, but Mirari seemed confused until she looked closer – there was a dark mist encompassing his body.

Mirari's staggered back. She struggled to find the right words to explain her shock and anger.

"W-Why?" she said. "You said you'd never use it."

"Mirari," Salathiel said, forcing her to look at him again. She gasped when she saw his hand reach out. At the sound of her cry, Shiba swept in and tackled her away. Gaven locked his arm around Salathiel's neck, effectively grounding him.

"That's enough!" Gaven said, seething through his teeth. "You've gone too far. Remove it!"

"You know I can't," Salathiel said, trying to pull Gaven's arm away. "He has to fight it himself." He twisted free of Gaven's grip and pointed a dagger at him. Gaven pointed his spear back, but Salathiel knew he wouldn't be the first to make a move.

Neo was writhing on the ground, his screams growing louder and more unbearable. Mirari covered her mouth and turned away. Now would be the time for her to do something, but what? Summon Cygnus? Could she do it?

Starlight, unfaltering now, took a deep breath, and focused on Neo's body and raised her illuminating hands.

"Don't!" Shiba yelled.

Starlight jolted back in shock. "But..."

Shiba fell to one knee with a hand clutching his chest. Groans escaped him as he writhed, each breath a laborious struggle, a faded look etched on his face.

"No one touch him!" Shiba ordered. "Nothing can keep him down."

Salathiel wasn't sure of that, but if he knew anything, it was that these two fighters were strong on their own, and together they created an unbreakable bond. He could tell Shiba was helping Neo in his own way, channeling strength and bravery through their bond. Dark aura would only buy him time.

Shiba staggered to his feet, holding his daggers at the ready.

"Kitten," he called out. "Are you with me or not?"

Salathiel turned to Gaven, and he seemed uncertain of the answer.

With a deep breath, Shiba stood tall and flowed into an offensive stance, as good as new. He didn't wait for a response. In a blink, he rushed toward Salathiel, drawing his attention. Salathiel threw his daggers, but Shiba weaved his through the air in a swipe too fast for mortal eyes to see. The deflected blades lodged into opposite walls, one a mere feet from Fangbane's head.

Shiba's confidence must've inspired some courage in Mirari. She unsheathed her sword and stepped forward.

"Stay back," Gaven said, gritting his teeth.

"Why?" Mirari hissed.

"That's an order!" He nudged toward the other direction. "Go help Neo."

Gaven was right. She was the only one who could help Neo right now. But Salathiel could see that the sight of dark aura was unsettling for her as if it was living inside her.

Shiba was inches away from Salathiel when he stepped to the side, catching Salathiel off guard. He twirled high and low in a deadly dance, grazing Salathiel's body multiple times. It forced him into a defensive block, but Salathiel knew he had to act quickly. He dropped low, swiping his leg under Shiba's feet, then jabbing his fist into Shiba's chest. Shiba staggered back, breaking the window behind him. It took him an extra second but he stood tall; it would take more than that to throw him off his feet.

Shiba adjusted his grip on his blades. He stood strong and menacing, and now Gaven had joined him by his side. It was an unlikely pair, but if anyone knew what Shiba was going through, it was him.

Gaven jumped toward Salathiel, swinging his blade down. The first slash missed, but it was quickly followed up by Shiba. Salathiel fell off rhythm for a beat, knowing that he had a slim chance of escaping the wrath of both region leaders. He felt a sharp pain across his ankle – scuffed by Shiba's blade. Then he felt a blow to his stomach by the blunt end of Gaven's spear. Salathiel faltered while trying to catch a breath.

He appeared to be at a checkmate, but Salathiel would continue to fight as long as there was breath in him. He waited until Gaven and Shiba lunged at him, then swiped his arm to the left. The earth rose and they collided with a thick root, dragged away by its force. They slammed against a wall, weapons dropping, and were quickly confined by smaller vines, sturdy enough that it would need something sharp to cut through their grip.

Mirari rushed to their aid. Raising her blade, she began slicing away at the vines confining Shiba and Gaven.

"The flames!" Gaven said with urgency.

"I-I can't," Mirari said. "I don't know how to summon it. She's not listening to me."

Salathiel heard a loud roar from behind. When he turned, he saw Neo charging at him with renewed energy. The mist around him no more. He couldn't tear his eyes from the sight, nor could the others, as if everything around them had stopped in time to admire the sheer strength of this fighter who conquered dark aura on his own. Salathiel didn't react in time as Neo grabbed his arm and punched his stomach. But it wasn't just a punch. Salathiel flinched, feeling black ooze flow out from his stomach. Neo had picked up one of the glass shards and lodged it into him. It was big enough to stay in his torso as Neo let go and launched him in the air. Salathiel hit the ceiling and fell back down.

The two fighters were now freed, and Shiba joined his partner's side. He chuckled, "I knew it was no match for you."

"It was quite a tickle," Neo said with a big grin. He rubbed his gauntlets together. "Let's finish this, Milord."

Salathiel held his breath, pulling out the shard from his stomach. The injuries didn't slow him down as he got to his feet. His will was as strong as the Knights', but even with dark aura on his side, could he win this battle?

Shiba wasted no time. He took off first, landing a glancing blow against Salathiel's waist. Salathiel blocked it, but he didn't have a free hand to deflect Neo's strike. Seething in pain, Salathiel spun away and readied his daggers.

The dance of blades and fists intensified, each movement a testament to everyone's mastery. Salathiel, wounded but undeterred, maneuvered with grace, countering each bolt with calculated precision.

"Is there truly nothing we can do?" Starlight said, turning to her husband. He had been entranced by the battle and ignored her as if he didn't hear her.

Mirari bit her lip. She must've also found it odd that he hadn't given any orders. Was he in shock? Or did he want to watch the battle play out?

Salathiel came to an abrupt stop, realizing a dagger had embedded itself in his leg. Shiba was leaning against the wall with a hand over a dagger that was firmly lodged in his shoulder. The fight was nearing its end, and Salathiel sensed that Shiba was a single shove away from defeat.

Gaven must've read the resignation on Shiba's face. He bellowed his name, but Salathiel was on Shiba in an instant. Neo stood tall in front of his partner, heaving like a bull. Charging head first, Neo met Salathiel in the middle. They collided with a force Salathiel didn't expect. He toppled backward and the dagger flew out of his hand. A sharp pain tingled up his spine when he collided with the ground, the brawler on top of him. There were more parts of his body that were crushed, Salathiel was sure of it. He just couldn't feel most of his body under pressure and pain.

Neo rose, his fist held above Salathiel, who was straddled between his legs. Salathiel tried to budge, but Neo had him in a tight grip. He gawked at the fist, now encompassed with transparent kore. He wouldn't survive that. Salathiel did the only thing he could do – reached his free hand into his belt. He swung a dagger up, slashing Neo's arm where his kore did not reach. Neo recoiled, his arm oozing crimson.

That was his mistake. Grabbing Neo's collar, Salathiel pulled him down. It looked like a strange move from afar, but Neo's colossal frame slackened, and the once iron grip weakened. With a swift maneuver, Salathiel extricated himself from Neo's clutches.

The brawler did not attempt to rise. His legs loosened and Salathiel slipped out. Breathing heavily, he rose triumphant. The surviving fighters darted their eyes between him and the fallen fighter, no doubt sensing a shift in the tides of fate.

As Neo's life force dimmed, Shiba dropped to his knees, huffing and wincing with a mournful melody. The room, now a silent witness to the aftermath, was filled with a harsh dissonance.

Remorse, like a shadow, crept over the spoils of victory. Even in his triumph, the weight of the moment bore down on Salathiel's shoulders. With a heavy heart, he shook away the haunting thoughts. Mirari's freedom required sacrifices, and he would see that they were made, even if it required his own. He had to.

He glanced at Gaven, the last person standing in his way, and he steeled himself for the perils ahead.

CHAPTER THIRTY-FIVE

Gaven heard Mirari's bloodcurdling scream as Salathiel stood up. Neo was lying face up with a dagger lodged in his heart. His cousin appeared crazed when he stood over the body with blood smeared over his face and clothes.

"Will you still continue to stand in my way?" Salathiel said.

Gaven could tell he felt no remorse. This wasn't an act. He truly wanted to kill everyone in the room, and Gaven was the one who let him in. Gaven seethed as his knuckles turned white, but when he stepped forward, the rage in his chest subsided. It was a strange feeling, but he had felt this before. The aura in the room had shifted, and it took a moment for Gaven to process the situation.

Twisting on her heels, Mirari smashed her fist into Salathiel's cheek. He was forced backward, head smacking against the wall, cracking the paneling. Starlight seized the opportunity to scramble to Neo and pull the dagger from his chest, heedless of the blood drawn from her hand from touching the edge of the blade.

She tossed the dagger to the side and scanned his vitals,

murmuring through her tears. Her hair curtained over his motionless face.

On the other side of the room Fangbane was still cowering behind a table. Though confining Mirari was his responsibility, he had certainly given up trying to contain her. Gaven took a second look at Mirari. She huffed labored breaths with her hands clenched. Her gaze didn't leave Salathiel.

Salathiel's expression had also changed. Unflinching and focused on her eyes, he carefully brushed himself from the ground, clenching a dagger in his hand. Mirari unsheathed her sword and pointed it at him.

Gaven couldn't see her face from where he stood, but he knew what had happened. Gaven could feel the coldness in her glowing eyes.

Salathiel lifted his chin, repulsed by Mirari.

"Cygnus," Salathiel said, unnerved.

"Puppet," Cygnus responded. Her voice, Mirari's voice, was light and airy but her words were as sharp as her blade. She spun her short sword around in a lazy circle.

Gaven wanted to call out. He wanted to demand that she release Mirari, that they didn't need her. But he knew his words would mean nothing. He had to get her back by force.

He thought back on Salathiel's words, and in this moment, there was no denying it. They wanted the same thing. Even if Salathiel took one of their own, there was a greater issue at hand. The unfortunate truth was Salathiel had the power to defeat Cygnus and Gaven did not.

Warily, Salathiel edged away from the wall. He had his hand out and a dagger separated him from Cygnus. Gaven yanked the blade out of his shoulder and crept closer so that he could keep his eyes on both of them.

Cygnus sneered, luminescent eyes glancing at the unsheathed dagger. For a moment her face went soft. Pleading, she asked, "Will you really harm your dear sister?"

It lit a scowl on Salathiel's face that Gaven had never seen before. He could see why Salathiel didn't trust Cygnus.

"Don't try to act like her!" Salathiel seethed and charged at her. She grabbed his wrist with such speed that Gaven almost missed it. Salathiel's weapon clattered to the ground as he cringed in pain, forced to his knees by her unrelenting grip.

Gaven surged forward, anger burning in his eyes. He knew he stood little chance against a goddess, but duty fueled his every step. Spinning his spear, he unleashed a loud battle cry and brought it down on Cygnus' arm. He expected her to move in time, and she did, releasing her grip on Salathiel.

"Don't play her games," Gaven said. "Focus."

Salathiel shuffled to his feet, readying another dagger. He was always the more even-tempered one. Even if they hadn't had a proper conversation in over a decade, this was how it had always been. And right now, Gaven needed him to play that role.

"I know," Salathiel hissed. Lifting his blade, he held it in front of his face. He called to her, "You may have convinced everyone else, but I see through your lies, Cygnus. Release her."

She sighed, sounding bored. "Or else?"

Salathiel darted forward, swiping his blade down with a sharp whistle. Cygnus blocked with more force than he was expecting and he lurched backward.

Using the back of a chair, Cygnus vaulted into the air and swung her blade down. Gaven intercepted the attack, blocking her sword with a barrier around his arm, and retaliated with a swift strike of his spear.

She gracefully somersaulted away and dropped low, unleashing a spinning swipe that Gaven had to avoid lest he lost a leg. But it left him exposed, giving her an easy critical hit when she ricocheted up and struck her fist into his face. He dismissed the injury with a shake of his head, clearing the blood away with the back of his hand.

She raised another fist, but it was abruptly jerked back by the vines surrounding her. They constrained her, limb by limb, until she was fully encased against the protruding stump at the center of the room.

"I know you're in there, Mirari," Salathiel said. He lowered his weapon, taking one step closer to her. "Listen, you have to fight her. You are the one in control. Not—"

A ball of fire rushed past his head. Salathiel held up his arm, and Gaven joined him by his side. They watched as flames gracefully rose from her hands, lighting up the vines around her. In a second, her body was freed and she stepped forward.

"I see you are no longer honoring our deal," Cygnus said, glaring at Gaven.

"I said you could fight Lachess," Gaven said. "Leave the rest of us alone."

Her eyes flickered to Salathiel. "Her pawn must go, too."

Cygnus struck out with her fire again, and Gaven summoned a barrier around the both of them a split second before impact. Cygnus had him on the defensive.

But not Salathiel. He bounded forward, swinging his dagger at Cygnus. She blocked it, but Salathiel drew another hidden blade with his left hand and took a swipe at her. Cygnus jerked back and a flutter of lilac strands drifted to the floor. She twisted and arced her knee at his stomach. Salathiel hunched over to absorb the brunt of the attack with his forearms.

The two sprung together and darted apart, exchanging a flurry of blows in a chaotic rhythm. They were moving fast, twisting and turning as they tried to get the upper hand on each other.

Gaven hesitated to jump in, not wanting to hurt Mirari or kill Salathiel. He watched Cygnus twist Mirari's gentle features as she thirsted for Salathiel's soul.

In a swift motion, Salathiel commanded the earth beneath Cygnus to rise, not as a barrier, but as a disruption to her balance. She wobbled, momentarily vulnerable. Salathiel twirled the fingers on his other hand. Something was beginning to form in his hand, something dark and eerie, but controlled. Gaven's eyes widened as he recalled the familiar sight. He swallowed any fear he had

Salathiel twisted his wrist and brought it down toward Cygnus. Before his hand could reach her, she pressed her foot against his chest and kicked him over her head. He landed flat on the ground, breath whooshing out of him in a choked gasp.

Gaven stepped forward. "Cygnus," he said. He hated saying that name, but he doubted she would respond to anything else. "That's enough. You've done enough."

She tipped her head back to look at him through hooded eyes. A cruel smile curled at the corner of her mouth. "That's where you're wrong."

She came at him with her fist pulled back. He was not afraid of a punch, but her hand had erupted in flame before she thrust it forward. Gaven crouched, barely missing the flame. He acted quickly and rolled to his left before another ball of fire led him to his fate. Rising to his feet, Gaven took two steps forward and carried his spear on the upswing. She pivoted and took a step forward. Her hand grasped the center of his spear and she pulled him forward. He flew across the room and broke a chair as he fell. Feeling the wrath of the goddess, Gaven could tell that Cygnus' agility was higher than Mirari's, but to also carry divine strength? He wasn't sure if he could pin her down.

Salathiel got back to his feet, but not for long before Cygnus grabbed him by the front of his shirt, hoisting him up. She hammered him with punch after punch. Salathiel blocked each blow but groaned under the force of each attack. On her last punch, she pulled her hand back longer, as it erupted in a flame before she thrust it forward. Salathiel held both his hands in front of him, generating dark aura in his palms, this time much larger. It cushioned the blow, but the force was enough to knock him off his feet. The air resonated with a thud as Salathiel crashed, breath stolen from his lungs.

"Mirari," Salathiel gasped, trying to speak. He didn't bother wiping his blood-stained lips. "I know you're in there. You can fight her. I know you can do it."

Cygnus clicked her tongue. "Aren't you wasting your breath?"

Salathiel gasped, hands scraping across the ground. Cygnus lifted her hand to pound him further, but he raised his own, sliding it past hers and twisting it. With his other hand, he thrusted his palm into her chest. A direct blow. The dark mist clung around her chest.

Cygnus lurched forward, trying to scrape away the mist. But it stuck like a swarm of bees, unyielding and persistent.

Gaven had a small dagger in his hand. If anything, it could slow down her attempts at freeing herself from dark aura. It pained him to use it on Mirari again, but it was necessary. He sprung forward, aiming the sharp blade at Cygnus. She jerked her hand up. The dagger plunged into the meat of her palm and Gaven's eyes widened with shock.

Using his weight, Gaven tried to bring the blade of the dagger closer to Cygnus. Growling, she clenched her hand around the blade and pulled it from his grip. Her other hand shot out and wrapped around his throat.

There was no warning – Gaven wasn't sure what he would have done if there had been – but between one blink and the next, fire erupted from Cygnus' hand, and Gaven didn't have time to react.

Salathiel jumped in between the both of them, his hands wrapped with dark aura, one hand reaching for the critical point in Cygnus' elbow and the other hand pushing Gaven backward. The pressure forced Cygnus to buck her arm. She missed her shot and loosened her grip on Gaven. She was seething with anger, and took another swing.

"Sal!" Gaven called out, stepping forward. But there was a

brief moment of pain as if his stomach acid was dissolving him from the inside. Gaven breathed heavily, dropping onto one knee. His vision blurred and flickered for a moment. Shaking off the effects, he focused on the stray wooden patterns on the ground. Eventually, he felt himself breathing again, and still feeling uneasy, he got to his feet.

Salathiel's arms were wrapped with dark aura. He used them as a shield to absorb Cygnus' fiery punch. It was barely enough. The dark aura dispelled, and he stumbled backward. While fetching for a breath, he turned to Gaven. There was sincerity in his eyes, and Gaven recognized it. It was as if Salathiel now accepted that they were all mere pawns in the cosmic game, and fate had already woven its cruel design into the fabric of the moment.

"Cygnus fears you for a reason," Salathiel said to him in a remorseful tone.

"What do you mean?" Gaven asked.

He reached for him, but in the blink of an eye, Cygnus' flames shot out and encased Salathiel in a spherical flame. Gaven was knocked back by the force. But Salathiel made no attempts to escape.

Gaven's heart pounded in his chest as he rose to his feet, the scorching waves of Cygnus' fiery wrath pushing against him like an insurmountable tide, each step forward a battle against the relentless force that sought to consume them.

"She knows her fate," Salathiel said. He closed his eyes and took a deep breath. Once formidable and proud, he now stood shrouded in the inferno. But as he returned his glare on Cygnus, a confident smile played upon his lips. "You were always meant to be the hero, Gav. Don't let me down."

Gaven desperately strained against Cygnus' power, his every muscle screaming in protest. The faces of those he had lost flashed before his eyes, and his mind echoed with his failures. The flames were mocking him, but his heart roared with the fervent hope that this time, against all odds, he could save the ones dearest to him.

With a gallant cry, Gaven gathered every ounce of strength within him and lunged forward once more, defying the scorching forces that sought to keep him at bay. Salathiel, Mirari – despite all that had happened since their paths diverged, they were family.

A pulsating force surged through the air, hurling Gaven back.

When he looked up, he saw the flames glow and dance with malevolent glee as they devoured Salathiel's essence like hungry serpents, licking away his very soul.

"Sal!" he called out. Gaven had to shield his eyes against the searing brilliance of the flame.

Through the blinding light, he managed to catch a smile peeking from Salathiel's silhouette, the final trace of family who had once walked beside him. And then, with a silent flicker, that silhouette vanished into the reddish flame. Its quiet departure echoed louder than any scream – a stoic acceptance of the inexorable fate that had befallen him.

When the flames pulled back, the air stood still, silent. Gaven wasn't sure how to feel. Even though Salathiel was absent for most of his life, he couldn't deny that he was a part of him – the courage he earned, the will to dream big, was all Salathiel pressing him to do better than before. He had left Gaven with one final task, a seemingly impossible one.

"Cygnus!" Gaven bellowed. He glazed his hand down his spear, illuminating it in a bright cyan glow. He was the Valiant Tiger. Though he might not be enough to outpower Cygnus, but he would give it his all. He had to. Who else could?

Cygnus faced her opponent, but her movements and gaze were tired. Her shoulders were slumped and she was struggling to catch a breath. Perhaps there was no need for Gaven to attack further, but he remained on alert.

Cygnus closed her eyes and collapsed. His eyes locked on her, and he waited for her to move. He didn't know if the goddess was still in control, and he wasn't going to take chances. He took careful steps forward, one after another, his spear at the ready.

Fangbane took no caution. He rushed to her, pressing his head against her chest. He then lifted Mirari's chin up, gently tilting her head to both sides.

"She's alright," he said. "I can sense her thoughts."

Gaven frowned and touched his heart. He didn't quite agree with Fangbane. Something felt different. Her energy was faint as if it was hanging on a thread. The sight of her made him uneasy, yet he was unable to look away. He didn't know if he should hold her, *if* he could hold her. He sighed. She was so far away. He didn't know how to reach her.

CHAPTER THIRTY-SIX

Gaven was sitting outside Mirari's room, leaning against the wall directly opposite to the door. For a while, it was just him and the silence of the estate. Starlight was in the other room looking over Shiba's injuries. The scratches would heal. It was his heart that needed a medic.

Mirari's door opened and Fangbane stepped out, gently closing the door behind him. He sighed, shoulders drooping.

"How is she?" Gaven asked dully.

"Still unconscious," Fangbane said. He lifted his hand to his mask and turned away from him. "I didn't think… This wasn't supposed to happen. I thought Salathiel was—"

"Save it, Fang." Gaven stared down the hallway.

Salathiel's words rang through his mind. Had he known this whole time that his plan would fail? Did he know that he was going to die at Cygnus' hands? Over and over his thoughts tumbled. There had to have been a moment where he could have changed things.

"Gaven," Fangbane said, sounding pained. "It wasn't your fault."

Gaven pushed himself to his feet. He scowled and pointed his finger at him. "You're right. It's yours. You wanted them to fight, and you got what you wanted. We lost good men because of you."

"Blaming me won't bring Salathiel back," Fangbane said. "Nor Neo."

Gaven clenched his jaw. How could he just accept that? He was right there. Salathiel died right in front of him.

As if Fangbane had read his thoughts, he answered, "You did everything in your power to save him. That's all you could have done. That's all any one of us could have done."

Gaven seethed, a storm of anger brewing in his eyes. "And yet it wasn't enough."

"Gaven—"

"I'll be in my quarters. Let me know when… when Mirari wakes up."

He trudged away and Fangbane let him go. Of course, Fangbane wanted to chalk Salathiel's death up to senseless tragedy. If this was Gaven's fault, it was only because he had trusted Fangbane. Salathiel was dead because Fangbane wanted it.

Back in his room, he stared out the window. Night had barely fallen. How was it still the same day? He felt like he'd been away for at least three years. Despite that, he didn't think he'd be able to sleep. In his bed, he stretched out across the covers, letting his booted feet hang off the edge. He covered his eyes with the back of his hands and tried to silence his thoughts.

Pulling his arm away, Gaven stared at the ceiling. What would he say to Mirari? She had Cygnus to worry about, and that was enough. The weight of Neo's death and Salathiel's blood on her hands would be too much for her to bear.

Gaven wasn't unfamiliar with death. He was a warrior, a veteran on the battlefield, and had spilt his fair share of blood. But it was different for Mirari. Even with all her training and being with the Knights for so many years, she was still gentle and kind-hearted. Underneath all that bravery, she carried reckless ambition and impossible hope. But all that strength was carried on thin ice. Salathiel's death could destroy her. No, it *would* destroy her if she didn't have his support.

Though he and Salathiel had got into an argument every time they'd encountered each other, Gaven didn't hate him. He couldn't. Salathiel was his cousin. His family. He knew the thoughts Salathiel had at the end, he wanted to protect Mirari, and possibly even him. For Salathiel and for himself, Gaven would stay by her side and help her get through this.

A sweet chirping outside his window surprised him. Through the glass, sunlight poured in. Mirari must still be sleeping – it was a bittersweet thought, and he quickly cleared his mind.

Gaven changed his clothes without any thought and stepped into the hallway. Moving mechanically, his feet took him in the direction of Mirari's room. Halfway there, he tuned back in, hearing a commotion coming from farther in the mansion.

Gaven hesitated at the junction that would lead to Mirari's door, but decided to turn away. There wasn't anything he could do for her right away. If there was danger, it was better that he addressed it away from her.

He headed to the front entrance. On the landing that over-looked the foyer, Gaven watched Erel and the Knights stumble through the door. Disheveled and windswept, they looked like they had been traveling all night. They hadn't even bothered returning their mounts to the stables. Hime noticed Gaven first. Sprinting halfway across the room, she called him.

"Where's Lord Fangbane?" she asked. "We got information that he's going to want to hear."

"Here," Fangbane said, wearily coming out of a side room. He glanced at Gaven but continued to address Hime, "Did you find something?"

"We know who the vessels are, but not just that. We misinter-preted part of the legend." Fangbane leaned in closer as Hime filled him in on their discoveries.

Erel exchanged a brief look with Gaven, and as though Lucan was the mind reader, he nodded at Gaven and then looked at Fangbane skeptically.

"We need to talk," Lucan said in a whisper. "Her brother might be danger." Gaven lowered his gaze as he continued. "If what we suspect is true and he's under Lachess' influence, then he must—"

Seeing the stiffness on Gaven's face, he asked, "What is it?"

"I'm afraid you're too late." Gaven said.

"What do you mean?"

Kylah stepped forward, her eyes wandering past the group and into the estate. She was the first to notice that something was off.

"Where's Neo?" she asked. "Where's everyone else?"

Fangbane and Gaven exchanged a quick glance. Fangbane rested a hand on her shoulder and pulled her in with the rest of the Knights.

"Kylah," he said, his voice cracking. "I'm so sorry. Something happened while you were gone." It was the kindest way he could put it.

In a lowered voice, Fangbane delivered the bad news to the other Knights. Gaven couldn't hear it, but he saw Hime gasp. Kylah covered her mouth and sank to her knees. Gaven couldn't see Fangbane's face underneath the mask, but he wondered if he was pleased or if he felt any remorse at all.

"Is… is that true?" Erel said. He knew she didn't need an answer. "And Mirari? Is she ok?"

Before Gaven could answer, Fangbane said, "Perhaps this conversation would be better had in the library."

On the way, they met Shiba as he came out of the infirmary. He was chalk white, pale enough to match the bandages around his leg and arm. A sense of dread dawned on Kylah's face when she saw him. Her eyes wandered to the door and she paced toward it without a second thought.

Starlight appeared in the doorway as if she knew Kylah was going to see Neo. She intercepted the distressed spellcaster with a firm hug.

"Let me through!" Kylah screamed, clawing at the door frame. Starlight stood her ground, holding onto Kylah tightly and patting her back.

"In time, dear," Starlight said, catching Kylah's tears on her shoulder. "Right now, you need to be brave. That's what he would've wanted."

"Why? Why?"

Shiba, without uttering a single word, gently pulled her away, leading her a few steps back from the infirmary door. His eyes were worn and faded, and the lines etched on his face betrayed the pain he, too, felt.

"I'm sorry," he said in a raspy voice that barely held any strength. "Come. We need to finish this fight… for him."

To Gaven's surprise, she allowed Shiba to guide her down the hall. These were the words Kylah needed to hear to put her into motion in the right direction. Meanwhile, Starlight refused to leave the room, arguing that her place right now was to take care of the fallen.

In the library, Gaven stayed by the window overlooking the courtyard and listened while Fangbane recounted the events of the previous night with an air of detachment. He had no choice but to tell them that Mirari was Cygnus' vessel. Not that they didn't know at this point, but perhaps they underestimated the level of destruction she was capable of. The Knights sat in silence. Gaven didn't know whether they were in disbelief or had accepted that what happened had always been a possibility.

After the bad news was delivered, Erel was the only one who had any soul left. She sat primly on the couch with her hands folded together on her lap as she began debriefing them of their findings.

"We strongly believe that Councilor Julie is Lachess' vessel,"

Erel said. "However, we have nothing to prove it. She conducts shady work under the table, dealings with merchants, weapon exchanges, and so forth. But she doesn't leave enough evidence for us to prosecute her."

"I don't think that will be necessary," Fangbane said. He was leaning forward, twiddling his thumbs. "The Council can't help us now. No legal proceeding will. I'm confident that Cygnus will lead us right to her. We need to—"

"Leave it up to the gods?" Gaven raised his voice. He rose from his seat and slammed his fist on the table. "And look where that got us!"

"I understand you're upset, but—"

"We lost two lives, Fang! Don't you see by now that Cygnus doesn't care? She will set this whole world on fire just to kill Lachess. She won't care if she has to kill every person along the way. Are you really just going to let her do that?"

Fangbane didn't seem to waver. He stared at Gaven and calmly replied, "Do you have a better idea?"

Gaven gritted his teeth. Salathiel *was* the better idea. If anyone could stop Cygnus, it was him. Erel got to her feet and laid a hand on Gaven's back.

"His Honor has a point," she said. She pressed on his back, inviting him to take his seat. Begrudgingly, he did. "The inscription that rests in the Belligmn Tribe says that Cygnus cleansed the boy and the town of dark aura." She caressed the scroll that could have saved Salathiel's life, then turned to Fangbane with a dire look in her eyes. "But she didn't cleanse them, she killed them. She has no regard for mortal lives. We would be daft to trust her."

That took the wind out of their sails. Gaven could practically see the despair creeping over them. After all, how could they defeat a goddess? With a flick of her hand, Cygnus could decide who lives or dies. That was the power of the Goddess of Fate.

"I see," Fangbane murmured. "Thank you for gathering this information."

"Poor Mirari," Hime said, clasping her hands together in silent prayer.

Kylah squinted at the window with swollen eyes and the bright sunlight streaming through the glass. She was clearly defeated, and Gaven doubted that she would be able to fight Cygnus. Judging from the way she was hunched over, her spirit was stripped from her body, and there was little left of the Kylah they knew.

"Now what?" Hime asked, her hands gripping the ends of her skirt. "What should we do?"

"What can we do?" Shiba mumbled. He was hunched over his seat, not once taking his eye off the mahogany table. His eyes had gone dull. Gaven had never seen the Shadow Soldier look so defeated, not even at Mecate's funeral. Then again, he had to face the physical recoil of the paragon's partnership, regardless of whether or not he could handle it.

Fangbane began, "My hope is that once Cygnus' purpose is complete, the destruction of Lachess, she'll no longer need Mirari. She will leave on her own."

Gaven laughed harshly. "Hope? That's what you're hinging Mirari's future on? You *hope* that Cygnus will just wander away when she's done with Mirari? You know what's more likely? I think this, all of this," he waved his hand, "has just been a part of your plan."

"My plan?" Fangbane said.

Gaven sneered. "Your plan to sacrifice Mirari. Salathiel was right. You don't care whether she lives." Somebody gasped. "This is what you wanted all along, isn't it? Everything up to this point. Sending the others away, bringing Salathiel here. You knew Cygnus would fight him. You *hoped* Cygnus would take over. But you were wrong about one thing. Salathiel wasn't Lachess, and in your error, you've killed two good men."

Fangbane didn't move in the slightest. Gaven wasn't even sure if he was listening. Finally, he swiveled around, directing his attention to everyone.

He said with a calm voice, "If Mirari cannot control Cygnus' power, then the best she can do for us is to let Cygnus fight Lachess."

There were more gasps in the room, and Dorain was the first to get to his feet.

"You take that back!" he yelled. "How can you treat her like some tool?"

"I care about Mirari as much as anyone else in this room, but if we want any chance of stopping Lachess, this is what needs to happen," Fangbane said, bringing his hands to his lips. He faced Gaven. "I know that I can't convince you otherwise, but no, this is not what I wanted. I am willing to listen to any alternative options."

The room went quiet and a frustration swept across the table. Fangbane's masked face drifted from one Knight to the next, but nobody had anything to say.

"If there's nothing else," he paused, as though waiting, "then I suggest we discuss preparations."

CHAPTER THIRTY-SEVEN

Mirari blinked awake with a gasp. Her sight, her senses, were muggy and covered in a haze. She was kneeling on the floor in a corner of Fangbane's study. Light shone from the window, but it quickly grew dark as if the sky became overcast. Her collar was tight around her neck; something was gripping the back of her shirt. Her whole body grew in discomfort – her body ached like the early days of training with Gaven. She realized why when she discovered she was covered in bruises and cuts. Her hand throbbed. She gasped seeing her palm speared through with a dagger.

Trembling, she seized the hilt with her other hand, her fingers wrapped tightly around the grip. She held her breath and cried out when she pulled it free. Crimson droplets trickled down, staining her legs. Her eyes widened when she got a closer look at the dagger.

It was Salathiel's. What had happened?

What do you think happened? The voice slithered through her head.

A chill went through her, dismissing the fog from her mind. She tossed the dagger aside and staggered to her feet.

"Sal?" She spun around. "Salath—" She hadn't noticed, but Gaven was behind her. His eyes were fixed on the ground, completely oblivious to her presence.

She took only a few steps before she froze. Fangbane was crouched next to a large body on the floor. Shiba's cloak covered the body's head and chest, but it was too short; Mirari could see Neo's legs. Shaking her head, she lifted her hand to her mouth.

"No," she whispered. "No, no, no."

She started at the body that couldn't belong to her friend. She could barely see anything through the tears streaming down her cheeks, hear nothing over Starlight's screams. Her own screams.

"Why?" she wailed. "Why?"

It was his time. He died nobly.

She looked behind her and saw a translucent figure. For the first time she could put a face to the terrorizing voice. She had long, wavy hair that fell to the ends of her white robes, and large turquoise gems adorned her head, neck, and arms. It was hard to hate such a beauty, but Mirari was reminded of her menace when Cygnus gracefully turned her chin.

"You were only supposed to take away the dark aura!" Mirari said.

You must learn to live with the hand you are dealt with.

There was nothing more she wanted than to strangle Cygnus. "You are the Goddess of Fate. You *have* a choice."

Cygnus lowered her head as if she were praying. It didn't matter to Mirari. It was clear to her that she was not sorry.

That is not how fate works, child. Do you truly think I act as I please? That I enjoy taking the lives of mortals?

"You can choose between saving someone or letting them die."

No, child. I cannot. Because if I judge how I see, I would plunge your world into chaos.

Mirari remained silent, realizing that was what Lachess did. Cygnus must've read the look on her face.

You understand now. Everyone has a time, but I do not determine it. I merely enforce fate. Lachess and I were designed to create balance, but she let pity get the best of her.

The sound of Sarkan's cries distracted her from her acceptance. He ran up to his mother and bawled in her arms.

"Don't look, sweetie," Starlight cried. "Don't look."

Fangbane embraced both of them tightly, and Starlight's tears trickled down his shirt. Gaven was somber. He was now looking directly at Mirari.

She reached out to him, but her hand went right through him.

"What did you do to me?" Mirari asked, pulling her hand back and staring at it.

Be thankful that you are still here. It'll only be a matter of time.

Cygnus' silhouette began to fade. Mirari tried to grab her before she disappeared, but her hand went right through her too. The room around her began to fade to black, her friends fading along with it.

"No, please," Mirari cried, searching for a source of light. Anything. "Don't leave me here."

But alas, it was only her and her voice, echoing in the pitch black. She couldn't even see her body, if she still had one. And time passed, but how long? She would never know.

"How is she?"

"Still resting."

"Still?"

"She needs time. She'll awake when she's ready." Silence. "I'm sorry. I have to go now."

"No, I understand. You and Sarkan, take care."

Three sets of footsteps. One faded and two approached. The footsteps halted and there was a long pause before she heard a sigh.

"You sure you don't need me?" Worry was evident in this feminine voice, just as it was in the previous one, but there was a speck of confidence in the way she spoke.

"If I'm gone, then someone needs to govern Althaea Main. I wouldn't entrust it to anyone else."

She heard her whisper, "Take care, Mirari," before the sound of her footsteps journeyed beyond Mirari's reach.

Mirari felt like she was floating on a bed of darkness. A candle flame burned just out of sight. She could feel the heat, but she couldn't see anything around the candle but black, nor could she move. She could only listen. That was preferable, knowing that she would only gain heartbreak from seeing the sorrow of her comrades. For now, she just wanted to rest.

"Mirari," a deep voice said with a sigh. She recognized that voice, but shied away from giving it a name. If she named him, she would have to think and remember why she was here and what she had done. "I don't know if you heard, but the other Knights are back. They want to see you so don't keep them waiting too long."

She felt a large hand wrapped around hers.

"I know you're blaming yourself right now, but it's not your fault. There's no way you could have known what she would do."

He's right, a voice said. It curled like smoke around her shoulders. It drowned out the living voice, filling Mirari's head with its words. *Don't feel guilty. Fate is out of your control.*

"Go away," Mirari snapped. But she couldn't hear her own words or feel her lips move. Was she thinking or talking? Could Cygnus even hear her?

The voice laughed. *Go away? You and I are one.*

"You are not me! You can't control me."

Mirari felt a sigh, a gust of wind flickering her candle.

You know your fate, Cygnus said. *The fate of the vessels. There's no point in resisting. Give in to me. Give in. Give in! GIVE IN!*

"No!"

"Mirari?" Gaven's hand tightened on hers. He sighed in resignation even as she fought to squeeze back. She was trapped in her body. The smoke that curled around her tightened like a vice, binding her. "I have to go now. We're preparing to fight Lachess here. Fangbane hopes the collateral damage will be kept to a minimum if the battle is at the estate." He exhaled heavily. "He thinks you're an acceptable loss. But you're not. We'll get through this. Together. We're here fighting with you."

The candlelight was growing. No longer was it a flicker. It began to fill her vision, a campfire, billowing thick, black smoke that held her in place. Gaven squeezed her hand once more and then let go.

"I'll be back soon," he promised. He didn't immediately leave. When he spoke next, the words were low, spoken close to her ear. "Whenever you're ready, I'll still be here." She felt a light touch to her hair and she wanted to weep. He left, but his words stayed with her.

Screaming in her head, she pulled free of the smoke trapping her.

"Release me," she demanded.

Child, you do not know the forces you are dealing with.

The campfire was now a bonfire. The blackness was beat back by the light, her coldness washed away by the sweltering heat. No longer asleep, not quite awake, Mirari stood in this void. The flames twisted and coiled, taking shape. She stared at a version of herself made completely of flames

"I think it's time you stepped aside," it said. The flaming face split where the mouth would be, revealing a wicked smile.

"No," Mirari said, shaking her head emphatically.

"No?" Cygnus said, drawing the word out. "Would you

prefer the damage to spread to all three empires. Or maybe even beyond that?"

"I'll fight her, as I'll fight you." This was her world. Her mind. She held her hand up and her sword was in her hand. Raising her sword, she stared Cygnus down. "We are not your playthings. We make our own choices!"

Screaming, Mirari launched herself forward. She swung the blade down. Cygnus caught it in her palm.

"This is why my flames can't be controlled by a mere mortal. You and Lachess are the same." Mirari jumped back, pulling her sword from the goddess's hand. "You act on emotion, and you rage against the inevitable."

Undeterred, Mirari surged forward, her blade slicing through air. Cygnus raised her hand in defense, only to be met with a cunning feint from Mirari, who ducked low and struck at her leg. The blade found its mark, but Cygnus was only off balance for a moment. The heat intensified and Mirari was forced to roll away, shielding her face from the blistering flames.

"You all struggle and resist, for what reason?" Cygnus continued, voice hardening with anger. "You are mortals. You know you will die."

Getting back to her feet, Mirari pointed her blade at Cygnus' face. "You'll die too."

"Futility at its finest."

Mirari shook her head slowly, realization dawning on her. "Don't try to deny it. You *can* die. If Lachess can die, so can you."

She scowled and seethed like the crackle of fire. "Be quiet!"

She struck out, launching a barrage of fiery bolts. Mirari dodged each blast, making her way toward her. Block, duck, lunge, step by step. Until she was standing in front of the goddess.

Cygnus slammed her fists down. Mirari barely got her sword

up in time to block it. "Do you fear it?" Mirari asked into Cygnus' twisted face. "Do you fear death?"

"I won't hear this from a mortal!" she screamed, blasting Mirari back. The sword flew from her hand, clattering to the side. "I am a goddess. I fear *nothing*."

"Nothing except your own fate."

Singed and bruised, Mirari struggled to rise, her weariness creeping into both mind and body. Yet, she knew she couldn't afford to falter.

Sensing Mirari's fatigue, Cygnus seized the opportunity, launching a swift and unexpected attack. With instinct guiding her, Mirari abandoned the thought of reaching for her sword. Instead, she took Cygnus head on, boldly clasping her blade between her hands. The heat scorched her palms, but she wrestled the pain.

"We know we're going to die," Mirari said, pushing with the last of her strength. "But it's what we do with our lives that makes every second worth it. Death is what makes life worth living. I am not afraid of death, and I am not afraid of you!"

Mirari watched her hands dissolve in the light of the flame. Strange. She stopped feeling pain, or was it that she was so far gone that her senses were fading?

She felt her strength fleeting away along with the rest of her senses, and she accepted it. A solemn peace enveloped her, knowing she gave it her all.

"You won't win," Mirari said, the sound of her own voice distant and muffled in her ears. She drew a final breath, the world around her a blur of incandescent light. In that moment, she thought she discerned the soft cadence of Cygnus' words, lost to her as the brilliance consumed her world.

I already have.

GAVEN WENT RIGID. His spear clattered to the ground. His heart felt like someone had reached into his chest, grabbed it and twisted it.

He heard Hime scream.

"Your Honor?" she called, taking a step closer to him. "Your Honor, what is?"

He crashed to his knees and hunched over. He sucked in a frantic breath and another. Black spots danced in front of his eyes. Panting, he grabbed his chest and curled into himself.

"Lady Starlight? Anyone? Please, get in here!"

Gaven heard a rush of footsteps enter the room.

"What happened?" Starlight asked.

"I don't know. He just collapsed."

Delicate fingers touched his wrist. "His heart is racing, he…"

He couldn't hear the rest of what she said over the sound of his heart pounding in his ears. But that couldn't be right. How could his heart race when it was pulled out of his chest? Worse than that, there was a prevailing coldness seeping into his bones.

"No," he rasped, pushing himself up to his knees.

"Gaven?" Fangbane crouched next to him, meeting his gaze. "What is it? What happened?"

"M… ra…" he said weakly.

"What did he say?"

"Mirari," Starlight said, grabbing his wrist again. He shook her off and tried to get to his feet. "Stay still. Where are you going?"

"Did something happen to Mirari?" Fangbane asked.

Shiba and Lucan were standing in the doorway. Shiba barely had any life left in him, but when Gaven met his gaze, all the blood drained from his face.

"It can't be," Shiba said, eyes widened.

"I have to… get to…" Gaven muttered, staggering forward. He tried to push Lucan aside, leaning heavily against him.

"What happened? Is she awake?" Lucan asked, grabbing his

arm and resting it over his back. Gaven didn't have the energy to respond, or that was what he told himself because he wasn't sure of the answer himself. They stumbled across the foyer and into the courtyard, hurrying toward Mirari's room. The rest of the Knights followed behind him.

They made it to the stairs, but Lucan stopped. Gaven was about to protest when he heard footsteps.

Mirari was slowly descending the stairs. She dragged her right hand down the railing, her untied hair falling like a curtain around her shoulders. Pausing on the steps, she leaned across the banister, staring at Gaven with those cold, glowing eyes.

Lifting her left hand, she asked, "Will you still stand in my way?"

Pushing off Lucan's arm, Gaven lurched forward. The sight of Cygnus fueled his strength. Though the physical pain was slipping from his body, there was still a gaping emptiness in his chest. And only one thing could fill it.

"Give her back," he said, flatting his hand across his chest. "Return Mirari."

"Give her back?" She tilted her head. "The Valiant Tiger can deny it all he likes, but deep down he knows the truth. Mirari is no more."

No more?" Hime repeated in a trembling voice. Limpid eyes pleaded with Cygnus.

"She has fulfilled her duty."

Gaven stepped back, retreating until his back hit the wall. Next to his hand, someone handed him his spear. Grabbing it, he leveled the point at Cygnus. He was gratified to see her eyes narrowing. To see her wary.

"I don't accept that," he said.

"Neither do I," Dorain declared, stepping up to the bottom of the stairs. "I won't give up on Mirari!"

"She's one of us," Shiba said, straightening his back and flexing his arms.

Lucan's face was pinched with disbelief. But, even then…

"You won't get away with what you've done," he said. He drew his blades and glared at Cygnus.

"What are you doing?" Fangbane called out from the back. He shoved his way to the end of the stairway in front of Cygnus and blew out his breath. "We shouldn't fight amongst ourselves. We…" Trailing off, he turned to Cygnus. "We should work together. We want to defeat Lachess too."

"I have no interest in working with a ruler who cannot tame his army," Cygnus hissed.

An arrow shot toward her, sharply whistling through the air. Fangbane dropped to the ground with feline agility, the arrow whizzing just above him. Cygnus shifted her head with an eerie calmness, and the arrow sailed past her ear, embedding into the stone wall behind her. Sighing, she smirked at Dorain with a predatory gleam in her eyes.

"If you all dare to resist fate like her…" She hopped up onto the railing, defying gravity with an otherworldly grace. "You will meet the same fate as her."

Gaven understood then that Mirari had fought Cygnus' control. Of course, she had. A flicker of hope ignited within him. She could still be fighting. As long as there was breath in his body, he would help her. Even if the ache in his chest said that it was pointless, even if Shiba's pity implied that even if Mirari fought, she hadn't managed to defeat Cygnus, he wouldn't give up.

He couldn't give up.

If he did, he failed her as her partner, and he had failed Roselyn. He wouldn't accept that, couldn't accept it. Not if he wanted to keep going.

Fangbane had crawled his way back behind his team and got to his feet. He squeezed Starlight's shoulders and said, "Take Sarkan and go. I'll be right behind."

Starlight shook her head. She stood tall, her hands clenched into fists. After all, she was a fighter too, and she knew better than to believe his lie. Fangbane lowered his head.

"I must stay with the Knights," he said. "This is my responsibility."

Sighing, Starlight pulled him in for a tight hug.

"Take care," she said before turning on her heels and running down the hall.

Fangbane rejoined his team. "Knights, think about what you're doing."

"I'm done thinking," Dorain spat, eyes blazed as he shot two arrows in quick succession. They were spread out enough that Cygnus couldn't just move to the side to dodge them.

So she leapt to the ground where Gaven awaited her.

She tucked her legs to her chest, spinning through the air. Mid-descent, she stuck her foot out and Gaven barely got his arm up in time to absorb the shock of the blow. He stumbled back and she drove her other foot toward his face. Her face – Mirari's face – was twisted with anger.

She bellowed, "Know your place!"

Lucan appeared behind her, light on his feet. With his hands clasped together, he drove them down at her shoulder. She rolled out of the way and tried to sweep his legs out from underneath him. Lucan jumped back, holding a dagger at chin-level.

"Shiba?" Fangbane called out, darting his eyes between the umbra and the goddess. "We need you."

"I'm trying," he said, voice strained as he put his injured hands to use. Gaven could see the shadows twining around her legs as effective at holding her in place as his own shadow would be. Gaven wiped blood from his mouth and glanced back at the Shadow Soldier. He could do better, but given his current condition, Gaven knew Shiba was giving it his all.

"Fang," Gaven called. "Can you sense Mirari at all?"

"I—" Fangbane gasped.

Chuckling, Cygnus stood tall. "I'd advise you not to do that again. Mortal abilities don't work on a deity." She approached them like a tiger sighting her prey.

She abruptly stopped, and narrowed her eyes. Fire streamed toward her – real fire – but she waved her hand dissipating the flames.

Kylah was a ways down the hall, but her power knew no limits. Glaring, she was crouched in a stance with one palm facing outward. She thrust another whirlwind of fire at Cygnus. It looked mighty powerful and would've consumed any normal person within seconds. With a swipe of her hand, Cygnus brushed it away, vanishing it like mist. Unfortunately, Kylah was fighting in Cygnus' territory.

"Not even the Witch of Aten can stop me," Cygnus said. The air was heating up with Cygnus' rage. She tossed her hair back with an arrogance that Mirari never possessed.

"Aten wouldn't approve of your ways," Kylah snarled, with a burning anger in her ruby eyes. "If anything, he sent me to stop you!" With a loud cry, she thrusted another fiery punch.

Cygnus swiped it away, but managed only a single step forward before something pulled her back. Her foot was stuck to the ground, secured by Shiba's shadow. Ice erupted around her feet, layer by layer, locking her in place. Hime was crouched on the ground, just out of Cygnus' sight. Her hand was outstretched and sweat was beading on her forehead. Kore may not work directly against Cygnus, but she was not invincible. She was *in* this world, tied to the limitations of mortals.

Dorain darted up the stairs and shot four large light arrows into the ground. The air crackled as the arrows lodged into the ground and formed a tight luminous cage around the goddess. She wouldn't be able to leap out of their grip without impaling herself on the arrows.

Like silk in the wind, Lucan gracefully slipped out of the shadows. Cygnus was within reach, and he grasped her head, tilting it back with a dagger to her neck. Cygnus didn't flinch.

"Mirari is gone," she repeated. She blinked calmly, staring up at the ceiling. "I am your only chance at defeating Lachess. Do you dare challenge your odds?"

Cygnus jerked her head back, slamming into Lucan's chin. His arms loosened just a bit enough space for her to lift her arms and wrap her hands around his bicep. With her otherworldly strength, she yanked him off his feet and spun him like a rag doll. She tossed him high and he crashed into Dorain. Kylah ran to their side, helping them sit up. Blood streaked down Lucan's face, but he was alive.

Heat, but not flames, flared around Cygnus. She pushed her weight against the ice until it began to crack. Her energy pulsed outward, shattering the glass and the arrows that confined her.

Before the Knights could catch their breath, Shiba lunged forward, a tempest of fury in his eyes. But she intercepted him with supernatural ease, seizing the seasoned fighter and flinging him over her shoulder with little effort. Shiba collided with Gaven, all the air rushing out of him from the force of Shiba's short flight.

Gaven pushed Shiba away and used his spear to get to his feet. He wanted to rush her, fight her properly, but he couldn't. He didn't want to hurt Mirari's body. Mirari was still in there. She was…

"It's true, isn't it?" Lucan said, getting to his feet. He teetered to the side, shock or pain keeping him off-kilter. "Mirari… she's—"

"Silence," Gaven snapped. Lucan's glasses were askew and his colorless eyes were wide open.

"You can't deny it forever," Shiba said. "I can see it in your face."

"Silence!" he said again. It didn't matter. They had to stop Cygnus here. There was no telling how many others she would hurt to achieve her goals. She was a fire, burning everything in her path with no care for the destruction she caused. Cygnus needed to be stopped because of what she could do, but also for Mirari's sake. Mirari, who had died trying to stop her.

"I've had enough of this," Cygnus said, echoing Gaven's thoughts. She straightened her back and held her fists down by her side. She stared at Gaven and asked, "Do you think "Councilor Julie" still exists? Lachess consumed her long before you met her. There is no salvation for the vessels. Once they've done their part, they're gone. I warned you, but you continue to stand in my way." She opened her hands and flames erupted in her cupped palms. "You remember *this*, don't you?"

The flames. Death in tangible form.

"Don't get too close to the soul flame!" Gaven warned, taking a step back.

"Her flames?" Dorain said, confused by his warning.

"They can burn away life."

Shiba glanced at him. "But she has limits, doesn't she?"

Gaven realized that Shiba was right. Up until now, she'd only blasted them with heat, conserving her flames. Killing Salathiel took a lot out of her.

"Then how do we defeat her?" Dorain asked.

"You can't," she said, waving the flame around. "Don't you understand that? You're wasting your efforts and my time." She stepped forward and lifted her arm, stretching toward them. The flames grew, engulfing her entire hand in the fire. "This is your last warning. Stand down or I will kill you all where you stand."

"What are we going to do?" Lucan asked. He turned to Fangbane, who had stood frozen this entire time. Then, he turned to Gaven. They all did.

He bit his lip. What *could* they do?

CHAPTER THIRTY-EIGHT

Cygnus took another step forward. The flames danced in front of Fangbane. He couldn't just give up and let her win, but at the same time, they didn't stand a chance of defeating her. With those flames, she could—

The flames extinguished. Gaven's eyes jerked from her bare fingers, up to Cygnus' bright eyes. She wasn't looking at them any longer. Her gaze was sightless, as though she was looking at something they couldn't see. Gaven hefted his spear, but didn't make a move. There was something unnerving about how she was standing, like a prey that had sensed a predator. Kea cried out sharply, soaring over the wall to land on Dorain's upraised arm.

"What is it?" Kylah asked.

"We're out of time," Dorain said, swallowing his nerves.

Fangbane could feel raw power coiling inside Cygnus. The same ominous aura was coming from the bridge that led to the Estate. It approached them like a tide of dark smoke – like two opposing elements crashing together.

Cygnus' lip curled and she made a fist. She gave a short nod. "She's here."

A shiver leapt down Fangbane's spine. He could read Gaven's thoughts – manic, angry and confused. This wasn't Soteria, or Laikos, or even Salathiel. This was the creature who held herself equal to Cygnus.

Cygnus sneered at Gaven. "Stand back, mortal," she said. "Do not interfere, if you know what's good for you."

Gaven growled, but a hand on his shoulder prevented him from saying anything. His anger didn't abate when Fangbane stepped up next to him.

"There's nothing you can do now," Fangbane said, gripping his shoulder.

"Am I supposed to just watch?"

Fangbane knew Gaven blamed him for what happened to Mirari. Whatever Gaven thought, now was not the time to hash it out. He could have stood next to Gaven, railing against Cygnus to leave Mirari alone. It wouldn't have made any difference. Cygnus would have consumed Mirari regardless of where they were or who asked her. What were the pleas of mortals to a goddess?

However, if it made it easier for Gaven to blame Fangbane then he would offer himself up – his own sacrifice to honor Mirari's.

"Yes," Fangbane said. "That's exactly what you, what we all have to do." He pushed Gaven until he was looking into the cold metal of Fangbane's mask. He was glad for his mask, to conceal his own pain as he spoke sharply to this grieving man. "Mirari is dead." Gaven flinched. "Don't let her sacrifice be in vain."

Retreating, Gaven jerked his shoulder away from Fangbane's grip. "Is it a sacrifice if it wasn't her choice?"

Curling his fingers, Fangbane dropped his hand back to his side.

"We can discuss this afterward," he said. "Don't interfere or all three empires will be at the mercy of the goddesses."

Gaven glared at him but seemed to heed the warning. Fangbane didn't dare move when Cygnus cast him an enigmatic look, leaving him to decipher the emotionless expression in her eyes.

The very air grew heavy. Then, Fangbane noticed that the walls began to groan and protest. A strange darkness spread over the sky, obscuring the afternoon sun. Cygnus' doing.

The door burst open and the woman Fangbane had known as Councilor Julie stood in the entryway. He stared at her, not intentionally – it was hard for him to turn away from the intense glow in her eyes that rivaled Cygnus' presence. Adorned in resplendent golden armor that gleamed with every step, Lachess approached the group with her scythe at the ready – a deadly extension of her will.

"I had enough of you!" Lachess shouted, her heels clattering with every step. She stopped at the center of the courtyard. "You only seek to destroy everything I've created. How wicked you are. How desperate you must be that you would try to rewrite what you were born to reinforce."

As Cygnus moved to the center of the courtyard, Fangbane grabbed Gaven's arm, pulling him back from the impending clash of goddesses.

The mirthless smile on Cygnus' face betrayed the intensity of the impending confrontation.

"I knew you would change your mind once I got rid of your pawn," she said.

"I gave you a chance, Cygnus," Lachess said. "Now I see that mercy was not an option." She tilted her head from side to side, loosening her muscles. She spun her scythe in a circle, blade cutting through the air with a chilling whistle. "You will meet your end today!"

"Mercy? You were hiding this whole time. You're afraid to lose." Cygnus' smile widened, sharp and cruel and like a dagger stretched across Mirari's face. "Continue hiding behind the mortals, Lachess. I dare you. You'll know exactly what I'll do to them."

"You can't just leave well enough alone?"

"That's what I've been trying to teach you this entire time!"

Lachess seethed and advanced. In the blink of an eye, she was inches from Cygnus.

No more words were exchanged as the two deities collided like a cataclysmic force of nature. The air was charged, crackling with energy at each blow. They paid no attention to the Knights, heedless to their safety of all in their path – just as the legend had said.

Fangbane felt the force unleashed in each exchange, enough to blow him off his feet. He raised his hand to shield his eyes from the debris, their clash shaking the very foundations of the courtyard.

"We can't stay here," Lucan called over the explosions. Gaven was reluctant, but he followed the others to observe the battle from the training grounds adjacent to the courtyard. A heavy stone statue was ripped from the ground and flung in their direction. Hime was quick to react and generated a barrier to protect them.

Cygnus summoned a column of flames trying to enclose Lachess. The Goddess of Devotion was undeterred. She broke the wall and slammed her fist into Cygnus' side. The flames sputtered, but Cygnus kept going.

Fangbane had, at first, been fascinated by the control she held over those flames during the siege. The grace in her movements had captivated him. He had wondered about the source. But knowing the truth, he quaked in silent fear.

A small pebble was flung in their direction, slicing Gaven's cheek. Hissing, he touched the cut. Blood beaded underneath his fingers.

"It's not enough," Fangbane said. "We need to retreat farther."

"Retreat where?" Shiba asked. He waved his hand toward

the manor and the cracks forming along the walls. "If we go inside, we'll be in more danger."

He was weary from his bout with Cygnus. Fangbane caught the meaning behind his warning.

We don't have enough people to stop them.

Shiba was right. Without Neo, their defenses took a blow, and without Mirari, they had one less fighter on their side.

Fangbane knew what Shiba wanted. During the battle at the Althaean Siege, Neo had tapped into his powerful kore, amplified by his partner bond with Shiba, to create a huge barrier. It had managed to contain the heat and force of Cygnus' flame, protecting the onlookers from being singed.

But they couldn't do that now. No fighter could replace Neo.

"To anyone willing to fight," Kylah said. She revealed a stash of yellow vials in her hands. "This will help boost our stamina. It ain't much, but it'll give us a fighting chance."

Fangbane could sense everyone's doubt that it would make any difference. Just like the battle at the Althaean Siege, they were merely spectators. They could only observe this duel. They were woefully out of their depths, watching these titans. Watching and hoping that Cygnus came out on top.

But Kylah was holding strong despite losing the love of her life, and the fire burning in her eyes was the spark of hope that everyone needed.

"If the Knights won't stop them, then who will?" Kylah said. "We need to contain this here and now!"

Dorain was the first to snatch a bottle. The potion went down his throat in less than a second and he showed off the empty bottle.

"If I'm going to die today, then I'm going to die fighting," he said.

Hime and Lucan straightened and nodded. Each taking a vial, they followed Dorain's lead. Shiba and Gaven each took a vial, and

Fangbane held the last one. Fangbane would do this duty as well. He had chosen to bring these people together under his leadership. He had to push them as far as they were able. His call, his leadership.

"I feel it," Shiba said. He got to his feet, rolling his shoulders.

It's my turn to save you. Gaven's thoughts were loud and a memory came to his mind. It was not of the Althaean Siege, but some time afterward. He was defeated, tired, and confined both physically and mentally by his peers. When he first laid eyes on the stranger who had saved him, it was familiar and refreshing. Knowing now why she had that effect on him, he wished he could've changed that moment – welcomed her instead of pushing her away.

Forcefully, Fangbane turned his back on Gaven's thoughts. He couldn't let himself be dragged into Gaven's pain.

He glanced at the goddesses in battle. Lachess had spun her scythe to slam the shaft down onto Cygnus.

"If you wanted to win, you should have taken the girl when she was a child," Lachess roared as her scythe came down.

Cygnus had some type of force around her arm, and it trembled as she struggled to counter Lachess' strength. She roared as she pushed back with her arm. She brought her knee up, catching Lachess in the stomach. Lachess stumbled back and lurched forward. In the time it took her to recover from the pain, Cygnus rolled to the left and sprung to her feet, recovering her sword in one swift motion.

Could Lachess be right? If she took control of Julie as a child, she had decades to perfect her new body and remaster her power. On the other hand, Mirari had fought Cygnus every step of the way. Cygnus wasn't prepared. Perhaps they had a winning chance.

Fangbane slipped the vial under his mask and poured it down his throat. He turned to Dorain and asked, "Can Kea create a distraction around Lachess?"

"What?" Dorain hissed, disgust in his voice. "We're helping Cygnus?"

"We have to. She's the lesser of two evils," Fangbane said.

"She kills mortals," Dorain argued. "She killed Mirari."

"I said two evils. Dark aura is a plague that even Lachess can't control. As long as Lachess exists, so will dark aura. Without Cygnus, we have no cure."

That got Dorain to hold his silence. While it was undeniable Cygnus could not be trusted, the Alliance had witnessed the destructive capabilities of Lachess' power. If they stood against the one being who could purge such darkness, where would that leave them? To Fangbane, there was no second guessing. If they let Lachess win, they would be unable to stop her later.

"They both need to go," Lucan said, clenching his teeth. "But Cygnus has a limit. Our odds of defeating both are better if Cygnus burns her energy on Lachess first."

Fangbane could sense that his argument was resonating with the Knights.

Dorain shook his head. Kea was resting on his shoulder when he lifted his arm, and she stepped up. "You heard him. Get ready."

Kea trilled loudly – a fierce battle cry – and took off, circling above them a few times before disappearing out of sight.

Fangbane pointed to a spot in front of them and another on the far corner. "Lucan, Hime, I'll need you on the defensive."

Lucan glanced where Fangbane had pointed and shook his head.

"You know that's not my proficiency," he said.

"We don't have a choice. It's our best option."

Lucan bit his lip and accepted the situation. Hime had already run to her position. She nodded back at Lucan and waited for his signal.

He stepped forward and sank to his knees. Rolling his shoulders, he pressed his hands on the marble floor. The ground shook and the air shuddered with the force of a shockwave of energy. A clear dome erupted over their heads, only noticeable by the slight way the air distorted around it. Hime raised her hands, enforcing the barrier's sturdiness with her kore.

Cygnus charged at Lachess, fists wreathed in flames as she drove her hands toward Lachess' face. Her visage was twisted and otherworldly. No one could mistake her for Mirari. This is what Fangbane remembered of that fight between Gaven and Cygnus.

The unrestrained brutality in Cygnus' motion was unprecedented. Fangbane suspected she'd been conserving her energy for this battle. She'd save her flames for Lachess because she didn't respect the Knights as opponents. A bitter pill to swallow, but theirs nonetheless.

With a swift turn, Fangbane faced the Knights, his voice laced with urgency. "Dorain and Kylah on high ground. You'll be on your own, so you must be mindful of your surroundings. Use cover. Become one with the shadows."

They nodded, obeying his command without question and sprinted toward the stairway. It wouldn't be easy convincing the last two fighters. Shiba and Gaven's faces were etched with pain and grief. They were the strongest of the Knights, yet suffered the biggest toll in this conflict. How much more life they have left in them?

"Shiba, Gaven," Fangbane called. "Please, I need your assistance."

Shiba huffed, drawing his daggers. It wasn't in obedience to Fangbane's plea, rather he was fueled with so much anger that he was ready to die for the cause. Without waiting for Fangbane's orders, he took a step closer to the goddesses. That was okay — going on the offensive was exactly what Fangbane wanted him to do.

But Gaven? He stood like a statue and Fangbane picked up trails of his thoughts. He was finally acknowledging that he was but a mere mortal trapped in the celestial clash that unfolded before him. The worst part was seeing the clash happen in Mirari's skin, and it broke his heart. Which side would he choose? Could Fangbane rely on him to fight with whatever strength he had left?

The only barrier protecting the Knights was beginning to pulse and strain. Lucan and Hime winced, heads drifting to the floor as they were stretched to their limits. How much longer could they maintain the barrier? Not indefinitely. They were at the mercy of the two goddesses, and it was just a matter of time.

CHAPTER THIRTY-NINE

Cygnus swung her sword in a wide arc, bringing the blade down on Lachess' neck. The screech of metal on metal echoed in Fangbane's head as Lachess blocked with the curved blade of her scythe. She spun her scythe and slashed it at Cygnus. Cygnus jumped back and sent forth a torrent of flames.

With barely a blink, Lachess sidestepped that attack. Growling, Cygnus charged forward again, unleashing a flurry of swift strikes. Lachess deflected each attack with minimal movement and countered each slash with precise strikes of her own.

Lachess and Cygnus continued exchanging blows, tearing up the courtyard.

The barrier was fracturing. Fangbane could see Hime repairing each crack as it formed, but it was like pouring water into a bucket full of holes. A futile endeavor. Fangbane couldn't stumble around trying to think of this fight like it was the same as Cygnus' battle with Gaven. There was a key difference – yes, Fangbane had a resource he didn't have in that battle. A goddess.

"Gaven," he said, waiting for the man to tear his gaze away from the two goddesses. "Please, work with us. Form earth around Lachess' legs, similar to what Hime did to Cygnus."

While they couldn't directly attack the goddesses with kore, they could affect the ground around them.

"You want me to help Cygnus?" he asked in a strange voice, not heavy with anger but genuinely bewildered.

"We have to." This was Mirari's divine purpose, but he knew something like that wouldn't convince Gaven to support Cygnus. Instead, he said, "We can't let Lachess continue or we will have something worse than the Althaean Siege to contend with."

A woman cried out. Fangbane's head whipped back to the fight to see Cygnus on the ground. Her sword had fallen from her grip and she had her arm up to shield her face.

Fangbane risked tearing away from the fight to give Gaven his full attention. He trusted Lucan and Hime to keep the barrier up for a little longer.

"Gaven," Fangbane urged. "You have to help."

He was stiff, unable to take his eyes from the battle himself. He was, no doubt, bitter and still reeling from the shock of losing Mirari.

Lachess' rage charged her scythe and it illuminated with a mesmerizing yellow light that left no doubt that it contained otherworldly power. It wasn't the form of dark aura they were used to seeing. This was the original source, the divine power of life.

"You're a hypocrite," Lachess seethed at her enemy. "You hate me for trying to change fate. Why do you try so hard to avoid yours?"

"I'm the hypocrite?" Cygnus laughed. She crouched into position and balanced her sword over her arm. A reddish flame crawled up the blade. "I'm not the only one trying to rewrite fate."

Fangbane looked at the top of the stairway where Dorain was crouched and peeking between the rails.

"Dorain, where's Kea?" he asked. There wasn't time to convince Gaven, but the rest of the Knights were here.

Dorain's gaze flickered to Gaven, but he nodded anyway. He pursed his lips and whistled. Kea swooped in from behind and flew up ahead, circling the goddesses. He pulled his bowstring back and waited.

Cygnus charged in first, taking a jab at her sworn enemy. Lachess stepped to the side, and Cygnus flipped her sword over her head just in time to block her swing. The room flashed in a bright, white light upon impact. She twirled and struck at her with the force of her body, and the Knights were blinded by the light again. Her third offensive didn't strike; Lachess had caught her wrist. She waited, enjoying the shock on Cygnus' face, before tucking her foot under hers and shoving her off balance.

Kea dived. She pecked Lachess on the head before snatching a lock of hair on her way back up. Lachess hissed, holding her hand over the back of her head as she locked her gaze on the bird.

Dorain let loose an arrow and it found its way to Lachess. She jumped out of the way. It was enough time for Cygnus to get back on her feet. Another arrow whirled at Lachess and she dodged it again, moving directly into Cygnus' fist.

"Good," Fangbane said. "Keep it up."

Cygnus tackled Lachess to the ground. They were no different than harpies fighting for their territory – clawing, brawling, screeching. Their high-pitched cries rung out in vibrations discomforting to the human ear.

"What if she loses?" Hime said with a pinched look on her face. She couldn't cover her ears no matter how displeasing it was. Without the barrier, they would be blown off their feet or scorched within seconds. Despite her pain, Fangbane saw the way her eyes turned sorrowful. Shiba was perhaps the only one who didn't express any doubt.

"We won't let that happen," he said. From the ground, his shadow twisted and molded. Shiba thrusted his hand forward and his shadow darted toward Lachess. Kylah took a deep breath and followed Shiba's lead. She removed her hands from her ears and reached into her coat.

The shadow circled Lachess' legs once before emerging from the ground and spiraling up her body into a tight hold. Lachess scowled and struggled to break free. Her hands erupted in a yellow blaze, ready to slice the shadow like a hot knife on butter. But her gaze shifted to the front, drawn to two green vials catapulted in her direction. A ball of fire followed from behind, and it collided with the vials inches before it reached her. Shards of glass and drops of green liquid splattered over her body and tore holes in her skin.

The shadow slipped away like the acid rolling off Lachess' skin, as did her resistance. She was bleeding in black, dripping with the same eerie substance that Soteria and Salathiel bore, but only for a second. With one deep breath, her skin repaired itself. Flawless skin showed where her wounds once were. Fuming, Lachess turned to the Knights. To her, the injury was considered a little more than harassment.

"What do you think you're doing?" she said. "Stay out of this!"

Her eyes carried a rage that Councilor Julie never possessed. It was hard to remember that up until now, they had known her to be human. Now, they were picking a fight with a goddess. If Lachess grew annoyed with their attacks, she could easily annihilate them. Fangbane knew their chances of repelling her attacks were slim. Could they rely on Cygnus to defend them? No, to assume that Cygnus would return their gesture, or have any sense of mortal conduct, would be naive.

Lachess whirled her scythe at them. It spun so fast that all Fangbane could see was a yellow orb hurling in their direction. He raised his arms over his face – not that it would protect him against such a force. The scythe lodged into the barrier, but only for a second before it shattered the dome, and the Knights were pulled off their feet.

The manor was taking the brunt of the damage. Cracks formed in the foundation. Chunks of wall crashed to the ground around them. Fangbane's home would soon be demolished. He knew this much. Sorren had warned him – everything he built would fall regardless if he didn't put an end to the goddesses' fight. Starlight and Sarkan's safety put him at some ease, but he wasn't inclined to let another Knight die. Not if he could help it.

Lachess launched herself at Cygnus. Eyes wide, Cygnus stumbled back a step, but she wobbled under an injured leg. She would not be moving another step. Lachess was a breath away when she stretched her arm out, reaching for Cygnus' neck.

Closer. Closer.

She drew up short. Startled, Lachess looked down. Her foot had sunk into the ground. Fangbane's gaze flew over to Gaven. He had his hand out. It wasn't much, but it was more than Fangbane had expected.

Recovering, Cygnus spun on her heel and struck Lachess across the face. Lachess' leg bent at an awkward angle, caught in the earth. In a second, Cygnus' hand was around Lachess' throat. It was reminiscent of Salathiel's death, except Gaven wouldn't be running to Lachess' aid.

Lachess shot up, wrenching her leg free with a painful pop. She tried to regain the upper hand, but Cygnus pressed her down with a sharp strike to her sternum.

A blast of dark energy blew Cygnus backward, but she quickly flipped back to her feet. Lachess was standing, but the ground was uneven, helped along by Gaven's kore.

"I've had enough of you," she said, panting. Black ooze dripped down the side of her face matting her hair to her dark skin. She pointed her hand at Fangbane and the others.

Hime and Lucan's barrier shuddered under the onslaught. It shattered and Hime gasped as she was thrown backward. Lucan formed a secondary barrier around them, just barely stopping the attack. Lucan was still standing, but now, without Hime's support, he was one kick away from being thrown in the same way.

"Are you with us now, Valiant Tiger?" Shiba said, turning to Gaven.

Gaven nodded, but not with the pride he typically had. His face flickered with hesitance, perhaps even unwillingness and fear. Still, no one understood duty better than the Valiant Tiger. Even if he didn't want to fight, his team knew they could count on him.

"On my lead," Gaven said, readying his spear. He charged toward Lachess first, and Shiba dashed close behind. Gaven targeted the ground between Lachess and Cygnus, and a thin pillar rose between them. Lachess took a step back. She was perfectly in the path of two daggers whirling at her. She batted them away with a quick swing of her scythe. Gaven swiped down from behind, and Lachess raised her scythe in time to catch his spear.

"Why do you stand in my way?" she asked. Her sapphire eyes were radiating, a level of anger they had never seen in her before. "Why do you side with Cygnus?"

"Because Mirari and I are one," Gaven said, pressing down on her weapon. "I don't care what you goddesses say. Torture us. Kill us. But I know," his blade inched closer to Lachess, "my fate is to be with her!"

Even if the others could not see it, Lachess' strength wavered for a brief moment. Fangbane wasn't sure why, but something in Gaven's words made Lachess realize something.

There was a bright flash of light – their weapons flew out of their hands and Gaven fell backward. By the time he got up, the goddesses were engaged in battle again. Cygnus launched forward, arms outstretched. Lachess caught her and they locked in a grapple, holding onto each other's hands. Cygnus slammed her head forward headbutting Lachess.

Though Lachess wobbled and almost fell backward, Cygnus

kept her grip on her hands, keeping her upright. She struck again and Lachess fell to her knees. Releasing Lachess' hands, Cygnus pulled back and hammered her foot down in the center of Lachess' chest. Even as she tried to get back to her feet, Cygnus kept her boot on her chest. She ground the heel in, her eyes alighting with raw fury.

"This is it," Cygnus said through gritted teeth. "You're finished."

Fangbane didn't have to read her mind – not that he could – to know exactly what she was going to do.

"Everyone, retreat!" he shouted. The words had scarcely graced his lips before the air began to heat up.

As flames emerged all over Cygnus' body, her lilac hair became burnished gold under the light of the fire. The flames were hot, so hot that even the air inside the barrier began to heat up.

Dorain and Kylah darted further into the mansion. Turning the corner, they escaped out the nearest window.

Shiba and Gaven narrowly got behind the nearest mantle that had fallen from the ceiling before a wave of heat pulsed past them. It was enough to knock Hime and Lucan off their feet, and the barrier shattered.

Shiba sprinted back, grabbing Hime's wrist along the way. He stopped briefly when they reached Fangbane.

"Go!" Fangbane said, pointing down the hall. Shiba looked down for a moment, at Lucan, before darting toward the training ground with Hime in hand. Lucan didn't budge. He recollected himself and glued his hands to the ground again. Fangbane pulled him up by the arm. "We have to go."

"But—" He stayed behind the mantle, peeking at the battle. Fangbane knew there was no chance of getting Gaven to retreat – not as a warrior, and certainly not as Mirari's partner. Gaven only had two options in his mind: avenge Mirari or die with her.

Fangbane lifted his hand to his mask as the metal warmed

against his skin. He and Lucan began to cough. The air was hot enough to sear their lungs. They could barely see the two goddesses through the flames. Cygnus was a bonfire, glowing in whatever was left of the mansion. Chunks of rock fell down around them as the estate buckled under the pressure of the flames and power.

"You think you've won," Lachess said, choking on the smoke. "But I can tell, finally, you understand why I did what I've done."

Sneering, Cygnus struck Lachess in the chest, over and over again. The flames around her foot grew hotter and hotter each time the sole of her boot connected with Lachess.

"I am nothing like you!" Cygnus said. "Don't act like you know me!"

"But I do," Lachess said. "You and I are one, and we are destined for the same fate. I have accepted mine. It's time you do too."

It was hard to see, but Fangbane swore he saw Lachess smile for a brief moment before the air shimmered and warped under the intense heat.

Gaven covered his mouth with one arm, the other waving at Fangbane.

"Go!" Gaven yelled, pointing toward the hall.

"We need to go," Fangbane repeated. He tugged on Lucan's arm again, and finally, he took a step back. "If anyone can defeat her, it's the Valiant Tiger."

May the Gods have mercy on us all, Lucan thought. He shook his head and took off at full speed down the hall. Though he nowhere matched Lucan's speed, Fangbane followed him. A large barrier shimmered through the hall – wrapped around the ground, walls, and ceiling – and guided their way to safety. Gaven was giving it his all. They had almost made it to the courtyard when an intense light surrounded them. Fangbane threw his hand over his head to shield his eyes. His ears ached as Lachess began to scream under the onslaught. Louder and louder, she wailed. The sound was so deafening that when it finally died down, the screeching echoed in his ears.

Gasping, Fangbane lowered his arm and turned to look. Dust from his decimated home obscured his vision, but the wind picked up, whipping it away. Inexplicably, that wind reminded Fangbane of Mirari. He pushed the thought aside and straightened.

The wind cleared, revealing Gaven standing before a single person facing away. He was blown back quite a distance, but remained standing. Leaning his weight on his spear, his chest heaved with every breath. Her – the deity that had won – hands were hanging loosely by her sides. Her head was tipped back like she was feeling the sun on her face. Both feet were braced on the ground. Underneath her heels, the ground was dyed black. A dark smudge was all that was left of her opponent.

CHAPTER FORTY

Gaven leaned against his spear, chest heaving with exhaustion. Holding up that barrier took the bulk of his strength, but the battle was not yet over.

"Did we do it?" Dorain asked. His voice cut the silence that echoed after Lachess' death cry. "Is it over? Is it finally over for real?" He took a hesitant step forward, looking around.

"I think so," Fangbane said. His face was still hidden by the damn mask, but Gaven could hear the smile in his voice. He was pleased. They all were, cheering and congratulating themselves for surviving a battle between two goddesses. Someone made a joke about Fangbane's decimated home. Laughter. It scraped his ears.

Objectively, Gaven knew this was just relief speaking. They were not so callous as to not care that Mirari and Neo had sacrificed themselves during this chaos. Gaven did not want to celebrate. He wanted to rage and scream. He felt like a traitor for helping Mirari's killer, even if it was for the greater good. Even if it was just choosing the lesser of two evils. He didn't want to choose. He wanted them *both* to pay.

Everything happened because of the goddesses. They played

it down at first – starting a war in the Tribe of Paragons, killing Mirari's parents – then they unleashed their power within society. The Althaean Siege, the uprising of the Blessed, everything pointed to them. They were supposed to be goddesses of balance, life and death, but instead they made humans their play things. When they balanced the scales, how could a life be worth less than another? How come Mirari didn't matter?

This may be a victory, but to Gaven, it was hollow and cheap.

Clenching his hands into fists, he averted his eyes from the revelry. He stuck his spear point into the ground. He made to move, but his foot nudged against the shaft. He was frozen, stuck staring. He had to get away. If it was all over, he didn't want to stay.

At the same time, he couldn't just leave. Could he?

Gaven sank to his knees, crushed under the weight of memories.

Her laughter.

Her gaze.

Her touch.

He had promised to be there for her, but where was he when she needed him most?

He felt a heavy gaze on him. Lucan was watching, but not really. He had lost his glasses at some point and his hair was falling around his face. He was as lost as Gaven felt. When he noticed Gaven looking at him, he blinked and focused. They stared at each other for a moment.

Lucan nodded and walked away.

Gaven wasn't a mind reader. He didn't know what that meant, but it felt like agreement and permission. He was also grieving for Mirari. Gaven's eyes drifted down to his spear again, sticking out of the ground. Taunting him.

He saw Cygnus standing across the hall. She had taken a few woozy steps away from the crushed Lachess, but hadn't moved too far. Evil would still lurk the earth if Cygnus were to walk away. He wondered if he would be able to do what Erel had managed. If he would be able to put his friend's body to rest long after her soul was gone.

He placed his hand on the shaft of his spear and used that to stand straight. He didn't release the spear. No one was looking in his direction. Even if Fangbane read his mind in that moment, he wouldn't know what Gaven was about to do. Even Gaven didn't know what he was about to do.

His feet kicked rubble as he approached the thing that controlled Mirari's body. He noticed details about her that he hadn't before. Her legs were shaking. Sparks of flames fell from her hands like sad little embers.

The spear was heavy in his hand. He hadn't felt the proper weight in years – the weight of death. There was no hesitation. He didn't even soften the blow when he met her eyes and thrusted his spear forward with a mighty cry.

Cygnus gasped, a punched-out sound. She followed the streaks of red pouring from her chest with her eyes. Seething, she grabbed the spear with both hands but lacked the strength to pull it out. Her grunts of struggle transformed into laughter.

"What does it matter?" she asked, a smile blooming across her blood-splattered face. "Only Lachess can kill me. I will still be reborn."

He twisted his wrist and dug the spear in deeper. A dark mist rose from his hands, slowly creeping up the shaft of his spear until it latched onto Mirari's body. He heard her gasp and shudder, but Gaven held the blade steady.

"It wasn't Lachess you were afraid of, no," Gaven said, watching Cygnus be consumed by the one thing that could end her reincarnation. "You're afraid of fate."

He pulled the spear back and it came out with a sickening squelch. Shuddering, he dropped it. He shook his hands free of his new power, sucking in incomplete breaths, then hid them from sight.

Gaven hadn't thought this through. How did he know that Salathiel had given him dark aura? He didn't. It was just a hunch. Yet he didn't regret it. If it was as Fangbane said, if she was just one of two evils, she deserved to die. She needed to die. He didn't care what happened to him, but Cygnus could not live any longer. Mirari's murderer wearing her skin – it was obscene.

Cygnus flattened her hand against the wound, but that was the least of her worries. Dark aura had wrapped around her body, surrounding her like a swarm of bees. She tried to sweep them away, but it was no use – it was feeding on her.

Gaven couldn't look her in the eyes – no, he didn't have the courage to say goodbye. Cygnus likely didn't have any strength left, otherwise she would've used the soul flames to dispel the mist. She would have to accept a fate she had tried to escape herself – death by Gaven's blade.

Cygnus' panic dissipated, as a humble smile crossed her face accepting the mist dance around her body.

"I am impressed," she said before closing her eyes. "Your devotion is… unyielding."

She fell over, her knees hitting the ground with a loud crack. Gaven stepped forward and caught her. He didn't think twice that it wasn't Mirari. A part of him still believed that it was her in his arms, and for just a moment, he convinced himself that it was the truth. He embraced her.

"Fate and devotion… are one," Cygnus muttered. Her breath was fading. "Lachess would have… rewarded you." She raised her unsteady hand and touched her heart. She coughed. Blood spilled down her chin. "As… will I."

Cygnus pushed him back with force and he sprawled out on his back, caught off guard. He pushed himself up. Cygnus was on her feet. Dark aura continued to swarm her as she turned her palms out and raised her head to the sky. The sad, wispy flames no longer dissipated when they left her skin. They fell like stones to the ground, spreading like a wildfire up her legs and across her torso.

Gaven pushed himself to his feet and ran from the red flames as they grew and grew. The fire expanded up, twisting and turning in a tornado.

Gaven reached the courtyard where the others were calling out.

"What happened?" Fangbane asked, running up to Gaven.

The tornado had set the mansion up in flames, but there was no sight of the tornado itself, or Cygnus.

"She's… gone," Gaven said. Fangbane and the others would believe he meant Cygnus. That whatever was left of her was being cremated in the burning fire. Cygnus would join Lachess as nothing more than ash and memory. There was nothing left to do but wait for the flames to die down.

But something glistened through the flames, catching Gaven's eye. It shone brightly like a lighthouse on a moonless night. At first he thought it was Cygnus' eyes, but it was a singular light. As the light grew brighter, he realized it wasn't red – it was purple.

A familiar purple. He was reaching for it before he even knew what it was.

"Gaven!" Strong hands grabbed him by his shoulders and hauled him away. Fangbane shouted over the roar of the flames. "What are you doing?"

"Mirari," Gaven mumbled. He tried to push forward. "That's… Mirari's. I have to get—"

Shiba slapped him across the face. Gaven hissed. He had no time for his games now. But seeing the remorse on Shiba's face brought Gaven back to the present. It reminded him that he wasn't the only one mourning.

"She's gone, Kitten," he said. Gaven shook his head. He couldn't accept it. He felt a hand grab his wrist and pull him back.

"She wouldn't want you to join her," Kylah said, shaking her head. "You have to let her go."

"How can I?" he said, voice swallowed by the flame's dull roar. He promised to stay by her side. He promised that she could rely on him even if everyone else turned on her. He promised to protect her.

He failed.

Another pair of hands was shoving him back. She pressed her full weight against him, and wrapped her delicate arms around his torso.

"She is in safe hands, Your Honor," Hime said. "The gods will take care of her." He could feel his shirt being stained with tears.

The building collapsed in on itself, crumpling down. The flames were extinguished like they had been snuffed out by the very weight of the fire itself. A hot gust of wind blew over them, and then it was over. The flames were gone. All that stood in its place was a statue made of ash, shaped like Cygnus, like Mirari.

He broke free of the loose grip and teetered forward. His hands were shaking as he reached out to the ashen statue, but before he could lay a finger on the figure, it collapsed, releasing a cloud of dust.

Sinking to his knees, he caught himself with his hands, feeling the fine ash beneath his fingers. Breathing harshly, he swept his hands through the ash, sweeping aside piles of the gray dust. This couldn't be it. It couldn't end like this. There had to be something left – something that proved that Mirari had lived and died.

"Your Honor," Dorain called out. He was the first to join Gaven in the wreckage, but he didn't dig. He simply watched Gaven desperately search for something, what he knew was nothing. Kea joined Dorain on his shoulder, and she let out a soft coo. "She's right. Mirari won't be forgotten."

The other Knights approached the wreckage. Lucan

crouched by Gaven's side. Placing a hand on his back, he said what Gaven feared.

"We have to move on," Lucan said. "It's what she would've wanted."

Gaven shook his head, pressing the back of his hand to his eyes.

"I failed her," he mumbled. Gaven lurched forward, pressing his head against the floor and curled into himself as if he were begging the gods for forgiveness. But he knew they would not grant his wish. Why should they? Mirari was born to be a vessel, a vessel for destruction. They would be happy that she and Cygnus were gone, and there was nothing Gaven could do to bring her back.

One Month Later

GAVEN INHALED the heavy scent of hay and horses. He walked along the stable, stopping in front of a gentle mare that belonged to Mirari. He opened the gate and the beast stretched its neck, nipping at his fingers when he didn't produce a treat. He ran his hand through her dark mane.

"Sorry, not today."

The groom was preparing Gaven's horse for his trip out of the fort, giving Gaven the chance to visit the mare, which he did whenever he passed through the stables. It was good to remember that he wasn't the only one who missed her. She had touched many during her life.

He had bittersweet memories of the Knights, an organization he once dedicated a vast amount of time supporting, but, if anything, he was thankful to have met Mirari because of them. The Knights' Estate was now a little less than a pile of rubble.

Gaven didn't know how Fangbane had explained that to the Council, but he was already rebuilding.

Meanwhile, the surviving Knights had returned to their original homes. Things had come full circle, back to the beginning before the Knights were assembled. Gaven was relieved that they finally saw Fangbane as the manipulative coward he was. That was only half true, but it was the truth he wanted to believe. The main reason why the Knights departed was more or less out of uncertainty. They had every reason to feel uneasy after what had unfolded. Not only were a good fraction of the Knights gone, but sacrificing one life at the cost of many, especially if that person didn't wish to be sacrificed, didn't sit well with most of them.

Gaven refused to speak to Fangbane. Whatever he was doing with the Knights, Gaven wanted nothing to do with it. His focus was on the now, on Althaea Main.

Shiba returned to his fortress, alone. The region leader of Avon gave orders and audited his troops as if nothing happened. To most people, that's how it seemed, but Shiba's unusual silence spoke volumes. Time after time, the Shadow Soldier lost people most dear to him. In Gaven's eyes, he was always stronger. Mecate. Neo. There was no doubt he was grieving, but at least he knew how to forgive and move on. That was something Gaven always admired in him, and something he hoped he could learn. But for now, Gaven couldn't forgive Fangbane, not after they had lost so many good lives.

Kylah didn't handle Neo's departure in the same way. She refused to talk about Neo, or let anyone talk about him for that matter, even Shiba. She rejected his offer for her to stay in Avon, something about facing her fears and living up to her shame. She didn't return to her secluded life in the Minettan forests. She went back to the beginning, her roots at the Tribe of Celtas. The likeliness of the Witch of Aten reaching out to the Knights again was slim, as was the likeliness of her overcoming her grief.

"Your Honor?"

He glanced over his shoulder, just seeing the top of the groom's head from his bow. The groom held the reins of Gaven's white stallion. "Your horse is ready."

"Thank you," he said with one last pat to Mirari's horse. The groom stepped out of the way as Gaven put his foot in the stirrup and swung himself upon his mount. "You're dismissed."

The groom bowed again and headed to the back of the stables.

Once he was out of sight, Gaven ran his fingers along the bridle until… there. He found it. A small scrap of paper tucked between his stallion's mane and the saddle. He pulled it free and scanned the words.

Eoin reported that there was news of a pocket of rebels harassing travelers along Endes Road. He and the Spirit Soldiers were investigating and would let him know if it was something the army or the Knights would be better suited to take care of. Gaven considered telling him to forget about the Knights. It would have to be something big to get them motivated to come back. But even if the world was plunged into darkness again, would they band together? Would they be as strong as before? There was no friendly giant holding them together, no brave maiden leading the way. It wasn't the same.

The High Priest was aging, and Princess Hime would soon ascend the throne. When that time came, it was clear what her priorities would be. While there was no doubt that she would become her own kind of hero for the people of Alta Hills, she would have no time to run around with the Knights.

Dorain was… out there. He was quick to disappear. No one knew of his whereabouts, definitely not Councilor Dareh. The distraught councilor didn't even bother blaming Fangbane or the Knights. He deployed a rescue team in search of his son, but a month passed, and the search was called off. Gaven had a hunch where the youth had run off to, even if Eoin didn't mention it. Dorain didn't want to be found, and he was in good hands doing what he loved doing the most – helping others.

In some way, it was good that the Knights were gone. For now, that was for the best especially since the Spirit Soldiers helped keep him connected to the people so often forgotten by the Council.

Unlike before with Laikos and Soteria's flashy attacks on the Council, the Spirit Soldiers were keeping a low profile, sticking to small ways they could help people. It wasn't the epic change Eoin had originally aimed for, but Gaven thought it mattered a little more.

Crumpling up the paper, he tucked it into his shirt pocket to be burned later. The low profile also kept them out of the Council's sight. If they were caught, there could be nothing that connected Eoin to Gaven. Not that the Council cared about anyone targeting peasants and villagers from the outskirts of society.

He tugged on the reins and headed out into the city. Althaea Main was thriving. Gaven's return after the battle between Cygnus and Lachess had been a quiet affair. It felt almost insulting, but he had easily slipped back into his role as region leader. Of everything that happened, it was the one thing that still made sense. In those dark days, he went through reports and signed papers by rote.

It was Erel who had dragged him out of his gloom. She'd joked that they needed to air out his office and he should take a trip to the plaza. She'd said it in jest, but hadn't let him decline. In some way, Gaven agreed. He was tired of reading shipment orders from the Hales, or in other words, from Lucan. He was just doing his job, but Mirari's family name brought discomfort every time he saw it.

"The people need to see you," Erel insisted as though she couldn't do that for him as well. That had been the first of his routine trips through the streets.

That first time had opened his eyes to the world again, bringing light to his gaze where Mirari's death had shrouded it in pain and sorrow. The Defiants and other evildoers among the Blessed were defeated and peace was slowly blooming back into the land like the rising sun. Not just in Althaea Main, but across all three empires.

His horse trotted down the street, heading toward the plaza. Loud voices drifted toward his ears. Not angry, just passionate. People called out to each other and merchants hocked their wares. The regular patrols weren't met with suspicion. Some people even greeted the guards as regular fixtures in the city.

To go on living as if their world wasn't almost destroyed by goddesses, as if the rebellions and riots never happened, was this the way it was supposed to be? Of course, it was. That was what he and the Knights were fighting for – to end centuries of animosity between empires, creating better lives for the unfortunate ones, becoming the symbol of peace that the Council failed to provide. This was what he wanted, but why wasn't he happy?

The noise around him mimicked the thoughts running through his head. He didn't have a partner anymore, no one to suppress the bad thoughts blazing across his messy mind. It was more than just that. He lost the people who stood by his side for as long as he could remember. Gaven had always thought he abandoned his younger self the day he left Minetta, but it wasn't true. That boy was always there, until now – he had gone with Salathiel and Mirari. That was a part of him he knew he couldn't recover.

His horse stopped at the center of the plaza, taking a drink from the fountain waters. Gaven tilted his head up. He did find peace and comfort in one thing: the new centerpiece. Erel must've known that visiting the statue was the only way to get him to leave fortress grounds.

It was somewhat controversial – erecting a statue of a Minettan on Althaean grounds – but it was non-negotiable. He didn't care what people thought of it. It belonged there. He painstakingly ensured every aspect of her appearance was perfect, just as he remembered. Her gaze lifted skyward, palm outstretched in a resolute gesture. Her hair entwined with the whims of the wind. With radiating grace, she stood poised, one foot confidently placed before the other.

She embodied bravery, a guardian of the people. Those who were graced to have known her agreed that she deserved to be remembered. Some still called her a Minettan, while others remember her as a Knight. But to Gaven, she was his beacon of hope, his eternal flame. He would even call her a goddess.

EPILOGUE

"Greetings, Your Honor."

"Lovely day, Your Honor."

"Can I interest Your Honor in my pottery?"

Gaven lifted his hand as he was riding through the plaza. He wasn't as friendly as Mirari, but it seemed that it was enough to just show up. Mirari had taught him that not all problems needed to be solved with death and destruction. Sometimes it was enough to just listen.

"Did you hear…?"

"…Tepis…"

"…not that great."

The current popular topic was Inigo and for once the mention of his name didn't make Gaven's blood boil. The insidious bastard was in some financial trouble and lacked even the Council's support to climb out of it. Evidently, the new Valenian Councilor was closely examining his business dealings and it wasn't going well for Inigo. The rumors had finally reached Althaea Main. It took a little longer, but Althaea's borders were becoming more open and friendlier.

A passing woman waved to him with a shy smile and he

caught the flash of a feather dangling from her ear. Nowadays, it wasn't so strange to see Minettans walking comfortably in Althaea Main. That wasn't to say there weren't the occasional troublemakers. They were less likely to emerge when they knew Gaven was patrolling, but it wouldn't do to let his guard down.

He observed the plaza, contentment washing through him. When he'd first taken the mantle of region leader, this was always what he'd wanted – peace and camaraderie. He was chastised for being a kitten without claws and pushing for change. It was a long road, but he thought he could finally see the end of it.

"Fancy some monkfruit? Two for one today."

These words were nothing unusual in the plaza, but it was the flash of lilac out of the corner of Gaven's eyes, just the right shade, that made his head whip around almost involuntarily. He'd be unable to rest if he didn't put this impossible notion behind him. Gaven would look and then go back to his patrol. He just needed to—

When he saw her face, he came away with a heavy feeling of disappointment.

He knew he had to move on, but could he blame himself if his soul wanted to search for its missing piece?

Shaking his head, Gaven pivoted his horse to continue down the plaza. Another woman with lavender hair was admiring a jeweler's goods. She had her back to him and Gaven resisted the urge to look this time.

Though, the way she stood, her height, her stance, everything was exactly like the woman he remembered. Shaking his head, he moved on.

"Ah, miss, miss. This bracelet would surely suit your tastes. It is made from the feathers of the finest harpy sparrow. What do you think?"

"It is very nice," she said.

The sound of her voice made him whip his head and pull his steed to a halt. No. It couldn't be.

He quickly dismounted, tying his horse to a hitching rail. Stiffly, he closed the distance between him and the jeweler. He couldn't take his eyes off her, even if he could only see the top of her head.

The merchant paled when he saw Gaven standing there. He bobbed up and down in a hasty bow.

"Your Honor! What great pleasure it is to see you today."

The woman turned and stared at him. He got a glimpse of her face, and it left him speechless. Seeing his uniform, she hastily took a step back and bowed.

"Apologies, Your Honor," she said. "I will be out of your way."

"No," he said too quickly, then added. "I-it's fine."

Her body was facing him, but she kept her head lowered. He must've been staring at the woman for too long when the merchant called for his attention.

"A-Are you looking for anything in particular, Your Honor?" he asked. Gaven blinked back to the present. He glanced over the merchant's goods before turning his head back to her.

"Is there one you like?" Gaven asked the woman.

"What?" She kept her head lowered. "I... I don't know..."

Gaven's eyes stopped on a bracelet with a feather charm. "That," he said, dropping a handful of coins into the merchant's hands. "I'll take that one."

"G-good choice, Your Honor." The man hastily handed the bracelet over.

Gaven turned and pressed the bracelet into the woman's hands. "Here," he said gruffly. "For you."

"Oh?" She examined the bracelet and smiled brightly. "You are a kind region leader," she said, tucking the bracelet close to her chest. She lifted her head, meeting his gaze with her dazzling irises, "Thank you."

On second glance, there was no mistake.

"I... Ah, yes." Gaven rubbed the back of his neck. He couldn't find the right words.

Everything – the sincerity in her eyes, the way her cheeks perked when she smiled, the graceful way she held the bracelet – was as he remembered. When she looked at him, his heart skipped a beat.

But was it her, or someone that looked like her? And if she wasn't who he thought she was, was it wrong to use her to fill the void in his heart?

He tried to convince himself it was a trick, a hallucination, wishful thinking. After all, he had watched her burn to ash.

She tilted her head. "Is everything alright?" she asked.

"Ah... yes." Gaven took a deep breath. "Do... you live in this section?"

"Ah, actually." She twirled her hair around her finger. "I am not from here. I hope that is—"

Gaven furrowed his brow. "This is your first time in Althaea Main?"

"I-I think so." Her voice was soft and contemplative. "I know that's a silly thing to say, but I have no memories of being here, but something drew me here. I don't know how to describe it." She blushed. "Ignore me. I don't know what I'm saying."

But Gaven couldn't ignore her.

"Can I help you?" She looked confused, tilting her head in that way she always did. He corrected, "W-with the bracelet, that is."

"Oh, yes. Thank you." She held her hand out and he secured the chain around the woman's wrists. He could feel the steady beat of her pulse against her delicate skin. "Thanks again."

"You're welcome." Her other hand was fiddling with a necklace dangling around her neck. His eyes widened. Once he had secured that necklace around that same throat. "That necklace..."

"This?" She moved her hand over it. It was different though

– the purple was cracked and the brilliant glow had long faded to a dull indigo. "I know it's broken, but…"

"But it did its job," he whispered.

"Sorry?"

"N-No. It's nothing."

How awkward it must've been for this woman to be caught in Gaven's musings. When his eyes met hers again, her face was beaming with curiosity. Could it be that she felt the same?

She stammered, "Do I know you? I don't, but I feel like I must."

He smiled, reaching out his hand. "Then we have a lot to talk about."

ACKNOWLEDGMENTS

When I started writing the Alliance series, *Edge of Divergence* was the only part I had completed. If you felt the impact of its twists and turns, then you understand my determination to complete this story. Some things changed along the way—some lives were spared (sorry, Neo). But as for Mirari, Gaven, and Salathiel, they were fated to reconnect just as they were fated to fall apart.

Why the sad ending? Because the Alliance series isn't about fighting for justice; it's about the inevitability of close friends and relationships falling apart. When your paths divide, you might wonder, "Why couldn't things stay the same?" It's natural to wish it could've ended up differently. Hence, this is a toast to everyone I've crossed paths with—online and in person—some I'll never see again, and countless others who will never know that they were acknowledged here. I cherish every memory of them, no matter how brief it was, and I wish them well in their future battles with fate.

Thank you for finishing this journey with me. The story may be over, but I hope the characters live on in your heart.

APPENDIX

FIGHTER CLASS – Fighters are trained in one of four styles:

Aegis – bow users in touch with nature and animals.

Celta – healers & spellcasters who are masters of *kore*.

Paragon – brawlers & warriors with close-combat weaponry.

Umbra – mixed-weapon fighters with self-defense techniques.

HALE INVENTIONS – The Hale family discovered they could process raw crystals containing energy, known as hāstals, and enhanced them with kore to create new technology.

Aulāce – indestructible shackles made with kore and alloys.

Aulōg – a lock coded with one's aura. Used to secure doors.

Clōve – a hāstal-sewn glove capable of communication.

Comstōne – quartz geodes that direct sounds to other stones.

Kinastōne – a barrel-shaped geode used to generate energy.

Kirinvā Stone – a hāstal rumored to offer protection.

Kōnvoy – a caravan that transports large shipping materials.

Lumastōne – a glowing pebble that replaces candlelight.

Oriōn – a cube that crafts a geometric replica of landscapes.

Renastōne – palm-sized stones that amplify healing abilities.

Visōr – a platform that mirrors images.

TERMINOLOGY – These jargons and commercial goods are unique to the land of the three empires.

Aster Spells – an advanced category of spells.

Aura – the spiritual energy unique to each individual.

Bitterworm – an invertebrate good for harvesting vegetables.

Buzzbean – a mixture of nuts and herbs used as tea.

Cepha Metal – a dense material that blocks psychic energy.

Cryphedeon – a disc-shaped herbal flower used for flavoring.

Featherpit – someone who wears feathers for fashion, directed at insulting Minettan culture.

Flatty/Flat-Faced – a derogatory word comparing two-faced Althaeans with the sides of a flat coin.

Galuchi Seeds – used as hunting bait to beckon wild animals.

Gotchen – a popular card game that often involves a wager.

Gritbear – a large omnivore with stocky legs and shaggy hair.

Iconel Alloys – materials used to improve durability.

Ilorinae – a territorial plant that can cause fainting spells.

Kamori Powder – pressed ash from the corpse of insects.

Kippin – a type of neutral tea that tastes like water.

Kore – affinity of elemental energy that one is born with.

Larmender – fortified wine made exclusively by House Tepis.

Lucifera Trees – tall and thin tropical trees with wide leaves.

Lorestone – a yellow sharpening stone.

Lumapetal – a herbal plant that grows in wet caves.

Mirithium – a common type of ore used to craft armor.

Muddleberry – a crimson-colored berry used to craft wine.

Norkfruit – a tropical citrus fruit with a purple skin.

Speedspike – plant seeds with a spiky surface.

Swine – a derogatory word used to describe Valenians, who live among nature and are bloated with wealth.

Talla – a symbol or drawing inked into skin.

Valkyrie – Obanian women who become fighters.

Yerna Hay – highly flammable grain crops grown in Valenia.

Zotweed – a mind-altering substance made of dried pedals.

RELIGIONS – It is a common belief that all life departs to either the spiritual world of Nagama or Inferna. If the Gods do not deem the soul worthy to join them in Nagama, they are sent to one of the seven flaming gates of Inferna.

Deity of Orism – Orists believe in one deity: Oris, the God of Judgment. He is primarily worshiped by Althaeans and celtas.

Deities of Quintism – Quintists, common among Minettans, worship only the five main Gods and Goddesses.

    Aten – God of Elements

    Cordelia – Goddess of War

    Sarkan – God of Authority

    Taurin – God of Land

    Urabe – Goddess of the Sea

Deities of Plethorism – Plethorists acknowledge the existence of hundreds of Gods and Goddesses, but a tribe in Valenia will often choose to praise one or two deities. The following are only a fraction of all known deities:

    Accolade – God of Reverence

    Candela – Goddess of Purity

    Current – God of Negotiation

    Cygnus – Goddess of Fate

    Erel – Goddess of Mercy

    Kanmor – God of Wealth

    Lachess – Goddess of Devotion

    Mersa – Goddess of Fertility

    Mirari – Goddess of Miracles

    Ophelia – Goddess of Health

    Xerxes – God of Power

    Verben – God of Wisdom

Dear Reader,

I am honored that you have made it to this page.

If you enjoyed this read, then please leave
an honest review. Your support
means the world to me.

Love,
Stefanie

Can't wait for the next book? Be the first to
read it when you **become a VIP Member**.
Join today and get free desktop wallpapers.

www.StefanieChu.com/vip

ABOUT THE AUTHOR

Meet Stefanie Chu, an award-winning New Adult Fantasy author and Seattle-based coffee and tea aficionado. Her diverse passions extend to birds, indie cinema, and the intricate flavors of Japanese cuisine.

Stefanie's journey through life has been as diverse as the worlds she creates in her novels. Having lived across Asia and Europe, she draws inspiration from the rich tapestry of cultures she has encountered. It's this global perspective that infuses her storytelling with a nuanced understanding of the complexities of the human experience.

Learn more at STEFANIECHU.COM

facebook.com/StefanieChu.Author

instagram.com/StefanieChu.Author

LOOKING FOR BONUS CONTENT?
THERE'S PLENTY OF IT!

- ORIGINAL ARTWORK
- DELETED CHAPTERS
- SWAG GIVEAWAYS

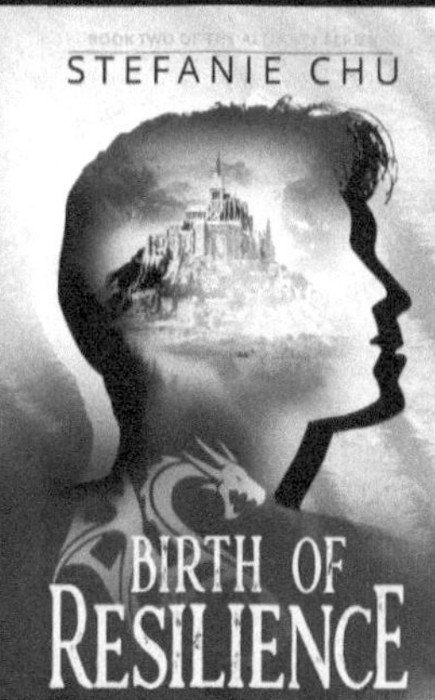

SIGN UP FOR STEFANIE CHU'S EMAIL NEWSLETTER AND
FOLLOW HER SOCIAL MEDIA AT @STEFANIECHU.AUTHOR

STEFANIECHU.COM/ALLIANCE

PRAISE FOR KNIGHTS OF THE ALLIANCE
BOOK 1 OF THE ALLIANCE SERIES

FINALIST FOR BOOK OF THE YEAR - *Indies Today Book Awards*
BEST EPIC ADVENTURE - *American Fiction Awards*
WINNER IN FANTASY FICTION – *Pencraft Awards*
1ST PLACE DEBUT AUTHOR - *Feathered Quill Book Awards*
2ND PLACE BEST FANTASY - *Feathered Quill Book Awards*
GOLD AWARD WINNER - *Literary Titan*
BEST NEW FICTION - *Firebird Book Awards*
FINALIST IN TEEN CATEGORY - *The Wishing Shelf*

THIS BOOK WAS MADE POSSIBLE BY
CANARI PUBLISHING

PUBLISHING. PRODUCTION. PRESS.
WWW.CANARI.SPACE